THE END OF THE
MAGI

Books by Patrick W. Carr

The End of the Magi

The Darkwater Saga

By Divine Right (e-novella only)
The Shock of Night
The Shattered Vigil
The Wounded Shadow

The Staff and the Sword

A Cast of Stones
The Hero's Lot
A Draw of Kings

THE END OF THE
MAGI

a novel

PATRICK W. CARR

BETHANYHOUSE

a division of Baker Publishing Group
Minneapolis, Minnesota

© 2019 by Patrick W. Carr

Published by Bethany House Publishers
11400 Hampshire Avenue South
Bloomington, Minnesota 55438
www.bethanyhouse.com

Bethany House Publishers is a division of
Baker Publishing Group, Grand Rapids, Michigan

Printed in the United States of America

Library of Congress Cataloging-in-Publication Data
Names: Carr, Patrick W., author.
Title: The end of the magi : a novel / Patrick W. Carr.
Description: Minneapolis, Minnesota ; Bethany House, [2019]
Identifiers: LCCN 2019024242 | ISBN 9780764234910 (trade paperback) | ISBN 9780764234804 (cloth) | ISBN 9781493421558 (ebook)
Subjects: LCSH: Magi—Fiction. | GSAFD: Bible fiction. | Christian fiction.
Classification: LCC PS3603.A774326 E53 2019 | DDC 813/.6—dc23
LC record available at https://lccn.loc.gov/2019024242

Cover design by Kirk DouPonce, DogEared Design

Author is represented by The Steve Laube Agency.

19 20 21 22 23 24 25   7 6 5 4 3 2 1

This book is dedicated to all the wonderful people at ACFW Middle Tennessee, for their encouragement, and to Chuck Missler, whose incredible lessons on the Bible exploded in my head and opened my eyes to wonder.

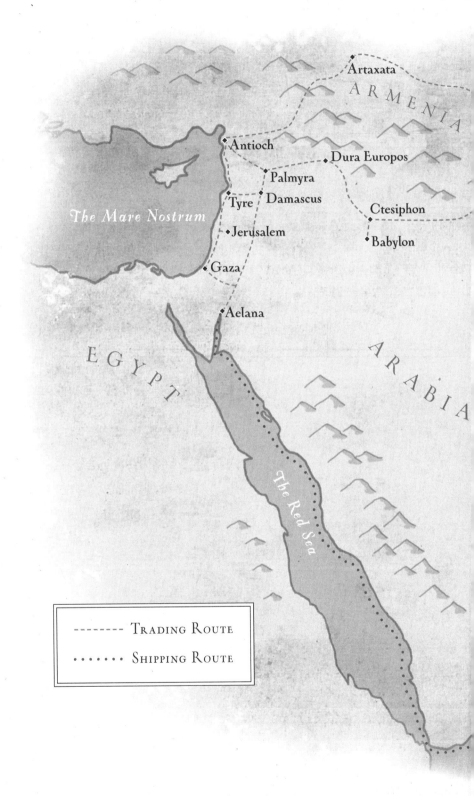

Artaxata

ARMENIA

Antioch

Dura Europos

Palmyra

Tyre Damascus

The Mare Nostrum

Ctesiphon

Jerusalem

Babylon

Gaza

Aelana

EGYPT

ARABIA

The Red Sea

- - - - - - - TRADING ROUTE

• • • • • • • SHIPPING ROUTE

CHAPTER 1

*Know and understand this: From the time the word goes out
to restore and rebuild Jerusalem until the Anointed One,
the ruler, comes, there will be seven "sevens," and sixty-two
"sevens."*

Daniel 9:25

BABYLON—537 BC

Any day now, Daniel thought, any day now they would
be free. He looked out over the brick parapet that could
hold ten chariots abreast toward the sluggish flow of
the Euphrates. Somewhere in the distance, beyond the vision
of his rheumy eyes, his dead countrymen lay buried in the sands
of Mesopotamia, doomed to rest in the land of their conquerors.

Regret whispered from him in a sigh before honesty compelled him to amend that thought. A few of the dead would
be disinterred to make the trip back to their homeland, their
descendants unwilling to leave any trace of their banishment
behind, any evidence of God's punishment.

A breeze carrying the scent of water and greenery came upon
him, unexpected in the midst of the heat of the day, a reminder
that even in this land of conquest, God still granted growth

and renewal. He turned and made his way west along the massive wall, past the towering garden with its stone troughs and water chains and sweating slaves, who sang the cadence of their imprisonment, watering the garden Nebuchadnezzar built for his homesick wife.

After nearly seventy years, the grandeur of Babylon no longer impressed him. Now he wanted nothing more than to journey west and return to the home he hadn't seen since he was thirteen, a desire he would have to surrender. With the long-suffering patience of his people, he descended the broad stairs toward the opulence of his quarters. Duties awaited him. Like so many before him, Nebuchadnezzar lay dead in the desert, while another king from another people, King Ahasuerus of the Medes, had found no fault with Daniel and would continue to find none.

Four days later, the quick slap of sandals approached him, lifting his head from the accounts of the satraps, the territorial governors. The urgent steps ceased, and snatches of frantic conversation from across the palatial room came to him. "Ezriel," he called to his assistant, "this carries the sound of news. See what it is."

Ezriel, nearly as old as he, levered himself up from his station and walked, back bent and shoulders rounded, toward the broad arch of the open doorway. A moment later the commotion grew louder, with Ezriel's voice adding its tremulous disbelief to the cacophony of the small crowd spilling through the door—men and women of every age, their faces lit.

Out of respect for his age, they let Ezriel lead them into his presence, their legs trembling to cross the space at a run. Tears tracked their way down Ezriel's cheeks, and he lifted his arms and face to the sky beyond the vaulted ceiling and cried, "It's done! We're going home."

Their joy no longer held in check, Daniel's countrymen surged forward to engulf him, embracing him and wetting his face and clothes with tears. "It's as you said . . ." Ezriel's voice broke with sobs. "Our exile is finished."

"We're going home, we're going home," the group chanted over and over.

More voices joined in, breathing the name of the city like a prayer: "Jerusalem."

He smiled and lifted his hands in thanks. "Never forget," he said to the gathering of people, "it is the Lord who saves, and His promises are sure." He caught the eye of Judah, strong and fierce in the prime of his youth, and nodded. But the man before him was too caught up in his relief and joy to heed the warning.

"Come, Daniel," Judah said. "Come with us down into the city. There will be a feast tonight such as our people have never seen in Babylon. We will eat and drink and make plans for our return."

Daniel kept his smile in place, careful to guard his words and expression. "In a moment."

Silence, imposing for the noise it followed, filled his offices after they left. Only Ezriel remained, looking at him with eyes as dark as the tar between the bricks of Babylon.

"I've worked with you for forty years," Ezriel said.

He sighed. "You always say that whenever you wish to scold me about something."

His assistant held up his hands, his eyes wide with feigned hurt. "Who am I to scold God's prophet?"

Daniel laughed despite himself. "You are my assistant and my friend. If not you, then who?"

Ezriel shrugged. "Several come to mind—Shadrach, Meshach, and Abednego."

"Hananiah, Mishael, and Azariah," Daniel said, but the familiar correction collapsed on itself. Even he often thought of his dead comrades by their Babylonian names. "And they have passed beyond the sphere of this world." Ezriel continued to look at him with suspicion. With a nod, Daniel said, "You've come to know me too well."

"Something troubles you," Ezriel said. "The others were too lost in their joy to notice."

"I'm not troubled. On the contrary, I doubt there is any man in Babylon whose heart is more joyful than mine."

"You have a strange way of showing it, old friend. Your heart neglected to inform your face."

He almost laughed. Such insights had made Ezriel indispensable for the last forty years. "I won't be going back."

His friend gasped. "Not going back? But you must. We buried Ezekiel in the sands of this accursed country nearly two decades ago. There is no one else to lead us. If you do not return, how shall we find our way?" His voice scaled upward. "Would you doom us by your absence to repeat the mistakes that brought us here? How—?"

Daniel raised his hand, palm out. "Stop. You exalt me beyond my station. If God desires a prophet for His people, He will provide one. For all we know, He may use you."

Ezriel's snort echoed in the chamber. "Did I interpret the king's dreams? Did I cast Belshazzar's blasphemy in his face? Did—?"

"Does any of that matter to God?" Daniel interrupted. "All of that was His doing, not mine."

"The people need a leader," Ezriel pressed. "They need a face, a name."

He knew better than to argue. Despite his protestations of admiration and service to him, Ezriel could be as stubborn as the most ill-tempered ass when he felt he was in the right. "You haven't asked me why I can't return," Daniel said.

His assistant's hand waved away his argument before he could offer it. "I'm sure you're going to give me some nonsense about being too old for the journey, as if there weren't a thousand men willing to carry you on their backs to Jerusalem."

Daniel levered himself from his seat without speaking, motioning Ezriel to follow him. He crossed to the wall of his office where broad cabinets ran its length. Neatly arranged stacks of papyrus and parchment filled the top of the horizontal surface. Locked doors kept records of a more private nature from prying eyes.

Pulling a key from within his robe, he unlocked the leftmost door and reached in to withdraw a sheet of fresh parchment, the ink hardly dry. "It's a copy," he said in answer to the unspoken question, "but this is why I can't go."

Ezriel's face blanched. "Are we cursed before we can even return?"

His friend's despair might well have been the sum of Hebrew existence, a cycle of favor and correction God visited upon His people. "The future belongs to God, but we've been given a task and we cannot afford to fail. Read it."

Ezriel cleared his throat, brought the top right corner of the parchment closer to his eyes, and began reading. "'Seventy weeks are determined for your people and for your holy city, to finish the transgression, to make an end of sins, to make reconciliation for iniquity, to bring in everlasting righteousness, to seal up vision and prophecy, and to anoint the Most Holy. Know therefore and understand that from the going forth of the command to restore and build Jerusalem until Messiah the Prince, there shall be seven weeks and sixty-two weeks. The street shall be built again, and the wall, even in troublesome times.'"

With Ezriel only halfway through the writing on the parchment, an obscure impulse of compassion or mercy compelled Daniel to pull the sheet from his hands.

"The Messiah?" Ezriel's voice wavered between disbelief and awe. "The King? When did this come to you?"

He shrugged, wishing to keep the rest of the prophecy from Ezriel's peering gaze. Locking the sheet back into the cabinet, Daniel steeled himself for the barrage of questions. "I will have copies made for you. When you return to Jerusalem, you must choose to whom you will entrust them."

But Ezriel refused to be so easily distracted. "What does the rest of it say?"

"You will know soon enough."

Instead of being comforted, his friend's face crumpled, accentuating the bend of his spine. "Again? Must we disappoint our God again?"

Daniel shook his head. "Not us, old friend. Don't take burdens upon yourself that don't belong to you."

"I don't understand," Ezriel said. "Why does it keep you from coming back to Israel with us? Did God tell you not to go?"

Daniel turned away, busying himself with pointless reports to give his hands something to do. "God's leading isn't always as obvious as having His messenger show up in the middle of your afternoon prayers. Sometimes He whispers so softly to your heart, you scarcely know He's spoken." He considered Ezriel's disbelief and faced his friend again. "Israel is caught between powers. The land of milk and honey is too sweet a prize for the rulers of this world to pass by."

"Doesn't God say He will protect us?" Ezriel said.

Daniel dipped his head in agreement. "Of course, but how many times in our history have we rejected Him? Do you believe it will be different this time? Have we at last become wise enough so that our children and their children no longer have to learn from their mistakes? Will they learn from ours this time?" He ran a hand over the age-spotted dome of his head. "God will use the nations around Israel to remind His people of himself. It might be Egypt, Persia, the Greeks, or some other power we've not yet encountered. To the rulers of this world it will appear as if we are nothing more than another conquest to be made, but God has a plan."

"What does it mean, your prophecy?"

"It is exactly as it sounds, a timetable for the coming Messiah-King. From the day the command is issued to rebuild the city of Jerusalem to the coming of the King is four hundred and eighty-three years."

"Why would God tell you this?"

There, Ezriel asked the question Daniel had buried in his heart since he'd first received the prophecy. The most obvious answer troubled him. "To make sure we don't miss it."

His assistant grew still, the rise and fall of his chest barely visible. His hands trembled, reaching toward him. "That implies we might."

"I intend to make certain we don't." The intensity of his promise surprised even him.

"How?"

Daniel smiled. "By using the power God has placed in my hands while I can. The king's magi are under my command. The order to rebuild Jerusalem, when it comes, will come from the seat of the power that rules the world. We will keep watch and wait for that day."

"And then?" Ezriel asked.

"We will count the days until the Messiah comes."

Ezriel's brows rose. "For almost five hundred years?"

Daniel nodded. "The magi will count the days until He comes, and we will be there to help anoint Him."

Ezriel turned a slow circle, his eyes searching the ceiling high above them. "And if the power of the world shifts away from Babylon?"

"Then the magi will follow it, serving whomever God chooses as ruler." He watched his friend consider this before he swallowed, his throat working against what he was about to say next.

"If you ask it of me, I will stay here with you and assist you however I may."

Daniel reached out and caught his friend in a fierce embrace. "You must return home for the both of us," he whispered. "There will be those who elect to stay here in the land of the Chaldeans. They won't know why; they may not even suspect it is God who has called them to remain. But I will find them and bring them into the magi, and they will become the elect within the elect." He released his friend and stepped back. "Go. I will come down to the city and join you as soon as I can. We should celebrate."

Only after Ezriel had left did Daniel retrieve the parchment with Gabriel's message upon it. As though it held the power to compel him, he found the rest of it, the part he'd kept Ezriel from seeing. Reading aloud but in a whisper, he said, "'And after the sixty-two weeks, the Messiah shall be cut off, but not for himself, and the people of the prince who is to come shall destroy the city and the sanctuary.'"

His heart labored as he read until it struggled to keep its rhythm. Finally he wrenched himself from his contemplation.

"We can only do what we can do," he prayed. "The rest, O sovereign God, is up to you."

He returned to his parchments and ink. There were preparations to be made. Somewhere in the distant future, the Messiah would be revealed.

CHAPTER 2

The light hung motionless in the western sky, too large and steady for a star and blazing pure white. Venus perhaps, Myrad thought, calling it by its Roman name. He stood unmoving in the desert, and after a time he noticed the light remained constant. He peered at the mariner's star hanging some thirty degrees above the horizon. The rest of the stars and planets circled their procession around the star seamen used to find their way, but not this one. It hung in the sky without moving. Curious, he continued to watch it, untiring. The light had no tail, so it didn't belong to that class of bodies known as harbingers, beacons in the heavens that brought omens of doom or prosperity, depending on the culture. Before long the night slipped away until the sky lightened from pitch to charcoal to slate to blue.

"What are you?" Myrad mused. "Are you important?"

A single voice came to him in answer, filling the heavens. "I am."

Without transition, he blinked and registered his bed and the walls of his room by the dim light of the candle burning on a small table. Scrambling from beneath his blanket, he grabbed the candle and limped from his father's apartment within the magi's quarters to the steps leading up to the city wall. This late, only the guards patrolling the city took note of his passing. Nothing about his dress or his staggered gait appeared to give them enough alarm to stop him for questioning. The magi were a power unto themselves, the practice of their arts inscrutable to others.

He made his way to the top of the wall while a desperate hope bloomed in his chest and he muttered supplications. "Please," he whispered.

Gazing westward, he searched the sky for the light of his dream, but the heavens were as he remembered, the constellations the same as any other night. The hunter, the bull, the hero, the twins, and the rest were all there to greet him as before. He stood waiting for the star or its voice to come to him, whispering his pleas.

He waited for an hour, ignoring the growing pain in his foot until dawn, but no light, no sound came, and his prayers to his father's god fell from his lips to the ground beneath the walls, unanswered. Defeated, he made his way in pain down the steps and back to his father's house.

When he entered, he found his father waiting for him. Gershom sat at the table, his hands clasped before him, the hands of a scribe, hands accustomed to writing. They were still now, completely reposed, and sought nothing of each other as Myrad's hands did. The two of them looked nothing alike, the Hebrew father and the Persian son. One was old with a graying fringe of hair clinging desperately to his head, the other a sparse young man of some nineteen years with dark hair and eyes typical of the Persians. Fear ate at him, setting his feet in motion despite his deformity while Gershom sat quietly. The two men were different that way as well. Gershom could wrap stillness and peace around himself seemingly at will, while his son struggled to be at rest even in his sleep. More than anything, he wanted to please his father.

"You woke early," Gershom said.

"I had another dream."

"Tell me about it." To the magi, dreams were the primary way their different gods communicated. Even among those who followed the god of the Hebrews, like his father, dreams were considered important.

Myrad sighed. "It doesn't matter. It's not a true dream. I went up to the city wall to check, but nothing had changed." He clenched his teeth around the rest of his words, but too many defeats pulled them loose. "You should have left me in the market with the traders and melon sellers."

"I saw something in you," Gershom said. "I still do. You remember what happened after you found out I was one of the magi?"

Myrad shook his head. Gershom had adopted him as his own son two years prior, when his mother joined his father in the sands of the desert. Next to that gift all other memories became trivial.

"You asked me questions about everything." Gershom smiled. "I never realized how little I knew until I met a merchant woman's son who thought I held the answers to all of creation."

Myrad nodded. He remembered now, yet he still didn't understand. Adopted out of poverty, the ranks of the magi would be closed to him unless he could prove the favor of the gods by having a true dream. "I'm not meant to be one of the magi. I'm half a dozen years older than the other apprentices."

"You have the heart and mind of a magus," Gershom said. "God gave you an insatiable curiosity, and I believe He called me to adopt you when your mother died." He leaned back to reveal the small sheet of parchment before him, his wispy circlet of hair fluttering with the motion. "It so happens I remember a dream myself. It seemed sufficiently different for me to write it down." Glimmers of hope danced in his father's eyes. "Tell me your dream."

Hoping despite himself, he recited his dream in strict chronological order without pause, as he'd been trained. Smiling, his father flipped his sheet of parchment over and slid it across the table for him to read.

Myrad couldn't seem to bring his gaze under control. His eyes kept leaping past the sentences to the end. Tremors in his hands sent the words jumping on the parchment. It took him three times as long to finish as it should have.

"They're the same," he breathed. "Exactly the same." Questions poured through him, but one stood above the rest. "Does it have anything to do with the calendar?" Every day since his adoption, he'd watched Gershom mark the passage of time on a calendar that tracked hundreds of years.

Gershom smiled but shook his head. "Impossible to know. We can inquire of the Most High, but if He does not answer . . ." His lifted hands punctuated the sentence. Gershom pulled him into a fierce embrace. "But, my son, tonight you will come with me. You will be counted among the magi."

Yet the habit of doubt refused to surrender so easily. "Will they believe you, Father? I wasn't born to you."

Gershom nodded. "Magi are forbidden to lie. They may not welcome you, but you will be admitted. And when your masters discover your curiosity and passion for knowledge, they will love you just as I do. Come. We have time for our prayers before we depart."

Myrad reached up to adjust the circlet slipping to the right to rest unceremoniously on his ear, another sign, and not the least, that he didn't belong. He removed the band of silver-copper alloy and squeezed it between his hands, hoping to force the emblem of power and influence into a better approximation of his head. The single palm engraved on it mocked him.

Gershom took the crown with his ink-stained hands and balanced it atop Myrad's head. "Until we have time to have it fitted to you, the trick is to carry yourself so it doesn't slip." His eyes crinkled. "And carrying your head high and steady will convey confidence."

Gershom grabbed his ceremonial quill and parchment. Then he retrieved a pair of jeweled ceremonial daggers, which he placed through their sashes. With a nod, his adoptive father turned him toward the door. "It's time. Remember, walk one step behind and to the right, as is proper for an apprentice."

They stepped out into the hallway. With his first ungainly step, the circle of metal resumed its accustomed position on his ear. His trousers couldn't disguise his deformity. Beneath the flowing silk his right foot was fixed, bent inward, forcing him to walk on the outer edge. Try as he might, he couldn't straighten it or keep the limp from staggering his gait for more than a few feet without pain. After the fourth attempt to keep the symbol of elevation atop his head, he gave up, determined to carry the crown in his hands until they reached the imperial court. His fingers brushed the engraved palm. Someday, if he rose high enough in the ranks of the magi, there would be five more to keep it company.

They rounded the corner, merging into a vaulted hallway decorated with tiles in a thousand shades of blue, and their solitude vanished. Everywhere Myrad looked, magi flowed toward the throne room where King Phraates IV, the Arsacid, the king of kings, held court. Brilliant colors rippled with their steps, every shade of the rainbow in evidence. Two men, walking close to each other and speaking in whispered tones, wore crowns bearing six palms.

"Father."

Gershom turned, his dark eyes, even more wary than before. "Yes?"

"Do you think I will ever attain the sixth palm?"

His hand drifted up to touch the four palms of his own crown. "Who knows? Perhaps you shall. It's not unknown for Hebrews to be elevated to the highest positions in the land. Do you wish to be one of the twenty? A satrap bears much responsibility."

Myrad looked at the men again. Something in their conversation must have concerned them. The man on the left schooled his features to stillness, but a muscle twitched in his cheek as he glanced over his shoulder at the guards following as if seeking reassurance. The man on the right brushed his hand against the dagger at his belt. The folds of silk parted enough for Myrad to see a plain hilt, no jewels or decorations, just functional leather.

Dropping his voice to a whisper, he nodded toward them. "Father, they're frightened. Why?"

Muscles twitched along his father's jawline. "Musa."

The king's concubine? What did she have to do with this?

A man with five palms on his crown stepped out of a side corridor, matching their pace. A moment later, when they came to another intersection, the man put a hand on his father's shoulder. "Gershom, a word."

His father pointed toward one of the heavy columns lining the passage, and they stepped aside into the shadows. "Masista, I thought you were in Antioch." They exchanged arm clasps, but the other magus's expression never warmed.

"Phraates had me recalled. He no longer wishes to oppose the might of Rome with might of our own." His face twisted. "He wishes a more conciliatory stance." He leaned in closer. "There are whispers," Masista added. "Musa means to be queen despite the vote of the magi." His eyes darted toward the recesses of the hall. "You need to leave Ctesiphon."

Gershom shook his head. "The magi have been kingmakers in Persia for centuries. Whatever Musa intends is of no importance. Why are you telling me this?"

The planes of Masista's face hardened. "We've become too much like the Romans. Our kings slaughter their way to power, and blood is spilled in the throne room. The influence of the magi has waned with the years. Augustus's concubine has the king's heart in her hand. Do you think mere tradition will stop them?"

Gershom straightened, his head lifting a fraction. "I'm not so naïve as you might believe. I have made preparations. If need be, Myrad and I can flee."

"Then go now. There are more soldiers in the palace than usual. Many more." The magus glanced once more over his shoulder and then left them, continuing toward the throne room without looking back.

"Who is he, Father?" Myrad was shaken by the conversation. "A friend?"

Gershom pursed his lips. "He's one of our emissaries to Rome and Armenia. Not necessarily a friend, but not someone to ignore either. Your apprenticeship can wait. I think a quick trip out of the city for a few days would be wise."

They started back toward their quarters, but before they made it to the previous crossway, soldiers in gleaming mail stepped into their path to block them. "The king requests the presence of all magi tonight," the soldier in the middle ordered. "No exceptions."

Gershom's hand found Myrad's arm, squeezing a warning. "Of course, Captain. I have forgotten some important papers in my rooms." He stepped to the side, but again the soldier blocked his way.

Gershom bowed. "Perhaps you would allow my son to retrieve them for me? He's not one of the magi."

The captain studied Myrad with a hard gaze that stopped at the circlet he held at his side. "The king demands the presence of all magi. Now."

Myrad tried to swallow the knot of fear in his throat, but it wouldn't go away. Politics in the empire could be ruthless and bloody. The magi were the stabilizing influence, the power behind the throne that smoothed tensions between clans. No king would attack his own magi, would he? He swallowed again, or tried to.

They turned a corner, and the corridor, already massive, opened, the ceiling fleeing toward the sky as echoes of a thousand conversations merged into worried murmurs. Ahead, a large vaulted arch led to the imperial throne room. Rank upon rank of cataphracts stood at attention before the doors, hereditary nobles sworn to fight for the satraps or the king. Each man wore scaled armor and a helm covering everything except the eyes, and each held a long spear in addition to the sword belted at his waist. Masista stood at the back of the crowd in front of them, then melted into it with a last look of warning.

Gershom stopped so quickly that Myrad walked into his back.

The buzz of voices in the entrance hall carried nervous undercurrents. He heard snatches of conversations, the tone becoming strident as they waited for admittance. Then the massive doors to the king's court opened, and momentary relief settled over the assembled magi as those closest stepped through.

His father didn't move but stood staring behind them at the way they'd come. Quickly, he turned away. Myrad shifted his weight to his good foot to look backward.

His father's hand found his shoulder. "Don't."

"What's back there?"

"Soldiers," his father whispered. "Many of them. Listen to me, Myrad. The magi are about to cast their final votes to confirm or deny Musa as queen. The votes will be taken in order of rank with the satraps first and the apprentices last. You must vote in opposition to me."

He shook his head. "I don't understand."

"I know and that's my fault."

"But—"

Gershom clutched at his tunic, pulling him forward. "Don't argue. Just watch me and vote in opposition, and pray no one will think to connect you to me. If nothing happens, then I'll explain."

"And if something does happen?"

His father touched the dagger at his belt. "Then find me. Now stand apart and go in with the last of the apprentices. We don't want the king's men to see us talking."

He stepped away, back toward the rear of the crowd as his father moved ahead. The satraps, all of them with six palms and personal guards, entered as the senior administrators, those with five palms on their crowns, queued up under the unblinking stares of armed men lining the entrance.

One of the men veered to the side as he neared the entrance, as if he might leave, but a soldier stepped in with a muttered command, his hand on his sword. The administrator, his eyes wide, slunk his way into the throne room.

Myrad backed away from the entrance, searching for others with a single palm on their circlet. Fear accentuated his limp. Muted laughter put a rod of iron in his spine, and he tried again to place the circlet on his head.

"You're wasting your time, city rat," a voice behind him said. "The circlet has rejected you."

He turned to see a younger apprentice eying him. His tarnished band of silver and copper alloy chose that moment to shift and slide toward his ear.

They edged toward the vaulted archway, and the buzz of voices died down as the entrance hall emptied. The echoes of conversation no longer blended together but became discrete, threatening judgment and condemnation. Behind him, row upon row of mailed soldiers stepped forward, blocking retreat.

Myrad entered, following the apprentice in front of him, his mind a jumble. Not all of the magi seemed nervous. Some laughed and joked among themselves. Perhaps he worried without cause. He took a seat on the rearmost stone bench arrayed before the king's dais. There, Phraates IV sat in splendor, the king of all the kings in the Parthian Empire. On his right sat Musa, the concubine given to honor the ruler of the empire by its greatest enemy, Rome and Emperor Augustus.

On Musa's right sat her son, a man close in age to Myrad. But the son wore as much arrogance as a king, and the looks he exchanged with his mother smoldered.

Silence fell over the hall.

"We are here to install Musa, my favored one, as queen,"

Phraates announced. His voice quavered with age, and he struggled to make himself heard, though any sound carried well in the hall.

"Such an interesting custom," Musa laughed, "asking your magi for permission. In Rome the emperor's word is law."

One of the satraps in the front row shifted as if to stand, but the man to his right put a hand on his shoulder, holding him down.

"Alas," Phraates said, "this is not Rome."

"O king, live forever," said the satrap who'd held his neighbor down. "Is it not good we are Parthians and not Romans?" His gaze shifted to Musa. "Did not the cavalry of Parthia leave tens of thousands of Romans dead in the desert and take the head of that vile snake, Crassus?"

The king nodded at the flattery, but Musa's eyes held murder.

"Is there not wisdom in much counsel?" the satrap asked.

Musa leaned over to whisper in the king's ear, her hand caressing his thigh.

"In some cases it is so," the king replied, "but the king should choose his queen."

The satrap dipped his head and sat. To his right, another man with six palms on his crown stood. His voice, deep and resonant, carried the tone of a man used to being obeyed. "O king, live forever. For centuries the magi have approved the marriage to the king in order to keep the empire strong. If it pleases the king, keep whatever concubines you desire. Only consider that Rome, having failed to defeat us by military might, will seek to compromise us by other means. Have they not suborned treason against us by placing pretenders to the Parthian Empire on the throne of Armenia?"

Rage twisted Musa's face for an instant, no more. When she spoke, her voice was as smooth and silken as the garments she wore. "If that is the king's wish," she purred, "I will abide by it and remain his devoted consort."

At her side, her son flushed. Without turning to him, she placed a hand on his shoulder.

"If it is *our* wish, you will abide by it," the satrap said.

Phraates's expression clouded, his face becoming as stone. His gaze swept across the magi like a scythe. In the instant Myrad's eyes met the king's, fear stilled his breath. He'd seen that same look in the marketplace, moments before men fought and died.

"Proceed then with the vote, magi." Anger gave the king's voice resonance.

Ten paces ahead, he saw his father bend over, his quill in hand, scratching at the parchment. Myrad shook his head. Gershom hadn't brought any ink.

A satrap Myrad recognized as the governor of Pamphylia stood and bowed to the king and Musa before addressing the assembly. "I request a formal vote to confirm Musa, the king's most favored consort, as queen of the empire."

A man Myrad knew as his father's superior, Katanes, master of the mint, stood and added his assent. "The issue has been debated for three days in accordance with the laws of the empire, which cannot be altered. Those against may stand." He resumed his seat.

A moment of silence passed. The two satraps who'd spoken against Musa at the beginning fidgeted in their seats, but no one stood. Her eyes glittering, Musa leaned over to whisper to the king. He nodded.

"You." The king pointed to a satrap sitting in the front row. "For three days you have argued against my taking Musa as my queen. Have you lost the strength of your conviction? Stand up."

The magus licked his lips but remained seated.

"Stand, magus!"

Slowly, he levered himself to his feet. "O king, live—"

"Silence!" Phraates's gaze cut across the room. He stabbed his finger at those who'd defied him, shouting and gesturing for them to stand at once. "You." He pointed at Gershom. "Stand!"

Myrad watched as his father joined the others at the command of the king.

"For three days I have suffered your insults against my crown and my queen." Phraates held out his hand. Musa placed a scroll in it. Phraates unrolled it, looking out across the throne room, his anger flaring into rage. "You have each been found wanting. Your places will be given to others."

He read a name from the scroll Myrad recognized as another of the satraps, but got no further. Chaos erupted in the hall as magi and satraps bolted for the doors. The king's soldiers drew their swords and rushed into the assembly, weapons rising and falling with the rhythm of a sickle. Screams and blood filled the air. Daggers flashed everywhere, the magi fighting both the soldiers and one another.

Feet thundered behind Myrad, and he spun to see more of the king's men charging from the rear of the throne room.

"Him!" a voice screamed as the soldiers drew near. The apprentice who'd mocked him stood five paces away, pointing. "I saw him with one of those who oppose the queen!"

One of the soldiers veered toward them, his sword back but coming forward.

The press of people kept Myrad from fleeing. He braced for the stroke that would kill him in an instant.

The other apprentice stared in horror, watching as the sword swung for him instead. His eyes never closed, not even as his head flew from his body.

One of the magi with four palms on his crown took the soldier through the neck with his dagger. Then he too was struck down.

Myrad searched the chaos. "Father!"

In front of him, three men fell to the floor in a tangle of arms and legs, kicking, punching, stabbing.

There! "Father!"

The soldiers were almost upon him.

Gershom turned, and their gazes caught. Myrad tried to yell, to tell his father to run, to hide. Anything.

His father's mouth formed words Myrad never heard. *Find me.*

Then a sword thrust into him. Crimson bloomed in his chest, and his father crumpled to the floor.

On the king's dais, Phraates, Musa, and their son looked on in triumph.

Myrad waited, his mind as numb as if he'd already died. The cataphracts finished their butchery, slaughtering the remainder of those who had defied the king. When the soldiers returned to their places at the front and rear of the hall, their mail splattered with the blood of the magi, Myrad stood paralyzed. Around him, perhaps a dozen other apprentices still lived of the two score who'd entered.

Phraates broke the silence into shards. "Be seated, magi."

It took Myrad a moment to force his knees to obey, a moment in which Musa's eyes found him. At last his knees buckled and he collapsed onto the stone bench.

"We have a vote before the council of the magi," the king continued. "Any who wish to vote against Musa as my queen may stand now."

Myrad cowered, hating himself.

"Excellent," Phraates said. "Is not the wisdom of the magi legendary, my queen?"

"Deservedly so." Musa looked out across the bodies of the fallen magi and giggled like a child who'd just been given a present. "Your throne room needs cleaning, O king. A suggestion?"

"Anything, my queen."

"Have the bodies dumped outside the palace. Let the beggars strip them for any items of value they may find." She gave the king a coquettish smile. A spatter of blood marred one cheek. "Then confiscate the lands of these traitors and add them to your own. It will be a gift and a lesson."

When the soldiers opened the doors, the remaining magi rushed from the hall, their steps just short of running. Only Myrad's clubfoot kept him from flight as his father's last message whispered over and over again in his mind.

Find me. Find me . . .

CHAPTER 3

Myrad crept through the halls of Ctesiphon, ignoring the blood spatters staining his tunic and the pain shooting through his ankle. Haste lengthened his stride, and his weight landed on the small part of his clubfoot. After two dozen paces he could feel the flesh beneath the callus beginning to bruise. After a hundred, pain flared in his calf.

He ignored it, flaying himself with images of his father falling to the ground while he watched. Out of sight of the other magi and their cataphracts, he ripped his magi's circlet from its lopsided perch. His face burned. He'd done nothing to help his father.

And he'd waited until he was safe before he pulled the crown from his head.

Tears gathered in his eyes, but he kept his head down, afraid his grief would give him away. Musa had looked at him. At him. He hurried past the administrators' offices, his father's workplace, and continued on until he came to their apartment.

Inside, a single candle still burned, the scent of beeswax drifting to him. An unexpected sound sent his heart to racing. Hearing it again, he realized the sound was only noises from the next apartment over. Quickly he closed the door and threw the bolt, leaning against it before sliding down until the floor stopped him. He buried his face in his hands and wept, wracking sobs that left him gasping.

After the worst of his sorrow had run its course, he stripped off his bloodstained clothes, poured water from a pitcher, and washed. The water flowed into the basin, red and smelling of metal. Drying himself with a clean cloth, he moved to his bedroom and dug through a cabinet until he found his most worn tunic and trousers, the only clothes he'd owned when Gershom adopted him. He strapped on his sandals and shuffled to the door, checking the candle. Midnight or close to it. Only an hour had passed since he'd come home.

Out in the hallway, no one stirred. A hush had fallen over the city as word spread, shocking to silence men and women who thought themselves powerful. Myrad limped through the halls with his head down until he came to the broad square outside the imperial quarters. Skirting the entrance set aside for the magi, he worked his way around the perimeter to the southern portion of the courtyard. News of the queen's largess brought beggars and scavengers flying to the plaza, a flock of crows and vultures eager to feed on the dead.

When he stepped through the broad arches into the courtyard, his stomach twisted in revulsion. Dead magi lay heaped on the stones, and the city's poor swarmed over the bodies, stripping them of clothes and belongings without regard. He watched as one man lifted a dead administrator to yank off his tunic, leaving the body to fall back to the stones with an audible impact. Myrad clenched his teeth but kept his head down as he entered the chaos in search of his father. With the crowns gone, there was no way to tell one magus from another. The satraps and high-ranking administrators had worn jewelry of great value. He watched as two men argued over a ring. Knives flashed in the torchlight, and they fell to the ground in a struggle for the prize, wrestling and slashing each other.

Myrad turned away, intent on finding Gershom. Fifteen minutes later, he'd checked every face without finding his father. Pairs of servants were still bringing out bodies, carrying them by the arms and legs and flinging them into the pool of torchlight where the crowd pounced on them.

When they dumped his father, a sob threatened to break free. Myrad squeezed his eyes shut to quell it and drew a deep breath. Limping forward, he pushed his way through the throng. Two women hovered over the body, searching his hands for rings, his neck for jewelry, but his father had never worn such baubles. Turning angry, the women clawed at his tunic and trousers, careless of the blood staining the silk. They flipped him over on his back, and one of them tore off the tunic while the other removed his trousers. A third woman darted forward to grab the sash that served as Gershom's decorative belt.

A small, folded piece of parchment fluttered to the ground. Myrad went to reach for it, but the third woman rushed over to snatch it up from the stones. He was close enough to catch her by the wrist. "I need that!"

She bared her teeth at him. "It will cost you."

"Please. He was my father."

The woman snarled and kicked Gershom's body, the blow rocking his father's head so that his dead stare briefly caught the light. "What do I care?" the woman spat. "Dead is dead."

Grief exploded within him. With his other hand he struck the woman across the face. He slapped her again and again until she let go of the parchment. He grabbed it, held it close to his chest. The woman lay on the stones of the courtyard, curled around his father's sash to keep him from taking that as well. Blood trickled from the split in her lip as she looked up at him.

The woman leapt to her feet and pointed her finger in accusation. "He's one of them that defied the queen!" she shouted.

Afraid of being recognized by the guards, Myrad fled away into the city, taking the twists and turns of the streets without plan until he was sure no one followed him, clutching the parchment as if it were his birthright. When hints of gray lightened the horizon to the east, he made his way back to his father's apartment.

Lighting another candle from the first, he unfolded the parchment. Blood stained the outer layers, but Gershom had folded it often enough to protect the message. When Myrad opened the last fold he saw the script and its mirror image written in red. He swallowed, understanding. Without ink, his father had cut himself to write a final message in blood. With no time to blot it, the original and its mirror stained the innermost folds. There were but three lines, four words total, one in Greek and two in Hebrew.

The first was *Rhagae*.

This he recognized easily enough. The city of Rhagae sat at the southern end of the Hyrcanian Sea and served as a stop on the trade route running from the Qian Empire in the east to the Roman Empire in the west. Centrally located in the Parthian Empire, it served as a major distribution point for goods coming from the surrounding empires.

The second word was Hebrew for *calendar*. There had been no time for his father to write an explanation, yet none was needed. Every day for the past two years, since Gershom brought Myrad into his household, his adoptive father had painstakingly marked the passing of each day at sunset on a stack of parchments. Every thirty days he would mark the end of another month in a different column in the center of the page. Only twice did he mark the completion of a year, a twelve-month span of three hundred and sixty days in a column on the far left of the page. Myrad often joked the calendar was Gershom's life's work.

"Several lifetimes, in fact," his father would say, smiling at his jest.

Myrad shifted his attention back to the bloodstained message. The last line on it, also in Hebrew, was *Amin Ben-Yirah*.

From the beginning, his father insisted Myrad add Hebrew to his studies of the more common languages of Greek and Aramaic. He displayed a gift for tongues from working in the market, and lately they had taken to speaking Hebrew to each other in halting phrases when they were alone. Ben-Yirah. He knew what the word meant, but he needed more. Was it a name, as it appeared, or was his father conveying one last message to his son?

As soon as the thought occurred to him, he dismissed it. While not physically imposing, Gershom had been the bravest man Myrad knew, even more because of his gentleness. He'd taken a stand against Musa despite the threat, and when he realized what was coming, used his dagger on himself to provide the ink to get this message to Myrad.

A flame came alight in his heart. Sitting there, knowing himself to be pitiful and powerless, he vowed to exact a price from Phraates and Musa. "Great or small," he whispered to himself, "somehow I *will* make you pay."

Outside the window, a cock crowed. He jerked at the sound.

Vengeance would have to wait, for now. The miracle of timing that kept his name off the list of those who had defied Phraates and Musa wouldn't save him. One of the survivors was sure to recognize him as Gershom's apprentice.

He filled a bag with his clothes, wrapping a linen tunic around his apprentice's circlet. The silver in it would buy food while on the road. He limped with haste to Gershom's room and opened his father's cabinet. Everything Gershom owned and held dear lay inside. Myrad gathered up his father's parchments, a stack with his calendar on top, and his stylus. No mark showed on the topmost sheet for the previous day. He made the notation, then wrapped it all in a piece of oiled leather and stuffed it in his bag.

Lastly, he opened a drawer and took out his father's purse, surprised at the weight of it. Loosening the drawstring, he found a collection of silver denarii and a few gold coins, Roman or Egyptian. Winking at him from their midst were an emerald and a ruby, small but brilliantly cut.

Gershom had lived a simple life, preferring the pleasures of conversation and food to the more exotic indulgences of the wealthy and powerful. What had he intended with such money? Myrad had no idea. This amount of money could easily buy his escape or get him killed.

He took half the contents and rolled the coins into a pair of trousers, making sure the bundle was tightly wrapped to keep the coins from jingling. He tucked the now-lighter purse deep into his tunic and adjusted his belt so it couldn't be seen.

Noise in the hall stilled him. He'd taken too long. Throwing open the shutter to the window, he slipped out onto a small courtyard and into the dawn. Head down, he made his way across it to an arched walkway leading east toward the sprawling outdoor market of Ctesiphon and freedom. Once, Myrad heard strident voices behind him at the window, but he kept his head down and his pace steady.

The walk across the city aggravated his foot even as the relative emptiness of the streets nagged at him. People were hiding, afraid to venture out. Distracted, he turned a corner and nearly ran into a pair of soldiers. A gasp escaped him and he quickly bowed, turning to shield his clubfoot from view.

"Watch where you're going."

"My apologies," he said and kept bowing until they showed their backs to him and walked away.

By the time Myrad entered the dusty grounds of the market, sweat drenched his tunic and was making headway through the bands of cloth that served as his belt. But the streets filled with people at last, and he took his first full breath of the day. He slowed, taking smaller steps and distributing his weight more evenly across the surface of his bad foot. The smell of roasting goat reminded him he hadn't eaten since before the magi gathered.

He bought enough meat and bread for the entire day. Wrapping the food in fig leaves, he placed half in his bag and ate the other half. He tucked the copper coins he got as change into his belt and continued east, searching the stalls.

He found the water seller farther on, where the market ended and the livestock pens began. He purchased two full waterskins, judging either would keep him for the day. Squinting into the morning sun, a vast sea of tents, camels, and horses stretched before him toward the horizon.

He didn't realize the danger awaiting him until he'd found his way to the horse pens.

CHAPTER 4

Myrad circled around the first horse pen he came to, working to avoid the manure and ruts that countless animals had left in the dirt. The horse trader had pitched his tent by the gate of the pen, a patchwork of stained canvas six paces across. The merchant himself, short but thick as a stump, sat in the shade of the tent's awning, observing the passersby. His beard stuck out in all directions in defiance, it appeared, of both gravity and grooming. Oddly the man reminded him of Gershom.

A stab of grief caught Myrad by surprise, stealing his breath. He stopped in the middle of the market, people passing all around him, and struggled to regain his composure. It took him a minute of warring with himself before he felt confident enough to breathe without sobbing. Biting his lip to keep it from trembling, he put on a show of confidence and approached the merchant. "I'm looking for a horse."

A smile lit the merchant's face, and he gestured to the seat next to him. "Then you have come to the right place, sir. Welcome to the pen of Eskander. Please, sit and tell me the tale of your travels."

Myrad moved toward the indicated seat, his mind working. Tale? He simply wanted to buy a horse and get away from here.

Focused on his reply, he didn't see the rut that caught his clubfoot and sent him tumbling. He pitched forward and by sheerest luck caught the bench next to the horse trader with his hands. Twisting, he seated himself.

Eskander's gaze slid from Myrad's face down to his feet. When he caught sight of the twisted foot, he blinked and then focused again on Myrad's face.

It might have been nothing. Over the course of his life, he'd seen every possible reaction to his deformity, from jeering to sympathy to amusement, to reactions similar to the merchant's—a guilty look as if caught peeping into the master's bedchamber.

Their eyes locked, and the merchant smiled, keeping his attention resolutely on Myrad's face, not even daring to look at Myrad's clothing to gauge his wealth.

"Tell me, young master, what sort of horse do you require?"

Myrad pointed to his feet and wiggled his clubfoot. "One with an even temper and a steady gait. As you can see, I have little interest in becoming a tamer of horses."

Eskander relaxed but still avoided looking at Myrad's foot. "Will you need a packhorse for your journey as well? Even with horses, prices drop with quantity."

Myrad forced a smile. "No, good merchant. The trip to Babylon hardly requires such." Babylon lay some forty miles south of Ctesiphon, the opposite direction from where he was headed.

"Why go to the trouble of buying a horse for such a trip? A boat would take you down the Euphrates just as quickly and be cheaper than buying and reselling a horse. For a denarius you could relax on the deck and drink wine all the way to the fabled city."

Had Myrad only imagined the merchant's emphasis?

He nodded, his mind racing. "Alas, Eskander, I have a fear

of water no amount of wine can cure. I can't swim, and there are creatures living in the river that make meals of the slow and infirm." He laughed, using the opportunity to check to see if all the merchant's guards remained at their posts.

Eskander rose, leading Myrad to the pen. Following, Myrad glanced over his shoulder to see one of Eskander's guards leaving his post, heading back toward the city at a jog.

He drew a shaky breath. Foolish. Anyone looking for him would know he would try to leave the city. All they would have to do was put the word out to the horse traders to be on the lookout for a man with a clubfoot. How long did he have before Musa's men came for him? It had taken him the better part of an hour to make his way from Gershom's apartment to the market.

"Either of those two would suit your needs, I think," Eskander said. The trader pointed to a bay and a sorrel standing near the gate of the pen.

Myrad gestured to the sorrel. "That one." The horse's color would blend better with the scrub and sand in the desert, but more important, it stood closer to the gate. "How much?"

Eskander nodded. "You have a good eye. Come, let us sit in my tent and we can discuss the price."

Myrad shifted on his feet to have an unobstructed view back toward the city. The crowd at the market was growing, and he saw no signs of anyone struggling to get through. He shook his head. "I'm sorry, good merchant, but I hope to make the trip to Babylon in a single day, which necessitates a quick departure. Let us haggle here."

Eskander stopped and turned. "As you wish, sir. Forty denarii."

Though he hadn't intended to bargain, the merchant's larceny was unacceptable. "*Forty*, you say? I'm going to ride it, good merchant, not race it. Any other trader would be glad to sell the horse to me for ten."

"Ah," Eskander said, "let me tell you the history of this fine animal."

He was stalling. "The day wears on," Myrad snapped. "How much?"

Eskander's face grew tight. "Thirty denarii. No less." He smiled. "I will be happy to wait if you need to go back into the city for the money."

There. This merchant *had* been paid to watch for him. No respectable trader would let a potential customer out of his sight. Letting profit walk away was anathema to their way of life. Myrad dug into his purse for the roman gold coin within. Pulling it forth, he placed it in Eskander's hand. "Bring me the horse, good merchant. Right away."

Eskander paused, then jerked his head in assent. "Yes, good sir." With a snap of his fingers one of his men came running. "Bring the sorrel out." He turned back to Myrad with a grin. "Will you be needing a bridle or blanket?"

Myrad sighed. "How much?"

"Only a denarius."

He shoved the coin into Eskander's open hand. "Here."

The merchant bowed. "Always a pleasure."

Myrad went around to the other side of his newly purchased horse and jumped off his good foot onto the thick blanket placed across the animal's back. It shied to the side and then settled. He set off with the merchant's gaze boring into him. For a few moments he dared to hope he'd gotten free of the trap laid for him, but a glance backward told him otherwise. One of Eskander's guards had mounted and was following him at a distance, trying to pretend disinterest.

When the man saw him looking, he turned away as if to examine some other horse trader's merchandise. Myrad kicked his horse into a canter, reining to the right to circle the nearest tent. Ducking beneath the ropes holding it in place, he turned three more times, bringing him back to the main thoroughfare. Eskander's man sat atop his horse just ahead, searching from side to side.

Urging his mount forward, Myrad trotted over to the guard and gathered the loose portion of his reins. As he rode past he leaned over and cracked the leather along the horse's hindquarters. Instantly the horse reared, throwing the rider heavily to the ground. The guard's face was a rictus of surprise, his arms flailing to catch his fall.

Myrad heard the snap of his collarbone an instant before the scream.

With the flat of his hand, he smacked his horse across the rump and held on as they raced away. A few miles later, he reined in and turned, searching.

There was no pursuit. He leaned forward to pat his horse on the shoulder. The sorrel tossed its head, its ears perking. It seemed Eskander had sold him a decent horse. Vastly overpriced but decent. "The thief probably thought he would get you back when the magi caught me," Myrad said to his new friend.

His horse craned its neck to look back at him with one eye. Myrad twitched the reins and dug his heels in until the horse took up a quick trot. Another mile outside of Ctesiphon, he came to the road running north and south. Scattered across the distance in both directions he could see long trains of camels heading away from the city. Many more would be coming and going through the course of the day.

His prayer came in two parts. First, that those following him would give up once they realized he'd escaped the city. Failing that, he hoped they would be forced to look for him somewhere along the road south toward Babylon. If he could stay ahead of their pursuit for the next week, the branches along the caravan routes would make finding him difficult.

Myrad reached down to massage his foot and amended the thought. He would be hard to miss for anyone paying attention. He needed a disguise. With his legs bent at the knees and gripping the horse's barrel, it was difficult to tell he was clubfooted. But as soon as he dismounted, even a casual glance would give him away. The twist in the bones and ligaments forced him to walk on the outside edge of his foot with a distinctive gait.

For a while he could indulge the hope of escape. He bent his head and let the grief he'd denied flow through him, his tears wetting the thick blanket. His horse cocked an ear back toward him but made no other concession to his sorrow. Myrad kept his head down and let the soft rocking motion of his horse's gait comfort him.

Afterward, he sighed and put his memories of Gershom behind a door with a twinge as though he'd dishonored his departed father. Still, he could and would grieve again later. What he needed now was concealment. Musa's men would be on the lookout for a lone rider. Grimacing, he dug his heels into his horse until they were moving at a canter toward the caravans plodding along the road ahead of them.

CHAPTER 5

The caravan, the fourth he'd overtaken, stretched ahead of him, each camel plodding after the one in front. As Myrad drew even with the rearmost guards, he tried to shed his fear and adopt a friendly air. Three previous caravans refused to let him ride anywhere close. He forced a smile, but the expression felt like it belonged to someone else. The mounted guards moving along at the rear weren't interested in Myrad's company.

The youngest of the guards, a boy a few years younger than Myrad and wearing a turban above a scattering of freckles, gave him a blank look. "Keep riding, stranger."

"I thought we could share the road together," Myrad said. He felt his smile wilting. "Where are you headed?"

"North," another guard answered, his mouth a line between a thin mustache and beard. They all had the skin coloring of Persians, and yet the tilt to their eyes told him their origins lay to the east and north of the Hyrcanian Sea. They were Parthians by birth, not just in name.

Myrad nodded as if their direction wasn't obvious. "As it happens, so am I."

"You can't ride with us," the boy said. "Not without the caravan master's permission."

"Perhaps I can persuade him. Who is he and where can I find him?"

"Walagash," the bearded guard said. He pointed. "Up there."

The boy shook his head. "You're wasting your time."

Myrad twitched the reins and trotted past at least a hundred camels—each with a sizable burden piled around a solitary hump on its back—until he came to a knot of men riding in the middle of the long train. One of them wore flowing robes in scarlet-and-white stripes and rode a horse larger than the rest. His bulk required it.

"Honorable Walagash?"

The man in robes turned to regard him. Myrad had seen big men before. Many of the cataphracts in Ctesiphon towered over him and carried more meat on their frames than he would have thought possible. Still, he'd never seen anyone who conveyed physical power the way this particular merchant did. Muscles bunched around his neck and shoulders, and his hands, easily twice the size of Myrad's, bore layers of scars across the knuckles.

Without blinking, Walagash's gaze took a leisurely route from Myrad's head to his feet and back to his face, ending with a glance at his horse. As for the merchant's face, it was much like the rest of him, gruff with stern features. Yet the gaze seemed to be seeking understanding through taking in the details, and the man's expression conveyed amusement rather than confrontation.

"You haven't come to trade," Walagash said. "What do you want?"

Myrad bowed. "Merely to share the road with your caravan until our ways part."

"A reasonable request. Why would I deny it?"

47

The question caught Myrad off guard. How should he respond?

"Yes," a voice on his opposite side said. "Why would he?"

Myrad shifted on his riding blanket to see the boy from the rear of the caravan riding close by.

"I see you've met Roshan," Walagash said. From somewhere deep in his chest came the deep rumble of a mountain laughing. "Roshan is the only member of my caravan who is more jealous of its safety than I am."

"You said so yourself, Father." Roshan reached up to adjust the thick folds of cloth serving as his protection from the sun. "Strangers on the road are dangerous. Send him away."

"Dangerous? He doesn't look dangerous." Walagash clenched his hand into a giant fist. "Are you . . . wait, what's your name?"

"Myrad," he said, then winced. He shouldn't have been foolish enough to give his real name.

"Life requires rules, but flexibility as well," Walagash said. "Return to the rear, Roshan. Let me speak with our visitor." He waited until the boy had ridden beyond earshot. "Roshan is of my tent, part of my household, and will inherit my caravan someday. To make a profit, a merchant has to be able to read people. Roshan is nearly as skilled at it as I am."

"I've heard it said that desperate men make for good customers." Myrad had heard the quote his entire life in the marketplace, from the lowest seller of melons to those offering the finest silks. "But I've always thought the most skilled merchants are those who can determine a customer's greatest desire and fulfill it."

"True." Walagash's expression sharpened, grew speculative. "You're acquainted with the rudiments of trade at the very least. Tell me, Myrad, which portion of the great road have you traveled and how often?"

Something in the merchant's demeanor warned him against trying to shade the truth. "I haven't," Myrad answered. "I was born and raised in the city, but I worked the marketplace with my mother for most of my life."

Walagash nodded. "An honest answer and well spoken, for you could have simply let me continue with my assumption."

Beyond the merchant's assurances, Myrad sensed the man was still testing him in some way. Walagash's gaze never wavered. "No," he said. "You knew I was no merchant."

Walagash cocked his head. "Also well spoken. Lone travelers on the road are uncommon but not unheard of. You may ride with us until sunset, but I won't extend my protection to you and I won't allow you to bring trouble on my caravan. Ride at the back."

Myrad returned to the rear to ride with the three guards posted there. Each of them rode with two bows, matching quivers, and long knives. Roshan eyed him with suspicion, while the man with the wispy beard, Aban, offered him a welcoming nod. Myrad was surprised to discover the third guard, riding on Aban's right, was a woman. Her name was Storana, who appeared to be of an age with Aban, about fifty, and only a fool would miss the ease with which she handled her weapons. Her face, weathered by sun and life, held traces of the beauty of her youth. When she caught him staring at her, her hand slid closer to her knife.

"My apologies," he said. "I've seen warriors among the Parthians before, but none of them were women."

She smiled at that and shed a decade from her face. "I'm not Parthian. I'm from Sarmatia."

Myrad recognized the name. The Sarmatians lived to the

north of the empire, part of the conglomeration of tribes most referred to as the Scythians.

"It's a fairly close relationship," Aban said.

"It is," Storana agreed, "but in Sarmatia, women are encouraged to be warriors. In fact, a woman so trained is forbidden to marry until she kills her first man in battle." She gave Aban a look that held a familiar affection.

Aban laughed. "It's fortunate for me your skills were considerable from an early age." He reached out and gripped her hand for an instant.

The caravan snaked its way north at a camel's walk. Try as he might, Myrad couldn't help but check over his shoulder for signs of pursuit. Had those seeking him followed his false trail to Babylon? Probably not. The deception felt clumsy even as he'd said it, and merchants were experts at spotting liars.

As though his worries held the power to conjure his fears, soldiers appeared in the distance behind them. Though there were only two of them, they came at a fast trot and would overtake the caravan in moments. If he attempted to flee, the soldiers would easily run him down. But if he stayed where he was, they would kill him as soon as they saw his sandals and the ruin of his foot. The desert swam in his vision, the air feeling too thick to breathe. He shifted on his blanket to see the guards staring at him, their expressions ranging from pity to suspicion. "If you hide me, I'll pay you."

Storana glanced at Aban, but Roshan spoke first. "Whatever you've done to bring trouble on yourself is your problem. Drop back or ride ahead, but separate yourself from the caravan."

Myrad looked to Aban, and after a moment's hesitation, the guard agreed. "If the god of the shining fire wills, you will survive. If not . . ."

50

The riders' approach ate at the distance to the caravan. Myrad's lungs constricted, and motes of black filled his vision. The caravan crested a hill, blocking them from the sight of the soldiers, and he kicked his horse into a gallop. But instead of fleeing, he reined in a moment later beside the merchant. "There are men coming, soldiers looking for me. If you hide me, I will pay you."

Walagash's face clouded. "No. Whatever trouble you have is yours to face. If I am caught hiding you, your troubles become mine."

Myrad's thoughts fragmented and scattered as the need to flee flooded through him. "Then don't hide me," he blurted. "Trade with me."

The merchant's brows rose, and the hint of a smile tugged at his mouth. "What sort of trade do you propose?"

"I need a pair of boots. I'll pay."

"Indeed?" The merchant smiled in earnest. "I'm intrigued. Aban!"

The guard rode forward at a gallop. Walagash gestured toward Myrad. "My fellow traveler here has a sudden, and I'm guessing a quite pressing, need for a pair of boots. I judge the two of you to be of a size. Are you interested in selling your spare pair?"

Aban nodded. "They're my second favorite pair, so I'm not sure he could offer me a price that—"

Myrad yanked open his purse and pulled out a gold aureus, a coin worth twenty-five silver denarii. "Here."

Aban's eyes widened. "Sold." He rummaged through the pack on the back of his horse, then turned to hand Myrad a worn pair of leather boots, pointed at the toes in the style of Parthian horsemen.

Walagash waved toward the rear. "You have your trade. Now drop back, away from my caravan."

Myrad reined in his horse, removed his sandals, and hid them in his bag. The caravan passed by him as he jammed the left boot onto his foot. Yet the right boot refused to slip over the ruin of his clubfoot. He grabbed the sides and pulled harder, but neither the boot nor his foot yielded.

The last of the camels walked past him. As the guards approached on their horses, Aban leaned toward him. "You have two minutes, perhaps three before the soldiers crest the rise behind us."

A panicked sob burst from Myrad. Think! What did the soldiers need to see?

He pulled a tunic from his pack and cut the sleeves from it. These he stuffed into the boot, filling it. Then he took his dagger and cut a slit from the inside hem of his right trouser leg up to the knee. He tied the stuffed boot with string so that it hung from his knee. He shoved his leg beneath the riding blanket, rumpling it to disguise its presence. He bent to tuck the loose ends of his trouser leg around the boot just before the soldiers crested the rise behind him.

He found himself a few dozen paces behind the caravan. Out of pity or concern, Walagash pulled the guards from the rear, leaving him isolated, perhaps to create the illusion Myrad was the sole guard assigned there.

As the guards drew close, Myrad spared a single glance toward them—no more or less than he supposed a caravan guard would do—before he let his gaze sweep over the scenery, trying to adopt an air of bored indifference. His pulse hammered in his ears. The riders passed by on either side, and after a cursory glance at his feet, they rode on.

Myrad didn't take his eyes off them until they had disappeared out of sight over the horizon. Aban drifted back until he and

Myrad rode side by side. "Walagash says you may ride with us for the rest of the day. But when we stop, our association ends."

On the northern horizon he could still make out the receding dust of the men hunting him. There would be more. If he couldn't find a better way to hide, he would die.

Two hours before sunset, the caravan came to the next oasis along the road to Rhagae. Up ahead, Roshan appeared at Walagash's side. The merchant gave the boy orders for setting up camp, which Roshan relayed to the guards. The camels and horses were picketed on the east side of the oasis, where sweating men pumped water from an underground cistern into a long trough.

To the north of their camp, another caravan, this one composed of horses only, also stopped for the night. Walagash stood a few paces away, eying their goods and their owner—a man in his sixties with close-set eyes and a strong nose—with what appeared to be curiosity, desire, and resignation.

"Who is he?" Myrad asked.

Walagash sighed. "Esai. He's a silk merchant, one of the elect. They sell the most valuable goods in the empire, but their ranks are closed. Unless one of them dies, or Phraates grants a commission to another, it's impossible to join their ranks." Walagash laughed. "Esai is a friend of long acquaintance, and yet I've never been able to persuade him to sponsor my request to trade in silk and I've tried more than once. I hope to set Roshan up in the trade someday." He paused. "When the time is right."

Myrad watched the other merchant, who stood there giving directions to his men. With a start, he realized the man was speaking Hebrew. The barest spark of hope came afire in his chest. "Is it so difficult to earn his recommendation, then?"

Walagash nodded. "Normally, it would be impossible. The recommendation is hereditary, and Esai is childless. I've tried to discover what he values more than silk, but if it exists, he's never said." He took a breath until his chest strained his striped robes and set off toward the silk merchant. Myrad trailed in his wake without invitation, hobbling to keep up.

"Greetings, Esai," Walagash called.

"Walagash," Esai said. "Fair weather to you."

"And to you. How do you fare?"

Esai shrugged and dipped his head. "Trade is good. The Romans are willing to pay almost any price for silk. But the bandits know this as well, and they're starting to work in concert. I've had to hire extra guards."

"Come to my tent. I have wine, and perhaps we may speak of trade."

Esai nodded. "A cup of date wine would help to wash away the dust of the road."

Myrad moved to follow Walagash back to his tent. "He seemed willing to talk at least," he said.

"He always talks," Walagash said, "but he never says much, despite my best efforts to ply him with food and drink."

"Would you mind if I accompanied you when you speak to Esai?" Myrad asked.

"What do you have to offer?"

"Esai is Hebrew, and so was my father. I may be able to discover what he most prizes."

"You may," Walagash said after a pause, "but that doesn't mean I'm granting you a place in my caravan."

Myrad slumped. He couldn't blame the merchant for his caution.

Two hours later, he sat in Walagash's tent, placed by the merchant at the entrance. Walagash and Esai sat in the center, drinking date wine and speaking of inconsequential things. Roshan sat on his father's right, the look on his face that of boredom. The small talk continued for another fifteen minutes. When the pauses in conversation stretched and became awkward, Esai rose. "Thank you for your hospitality, my friend. I must be leaving now. It's almost time for evening prayers."

Walagash held out his hand. "We've yet to talk trade. Won't you tarry a few moments more?"

Esai grimaced. "To what end? I trade the most valuable commodity in four empires. I have all the wealth a man needs and have no interest in trading anything else." He edged toward the tent flap.

"Enough, Father," Roshan said. "You know I have no wish to trade in silk. Robe me with the red and white of your colors and that's enough."

"Might I accompany you, honored Esai?" Myrad asked. "I haven't shared evening prayers with anyone since leaving Ctesiphon."

Esai's generous eyebrows betrayed his surprise. "You worship the Most High?"

Myrad bobbed his head. "My adoptive father was Hebrew. Three times a day we would pray to the Most High and read from the Torah."

Esai's lips trembled in time with his hands. "Then you are blessed beyond all men. I would give almost anything to have a Torah with me."

Walagash called Myrad's name, waving him over. When he drew close, the merchant tapped his ear.

"The Torah is the holy book of the Hebrews," Myrad murmured, stepping back.

"If it is a book you wish," Walagash said, "I will get you one. I'm sure one can be bought or copied."

Esai shook his head. "You don't understand, Walagash. The Torah is perfect."

"How so?"

Esai sighed. "You understand a letter in an alphabet can represent a number as well, yes?" At Walagash's nod, he continued. "The only people allowed to copy the Torah are scribes designated by the high priest in Jerusalem. When they are done with a page, they add the letters and check the sums both horizontally and vertically, comparing them to the original. If even one of the sums is wrong, they do not correct the page. They burn it and start over. If you think it is difficult to get me to part with my silks, you haven't seen me trying to get a synagogue to part with their Torah. There are some things money cannot buy." Longing filled the Hebrew's expression.

Myrad moved forward again, settling himself beside Walagash to make his allegiance plain. "Why do you want a Torah of your own?"

The old man's eyes clouded. "My travels do not take me to the land of my fathers, and synagogues along the route are rare. Even in those few cities boasting a synagogue large enough to have their own Torah, the frantic schedule of a merchant rarely allows attendance, leaving me parched and hungry. The word of the Most High God is like bread and wine."

Myrad held out his hands to the merchant, fearful he might leave. "Please, stay a moment longer. I shall be back shortly."

He hurried from the tent to his belongings, mouthing the words of a prayer. He opened the bag that held his father's papers and pulled the thick bundle of parchment sheets from their protective wrap. Setting aside the calendar, he leafed through the remaining pages one by one until he came to a sheet with the heading *The Book of Beginnings*.

Doubt flooded through him. Gershom valued his Torah above all his other possessions, but it had taken Esai's powerful desire, a stranger, to prove to Myrad its great worth. What right did he have to trade it away? For a long moment he wavered. Surrendering his father's Torah tore at him like losing Gershom all over again. Yet he wanted to discover what his dream meant, and for that he needed to go on living. "I'm sorry, Father." He clutched the Torah to his chest and returned to Walagash's tent, where Esai stood, obviously trying to leave. Only Walagash's bulk blocking the entrance kept him there.

"Here." Myrad held the first page up for Esai to see.

The merchant gaped, his hands feeling for the stool behind him. "You have it? Here? But how?"

"How isn't important," Myrad said. "That I do have it and am willing to trade for it is what matters."

Seated at last, Esai's head bobbed with impatience. "It's complete? May I inspect it?"

Myrad handed his father's Torah to the merchant, who spent half an hour leafing through it, devouring the words. At moments he would stop, his fingers brushing the page as tears gathered in his eyes. "It's all here," he said and lifted his head to look at Myrad. "Please tell me it's not stolen. As much as I desire it, I will not deprive another of the words of the one true God."

"It was my father's," Myrad said. "He . . . he passed away a while ago, and as his only son it has come to me. It is mine, Esai, and I have the authority to trade for it."

The merchant nodded slowly. His hands clutched the edges of the parchment as though unwilling to part with it. Myrad held out his own hand, and very reluctantly Esai surrendered it. "Name your price, Myrad. I will pay anything I am able."

"But you don't have what I want, Esai." He motioned toward Walagash. "He does." Without waiting to be invited, Myrad retrieved his stool from his spot by the entrance and brought it over to sit with the two merchants, creating a triangle. He didn't doubt the symbolism of the gesture would be plain. "I propose a three-way negotiation. I am willing to let Walagash bargain on his own behalf as though he owned the Torah. If the two of you come to an agreement, I will then bargain with Walagash for what I desire. If we reach an agreement, I will deliver the Torah to you."

"No," the silk merchant said. "What you propose is overly cumbersome. You own the Torah, and I am not without resources. Come, deal with me directly."

The suggestion held merit, but when Myrad drew breath to agree, a voice within put him in mind of his dream and he demurred. Surprised, he refused. "No. Walagash has what I require."

Esai licked his lips, his gaze fixed on the stack of parchment sheets in Myrad's lap. "Very well. Let us begin."

Walagash looked from Myrad to Esai, his eyes darting with speculation. "I desire two things. First, I wish the finest silk in your packs for Roshan. I will pay a fair price."

"A simple thing," Esai said. He eyed Roshan. "I have a deep blue cloth that flows through the hands like water. It's cool in the summer and warm in the winter. It is the best I have and worth more than its weight in gold. What else?"

"Second, I wish for you to bring me into the silk trade."

Esai gaped, and a short burst of laughter filled the tent. "You ask for a shekel and then demand a talent, Walagash. The silk trade is closed. I have no power to open it."

"But you do. You have no children and the trade is inherited."

The other merchant's eyes grew wide. "You wish to enter my household?"

"It is common enough. Adoption confers legitimacy throughout the world. In the Roman Empire an adopted son is given even more status than a natural-born one."

Esai stroked his chin. "You have a reputation for shrewd bargaining. Is it deserved?"

"I like to think so."

Silence settled over the tent as the two men regarded each other. "I think we can come to an agreement," Esai finally said. "I am willing to offer you the opportunity to enter the trade in exchange for the Torah, an opportunity only, perhaps a run from Margiana to Palmyra with a middle grade of silk."

Walagash gaped. At last he said, "The *opportunity* you are offering is to send me to one of the largest trading towns in the world . . . with a middle grade?"

Esai nodded. "The quantity will be substantial enough to allow you to exercise the skill you claim. If you prove adept, then we can arrange an adoption to satisfy the laws of the empire and execute secondary agreements in the nature of a partnership."

Walagash frowned. "Even if I am successful, what would keep you from dissolving the partnership?"

The two men negotiated at length. Midway through, Walagash summoned his factor, who brought in a small writing table with pen and parchment. The frantic scratching of the factor's writing struggled to keep pace with the stipulations each merchant sought from the other. Two hours later, they were done.

After the two shook hands, Esai faced Myrad, his eyes burning. "May I have it?"

"No. I still have to negotiate my price from Walagash. If we're successful, I will bring it to your tent in time for evening prayers."

The merchant turned to Walagash. "Give him whatever he requires."

After he left, Walagash dismissed his factor, but Roshan remained. He stared at his father, his expression verging on anger. "I told you, Father. I never wanted silks, only linen in your colors."

Walagash's eyes held affection, even empathy, but resolve as well. "Shouldn't a father wish the best for his children? Now, I need to speak to Myrad alone."

CHAPTER 6

I nstead of speaking, Walagash rose from his seat to refill his goblet with date wine. When he returned, he held another out to Myrad. "It would be improper to refuse a fellow merchant refreshment before negotiations."

Myrad laughed. "I'm not a merchant."

"But you are," Walagash said. "You proved that the moment you gave Esai what he desired in exchange for what he offered, and you followed it with as shrewd a piece of bargaining as I've ever seen. Now, what do you want from me?"

The wine, sweet and smooth, tickled his throat and sent warmth to his belly. He took another sip, and the light from the brazier in the tent took on a softer glow. "What do you have to offer?"

"I think you have the makings of an excellent merchant," Walagash said. "The look on Esai's face when you took the Torah from his hands told you everything you needed to know. If you want to measure how much something means to a man, give it to him and then take it back."

Myrad took another drink of the wine and a knot of worry he'd carried since fleeing Ctesiphon loosened, but grief poured in after it. More than anything he just wanted to see his father again. The light from the brazier wavered now. "You have the silk trade if you want it," he said. "What can you offer me?"

"I only seek to know what it is you most desire."

Myrad blinked and looked down at his goblet. Strange, it was full again. "I want to see my father." The normal spaces in his speech disappeared, and his words leaned on each other as if they couldn't stand up on their own.

"What happened?" Walagash asked.

"They killed him."

"Who killed him?"

He couldn't seem to pull his chin up off his chest. "Musa and Phraates, but mostly Musa."

Walagash dropped a mix of curses onto the floor of the tent.

The room floated in Myrad's vision. "I shouldn't have said that."

"A merchant is a fool if he trades in ignorance," Walagash said. "Who was your father, Myrad? And who are you?"

He looked at the empty goblet as if it had betrayed him. "Date wine is stronger than I remember."

"Who are you?" Walagash repeated.

He'd said too much already, and yet he needed someone to trust. Walagash would connect the pieces of their conversation together as soon as word of Musa's slaughter reached his ears. "My father was Gershom, minister in the treasury of the king and one of the magi." He lifted his gaze from the goblet to Walagash. "On the day of my induction, my first day as an apprentice, Musa and Phraates killed every one of the magi who didn't support their marriage. Musa is queen now in Ctesiphon."

Walagash's eyes widened. "That Roman concubine is *queen*?"

Myrad raised the goblet in salute and laughed. Sharp. Bitter. "All hail Rome."

"Is Phraates mad? He's given the Romans a foothold in the throne room of the empire."

Myrad nodded, though the motion felt exaggerated.

"You escaped, then?"

"The vote happened earlier, before I was made a magus. I left before they could make the connection between Gershom and me. They think I fled to Babylon." He hoped this to be true, but he said nothing of his doubts to Walagash. "I need to get to Rhagae. They're looking for me." He shook his head. "I'm not sure why."

"It's Parthia, Myrad. The kings here kill their own: fathers, sons, brothers. They're not in the habit of leaving political opponents alive."

"I'm nobody."

"You're a witness to a slaughter that could divide loyalties in the empire," Walagash said. "Who knows what fable they'll spin out of this?" He paused. "You didn't need me. You could have bargained with Esai directly to take you safely to Rhagae. Why didn't you?"

Myrad shrugged, or thought he did. The wine made his body feel heavy. "I'm not sure. You knew I was on the run as soon as you met me. I could see it in your eyes."

"And so you bargained with Esai to give me what I most desire."

"Yes." The answer took longer than it should have. "I need to hide. My father told me to go to Rhagae."

Silence settled over them, and he might have dozed for a moment. Myrad's next clear thought was of Walagash carrying him with ridiculous ease to place him on a sea of cushions. "By the god of the shining fire, for this I will take you under my protection and as far as you need to go."

Myrad extended his hand toward the merchant. "We have a bargain."

Walagash's grip swallowed his.

"I need to get the Torah to Esai," Myrad mumbled. Even his words felt heavy. "He'll be waiting."

"I'll take care of it," Walagash said. "Sleep now."

He didn't need to be told twice.

Someone, Myrad felt sure, was using his head for a drum. The beat was steady and timed in perfect cadence with the rhythm of his heart. Where was he? He lay still, waiting for awareness to come and the pain to subside. He worked to pry his eyelids open and saw the white and red of Walagash's tent. The stripes writhed in his vision.

When he sat up, the sudden movement brought a flash of white-hot pain stabbing across his temples. Limping his way out into the late winter sunshine, he saw Roshan and the merchant's guards had already struck most of the camp. Horses nickered and pranced in the crisp dawn.

He didn't know Walagash was behind him until he heard the rumble of his voice at his elbow. "May peace be upon you."

Myrad jerked at the sound and immediately regretted it. "And upon you." He massaged the sides of his head. "That wasn't just date wine, was it?"

Walagash smiled without any trace of apology or regret. "The caravan is more than just my livelihood. It's my family and friends. I needed to be sure of you before we struck a bargain."

Memories of the prior evening came crashing into his awareness. "I can't stay with you, Walagash. It was wrong for me to ask."

"How so?" The merchant's smile took on an edge. "You cannot renege on our bargain. The Torah has already been delivered to Esai and he has departed on his way to Palmyra."

"He can keep it, and you can have the silk trade. But Musa's men will be checking the other roads leading away from Ctesiphon, and when they realize I didn't go to Babylon . . . what will happen to your caravan if they catch me with you?"

"How do you know they'll find you?" Walagash asked.

Blood rushed to his face in embarrassment. "They know what I look like."

"You're well-featured enough, but hardly remarkable, Myrad. We will dress you as a guard. There must be any number of young men on the trade routes who look like you."

His face burning, Myrad pointed at his deformed foot, his finger jabbing the air. "I'm hard to miss."

"Ah, I'd forgotten."

"That must be nice," Myrad said. "The magi haven't. When I left Ctesiphon, the horse trader recognized me by my foot. Then he had me followed out of the city."

Walagash frowned. "I'm not going to let your misfortune keep me from my dream."

"Haven't you been listening to me? You can have the silk trade. Musa's men are probably coming this way right now."

"Probably, and their horses are certainly better than yours," Walagash said. "Do you think you can outrun them?"

"I think there's help waiting for me in Rhagae."

"That's two weeks away." Walagash stepped back, studying Myrad's twisted foot in silence.

Myrad clenched his fists. All his life, people stared and pointed at his foot and awkward gait. "There's nothing more to—"

"Hush," Walagash said. "I'm thinking." A moment later, he brightened. "Roshan!"

When the merchant's son appeared at his elbow, Walagash pointed at Myrad's foot and spoke as if there wasn't a person attached to it. "We need a disguise for that, at the very least for horseback, but walking would be good as well."

Roshan shot a look filled with suspicion at Myrad. "We're wasting the coolest part of the day, Father."

"True enough. Can you put something together while we ride?"

His son's shoulders dipped a fraction. "Probably."

"Excellent. Myrad, you will ride at the rear of the caravan with Roshan, Aban, and Storana."

The rear. Myrad nodded, his mind working. If and when Musa's men found him, he could pretend he and those in the caravan were nothing more than travelers with a common destination. No accusation would come against Walagash.

The guards struck the tent, and soon after they were mounted and moving, their pace dictated by the swaying line of camels plodding across the desert. At the rear of the caravan, Roshan issued orders. "Myrad, ride on my left. It will make it harder for anyone to see your right foot. Give me the boots you bought from Aban."

He slipped the left one off and handed it over along with the right one.

Aban smiled. "That's the most profitable deal I've ever made."

Roshan grunted. "You're not the only one. Father's just negotiated the trade of a lifetime." The boy's tone was neutral, but there was a twist to his lips as he said it.

Throughout the morning, Roshan worked as they rode. His questions about Myrad's foot set his face to flaming, though there was no scorn coming from Roshan or the guards.

"Show me how far you can bend your foot," Roshan said. He held the boot in one hand, a knife in the other.

Myrad lifted his leg and moved his foot as much as he could in every direction, which wasn't much.

"That's it? This is going to be a challenge." He made no move for a long while, just stared thoughtfully at the boot and Myrad's foot.

Uncomfortable beneath his gaze, Myrad's patience dwindled. "Aren't you going to do anything?"

"It's easier to fell a tree if you sharpen the axe first."

"What?"

Roshan sighed. "We don't have an unlimited supply of boots or time. I need to plan this out." With a nod he cut a long vertical slit down the length of the boot and then a horizontal cut along the instep from the toe almost back to the heel to create an upside-down T-shape. "Here," he said. "See if you can slip this around your foot."

Myrad took off his sandal and wrapped the flaps of boot leather around it. He saw the problem almost immediately. "You'll never get the leather to stitch back together."

"We're not trying to. We just need a disguise. Give me the boot."

Myrad surrendered it and started to put his sandal back on.

"Don't," Roshan said. "You'll just have to take it off again."

Gritting his teeth, he reached down to drape his horse's riding blanket over his foot.

"It bothers you, doesn't it?" Roshan asked. He produced a smaller knife to poke a series of holes on either side of the cuts along the boot.

"It might not if I weren't being reminded of it all the time."

With the holes completed, Roshan took two long strips of leather lacing and handed them to Myrad, along with the boot. "This is the best I can do without better supplies and tools, but it should be enough to fool anyone who sees you on horseback."

Storana jerked around, shifting on her riding blanket. "Soldiers behind us," she said. "Coming fast."

Aban barked in laughter. "Someone wants you badly, it seems."

Roshan growled curses in a variety of languages. "Get the boot on. Hurry."

Bent double as he tried to lace the boot around his misshapen foot, Myrad listened for the sound of horses. Roshan dropped another curse to keep the others company.

"Aren't you done yet?"

"It's not as easy as it looks."

Aban's voice drifted down to them. "They're getting closer."

"Can they see us?" Roshan asked.

"Perhaps not yet, but any moment now."

"Let me help you," Roshan said and grabbed Myrad's foot. Quickly he laced the boot together, skipping every other hole.

"Here they come," Aban said just as Roshan dropped Myrad's newly shod foot and straightened.

"Move over to ride on my right," Roshan said. "Make it look casual, as though you just want to check the camels on that side."

"But they'll see my foot," Myrad protested.

Roshan huffed. "We want them to. If we look like we're trying to hide it, they'll look more closely."

And it will be easier to pretend I don't know you if they recognize me. Myrad guided his horse over to the right without glancing back. A squad of soldiers galloped up to the rear of the caravan before splitting to ride along each side. A squat man with a puckered scar across his forehead rode toward him, searching. When he drew even, his eyes narrowed at the sight of Myrad's horse.

Myrad slouched, pretending disinterest. They should have

swapped horses. With an effort, he kept his gaze level and his right foot tucked in tight against his horse's flank. The soldier looked him in the eyes, then down at his foot where it dangled below the riding blanket, and then back at the horse.

Out of the corner of his eye, he could see Roshan watching. Only one of the boy's hands was visible. The soldier squinted, his hand drifting closer to his sword.

A cry from another soldier farther ahead broke the silence, and without a word the first soldier dug his heels into his mount and galloped away. Myrad waited until the men had vanished over a distant hill before he drew a deep, shuddering breath.

Throughout the rest of the day, they made adjustments to the boot and laces until it fit well enough to be indistinguishable from its mate. An hour before sunset they pulled into the next oasis, where Walagash called for Roshan and Myrad. The two of them rode forward together, past the date palms marking the boundary of the oasis and toward the watering troughs for the animals. Walagash stopped but didn't dismount. "We have a problem." His eyes flicked to his right, toward a stand of trees. "There's someone watching us."

"One of the soldiers?" Roshan asked.

"I think so. He's not the sort of fellow you can miss. He stepped back into the shadows as soon as he saw me."

"What did he look like?" Myrad asked.

"Unpleasant, with a long scar on his forehead."

Myrad swallowed. It took more effort than it should have. "That's the one who passed me earlier."

"All right," Roshan murmured. "Keep him on your right and get inside the tent as soon as we raise it."

Walagash grunted. "He's waiting to see you walk. Can you do so without limping?"

The merchant couldn't possibly know what he was asking, but Myrad nodded anyway.

"Go back to the rear of the caravan with Aban and Storana," Walagash said. "I'll get the other guards working on the tent. That will buy us some time." He sighed. "I should have thought of this."

"What?"

"They're covering the oases. It doesn't matter which way you choose to run, if Musa's men can get ahead of you—and they can since they have better horses—they can post a man or two at each oasis and catch you whenever you show up. It's not like you can ride across the entire desert. No one survives out there."

Myrad could feel the soldier's gaze on him, waiting.

He headed back to the rear of the caravan, sweating in anticipation. As a child, he'd tried to walk like others, desperate to be like them. Adopting a normal gait sent stabs of pain through his ankle. The farther he went, the worse the pain got. He'd never made it more than a couple dozen paces.

That wasn't going to be enough to fool anyone.

CHAPTER 7

They plodded closer to the center of the oasis. Walagash shouted orders that Roshan echoed to get his father's tent erected and the animals watered. Myrad told himself over and over he could do this; he could walk like a normal person. Only a short distance separated him from the tent, a paltry stretch of ground to cover, but his heart pounded against his ribs and called him a liar.

"Ride as close as you can to the tent before you dismount," Aban told him. "Only a few steps."

Up ahead, he could make out the silhouette of a man watching them from the shadows. "I can't. If I ride up to the tent and duck inside, he'll know I'm trying to hide something." He estimated the distance from the watering trough to Walagash's tent, at least fifty paces. Sweat broke out on his forehead, and a line of it trickled down his back. *Fifty*.

Storana rode in close beside him. "We will be with you," she said. "If that soldier attacks you, we will give him to the crows."

Myrad clutched at the guard's reassurance, but it didn't work. "There are too many people here. If you try to protect me, Musa will have you killed as well. It's only fifty paces."

But even as he said this, he realized his estimate was likely short. As they arrived, all the other guards dismounted and helped water the animals, moving the camels to the trough where they could drink before taking them to one side to tether them to the picket line for the evening. They inched closer, his heartbeat roaring in his ears.

"O God," Myrad whispered, "help me." At the tail end of the caravan, he would be at the farthest point from the trough. Beside him, Aban and Storana reined in, each turning their horses to let them drink.

"Are you ready?" Aban asked.

At his nod, the three of them slid off to stand by their mounts. Myrad felt the soldier's eyes on him but kept his eyes on his horse and angled his body so that no one could see the inside of his boot. Long before he could ready himself, it was time to picket the horses. He followed Aban's slow, measured pace to the line, forcing himself to adopt the man's gait, a horseman's swaying walk, while counting. Storana came behind, shielding him.

Pain shot through his ankle, telling him to shorten his steps. He struggled to keep his face expressionless, but by the time he reached the picket line, his breath hissed with every step, and tears mingled with the sweat running down his cheeks. He stooped to fasten his horse to the line and then returned. Aban stepped in on his right.

"Courage, Myrad," he said. "The life of any man is not without pain. Distraction helps. Tell me of some joyful thing."

"My abba," he said. "Gershom." His voice broke into pieces. "He took me into his household. He gave me a home and a name after my mother died."

Aban nodded. "A righteous man. Tell me more."

He tried, but bolts of searing pain shot up his leg with every step. When they came to the line of camels, he buried his face into a camel's shoulder and cried.

"Come," Aban whispered too soon. "We must take the camels to the picket line."

"Jamshed!"

The shout broke through his weeping. Myrad looked up to see a red-faced Walagash, glaring at him and screaming. "Yes, you son of a dog! I'm talking to you, Jamshed. What have I said about trading behind my back. Get in there!" He pointed at the tent.

Myrad understood. The soldier couldn't help but watch, but Myrad only needed to cover the distance to the tent now. Seventy paces. He set out, hopeful, but after twenty he was ready to surrender himself to Musa's man and die. He looked up at Walagash where he stood by his tent, still playing the part of the angry merchant, yet deep in the man's eyes Myrad saw comprehension.

They both knew he wasn't going to make it.

He ducked his head, nearly stumbling over a rock he couldn't see through his tears, and gasped as pain flared through him. He looked up. Forty paces remained. He laughed, but it sounded more like a sob. It might as well be forty miles. "One more step," he whispered as he put his right foot on the ground again.

Tremors wracked his legs, and his jaws ached from clenching.

"Curse you, Jamshed!" Walagash yelled. "When I call, I expect you to come running."

Ten paces from the tent, Myrad stopped. His right leg refused to bend. One more step and he would fall on his face. So close . . .

Walagash stood in front of him, helpless and glowering.

Hoping the merchant would understand his intent, Myrad took a deep breath. "A man has a right to make a living!"

It should have been impossible for a man that big to move so fast. Walagash was on him before he knew it. One of the merchant's oversized hands knotted in his tunic, lifting him from the ground. Relief poured through him as his weight came off his foot. Myrad watched as Walagash's other hand formed a fist.

"You dare to defy me?" he shouted.

Myrad saw the merchant's fist coming for his head. He twitched in his grasp, knowing he couldn't get away.

The world went dark, taking his pain with it.

When Myrad came to, night had fallen.

He blinked and winced, rubbing the knot on his right temple. Walagash sat on a stool nearby, his hands folded in his lap in placid unconcern.

"Is the soldier still out there?" Myrad asked.

"No. Two more caravans arrived after ours. Musa's man is at the inn now, spending his money on wine and other amusements."

"Thank you. I couldn't make it."

"I know. I've seen men in battle when they come to the realization they're going to die. You held that same look in your eyes."

Myrad pointed at the merchant's hands. "Is that how you got the scars?"

Walagash laughed. "No. Those came later. Before I became a merchant, I wrestled in the arena." His expression became somber. "There's money to be made if you're big and strong enough."

"You didn't enjoy it?"

"No." He grew quiet. "I think any man who does has something broken inside of him. I saved every denarius I could until I was able to buy my way into trade. No one was more surprised by my success than I was. Mostly I just wanted to stop hitting people. I tried not to hit you too hard, but it's been a long time since I've struck anyone."

Myrad pulled a long, shuddering breath into his lungs. "Now what?"

"I've sent men to the inn. They'll buy this soldier enough drink to loosen his tongue and discover what he knows. Regardless, Musa's man will be unable to rise with the sun tomorrow. We'll be gone before he awakens."

"That's not what I meant. If they have men posted at every oasis, they will catch me sooner or later. I can't keep this up."

Walagash turned his head toward the entrance of the tent and called Roshan's name. Soon his son stepped inside but stayed near the entrance. When the merchant beckoned his son closer, his steps were slow and reluctant.

"We need something for Myrad's pain," Walagash said. "What can we get?"

Roshan glanced down at Myrad's foot as though it were a mere thing instead of living flesh. "There's always poppy sap in the oases."

Walagash shook his head. "No, only as a last resort. He's got to be able to walk."

Roshan lifted his hands. "Camphor oil? It's mild, but it might take the edge off."

Myrad nodded. "I've used that before. It helps, some."

Walagash didn't look convinced. "What else can we do?"

Roshan shifted in obvious discomfort. He stood with his body turned halfway toward the tent flap as if he couldn't wait to leave. "We could bind the ankle with cloth and fold rags into the instep of his boot to give him more support."

"That sounds good." Walagash nodded. "Tend to him, Roshan.

I wish to see if Aban and Storana have learned anything from Musa's man."

Roshan stiffened. "Shouldn't someone else do it?"

Walagash didn't respond, but a quiet, tense stillness came over him as he stared at his son. Finally, Roshan ducked his head and left the tent, his sandals striking the ground in frustration.

"Does he dislike me?" Myrad asked.

"Roshan never wanted the silk trade. Having it means meeting the expectations that go with it."

"I don't understand."

The merchant rose from his stool and lumbered over to the tent flap. "You will in time. Someday."

Roshan returned a few minutes later, carrying strips of linen and a stoppered bottle. Without looking Myrad in the eye, he knelt and unbound the lacing of Myrad's right boot before removing it. Lifting the deformed foot, Roshan set it on a thick cushion. For a long moment, Roshan stared at it until heat spread in Myrad's face.

"It's not going to change," Myrad said.

Roshan finally looked at him. "You must have done something to anger the god of the shining fire."

Again? How many times must he have this same conversation? "The Most High God is not the god of the shining fire. I was born this way. What sin can a child commit in his mother's womb?"

Roshan shrugged away the question, taking the bottle of camphor oil and pouring it in his cupped hand. He began massaging Myrad's foot, using both hands to work the pungent oil into the flesh all the way up to the knee. "If what you say is true, then perhaps your parents must have done something."

His relief vanished. "Perhaps they did. I never knew my father. Gershom adopted me two years ago. I'm still learning the ways of my God."

Roshan didn't respond for a moment. "Is he so different, your god?"

"Yes. I mean no." He sighed. "It's hard to explain."

Roshan smiled but didn't meet his gaze. "It sounds like it."

Myrad took a deep breath. "I grew up worshiping the god of the shining fire the same as most people in Ctesiphon, but I don't think any of us took it seriously. We might have visited the eternal flame once or twice my entire life, even though we lived just a few streets away. My mother was a poor merchant in a community of men and women like her. What we really worshiped was commerce. If you don't sell, you don't eat. She died two years ago. That was when Gershom adopted me."

Roshan cocked his head. "Why?"

"I don't know. Ever since I can remember, he would come to the market and buy melons from me and my mother, even when they weren't as good as others. He always paid a bit more than she asked. As I grew older, we would talk and he would answer my questions, questions about everything. Mother would tell me to stop bothering him, but he seemed impressed. After Gershom adopted me, he told me there was another god, the Most High."

Roshan nodded. "The god of the Hebrews."

"You've heard of Him?"

"We're merchants of the great road," Roshan said. "We've heard of almost everything." He took a long strip of linen and began wrapping it around Myrad's swollen ankle.

He thought of telling Roshan about Gershom's calendar, but a nagging voice inside him argued against it. The heat and the scent of camphor oil tempted him with offers of sleep, and he nestled back into his blanket as Roshan tied off the wrap.

"Thank you." Talk of Gershom had opened a hole in his chest. More than anything at that moment, he wanted a friend. "I'll tell Walagash how much you helped me."

Roshan shrugged, then dropped a roll of linen at Myrad's feet. "Use that to pad your boot." He paused before adding, "I wish you'd gone with Esai. My future was set the moment my father obtained his heart's desire." And without another word, he left the tent.

For the next five days, the combination of camphor oil and bindings allowed Myrad to walk normally enough to fool the soldiers posted at each watering station, but each day the pain worsened and took longer for him to shed. On the sixth day, with at least eight days' travel still ahead to Rhagae, Myrad clawed his way to wakefulness from dreams invaded by scenes of torture to see the tent already struck and the sun well up from the horizon.

Aban brought him his horse. "Courage now."

The words must have been meant for someone else. Out of the corner of Myrad's eye, he saw the guard look to Walagash and give a small shake of his head. When the caravan started out of the now-empty oasis, even the gentle gait of his horse set his ankle to throbbing. He dropped into a state of semi-wakefulness where time crept, measured by the intervals between each stab of pain.

Two hours after midday, Storana roused him by shaking him by the arm. "Eat, Myrad." Her hand darted into her pack to offer him flatbread.

He couldn't remember his last meal, yet food held no interest for him. He held up a hand in refusal.

"You must." Storana thrust the bread at him. "You cannot heal if you don't eat. Pain is a burden that can be borne like any other."

Myrad took the bread and ripped off a bite with his teeth. Satisfied, Storana drifted away. He left the bread unfinished but couldn't seem to drink enough. Beneath the sea of pain, part of his mind noted that he seemed to be sweating more than usual.

They were still an hour from the next oasis when Aban rode forward. Soon afterward, Walagash and Roshan came into view, the merchant scowling at everyone around him.

"He's not going to make it," Aban said.

"I see that," Walagash snapped. "You have it?" he asked Roshan.

When Roshan nodded, stiff disapproval filled Aban's expression. "You'll cripple him."

"He's already crippled. If he's discovered, he dies. We all die."

Myrad forced himself out of his stupor. "What are you talking about?"

"They want to give you *hul gil*," Aban answered. "The joy plant."

He frowned, the name unfamiliar to him. "What is it?"

"Poppy-seed tea."

That name he knew. He couldn't help but know it. The streets of Ctesiphon, Seleucia, and Babylon were littered with the human detritus of those who'd surrendered to it. After a time—weeks or months or perhaps a few years—it killed them. Myrad drew a shuddering breath. Better that than the pain. "Give it to me."

"Walagash," Aban said, "there must be another way."

"Then tell me what it is." When he didn't reply, Walagash continued, "Stay with him. Remind him often to walk normally. If he falls, carry him into my tent at once. There are enough people on the trade routes who have given themselves to the tea to make one more unremarkable."

They halted the caravan, and Myrad watched Roshan through a pain-filled haze as he dismounted and rushed forward to a camel loaded down with their supplies. He dug through the packs, his hands submerged in their contents, until he pulled a small glass bottle free. A moment later he produced a heavy earthenware cup.

"How much do you weigh?" Roshan asked him.

Myrad answered with a slow shake of his head, grimacing. Even that motion sent lightning bolts of pain up and down his leg. "I don't know. Why would I need to know that?"

Walagash answered for him. "Two and a half talents, minus a mina or two. I carried him."

Roshan nodded without looking at his father and carefully measured out a dose of tea, which looked pitifully small.

"Is that enough?" Myrad asked.

The boy bit his lip. "Possibly too much."

Myrad took the cup and drank without hesitation. The agony in his leg had beaten him.

"Don't reveal yourself," Walagash told him. "You must walk without a limp."

He handed the cup back to Roshan. Already the horizon swam in his vision, the colors of dun and blue waving sinuously as if he were looking through a sheet of running water. Then the drug pulled him under.

CHAPTER 8

Time stretched and compressed, marked by periods of light and dark that passed without counting. Had Myrad been able to number their intervals, he still wouldn't have trusted the sum. Night and day chased each other, short or long depending on the mood of the drug. He woke at one point on his horse's back, the desert hills rolling away from him. With a shock he realized he couldn't recall Gershom's face. He squeezed his eyes shut, working to bring his memories into focus, but the images blurred and his father's features became indistinct. Myrad put his face to his horse's mane and wept.

Then there came a day when the pain burned away the drug's sleepiness and he found himself staring at the stripes of Walagash's tent, gasping for air. An unfamiliar face filled his vision, staring down at him. Myrad squirmed away, his hands groping. But his knife, even his clothes were gone.

"Calmly," the man said. His eyebrows were extremely long. "Poppy tea leaves its mark on the body and the mind alike."

Walagash's voice came from outside his field of vision. "Be at peace, Myrad. He's a healer. We're in Rhagae now."

They'd made it. He took a breath filled with pain and an aching need he couldn't identify. "How long have we been here?" His voice croaked. Twisting on a pallet, he saw Walagash and

Roshan sitting behind him. They fidgeted, like a man and a boy who'd been seated for too long a time.

"Only a day," Walagash said. "Yet that's the wrong question."

The poppy tea no longer numbed him, though his senses felt blunted, dull. "What's the right one?"

"How long will it be until you're healed."

The physician shrugged. "If he stays away from the poppy tea, that portion of his trouble should dissipate in another day. The leg is another matter. The tissues around the bone have been strained to the breaking point. If he uses a crutch, time will restore it eventually, but I have no cure for a clubfoot."

"How much time?" Myrad asked.

"Four weeks, perhaps six."

"No," Walagash said. "We can't stay here that long, and a crutch will arouse suspicion."

His comment had no impact on the healer. "Then you'll have to leave him behind." He stood, packed up the implements of his trade, and left.

"I never planned on going any farther than Rhagae."

"Plans change with need," Walagash said. "There were soldiers along the entire route here."

Myrad managed to sit up a few moments later. After the room stopped spinning, he gave what reassurances he could. "My father told me to come here. There must be someone he wants me to find." He searched the tent for his clothes before spying them at his feet. The tent flap was closed, so he reached down to toss aside the blanket covering him.

Walagash's hand covered his. "You need to rest. If your friend can be found, I will find him."

"I'll do it," Roshan offered. "If you go, Father, you'll be remembered. You have a tendency to make an unforgettable impression on people. I'm just a boy." He smiled and his eyes twinkled. "No one will notice me."

Myrad tried again to stand, but Walagash's hand kept him on the cushions. "What's his name?" the merchant asked.

Myrad surrendered. "Amin Ben-Yirah. If there's a synagogue in Rhagae, start there." He didn't tell them what the name meant.

Walagash kept Myrad pinned beneath his blanket until Roshan left. Then he handed Myrad his clothes. "Rhagae is a big city. There are any number of people who walk with the aid of a crutch. I'll find you one. If the god of the shining fire is willing, you'll be able to pass unnoticed." He left, closing the tent flap behind him.

By the time he'd finished dressing, a fresh layer of sweat bathed him, and a thirst for poppy tea filled him—even a sip or two to take the edge off his pain. He searched the interior of the tent but found nothing other than a waterskin he drained within minutes. Hopping on one leg, he made his way to a stool to wait.

Walagash returned first, his hands clutching a heavy crutch made of some dark-grained wood. "Here. Try this."

Myrad had never used one before, yet he'd seen countless others with one. War and disease left any number of men and women lamed. He tucked it beneath his right arm and took a step with his left foot. Swinging the crutch and his right leg forward in unison felt strange, but after a few moments he managed to navigate the perimeter of the tent in slow, deliberate steps. "Why are you doing this?" Myrad asked.

Walagash's face, large like the rest of him, broke into a smile. "It's just a crutch."

"You know that's not what I meant. Why help me find Ben-Yirah?" He swallowed and then forced himself to put words to his fear. "I'm not even sure he's here."

Walagash's eyes grew thoughtful above his smile. "I swore to take you as far as you needed to go. I deal shrewdly, but I've never given less than promised. I won't start now."

Myrad's gaze slipped to the floor of the tent. "But I'm not even sure where I need to go. My father and the life he planned for me are gone." Even as he said this, a nameless desire filled him, urging him to action. But what?

"You're young," Walagash said. "The inclinations of the heart change with the seasons of a man's life. At least allow me a day to search for your father's friend. Come," he said, breaking the mood. "You've eaten little in the past few days. You must be hungry."

He and Walagash left the tent and went into Rhagae. It was late afternoon when Myrad stopped to take in the view. Gone were the rolling deserts of Ctesiphon. Mountains rose to the north, the valleys between them lush and green.

Walagash caught his stare. "This is what keeps me on the road. The ever-changing earth in all its beauty is like a woman in her moods—sultry, serious, playful."

"Where is your wife?" Myrad asked, a little surprised the question never came to him before.

"She died," Walagash replied, his tone wistful.

"It was a long time ago?" Myrad asked.

The merchant nodded with a little smile. "You read people well. That's the beginnings of a good merchant. Yes. After Roshan was born, Adrina conceived again, but mother and child were lost. I have tried to be both mother and father to Roshan."

"I'm sorry," Myrad said. "I shouldn't have reminded you."

"Don't be. I like remembering her. Roshan is like Adrina in many ways."

They worked their way toward the market with frequent stops.

Myrad's arm hurt with the effort of using the crutch, but the pain was nothing compared to before and it served to distract him from his craving for poppy tea.

They found a vendor selling roasted goat and flatbread. After purchasing their meals, they sat and ate in silence. Myrad worked his way through every memory he had of Gershom, from the time he first met him to the day of his death, lifting them up to the Most High God as an offering and a prayer. Walagash sat across from him with a faraway look in his eyes.

When they returned to the tent at sunset, Walagash departed. Alone, Myrad knelt to offer his prayers to the Most High, feeling Gershom's absence as a wound. Then he retrieved the calendar. How long since he'd marked the days? He didn't know. Amending his prayer, he tried to correct the count, but precision eluded him.

Walagash returned then, followed by Roshan. "It's bad," Roshan said. "There were soldiers at the synagogue, asking after a clubfooted man, and no one there knew anyone named Ben-Yirah. A few of them laughed at the name. They said it was a joke. Then I walked through the markets and visited every Hebrew's stall I could find. No one had heard of a Ben-Yirah. No one."

Myrad shook his head. "That doesn't make sense. Why would Gershom send me to look for someone who doesn't exist?"

The tent flap fluttered. When it stilled, a clean-shaven man with dark curly hair stood just inside. His appearance and clothes were unremarkable, and he could have been anyone on the street, Persian or Hebrew, except for the eyes. Deeply set and restless, they did not simply see. They darted or glared at people and objects alike.

"I saw you at the synagogue," Roshan said.

"I am Ben-Yirah," the man answered, but his gaze never left Myrad. "Tell me what happened to Gershom."

In halting sentences and without any emotion that would betray him, he described Gershom and the last meeting of the magi. Ben-Yirah sighed. "I feared as much. The kings of Parthia lack the wisdom of Nebuchadnezzar or Cyrus. Gershom was never a threat to them, no matter how he voted."

Myrad stared at Ben-Yirah. He could see nothing of deception in the man's expression, only an intensity that put him on his guard. "Why would Gershom send me to you?"

The man smiled, his eyes almost disappearing. "My real name is Hakam. Ben-Yirah is a signal, a warning. Along with your father and others, I keep the calendar. Do you have it?"

"Calendar?" Walagash asked.

Myrad didn't reply. Instead, he removed the papers from his bag and pulled the calendar out from among them, offering it to Hakam.

The stranger gave it the merest of glances before speaking. "You've marred his work. I see there are two days unaccounted for." His accusation came out in staccato, a voice speaking at Myrad instead of to him. "Don't you understand? It has to be perfect."

"I tried," Myrad said. "But ever since I left Ctesiphon, I've had Musa's men after me."

Hakam dismissed the excuse with a wave of his hand. "The calendar of the Most High does not permit such excuses. The count must be *exact*." He tapped the papers, revulsion twisting his expression. "You're just an apprentice. There's no reason for Musa or Phraates to expend their efforts on you."

"It's true," Walagash said.

"Because he said so?" Hakam sneered, his eyes still on Myrad.

"Because we got one of the soldiers at the oasis drunk enough to tell us what he was doing," Roshan said, his voice hot. "He said he'd been ordered to find a clubfooted apprentice to the magi."

Hakam dismissed Roshan with a shake of his head. "Did he say Musa ordered it? Why would the queen waste her time on you, Myrad?"

The question cut. "I saw what she did," Myrad said. "I'm a witness."

Hakam waved away his argument. "So did hundreds of others. Musa and Phraates don't care about witnesses; they want them. Word reached us here in Rhagae days ago of what happened. Emperors rule by fear. The more you spread the story of your father's death, the more you do Musa's work for her."

"There were soldiers at every oasis and way station along the route from here to Ctesiphon," Walagash said. "They were after him."

"There must be some other reason. Did you steal something?"

"No." The accusation burned. "I took only what belonged to Gershom. I'm his son."

"He never mentioned you." Hakam's gaze swept over Myrad's features. "You don't have his looks or his coloring."

"He adopted me. Two years ago." For some reason Myrad couldn't put words to, he wanted Hakam's approval. Or at the very least, his acceptance.

Walagash came to Myrad's defense. "In some cultures an adopted son is as highly valued as a natural one."

Hakam shrugged. "Yes, some cultures, like the barbarians in Rome. But the Hebrews prize blood above all else. Since Gershom didn't tell you why you needed to seek me out, I will not risk myself with you. Do you know why he taught you to mark the days?"

"I will keep the days like my father before me and his father before him," Myrad said. "Gershom was my father. He taught me Hebrew and told me about the sixty-nine weeks."

Hakam blinked. "Sixty-nine weeks? What did he tell you exactly?"

Gershom had told him the words of Daniel so often that Myrad could have recited them in his sleep. The prophecy was part of him, inextricably linked to his identity as Gershom's son.

Hakam listened as the words spilled from him, but when Myrad stopped, he stood, his head cocked as if he expected more. For a long while, Hakam didn't speak. When he did, it wasn't what Myrad expected.

"There's nothing about the prophecy that's a threat to Musa or Phraates or anyone else. The Messiah-King isn't supposed to appear for decades yet. What did you take from Ctesiphon?"

"I told you. Just the money Gershom had saved, and his papers." Myrad glanced at Walagash. "He had a copy of the Torah that I traded for safe passage."

"The calendar is in your hands, and you traded away the Torah?" Hakam pointed. "What did you just put back in your bag?"

A hole opened in the pit of his stomach. "I don't know."

Hakam growled something in Hebrew Myrad didn't recognize. "Foolish boy."

The four of them looked at Myrad's bag as if it contained some demon intent on springing forth to devour them. Myrad opened it and removed the papers. There were half a dozen and they were written in Greek, but the language was beyond him. He handed them to Hakam.

He looked at the first one, then the second, then the rest. His hands moved faster and faster, flipping pages as his brows rose until the whites showed around his eyes. *"What have you done?"*

"I was in a hurry," Myrad said. "I needed to get away."

"What do they say?" Walagash asked.

Hakam stared at the papers in amazement. "Gershom worked in the treasury of the king, helping to oversee the mints. These are letters of transfer. With them a man could walk into any mint in the empire and empty it." He looked again at Myrad, his expression stopping short of compassion. "This explains the soldiers searching the city."

Walagash shook his head. "Couldn't Phraates simply issue new letters, replacing the old?"

"Yes," Hakam said, "if he knew the old letters had been stolen. If you were master of the mint, would you want to tell the king the letters of transfer to every mint in the empire are missing?"

"Can't we just return them?" The looks Myrad received from the others, even Roshan, told him how bad an idea that was.

Myrad started at the sound of Walagash's sudden laughter. No one else joined in but watched him in surprised silence. Finally, the merchant wiped the mirth from his eyes. "I hope word of this never gets out," he said. "All you wanted was safe passage to Rhagae. Now I discover I've been out-traded by a mere apprentice. Ha! It will be a miracle if I get out of this with my life."

"Katanes is head of the treasury," Hakam said, ignoring Walagash's comment. "How did he vote?"

Myrad thought back and replayed the scene in the throne room for the thousandth time. "Katanes stood with those wanting to install Musa as queen."

Hakam nodded. "After the king and queen, he's the most powerful man in the empire. Something must have led Gershom to keep the letters of transfer in his personal possession. My compliments, Myrad. With Gershom's death you've managed to become one of the most dangerous men in the empire—at least until Katanes and his men find you and kill you."

His mouth went dry. "What do I do?"

Hakam shrugged his indifference. "Get to the eastern edge of the empire as quickly as you can. The eastern satraps never fully supported Phraates, and they'll despise the idea of a Roman queen. You should be safe there."

"I had a dream I don't yet understand, and I must keep the calendar."

"The calendar is for Hebrews," Hakam said. A sudden passion lit his face. "The Messiah-King will come in my lifetime and then Judea will be free."

Walagash rose to escort Hakam from the tent. After, he said to Myrad, "I swore by the god of the shining fire to take you to safety. I keep my vows. Once we reach Margiana, you can travel by caravan to anywhere in the world you wish to go: Khushan, Qian, Judea, even Rome if you wish."

But Myrad wanted only to return home, back to Gershom, his father, and the life they'd had together.

CHAPTER 9

They slipped away the next morning just as the sun broke the horizon. Rhagae receded behind them, and with every step a tiny bit of worry lifted from Myrad's shoulders. Once again he'd evaded capture, yet he couldn't escape the feeling that sooner or later his luck or favor would run out. When they came to the next oasis, just after midday, Walagash called Roshan forward. Instead of slowing, the caravan increased its pace.

"We're not stopping?" Myrad asked when Roshan returned.

"No. The next way station is close enough for us to make it before nightfall. My father wants to put as much distance between us and Rhagae as possible. We'll water the horses here and catch up." Aban and Storana both nodded, and as one they galloped ahead toward the oasis.

After the rolling beat of their horses' hooves faded, Myrad turned to Roshan. "Thank you."

"For what?" the boy asked.

"Helping me find Hakam."

Roshan spat. "His kind is everywhere. So concerned about whether or not you're Hebrew, he never considers you as a person. You can no more change the circumstances of your birth than I can. If this 'Most High God' really exists, then he will look in your heart, not at your skin." Roshan glanced down at Myrad's leg. "Or your foot."

They kept to the same schedule for the next four days, early out of camp and late into the next oasis. The horses began to flag, walking across the hot sand with their heads drooping toward the ground. Even the camels tired, becoming more temperamental. Lines of fatigue showed on Walagash's and the guards' faces, and the lighthearted banter that usually accompanied their travels vanished.

Yet Myrad breathed prayers of thanks. Every minute he spent on horseback was a minute he didn't have to spend on his crutch or his foot, and he gladly traded the pain for the fatigue that came from their rigorous travels. The stabbing ache receded from his leg until it shrank to a knot in his ankle.

Then, nearly a week out from Rhagae, despite their haste and Myrad's prayers, their luck ran out. "We have a shadow," Aban said. The last light of dusk cast the oasis in shades of dun and charcoal.

"Perhaps several," Storana added.

Roshan searched the pack behind him. He pretended to pull some insignificant object free and rode forward.

Myrad kept his attention focused ahead, pressing his right leg against his mount to keep his foot disguised. "What do I do?"

"Wait and watch," Aban said.

The caravan slowed as they pulled the camels and horses aside for water and feed. Out of the corner of his eye, Myrad watched as the rider circled around to the left to enter the oasis from the opposite side. Aban dismounted and handed his reins to Storana. He slipped into the shadows, flitting from tree to tree.

Myrad sat on his horse, his eyes searching the area, but he saw no soldiers and none of the other people milling about gave Walagash's caravan more than a cursory glance. Before he could talk himself out of his decision, he dismounted and handed his reins to Storana.

"This is unwise," she said. "You're not built for stealth." But she made no move to stop him.

In the dark, with only occasional torches and the light of the inn ahead to guide him, progress was slow. He bypassed the arched entryway and circled around to one of the open windows. Keeping his face out of the light spilling through the opening, Myrad searched for Aban and found him a few moments later, reclining on a stack of cushions to one side, sipping date wine. Aban's gaze wandered over the room with seeming disinterest but came to rest on a particular spot more often than any other. Myrad tried to see what it was, but several carvans already filled the oasis and the inn teemed with guards eager to wash the dust from their throats.

He waited, his arm going numb from supporting his weight on the crutch. Customers filled the low tables and an elevated counter running the length of the room by the kitchen. Noise and smoke punctuated the conversations. When a pair of men left the counter, Myrad got his first clear view of Aban's target, a man whose face he knew.

Turning, he scuffed along with his crutch across the uneven ground to the entrance and through. Aban rose from his place and started toward him, but Myrad waved him back. The man he recognized might have sensed his stare. Perhaps he'd heard the sound of Myrad's crutch behind him and guessed what it meant. Whatever the reason, Myrad was still three paces away when he turned.

His eyes registered recognition, though his face showed no reaction. Instead, he swung back to the counter and took another drink of his wine.

The beat of Myrad's crutch sounded in counterpoint to his heart. He took the empty spot at the counter next to the man and paused to fill a goblet with date wine. His hands shook. He lifted the rim to his lips, intending a sip, no more, to wet his throat. But the drink, unexpectedly cool in his mouth, warmed his belly and calmed the frantic racing of his heart. When he put the goblet back on the counter, it was empty.

"Allow me," Masista said with a nod, refilling his cup.

Myrad bowed his thanks. Over Masista's shoulder, Aban positioned himself closer, his hand creeping toward the dagger at his belt.

"You remind me of someone," Myrad said.

"A friend of your father perhaps?" Masista asked.

"Perhaps a friend, or possibly a man with a common enemy. Is the enemy of my enemy necessarily a friend?"

"I suppose that would depend on the enemy," Masista said. "But I would hope so." His eyes betrayed the circumstances of some extremity that had driven him from Ctesiphon. They darted to either side, always searching.

Myrad took another swallow of wine, savoring the warm sensation that eased the pain in his leg. He let his eyes wander from Masista's drink to his head. Like most, his hair was dark and thick, but without a leather strap to keep it from his face and neck. "You're not wearing your cr—"

Masista's hand caught Myrad's wrist in a desperate grip. Aban rose. With his free hand, Myrad knocked his goblet over, sending the wine splashing toward their laps. Masista jerked to avoid the dark liquid, breaking eye contact, and Myrad shook his head.

Aban settled himself back at his table, but the dagger was in his hand now. "My apologies for my clumsiness," Myrad said. "For a moment you reminded me of someone else. Are you here for trade?"

Masista bobbed his head, smiling amiably, yet he sat on his stool like a coiled viper. "I am, but regrettably few merchants trade in the commodity I most desire."

"Perhaps you will favor my master with the opportunity to supply your needs. I have found him to be a man of discernment, and he carries a surprising array of goods."

"Perhaps," Masista said and turned away.

Myrad allowed himself the leisure of refilling his goblet and downing it before pushing himself from the counter. "My master abides in a red-and-white tent." His eyes locked with Aban's and then flicked toward Masista, hoping the message was clear.

He made his way out of the inn and back to Walagash's tent. The merchant waited inside, his face and posture the picture of unconcern, but his eyes glittered. Roshan stood to his left, shifting his weight from one foot to another.

"It would be wise to seek counsel before you put the rest of us in danger," Roshan snapped.

"The danger was to me. If there was danger to the rest of you, forcing Masista to seek me out in your tent would have tied us together in his mind."

Walagash pointed Myrad to the stool across from him. "Where's Aban?"

"He stayed behind to watch." Myrad eased himself onto the stool. "I believe both of them will be here shortly. I invited Masista to trade."

"So you protect us by meeting him alone and then throw that protection away by inviting him here?" Roshan asked.

Myrad nodded. "If he meant to kill or betray me, he would have done it already. He's one of the magi, and in the eyes of Musa and Phraates I'm a traitor." He paused and shook his head. "Masista's frightened, but I don't know why. He voted to install Musa as queen."

Walagash raised a hand to forestall Roshan's next objection. They waited in silence by the light of the small brazier. An hour later, they were still waiting. The date wine no longer warmed Myrad, and he found himself fidgeting as much as Roshan. Walagash sat on his stool brooding, his expression unreadable.

At last, Masista stepped through the tent flap, and although no one greeted or beckoned him, he joined them in the center of the tent. Aban and Storana appeared a moment later. Walagash pointed and made a circling motion, his desire plain, and they ghosted back into the night.

"No on will hear us except my most trusted," Walagash said.

Masista eyed the tent's closed flap. "And how do you know they are worthy of trust?"

"My guards are my family," Walagash said.

"Here in Parthia we betray family as quickly as friends."

"Magi and nobles perhaps," Walagash said. "Now, what do you want?"

Instead of being insulted, Masista smiled, dipping his head. "It's rare to meet a merchant who is so . . . forthright. I'm here to trade." He turned to Myrad. "Your father's death leaves the burden of your care to me, and I will shoulder it if you will allow me."

"The burden of care," Walagash mused, his eyes narrowing. "Myrad is part of my caravan. I will negotiate on his behalf."

Masista started in surprise. "You have brought him into your tent?"

96

Now it was Walagash who dipped his head. "I see our ways are known to you."

"Father," Roshan said, "you ha—"

"Go and check the perimeter, Roshan," Walagash interrupted, his voice firm. "At once."

Roshan spun on one heel and stalked from the tent.

CHAPTER 10

Walagash leaned forward, looming over them, his attention centered on the magus. "You speak of a burden of care, but you said you came here to trade. I'll ask you once more, what do you want?"

Again Masista looked to Myrad. "Musa has blinded the king. You've seen it. If she's not stopped, all of Parthia will fall under Roman rule. Is that what you want?"

"No," Myrad answered. He still had no idea why the magus continued to appeal to him.

"Roman or Parthian, what's the difference?" Walagash said. "General Surena crushed the Romans at Carrhae and was killed by King Orodes for his efforts. Phraates killed his father and a score of brothers and half brothers to secure the throne. Together, he and Pacorus drove the Romans from Syria and Israel and set up Antigonus as king of the Hebrews. But the Romans reclaimed their territory a few years later and killed Antigonus for his folly." His gaze shifted back and forth between Masista and Myrad. "And they just didn't kill him; they crucified him as an example to any who might defy Rome. So, magus, what difference is there between Rome and Parthia?"

Masista ignored the question, instead addressing Myrad as if the two of them were alone in the tent. "Musa killed your father.

She and Phraates struck him down for daring to put the needs of Parthia before the desires of Rome. Would you abandon the man who adopted you? Doesn't Gershom deserve justice?"

Heat flooded into Myrad's face and his heart beat accusations against him, reminding him of his vow. He jerked his head in agreement.

"Be very careful, Myrad," Walagash said.

Again, Masista brushed off Walagash's words. "I was there as well, Myrad. Your father didn't even try to defend himself. The king's soldiers slaughtered their way through the front rows of the highest magi and their guards, those who might have offered real resistance to Musa. But they didn't stop there. Musa's thirst was not so easily satisfied. The soldiers kept coming, killing defenseless men, good and faithful administrators like your father."

Myrad stood and faced Masista, though he couldn't remember rising from his stool. His breaths came in ragged gasps, and his hands ached from the clenching of his fists.

"No good can come from this rage," Walagash said.

His warning slid from Myrad, unheeded.

Masista went on. "It wasn't enough just to kill innocent men. No. Musa wanted more. She ordered the servants to gather the bodies, including your father's body, and throw them into the streets so the beggars and thieves of the city could pick over them. I watched, Myrad. Your father was my friend. I watched the detritus of Ctesiphon strip his body naked and fight over his clothes with no more regard than they would give a dog."

Tears blurred Myrad's vision. "She took everything from me."

"Then help me defeat her," Masista said.

"Anything."

"And now we come to it at last," Walagash said.

Masista confronted the merchant, his voice rising. "Would you deny him his birthright? Does he not bear a duty to avenge his father's death?"

Walagash shifted in his seat toward Myrad, holding up a huge fist for him to see. The knuckles were covered with so many layers of scars, the skin resembled a turtle shell. "It took me a very long time to learn that this"—he waved his fist in the air—"will only get you this." He held up the other fist. Both were equally scarred.

"Phraates and Musa entered the streets the next day," Masista continued. "Even the death and dishonor of those they hated was not enough for them." He swallowed. "I will not tell you what they did, but they defiled the bodies of all those who had stood against them."

"Enough!" Walagash's voice cracked. "Please . . . what do you want?"

Masista nodded. "Winter is breaking. Within a month, Phraates and Musa will leave Ctesiphon and travel north to their palace in Hecatompylos, but we will be there before them." A grim smile brought a gleam to his eyes. "The main treasury is there. When they arrive, they will find their silver gone, spirited away. They believe all their enemies to be dead. By the time they learn we have rallied the eastern satraps, the true Parthians, it will be too late."

"You want the letters of transfer to the mint," Myrad said. "How do you know about them?"

"Katanes is frantic to find you. After I voted with him to support Musa, he confided in me. Since I know what you look like, my offer to help was graciously accepted. Those few pieces of parchment could turn the tide against Musa and Phraates."

100

Walagash sighed. "And what do you offer in exchange for your revenge?"

"For his part, Myrad will be numbered among the most powerful when the new king takes the throne. A crown of six palms will be yours, Myrad, along with lands and slaves. With the ear of the king, you could ensure slaughter such as Musa's never happens again."

"What else do you offer?" Walagash said.

Confusion clouded Masista's expression. "I am offering lands and titles and the opportunity to see justice done, merchant. What more could the son of Gershom desire?"

"What more indeed?" Walagash said. "Leave now. You will have your answer in the morning."

"Wait," Myrad said, drawing the attention of the two men to him. "I have a question." He faced Masista squarely. "Why are you so afraid?"

The magus attempted a dismissive smile, but his eyes betrayed him. "What reason could I have for fear?"

Within the culture of the magi it was forbidden to lie, but centuries of following the stricture served to make them masters in the art of evasion. "That's not an answer," Myrad said. "You're not wearing your crown. You had five palms and all the authority that went with them. I will not help you unless you answer honestly."

"Musa was suckled on intrigue since birth," Masista spat. "She made a show of killing her enemies, and the morning after their bodies were dumped in the street, she ordered her men to search their rooms. You should have taken all of Gershom's papers. You left behind bits of correspondence between Gershom and me. One of them mentioned Musa in uncomplimentary fashion. Though I voted for her as queen, that was enough to condemn me. Magi are flooding from Ctesiphon and the rest of the western cities to flee east. Another war for the empire is coming, but we have a chance to strike a blow before we leave, a blow that will turn the tide in our favor. Give me the letters and I will make her pay for Gershom's death."

Myrad shook his head. "Give? No, I made a vow to make her pay, big or small. I want to be there when you take her ability to fight. I can help you. I made the trip to the mint with Gershom several times. I can tell you what to expect."

Masista's eyes narrowed, and at last he nodded. "Let it be as you say."

Walagash sighed, then clapped twice, the noise like tree branches breaking. Aban and Storana appeared at the tent's opening. "Escort our guest to the inn," Walagash said. "Our negotiations are done for the day."

Masista moved quickly to the entrance but then stopped and turned. "I miss Gershom as well," he said. Then he disappeared.

Except for the two of them, the tent stood empty. "You have a way of seeing to the heart of a man," Walagash said to Myrad. "But you should be wary of those who offer the future against the present."

"I don't understand."

Walagash took a deep breath. "Masista has nothing to offer you now, only vapors and smoke, hopes for revenge and power in the future."

"You advise that I reconsider and refuse his offer?" Anger still churned in his gut, but there was no target, no outlet for it. "You think I should just forget my father and ride around the country in a caravan?"

"On the contrary," Walagash said. "I think you should give the magus everything he asked for. And then let him go. The

102

letters from your father are a trap. If you do not give them to Masista, he can simply denounce you and take them. Once he has the letters, he has no need for you, and anything he does with them will draw the pursuit to himself."

Myrad shook his head. "He tried to warn us that day in Ctesiphon, told us to turn back before we went into the throne room. Only it was too late; the king's soldiers blocked the hallways behind us. No. I'm going to help him." Even as he said it, doubt whispered to him. Is this what Gershom would want him to do?

Walagash looked at him over his steepled hands. "Because you want revenge."

His tone cut, and a hard knot formed in Myrad's chest around his grief. "Gershom took me from the street and gave me a name and a life. Musa and Phraates took all of that."

"And you want to give her your life as well? Come with us, Myrad," Walagash urged. "Leave revenge and politics behind. Soldiers and kings die. Merchants continue. We don't take sides, and because of this we are left in peace."

"I saw him," Myrad said. "They left him naked in the street." He swallowed. "I left him there."

Walagash breathed a sigh lasting a dozen heartbeats. When it ended, he looked to be a smaller man. "I will not help you raid the mint in Hecatompylos. That was never part of our bargain. But this I will do for you. If you make it out of the city with your silver, you may find us on the main trade road heading east. If not there, then search for us in Margiana. You will always be welcome in my tent."

Nothing further was said, and before long Roshan appeared. Father and son left the tent, speaking in hushed tones. Walagash's warning about Masista sent him to his pack. He needed a guarantee of safety. He took out his father's papers, reading through them as best he could until he found the one he sought. This he removed and placed at the bottom of the pack, hidden beneath his spare tunic and trousers. The others he left at the top, undisturbed.

Exhausted, he sought his blanket and then lay down to sleep. His imagination conjured visions of revenge and bloodshed upon Musa and the king, but the thought of leaving Walagash's caravan opened a hole in his heart his savage imaginings couldn't fill.

Four days later, Myrad sat atop his horse on the outskirts of Hecatompylos, the summer home for the kings of Parthia and the site of one of the mints. To the east, a thinning cloud of dust marked the departure of Walagash's caravan. Masista nodded his satisfaction. "The pace of the caravan would only hold us back. Camels are sturdy but slow."

Myrad counted the number of beasts Masista had purchased. There were at least twenty camels, along with an even greater number of horses.

"Do you understand what you are to do?" Masista asked.

"Yes," Myrad said, but he couldn't suppress a thick swallow. Other magi, some he recognized from Ctesiphon, sat on their mounts in company with Masista. All of them wore their crowns and had mustered every soldier and cataphract owing fealty to them they could. To Myrad, they appeared a fearsome company.

Masista gnawed his lower lip every time he looked at them. "Too few," he said more than once. "But hopefully enough to allay suspicion. It's a pity we won't be able to empty the mint completely."

Just within sight of the towering walls of the city, Masista signaled a pair of soldiers who untied the spare horses and departed east into the desert, leaving the rest of them to continue. As they approached the gates, Myrad tried to look his part. Unlike Ctesiphon, which cowed its visitors with its towering parabolic entrance, Hecatompylos exuded a squat strength. The city encompassed a low rise, its broad walls sketching a rectangular perimeter wide enough for four chariots to ride abreast. As they rode down the main road toward the center of the city, massive temples adorned with dozens of towering columns in Greek fashion passed by them on either side, the largest reserved for the god of the shining fire, the closest the Parthians came to an imperial religion. There, priests tended a blaze that never died so that adherents might come and offer their sacrifices and prayers. Gershom taught Myrad there was only one true God, the Most High, but did He hear the prayers offered to the others?

He thrust those speculations away. If he wanted to live to see his revenge, the task at hand demanded his full attention. They passed through the shadow of the palace. Steps led up to the base, which loomed thirty feet or more above them. The king's residence surmounted the plaza created by a staggering retaining wall. He gaped at the monstrous construction.

"Keep your eyes ahead," Masista hissed. Around them the other magi, cataphracts, and soldiers paid the palace no mind. Their goal lay deeper into the city. With an effort, Myrad pulled his eyes from the mammoth structure and fixed his stare over the top of his horse.

They came to a building constructed of great blocks of granite, guarded by grim soldiers in heavy mail. Masista rode forward. "Inform the master of the treasury the magus, Masista, is here to see him."

One of the soldiers disappeared into the shadows of the interior. A moment later, a man with six palm leaves on his circlet came forward. His eyes were mere slits, a consequence perhaps of permanent suspicion. "I am Sadeq," he said.

"Greetings," Masista said. The magi pitched his tone to match the treasury master's expression. Without ceremony, he held the letter of transfer out for inspection. When Sadeq took it, he added, "Katanes begs your pardon for the irregularity."

Sadeq nodded absently as he read the authorization. Then he looked up. "That's a lie."

Myrad's heart struggled to keep its rhythm. Another dozen or more soldiers appeared from within the treasury to join those at the gate.

"No," Masista said. "It's the truth. He did say that, but I don't think he meant it."

The hint of a smile ghosted across Sadeq's mouth. "You know him then. Perhaps you can explain this unscheduled transfer to Seleucia?"

Sweat trickled down Myrad's back, which had nothing to do with the heat of the day. Yet Masista sat patiently on his horse, a look of unconcern on his face. "Magus Katanes did not deign to tell me, but I assumed it was because Musa has been made queen. It's rumored King Phraates—may he live forever—has decided to commemorate her elevation by having coins minted with her likeness on them."

Sadeq's expression soured. "Doubtless she'll take a title. Perhaps 'queen of queens.'" He gazed out over the men and horses gathered before them. The group which seemed so large earlier now seemed pitifully small. "Bring your camels," Sadeq said at last. "My men will load them."

Myrad breathed a sigh of relief as they moved into the courtyard of the treasury. Sadeq's men emerged in a line from the interior of the treasury building, each sweating under the load of a talent of silver. Masista's men dismounted and loaded each camel with six talents, fastening them together with heavy ropes so that three hung on each side before covering them with thick blankets.

The process took hours. Myrad watched from his position, kept on his horse by his infirmity and his role as scribe for each talent taken from the treasury. By the time they were finished, it was nearly noon and they'd lightened the Parthian treasury of over one hundred talents of silver. Masista ordered the camels in a ponderous circle and began their departure.

"A moment, magus." Sadeq's voice cut across the courtyard.

Myrad jerked his horse around and trotted over to the magi. "You can't leave," he hissed under his breath.

"Are we discovered?" Masista whispered. Around them, Masista's men shifted on their horses, casual, but their hands strayed closer to their weapons.

"The receipt," Myrad said. "Each delivery of metal has to be accounted for by both sender and receiver. Otherwise the men shipping it could take some for themselves."

Sadeq approached them from the entrance to the treasury, his expression hard.

"You're sure?" Masista asked.

"Yes." Myrad schooled his hands to stillness, away from the knife at his belt.

Masista caught the gaze of his men and gave them the slightest shake of his head. Then he dismounted and bowed. "Your pardon, honored Sadeq. I still require the receipt to the master of the mint in Seleucia."

"Indeed." Sadeq offered a sheet of parchment with the tally

and his seal on it. "Otherwise they might think you've kept some of the king's silver for yourself. If the queen suspected you'd deprived her of the coinage bearing her likeness, she would be . . . displeased." He favored Masista with a thin smile. "I hear her temper is noteworthy."

Masista bowed, taking the receipt that validated their theft. "I have seen both it and the consequences of it. You have heard correctly."

They departed, the camels passing single file through the narrow arch of the treasury. The city spun in Myrad's vision, and his hands shook on his horse's reins. They exited the city the way they'd entered, with four cataphracts posted in front and two in back and soldiers filling the space between, their bows strung and a quiver of arrows at the ready. When they rode past the palace, Masista chuckled. "Phraates and Musa will never know their own silver has been used to finance their enemies."

"They will," Myrad said. "When the head of the mint fails to send confirmation of receipt of the silver we've taken, Sadeq will know he's been robbed."

Masista laughed. "Ah, but if he tells anyone, his head is in danger."

"When," Myrad said. "The king's vizier will come to take an accounting and discover the missing silver. That is, unless Sadeq can cover over a hundred talents of silver from his own accounts."

Masista peered at him, his eyes speculative. "Your aid at the treasury was timely. You've struck a great blow against Musa. Now, would you like to strike another?"

The mention of Musa's name and the image of his father's death would be inextricably linked forever. One went with the other without fail and always would.

"You have similar letters of authorization for the other mints," Masista prompted.

Myrad paused to consider the camels, stalling. "Even if our theft isn't discovered for some time, won't your absence from Ctesiphon arouse suspicion? The queen, or Katanes, is already looking for me. They will be looking for you now as well."

Masista smiled as they passed back through the gates of the city to head southeast. "Speed is our friend. If we can outrace word of my departure, we can plunder the other mints before Katanes makes the connection."

Now Myrad understood. "The horses."

"Exactly," Masista said. "Even if they discover we've robbed them here at Hecatompylos, they'll be searching for camels."

But the theft failed to give Myrad the satisfaction he hoped for. An unexpected shame filled him, as if he'd dishonored Gershom's memory. "I won't be going with you. Take the letters. I have a dream I need to understand and a calendar to keep."

Masista pursed his lips below a flat gaze. "A pity. You would have been useful."

An hour later, they left the road to make their way into the desert, heading due south toward a solitary mountain. After another hour they met the two men they'd left behind with the horse train. Masista's soldiers dismounted and began shifting the silver from the camels to the horses, fastening two talents to each horse. When they were done, there were three times as many horses carrying burdens as there had been camels.

"What will you do with the camels?" Myrad asked.

"We have no further use for them," Masista said. "We'll put them to the sword here where they won't be discovered for some time."

The thought of killing the animals troubled him. "Someone

is bound to wonder why there are so many vultures in the air above this place. The tale might reach the city."

"This far away?" Masista asked. "What then would you suggest?"

"Strip them and set them loose. Any caravan finding them is more likely to take them for their own, and they'll do so without speaking of it since they won't want to find the owner."

"Wisely argued," Masista laughed. He wheeled his horse and ordered his men to strip the camels and set them free. The animals lumbered away to forage for whatever scrub they could find. "There," Masista said. "It is done."

But the magus's expression mocked him somehow. Shadows from behind fell across Myrad's vision, and a moment later he heard the whispering hiss of steel against leather. Then a pair of sword points pricked the skin of his back. He didn't move and kept his hands very still on the reins, terrified his horse might shy and the swords impale him.

"Our race across the desert is long and not without risk," Masista said. His voice held no tone or timbre that carried threat. "We're going to need every spare horse. Dismount. Now."

Myrad kept his voice even. "If not for my advice, you would have been discovered at the treasury."

"And for that you have my thanks," Masista replied. "And your life. But the time for subterfuge has passed. Are you a cataphract? Have you been raised to the bow and the sword since you were a boy? A broken pot may be useful for a time, but when its usefulness has passed, it must be discarded."

The threat of the swords remained. Masista's expression, though neutral, gave no hint he might be open to further bargaining. They'd already bargained, and Myrad had surrendered everything of value he owned. He'd even shown Masista how to escape detection at the mint. Here at the moment when he'd begun to fulfill his vow to avenge his father, Masista's betrayal would kill him.

Sliding to the ground, away from the swords of Masista's soldiers, Myrad managed to grab his sack of spare clothes before one of the soldiers seized his horse and led it away from him.

"You promised me vengeance," he said.

Masista's wide-eyed gaze mocked him. "And you've achieved it. By surrendering your horse, you've helped to ensure it." He dismounted and closed the distance between them until their faces were inches apart. Then Masista leaned over and took Myrad's bag from him. "And you will continue to ensure it." He opened the sack and took Gershom's papers that lay on top, then tossed the bag back to Myrad as he remounted.

Myrad told himself not to speak, but this magus had promised him vengeance and then ensured he wouldn't live to see it. He couldn't remain quiet. "If I live, you'll regret it."

"What will you do?" Masista smiled. "Run—my apologies, walk—back to the treasury and reveal us? You would be the first to die. A word of advice, young apprentice. Leave this part of Parthia as quickly as you can. Katanes is looking for you." His smile grew. "If you make it out of the desert, you could return to a life of selling melons in the market. But I wouldn't advise doing it in Ctesiphon or Hecatompylos."

Myrad turned his back to the magus, unwilling to look at Masista any longer, but the sea of scrub and sand in front of him was just as pitiless. His gaze fell across his crutch, still fastened to the side of his horse. Desperately, he hobbled toward it, his arm reaching. With a curt shout, Masista ordered his men to ride, and they thundered east across the desert, taking his crutch with them, a last insult.

He stood and watched them go, bearing as much weight as he could on his good leg. "He's killed me," he said out loud. There was no one and nothing that might offer a rebuttal. Scattered around him on the sandy earth were bits of rope used to tie the camels together. A couple of the rough blankets that had padded their load littered the ground as well. The camels themselves had wandered away.

His first thought was for his father, but on its heels came an image of Walagash. "I'm sorry," he mumbled, but whose forgiveness did he seek? His father's? Walagash's? Both?

Soon the sun touched the horizon, and a chill breeze swept across the sand. Myrad shifted his feet on the hard-packed sand and peered northward. The city lay three or more hours distant by horse, a day by camel, and forever for a man with a bad foot. Even if he could walk there without his crutch, a lone man entering the city on foot would attract attention. Limping into Hecatompylos would be tantamount to waving a sign for those looking for a clubfooted man, and anyone who came upon him on the road could rob or kill him with ease. And away from the road, there was little chance of his encountering anyone.

Not far away, an outcropping of rock thrust upward from the sandy earth around it. A pair of lizards sunning themselves scurried beneath it at his approach. He'd heard of men reduced to eating camel or lizards, but hunger wasn't his most pressing need at the moment. His waterskin was gone with his horse. Thirst would kill him long before hunger. He pushed the thought aside. Thinking about water held no power to conjure it. If he could just get to the city, he still possessed enough money to buy a decent horse.

But he had to return without attracting attention. Sadeq and any number of his men would recognize him. Passing through the city was out of the question. He would have to skirt its southern wall until he came to the trading grounds, but first he had to get there.

His gaze drifted from his knife down to his deformed foot. Again. How many times in his life had his deformity betrayed him? Gershom's adoption, that act of selfless love, forever changed Myrad's vision of himself. His father had taught him that all men were blemished. Some were just fortunate enough to carry their infirmities on the inside. He tried to flex his right foot, but the bones and ligaments were frozen from birth into their blighted shape. "I would be happy to trade," he whispered.

His body yearned for sleep. He hobbled over to the discarded camel blankets and dragged them back to his rock. Lying on one and covered by another, he brought his bag of clothes up onto the hard stone, put it under his head, and slept.

After a time, he plunged deeper into unconsciousness like a man falling from a great height into nothing. Images came to him without order or meaning. Gershom, Musa, Walagash . . . Without transition he found himself standing beneath a full moon, the dunes bathed in argent. The night sky had been a friend to him ever since Gershom adopted him, its familiar constellations named according to Greek beliefs or Hebrew. But that was before Musa murdered his father. Now they were nothing more than points of light, as cold and distant from his predicament as God. Unwilling to face their indifference, he looked down at his feet.

Wonder stole his breath, stilled his heart. He stood beneath ten thousand points of light strewn across the heavens like shining bits of sand in the firmament, his bare feet *flat* on the rock beneath him. Both feet. Slowly—he dared not look away or even blink—he flexed his right foot. It moved as easily and surely as its companion.

A voice whispered across his ears, a feathered touch against his skin. "Look."

He started. He scanned the firmament above, counting the twelve constellations Gershom had taught him represented the twelve tribes of Israel. He stopped, his restored foot momentarily forgotten. There in the western sky hung the light of his dream. As he watched, time sped and the stars of heaven spun around the mariner's star creating concentric circles of light. But not the light hanging above the horizon to the west. It rested there, unmoving, in defiance of its brethren. He stood staring at it, unblinking, as the rest of the stars painted arcs in the sky.

"You will go to the city of the dead," the voice said.

He awoke, still lying on the blanket he'd salvaged from the abandoned camels, still wearing the boot to disguise his deformity. He tried to flex his foot, but it didn't move. It couldn't, of course. Anguish and loss pierced him and he wept until sleep took him again.

CHAPTER 11

Myrad woke up in the gray light of predawn, a full moon still shining low in the west while hints of rose and orange showed in the east. Through the opening between a pair of low dunes he spotted one of the camels, its legs beneath it, its eyes closed. His first reaction was one of disgust. He needed a horse. Then he noticed the bits of rope Masista's men left in their wake. Moving slowly, his blemished foot offering him no other choice, he gathered as many pieces of rope as he could find and approached the animal.

To his surprise, the beast didn't move. In fact, it hardly took notice of him as he tied one end of the rope around its neck and the other around a rock. Limping back, he pulled the blanket from the rock and approached the animal once more. This he fastened to the camel just behind the hump with two pieces of rope around its middle, a task made more difficult by the beast's unmoving indifference. And it didn't appear to care as Myrad went facedown on the sand to push the rope beneath its belly. With two shorter pieces of rope, he fastened a bridle and reins. Still the beast sat in placid contentment.

"What shall I call you?"

When the camel didn't answer, Myrad realized sun or thirst might have gotten to him already. He'd half expected a response.

His best hope for survival didn't even look at him. He wasn't fooled. He knew enough of these animals from his years working in the market to beware of their mercurial nature. Luck or fortune had managed to present him with a mount and a means to steer it, but he would still need a goad. Searching the ground, he selected and discarded a series of sticks, all of them too light or too short. Wandering farther away, he chanced upon a dead wayfaring tree, hardly more than a sapling before drought and wind killed it.

For the second time, he considered the likelihood that he might still be dreaming. Wayfaring trees didn't grow this far from the mountains. The sapling looked to have been a year old or more before it died. He tried to imagine the possibility of its seed taking root and receiving enough water here in the desert for it to grow for a year. After a moment, he gave up. Sitting on the ground, he hacked away at it with his knife until he'd fashioned a goad roughly four feet in length.

Looking up, he saw another camel sitting in repose a few paces away. "They're animals of association," he said to himself. As before, he approached slowly, avoiding eye contact or quick movements, and tied the rope around its long neck, just beneath the head.

Brandishing the goad but not striking the animal, he raised his arms. "Ha-yup!" To his surprise, the camel lurched its way to a standing position.

In the end, the press of time and the lack of rope determined his actions. Thirteen of the original twenty animals remained within a couple hundred paces of the spot where Masista abandoned him. He managed to tie them into a semblance of a train, although he'd yet to mount and ride the lead animal. Worse, the sun had risen and beat on him with the force of a hammer, yet for some reason he delayed to assign each animal a name. It seemed fitting somehow. Thirteen. In a moment of whimsy he attributed to the heat, he eyed the lead camel and bestowed upon its indifferent visage the name "Jacob." Then he went down the train, naming each camel until he came to the thirteenth and last, a beast that appropriately appeared to be younger than the rest. "Benjamin," his voice croaked with the effort.

Already his tongue refused to wet his parched lips. Resigned to dying but too stubborn to surrender, he passed the tribes of Israel back to the lead camel.

With Gershom's adoption two years prior, he'd learned how to ride a horse. Never had he mounted or ridden a camel. The awkward, uncomfortable gait of the beasts was legendary, the very reason they were used for hauling goods while merchants accompanied them on horses. Only the most desperate and poorest of merchants rode camels.

"That I am," he whispered. He paused to change clothes, his mind conjuring images of guards recognizing him by his garb. Resting at the bottom of his pack, beneath his rolled-up tunic and trousers, was the last piece of parchment, the letter of transfer from the mint in Nisa. He stared at it, thinking. "With this I could be one of the richest men in the empire, and yet I'm probably going to die of thirst in the desert." He wrapped Gershom's legacy in his dirty trousers and put them both back in his bag. His spare tunic he fashioned into a turban to protect his head from the sun. Then he uttered a prayer to the Most High God and seated himself just behind the hump of the lead camel. But as soon as he brandished the goad, the animal grunted and shifted, throwing him to the ground. His head struck the hard-packed earth, and his vision dimmed to a pinpoint. When it cleared, his mount sat on the ground as before, daring him to ride.

He actually got the animal to stand the next time, but then slipped off the back midway through the awkward rocking motion to land on his behind. The camel twisted its long neck around to look at him and grunt.

After another hour, and after gaining a number of painful bruises, he finally emerged from between a pair of dunes and steered the camels north back toward the city of Hecatompylos.

The sun, directly above and behind him, transformed the desert into a furnace, but every time he urged the camels to greater speed, they immediately slowed again. Defeated, he curled into himself and began counting the plodding strides of his mount. Each appeared to be a pace in length, perhaps a bit more. He tried to use the beat of his heart to estimate the strides per hour, but his mind refused to consider such diversions. His mouth was as dry as the sand.

The sun was still up in the sky when he stopped sweating. He knew what would surely come next. Soon his head would begin to pound and his stomach would rebel, vomiting what little food and water it still held. Then he would lapse into unconsciousness and die.

"I won't make it to the city of the dead." His voice came in a breathy croak he barely heard. "They were all just dreams."

Exhausted, he lay forward on his mount and kept watch for some sign of the city. Though he fought to stay awake, he slipped into a fevered dream of random images without context or meaning.

"Hi-ya!"

The sound slipped from him, but an instant later water wet his face and lips. He lifted his head to a world spinning in delirium. It was only after he surrendered to it that he realized he was lying on the ground with a rope wrapped around his wrist. Everything hurt.

A guard leaned over him, blotting out the sun, and water splashed over him again. *Water.* The man stooping over him had water. The guard lifted his head, offering the waterskin. Myrad clutched at it, working to make his hands obey. It took two tries, and when he managed to drink, the water came so fast that he choked.

"Careful," the guard said. "You should know better than to try to cross the desert alone. What were you doing out there?"

Myrad continued to drink until his stomach felt heavy. He struggled to a sitting position. In the distance behind the guard and his horse, a caravan was snaking its way toward a walled city. *Hecatompylos.* He'd made it.

"Thieves," he said at last. "They took our goods and left me for dead in the desert. I gathered as many of the camels as I could and made for the nearest city."

The guard nodded. "You're lucky to be alive. Another hour and I'm not sure I could have revived you." He straightened, glancing toward the caravan. "I have to get back. You can keep the skin."

The guard mounted up and headed back to his caravan. Myrad took another pull from the waterskin and tried to shake the effects of too much sun from his head. How long had he been unconscious? Prolonged exposure made it difficult to distinguish color, bleaching the hues from the landscape and the city in the distance.

Once he'd regained his perch on Jacob, his camels caught sight or wind of the caravan in front of him and followed. Twice he looked up at the city wall to see soldiers peering at him, a lone man riding a camel and leading a short train without goods into the city. He kept his head down the rest of the way in.

The trading grounds of Hecatompylos sprawled across the low hills on the south side of the city. Without reason to hope for it, he searched the encampments for a red-striped tent but saw not one belonging to Walagash. After questioning a few of the merchants, he found the pens of Morteza, a dealer of camels with a blue open tent whose furnishings, braziers, wooden chests, and tables gave it a look of permanence.

After several moments trying to get Jacob to understand they'd arrived and he wanted it to kneel, Myrad finally dismounted. Thick rugs covered the ground within the merchant's tent, and the smell of tea and honey filled the space.

"Greetings, most favored one," Morteza said, addressing the air just to Myrad's left. Thin as a spear, with a beard shot with gray, he nonetheless exuded a boyish enthusiasm in defiance of his wrinkles.

Myrad checked over each shoulder. There was no one else within earshot. "Why do you call me 'most favored one'?"

Morteza chuckled. "Are you not? You have emerged from the desert and the dangers of the road with no goods, no soldiers, and no injuries. Come. Sit."

Myrad tied Jacob to a stake and limped over to sit next to the merchant.

"Ah," Morteza said, "I see I was mistaken. You've hurt your foot." He waved a hand in the air. "No matter. You are still most favored. Alone on the road with bandits about, you should be dead. How may this one serve you, young master?"

A soldier walked by, and Myrad was quick to adjust his feet to hide the stitching on the inside of his right boot. "I wish to sell these fine animals, good merchant. Though they are more agreeable than most of their kind, their gait is a trial and I have a need for greater speed."

The man's generous eyebrows climbed upward. "You as well? Two in as many days. Most come to buy, not to sell, but no matter." He turned to call into the tent. "Yasmina, come. We have a customer."

A young woman emerged from the shadows into the afternoon light. A hand shorter than Myrad, she peered at him with startling green eyes in a heart-shaped face that gave her mouth a hint of amusement. Morteza stood, surrendering his seat. "He is favored," he told her, "and young. Deal fairly, my daughter. I will get the tea." He disappeared into the tent.

"You run the negotiation?" Myrad asked before he could stop himself.

Instead of taking offense, Yasmina laughed. "It's not so unusual. Morteza saw early on that I negotiate more skillfully than he does."

The merchant emerged from the tent carrying a tray with a steaming pot and three cups. "The truth is, I could no longer abide your wretched tea. By the god of the shining fire, I've never met anyone who made a more bitter brew."

Yasmina lifted a cup and saluted Myrad with a nod. "And his eyes grew too weak to spot the flaws in the animals we purchased."

"Humph, it can't be denied," Morteza said. "My daughter's eye for animals, even the two-legged type, is quite discerning."

Myrad took a sip and nodded in appreciation. "This is quite good."

Morteza tapped his generous nose. "The skill lies here."

"Tell me about your camels," Yasmina said. Her eyes flashed green like new grass. Myrad could think of more than one reason why she might be a better negotiator than her father.

"They're well-tempered," he replied, "and not difficult to manage."

"Then why sell them? There are merchants here who would pay you to haul goods to Ctesiphon or Margiana. With luck and a little time, you could be a merchant in your own right."

He thought of Walagash. "I know too little of trade."

She cradled her cup to her chest and stood. "Let us see your animals then."

Myrad walked over to the first camel. Yasmina slowed her pace, allowing him to keep up.

"This is Jacob," Myrad said. "He carried me."

Her delicate brows rose in surprise. "You named them?"

He shrugged. "I didn't want to call each of them 'camel.' They wouldn't have known which of them I was talking to."

She laughed, and he found himself joining in. "Jacob seems a strange name, but nice enough. What would you have named him if he'd been bad-tempered?"

"Esau," he said without hesitating. She only nodded, missing the reference. He continued on, introducing Yasmina to the tribes of Israel.

"With thirteen camels in your possession, you could apprentice yourself to a merchant who could teach you."

"Twice now you've encouraged me to make a decision that would deprive you of trade. Why?"

"In truth, you're the second man in as many days desiring to trade his camels for horses. We have more camels now than we can move in a month. We took hundreds from another merchant. I won't be able to offer you what yours are worth."

He didn't know whether this was the truth or simply a bargaining tactic. "Then I'll take what you can and be thankful for it. Will it be enough to buy a good horse?"

"I can't speak for the seller of horses," Yasmina said. "Come, let us return to the tent. I don't doubt your animals are well-behaved, but camels think it amusing to spit."

They rejoined Morteza. "Have you come to an agreement, my daughter?"

"Perhaps, Uncle. I can give you ten tetradrachms for all thirteen camels." She held her hands palms up. "Ordinarily it would have been closer to twenty. Even so, a decent horse usually costs eight tetras."

He had that and more hidden in his pack if needed. "Perhaps you could provide information as well. Do you know the merchant who traded all his camels for horses?"

"Yes, his name is Walagash. We've dealt before, he and I."

Myrad's heart sank. He'd hoped to meet up with his friend on the road east and ask to join his caravan once more. Now Walagash was at least three days ahead of him and traveling fast. "He's a friend. Did he say where he was going?"

Yasmina shook her head. "No, I'm sorry."

He took this in. The sale of three hundred camels and the purchase of a corresponding number of horses would certainly affect the market, at least for a time.

He spent the night at the inn closest to the tent of Morteza and his daughter-niece. No dreams, no voices, or visions of impossible skies came to him, no healed feet that would make him whole. He woke just before dawn and hobbled out to the pen where he'd tied his horse. A sound from behind surprised him and he spun, his hand on his knife.

Yasmina stood two paces away, her hand extended as if he were an animal that needed calming. In the other she held a bundle. "Morteza's nose does not fail him, but his eyes do not see so clearly as mine. The desert leaves its mark on a man, and there are few reasons why anyone would dare cross it alone." She held out the bundle. "There's enough food here for a hard day of riding."

"Thank you," he said, taking it. He pointed at his horse. "How much can I ask of him?"

She stepped forward, ran her hands down the horse's legs, and checked the frog of each hoof. Taking the horse by the bridle, she peeled back the upper lip to examine its teeth. She pursed her lips. "No one's going to confuse him with Pegasus, but then you wouldn't want a racer anyway. They're too fragile and temperamental for your needs."

"What is it you think I need?" he asked.

She raised one shoulder, then let it fall. "To stay ahead of someone or to catch up with someone else. If you keep him at a trot, you can make three way stations a day for a time," she said.

"How many days will it take me to get to Nisa?" The question startled him. Until that moment he hadn't decided whether he would go to the city of the dead or chase after Walagash. But as much as he ached for the friendship Walagash and his caravan offered, Gershom was his father and they had shared a dream, a true dream.

"Eight days, perhaps nine," Yasmina said.

Myrad bowed. "Thank you. You've helped me far more than your purchase of a few camels. I'm in your debt."

She nodded. "Morteza imagines he can smell evil on a man,

or good. He likes the way you smell. There's no lack of caravans to ride with, no matter which direction you're going. Push him to a gallop if you pass close to a forest alone. Bandits hide there. Just make sure you let him walk afterward." She teased him with a smile. "You have a penchant for naming your animals. What will you call him?"

"Areion."

"The talking horse of the Greeks?" She laughed. "Do you think he's going to speak to you?"

"Only in my dreams."

CHAPTER 12

It took him eight days to cover the distance to Nisa. The last day he let Areion walk since they'd stopped the previous night at the closest way station. Either his pursuers had given up the search for him or they were looking in the cities of the west. None of the men or women at the oases or watering stops appeared to be searching for a man with a clubfoot. Of course, he'd taken pains, intense pains, to walk like a normal man for the few steps required.

The city of Nisa appeared as though it were hurrying to become a ruin. People walked the half-empty streets at ease with the horses passing through, and the market covered only a portion of the stone-covered plaza set aside for it. Once the capital of the Parthian Empire, the city was now little more than a repository for its dead kings.

"The city of the dead," Myrad mused. No voices or visions came to him during the ride from Hecatompylos, not even on those nights he'd been forced to sleep by the road with nothing but Areion and the stars for company. For hours each night he'd peered into the heavens searching for a star that never appeared. Shaken by its absence, he came to doubt his divine instruction. Perhaps his vision was nothing more than the fevered dreams of thirst. When he tried to insist on its reality, his mind hurled questions at him like darts.

Why would God use a clubfooted man to accomplish His ends? Why would the God of the Hebrews talk to a Persian? What arrogance made him presume to consider himself one of the elect?

On they went, hammering at him, but after a time their relentlessness became their undoing. His essential nature reasserted itself and he found himself answering each attack with a shrug. "I may not be one of the magi, but I'm alive and I'm free when I had no right to expect either."

Faced with the choice of considering himself cursed or lucky, he chose the latter. He mounted Areion and rode toward the eastern quarter of the city. There, he found a decent inn where he could stable his horse. He ventured just far enough into the market to purchase a change of clothes before making his way to a bathhouse. Standing on the mosaic tile in the anteroom, he shrugged himself out of the tunic and trousers he'd worn since the desert outside Hecatompylos. His temptation was to throw everything away except for the boots, but after a moment's reflection he folded them and placed them on a shelf beneath the set he'd purchased. Conscious of his clubfoot and the stares it brought, he passed into the warm room and descended into the pool where he let the water and conversation wash over him in equal measure.

Images of Walagash, Aban, Storana, and Roshan buffeted him. He'd been a fool. Walagash, along with most of his caravan, had extended friendship to him and he'd thrown it away for a chance at revenge. Myrad would have laughed if it weren't so pathetic. Of course, Masista had stranded him in the desert. Even if he hadn't, what would come of Musa's hypothetical defeat? Would Gershom care?

No. Gershom was dead. If the dead simply ceased, they didn't care. If Gershom lived on in the presence of God, he still wouldn't care, which led Myrad to an inevitable question. In an empire defined by ambition and murder, why should *he* care? If recent history was anything to go by, Phraates, Musa, and her son would all die violent deaths at someone else's hand, who would go on to die a violent death in turn.

He bobbed along the edge of the pool until he came to a clay dish holding cakes of soap. By the time he'd washed himself, he had a plan. If God did not speak to him here in the city of the dead, he would ride east to Margiana and seek out Walagash to offer himself to any service the merchant might offer.

Cleaned and clothed, he reclined on a low couch in the inn's serving room, sipping date wine after his meal and congratulating himself on his plan. If God or imagination failed to give him clarity of purpose here in Nisa, he would find it in Margiana. Downing the last of his wine, he rose and made his way to his room, where he fell onto his bed and slept.

He drifted through his dreams, content, until he found himself in the desert gazing once more at a bright, unblinking light above the western horizon. "Behold," the voice said, "the star of the Messiah-King." He stared at the light until the voice came to him again. "Go and see."

He awoke to a dark room, the small slit that served as a window showing nothing but a matching hue of black. He bumped his shins in search of his clothes but didn't care. The dream had given him a renewed sense of purpose and in an obscure way had brought Gershom back to him as well. He jammed his boots onto his feet and hobbled out to the street.

There was no doubt in his mind what he was looking for, but the inn and the surrounding buildings blocked his view. He ventured into the main thoroughfare that ran east-west through the city and turned to search the sky, impatient, but before he could look, he heard voices.

"Myrad?"

Shadows approached him from the darkness, and he took a step back. *Fool.* He'd left his knife and cane in his room. "Who's there?" The figures came closer, bearing candlelight. Faces became distinct, but only the man to the right of the candle resolved into familiarity. "Hakam?"

The man stepped closer. "Why are you here?" The dim light accentuated the mournful cast to his eyes, and his voice sounded vaguely distrustful.

"I had a dream," he said simply. If Hakam mocked him for it, well, no matter.

"What dream?" Hakam demanded. Anger and surprise wove through the question.

He sighed. "The same dream that led Gershom to proclaim me as magus. The dream of a star, but each time I awake, it's gone. It's only in my dream."

"Look." One of Hakam's companions pointed over Myrad's shoulder.

There, low over the western horizon, a steady light blazed pure white without twinkling. They stood, eight by Myrad's count, gazing toward the west at a star that hadn't been there the night before.

"That's no dream," one of them said, his voice light, amused.

"Let us go in," the man holding the candle said after a long moment. "The star isn't going anywhere, and I wish to hear the tale of this dream."

CHAPTER 13

The man bearing the light led them to an inn across the street from Myrad's. He could only shake his head at the coincidence. They went into the serving room where they lit candles and one of the men disappeared into a back room, then reemerged carrying a pitcher of wine and cups. The man holding the candle gestured Myrad toward a chair at the head of a table before turning to Hakam.

"The two of you are acquainted. Introduce us."

Hakam's mouth twisted, but he acquiesced with a nod. "This is Myrad, a young Perisan man of Gershom's acquaintance." Then he pointed at the others in turn, making introductions. "Dov. Eliar. Mikhael. Harel. Shimon. Ronen. Yehudah."

Myrad worked to commit each man's name to memory, yet fatigue and darkness gave the events a surreality that made him question if he'd truly awakened. Yehudah, the man who'd borne the candle, gestured to Myrad with his cup. "Tell us everything. Leave nothing out." The others nodded in unison.

"No," Myrad said. "I do not trust you. I trusted a magus once before and I nearly died."

Yehudah smiled at that, his face a mixture of strong Hebrew features with the coloring and tilt to the eyes of the horsemen of eastern Parthia. Myrad noted he was of an age with Hakam, perhaps ten years older than himself. He wore his authority among the other men as naturally as his silk tunic. "Why do you name us magi?" he asked.

Myrad almost laughed. "You dress like them, and there's a way each of you have of holding your head, as though the palms of your authority are still on your brow even though you're not wearing your circlets. How many palms can you claim, Yehudah?"

"Six. I hold the satrapy for part of Bactria. At least I did until my allegiance with Gershom was discovered. Tell us what assurances you require that would gain your trust."

He shook his head. Neither Hakam nor Yehudah, nor any of the rest of the men gathered around the table understood. "I don't think you can give me what I want."

"Please, let us try," Hakam said. But his tone sounded akin to a command rather than a supplication.

"Now you believe me?" Myrad cocked his head and spat to one side. "You dismissed me because I'm not Hebrew and because I missed two days on the calendar, even though you knew nothing of what I'd done to escape. I have no wish to be in your company, *magus*."

"I will not be lectured to by a—"

Yehudah held up a hand, and Hakam fell silent. "Gershom was a good man and a friend. I share your grief. He died because he shared our mistake."

While Myrad wanted nothing to do with Hakam or the magi, Gershom had always praised his curiosity as a virtue. "What mistake?"

Yehudah sighed. "Since the time of Daniel, we were servants of the prophecy, numbering the days, but we forget his lesson. He rose to prominence in two empires because he served God and was elevated. We allowed ourselves to become embroiled in the politics surrounding Phraates's choice of queen."

"It was the right choice," Hakam said. "The woman is evil. How can the Messiah rule if the entire world has been crushed beneath the Roman heel?"

"No," Yehudah countered. "The choice was wrong. Daniel's example was there before us. So was Nehemiah's. Serve with humility." He turned back to Myrad. "Gershom, like the rest of us, confused service with allegiance. He wanted to save the empire from Musa's influence, but empires can't be saved. They come and are washed away by the inexorable tide of history. Egypt, Assyria, Babylon, Persia, and Greece are dust. Khushan, Qian, Rome, and Parthia." His hands waved the air, dismissing their images. "They will all be replaced by empires that will fall in turn."

Myrad took a sip of wine. Yehudah's list sparked a dangerous question, but he wouldn't shy from it. "Then what good is this Messiah-King? It's just another empire to be washed away."

Yehudah shook his head. "The empires of men are transient, ephemeral as dew, but God's kingdom will last forever."

"Why do you care so much whether I join you?"

"Because from the moment I saw you in the street staring into the west and Hakam called your name, I knew God had chosen you." He motioned around the table at the other seven men. "Why do you think we're in Nisa?"

Still, Myrad wasn't ready to trust them yet. "Daniel's test then," he said finally. "Tell me my *entire* dream with its interpretation and then you can tell me what you think I should do about it."

Yehudah smiled. "As you wish. This is the—"

"No," Myrad interrupted. "Not you." He looked around the

table at the other men until he found one who reminded him most of Gershom, a middle-aged man with a fringe of hair. "Him."

Eliar pushed to his feet and faced him. "This is the dream you've had three times now," he began. "You found yourself in the desert gazing at a light in the western sky. The light burned, too large and too constant to be a star and without the tail that would proclaim it a comet. The light held steady in the sky, as unmoving as the mariner's star, though it hung low in the horizon. A voice came to you and told you this was the King's star. Here lies the meaning: The King, the Messiah, has come to Israel, and the appearance of the star announces His arrival." Eliar smiled, and his eyes shone in the dim light. "This is the dream, and its interpretation is sure."

Like an unexpected wave crashing against the sand without warning, the revelation and interpretation of his dream undermined his objections. "What does it mean? Hakam said there were decades left before the Messiah comes."

"God will make His purposes known," Yehudah said. "In the meantime, I would like to hear your tale."

With a sigh, Myrad nodded. "The dream came to me the night before the slaughter of the magi," he began.

When he finished nearly an hour later, Hakam was the first to speak, staring into his cup. "Masista's true allegiance against Musa must have been discovered." He raised his head to look at Myrad. "He led you across the desert because he didn't dare use the roads. Phraates and Musa are consolidating their power in the west." He glanced around the table. "Most of us were already on our way east when we received the dream to come to the city of the dead."

"But why here?" Dov asked, the oldest of the men present.

Myrad listened as each of the magi offered reasons that were just as quickly dismissed.

"We'll have to wait here until the meaning becomes clear," Yehudah said after everyone fell silent.

"We can't stay here," Mikhael said. "Musa's soldiers are no more than two days, perhaps three, behind us."

"I think I know why we're here," Myrad offered. "The letter to the treasury in Hecatompylos was one of six I found among Gershom's papers. Masista took the rest, but I have the one for the mint here in Nisa."

Quiet settled over the room, each man unwilling to be the first to speak. In the end, it was Ronen who broke the silence. "There are gifts mentioned in the Torah, the symbols for God's chosen."

"Gold," Hakam said, his eyes burning. "For the king."

"Frankincense," Harel said. "For our priest."

"Myrrh," Ronen added. "For the prophet of the people."

"What about the calendar?" Myrad asked. "The King doesn't come for another thirty years yet."

"Doubtless the meaning will become clearer in time, when we see him," Yehudah answered. "For now, our next steps are plain. We will use Gershom's writ to withdraw as much silver from the mint as possible, then use the money to bring our gifts to the King."

"We won't be able to get them here," Harel said. "And Phraates's soldiers are coming."

"I know." Yehudah nodded. "We will have to go to Margiana."

Margiana. A thrill of hope coursed through Myrad at the prospect of seeing Walagash and his friends again.

CHAPTER 14

It took them over a week to travel to Margiana. All eight of the magi, plus the cataphracts belonging to those who possessed such, had been required to relieve the mint in Nisa of its silver. Three days out of the city, a towering cloud of dust approached from the east.

"Sandstorm?" Myrad asked.

Dov squinted, his head thrust forward. "It's too small, and the storms usually pass west to east. Yehudah! Horses!"

They left the road, making for a copse of cedar trees where they hid. Myrad expected to see a column of horses any second, but while the cloud continued to approach, its cause remained hidden. Half an hour later, he heard the rumble of countless hooves. Fifteen minutes more and he saw a column of cataphracts and horse soldiers stretching into the distance. He tried to number them, but the column moved at a trot and dust obscured his vision. "I can't count them all."

Dov smiled, his eyes crinkling with amusement. "Try this. Number them as accurately as you can while I count to ten. Then, instead of counting the soldiers, we'll count the seconds."

Myrad blinked. The idea was simple but brilliant. When he said so, Dov nodded. "Precision is an admirable goal but not always needed." He pointed. "Orodes is making a bid for the throne in earnest. It would be good to know whether this is a feint or a thrust."

After the last of the soldiers disappeared over the horizon, Myrad sought Dov's interpretation. "Eight thousand, give or take a few hundred. What does it mean?"

Dov mused in silence, his lips pursed. "There are too few men to attack any of the major cities, but a sizable force nonetheless. Perhaps the clan of Orodes is content at this point to keep Phraates in the west."

"Why?"

The magus shrugged his ignorance. "Who can say? Perhaps he's waiting for some other stratagem to tip the scales in his favor."

They rode due east for ten more days until they passed through a gap in the hills and came in sight of a circular earthwork surrounding the largest trading city in the Parthian Empire. Myrad stared at it in wonder. The size of the redoubt defied imagination. Words failed him as he gaped. "Why?" he managed at last.

"There's enough wealth flowing through the city of Margiana to build a small empire," Yehudah said. "The walls were built to remind the Khushan this portion of Bactria belongs to Parthia."

"If we can keep it," one of Yehudah's cataphracts said.

The magus dipped his head, conceding the point. "True enough. This is the eastern limit of Arsacid power. Here, all the caravans from Bactria, Qian, Indus, or Khushan must sell their goods to Parthian traders. This city is the eastern focal point for the empire's wealth. That makes it valuable to its enemies as well. It is said anything can be found within its earthen walls."

"Is it true?" Myrad asked. "Can a man find anything there?"

Yehudah laughed. "So long as it can be hauled on the back of a camel."

They circled around to join the line of caravans waiting to

enter. Dour-faced soldiers mingled with merchants and rode in bands through the streets. Even so, the flow of beasts bearing goods proceeded without ceasing. Where one caravan stopped, another began, the slowly rocking gaits of the camels taking or bringing goods to Margiana.

"Are there always this many soldiers here?"

"No," Yehudah said. "And many of these men are mercenaries from Khushan or Scythia. Orodes has no intention of losing Margiana to Phraates."

They passed multiple pens of horses and camels for sale, dwarfing those he'd seen in Ctesiphon and Hecatompylos. Myrad's head spun as he searched for a red-and-white-striped tent, but the sights and sounds of Margiana overwhelmed him so that he soon gave up looking for it.

It took them another hour of riding through the press of people and animals to come to the more permanent part of the city. After a few questions of a local merchant, Yehudah guided them to a gold-and-silver dealer in the north quarter.

"Myrad and I will negotiate," Yehudah said, "while the rest of you stand guard."

"Why me?" Myrad asked.

"You have an honest face. Any merchant who wishes to remain in business won't base their judgment on appearances only, yet I've never met a man or woman who didn't trust their eyes first and their other senses last." He pointed at the door. "Our gold merchant here is a middle-aged woman, Zarya. I believe your presence will make her more amenable to bargaining."

Myrad stopped. "Why? Because I've got a clubfoot?"

To his surprise, Yehudah nodded. "Yes. Zarya will want to mother you because of your youth, and she'll want to care for you because of your foot."

Unlike other merchants, Zarya kept no goods in her shop. Instead, scales and weights rested on a wooden counter made of heavy planks and topped with a plate of copper. There were no chairs in the shop, and Myrad could smell no hint of tea. Evidently, the customs of trade didn't apply to gold merchants. Somber-looking guards stood at the door with their weapons drawn.

"Peace be with you," Zarya greeted. "How may I be of service?"

Yehudah bowed. "We have a quantity of silver we wish to exchange for gold."

"Very well. Khushan, Parthian, or Roman?"

"Parthian," Yehudah said with a smile that wasn't returned. "Denarii and tetras."

Her eyes shifted, calculating. "Reasonably pure, the exchange is fourteen to one by weight for Roman, and thirteen to one by weight for Qian."

Yehudah's eyes narrowed. "The exchange in Seleucia is thirteen to one for Roman."

The merchant lifted her hands. "We're closer to Qian than Rome. It's more difficult to get Roman coinage this far out. You'll find the other merchants' prices are the same as mine."

"Why then should we deal with you?"

Zarya smiled for the first time, revealing lines in her face even as it made her look younger. She waved at the counter. "My scales are honest. I allow my customers to check them before we weigh your trade, and I even let you choose which side you use. For that matter, I will let you use both sides to show they measure weight the same. We shall use the same weights for your silver and my gold."

Yehudah nodded. "Demonstrate, if you would."

Zarya placed a tiny weight on the left pan of the smallest

scale and it tilted slowly toward that side. She placed the matching weight on the other side and the balance righted. She then swapped the weights with the same result. Finally, she shifted to the largest scale and repeated the demonstration with a full talent of weight.

"That is satisfactory," Yehudah said. "Your larger scale will be useful. We have quite a bit of silver to trade."

Zarya smiled, amused. "This is Margiana. I'm sure I can accommodate you."

Yehudah moved to the door and signaled the others. By the time they had unloaded half the horses, Zarya's nonchalance began to fray at the edges. When they finished, she ordered everyone out of her shop except for Yehudah, Myrad, and her two guards. "What did you do, Yehudah?" she asked.

"Do? We merely wish to trade a quantity of silver for gold."

Zarya paused, staring at him. After a brief moment, she said, "You know, there are rumors circulating that we're about to have another fight for the throne." She pointed at the large pile of silver on the floor. "If word spreads you've stolen from the empire, no one will deal with you." She gave a sardonic laugh. "It appears as though you've stolen half the silver of Nisa and dumped it on my floor."

"I assure you, it's not stolen," Myrad said. "It's recompense."

Zarya's eyes widened. "By the light of the shining fire! It *is* stolen?"

Yehudah tried to silence him with a glare, but Zarya interposed herself between them, close enough to touch. "Go on," she said.

Shifting to escape Yehudah's censure, Myrad faced her. "King Phraates and the queen, Musa, killed my father and every other magus who defied them. They dumped their bodies in the street

139

and claimed their lands and servants as their own." He nudged one of the bags of silver with his foot. "This is only a partial payment, but it will have to do."

If he thought his admission would satisfy the gold merchant, he was wrong.

"How much of it did you take?" Zarya asked.

"Seventy-five talents," Myrad said.

Yehudah rolled his eyes, and Myrad caught snatches of a Hebrew prayer. "They won't miss it."

Zarya's mouth opened and closed a few times before she spoke. "How can they not?"

"Because we had the transfer order to take it," Yehudah said. "His father was one of the magi in charge of the mints. The master of the treasury in Nisa believes we've simply executed a transfer, which we've done. As far as you know, we have come by it lawfully."

She shook her head. "That won't help me if they come looking for it."

"They won't," Yehudah said. "Those rumors you've heard are true. The eastern satrapies are banding together to resist Phraates and Musa. There's going to be war within the empire again."

"May the god of the shining fire have mercy on us," Zarya said. "Why can't the magi pick a king who's not already half crazy?"

"They did," Yehudah said, "but every king who comes to power seems to think he needs to marry his sister. After a few generations, the children are all crippled with insanity and disease."

Silence filled the room as Zarya looked back and forth from them to the silver heaped on the floor. Her lips tightened, a prelude to denial.

"Fifteen to one," Myrad said before she could refuse.

She blinked, turning to Yehudah. "You agree to this?"

"I do, with the provision you tell no one what you've heard."

"I wouldn't have anyway. A gold merchant who spills her customers' secrets spills their blood. Her blood follows in short order."

Yehudah picked up the first bag and dumped its contents onto the counter for Zarya's inspection. "We will leave half the gold on deposit with you until tomorrow. The rest we take with us."

Zarya nodded. "I trust you'll be leaving soon."

"You can rely on it," Yehudah said.

As Yehudah went to grab the next bag of silver, a sudden inspiration came to Myrad. He leaned closer to the gold merchant. "A question, if you would. Where might I find the silk merchants?"

CHAPTER 15

They exited with the sun a pair of hands above the horizon, but already torches sprouted up along the still-busy streets. Yehudah caught Myrad's questioning look and explained, "Margiana never truly sleeps. The merchants do business well into the night, and most of the inns never close, a fact which makes it dangerous."

It hardly needed to be said. Amid the bustle of the vast marketplace, hungry, unblinking stares followed them. As Myrad shifted to mount his horse, a face ducked behind the façade of a nearby building. For a split second, memory tugged at him, but the glance was too brief and too many other faces intruded upon his awareness. "I think we're being followed."

"Possible," Yehudah said without concern. "If we stay together, my cataphracts will discourage any potential thieves."

Yehudah led them to the southern portion of the city, where the spice traders occupied a series of buildings nearly as formidable as those of the gold merchants. "There are spices here worth more than their weight in gold. If you're caught stealing cinnamon, cardamom, or—may God help you—saffron, you lose not a hand but your *head*."

A thousand scents blended in the night air, making Myrad light-headed. They stopped before a shop resembling a dozen others. Something about it must have appealed to the magus. Myrad dismounted to follow Yehudah inside. "Our God gave us favor with the gold merchant," he said before they entered, "but perhaps it would be better not to burden the spice merchant with our history."

The spice merchants, a man and woman with the look of siblings, moved about their small shop with the well-practiced choreography of dancers. "How may we be of service?" the woman asked as the man placed a jar in the single empty spot on the shelf. "We have a supply of the finest saffron from Indus, as well as white-and-red peppers from Bactria." She pointed to a container with a reddish-brown powder in it. "And we've just received a shipment of cinnamon from Egypt."

"Excellent," Yehudah said. "We would like to buy a quantity of myrrh oil. Do you have any?"

The woman frowned. "Caravans from Ethiopia are infrequent visitors, but there are enough Hebrews here to make the oil worth holding. How much will you require?"

"A thousand shekels by weight," Yehudah said.

She jerked in surprise. "My condolences, good sir. I grieve with you. Your losses must have been great."

Yehudah smiled. "You misunderstand me, honored merchant. The myrrh is a gift."

Confusion replaced commiseration. "Strange, to present someone with embalming oil."

"It has other uses," the man interjected. "There are even those who drink it with their wine."

"Indeed," Yehudah said. "I will present the gift and let the recipient decide how to use it. Do you have enough?"

The woman nodded. "Barely. I will have to get word to the caravans headed south to bring more. What else will you need?"

143

"Frankincense, if you please."

"I have a quantity from Sheba. Will you want it as an oil as well?"

"No, the dried form will be fine. But I wish to burn a sample."

"Of course," the man said. He disappeared into the back room and returned with a pebble of translucent yellow resin.

"With your permission?" Yehudah asked.

The woman nodded and weighed the sample while the man disappeared once more and then returned bearing a plate with a glowing coal upon it. The woman placed the nugget on the ember, and tendrils of smoke drifted upward. Yehudah fanned the smoke with one hand, inhaling deeply through his nose. Myrad mimicked him. Aromas of earth, wood, and sweet spice filled his senses. He closed his eyes, drifting, before Yehuda's voice brought him back to the shop.

"That's wonderful," he said. "We'll need five hundred shekels by weight."

The woman again showed her surprise. "We'll have to go to one of the other merchants to complete your order. A gift fit for a king."

Neither Yehudah nor Myrad moved for a long moment, and the woman cleared her throat. "The quantities you require are expensive."

"I understand," Yehudah said. "How much?"

While they haggled, Myrad thought of Gershom. His father never mentioned spices or resins in connection with the Messiah, only the necessity of marking the calendar. Yet these magi seemed to be in unspoken agreement concerning the gifts, even regarding the quantities of gold and spices required. Accompanying Yehudah and the others left him with the feeling of being in some Greek play where everyone but he knew their lines and actions. What was he missing? Where could he go to find the answers?

After they made their purchase and departed the spice merchant's shop, they headed for an inn in the southern part of Margiana. Again, Yehudah found his way with easy familiarity, knowing which inns offered a private room where they could speak without fear of being overheard. Myrad followed, but the prickly sensation he'd felt outside the gold trader's returned. When he spun, hoping to take any watcher by surprise, no one moved and none of the faces tugged at his memory. Frustrated, he trailed Yehudah into an inn on the edge of the city, slipping just inside the door to hide in the shadows and wait. A figure across the street, obscured by a cart, watched the entrance. After a long moment, he turned away. Myrad followed. He caught sight of the figure once more. Whether the man sensed him or simply outpaced him, he didn't know. Regardless, at the next street he lost sight of him.

Myrad found his way back to the inn, where Yehudah and the rest were waiting. The magi reclined in a circle around a low table with their heads forward, talking in low tones.

Dov was the first to see him and waved him over. "Come, we've been waiting for you. We have important business to attend to."

They opened a space for him. "Business?"

"We've yet to determine who will go to Judea," Yehudah said.

It took Myrad a moment to understand. "Aren't we all going?"

Dov shook his head. "That is not our way, and after our mistake with Phraates and Musa, we thought it better not to assume God's favor."

"I don't understand."

By way of answer, Yehudah rose and disappeared down a

hallway. He returned carrying a wooden bowl containing a set of small black stones. "As far as we know, we are the last of the magi counting the days. If we die, the prophecy will be lost within sight of its fulfillment. And so we shall cast lots to determine who goes."

Myrad studied the dark, smooth-looking stones. Each one bore a Hebrew letter in white, beginning with the stylized X-shape of the first letter, aleph, and ending with heth, the eighth letter.

"Each of us will choose blindly," Yehudah said. "If a man draws the aleph stone, that means God has chosen him to go to Israel. After each draw, the stones will be tossed again."

"One chance in eight?" Eliar asked. "With those odds it may be no one will be chosen."

It seemed Yehudah was going out of his way to thwart the mission, but his smile and the gleam in his eyes told a different story. "If I had all twenty-two letters, I would use them. Are we agreed?"

The magi clustered around the table all nodded.

"Good. I will go first," Yehudah said. He handed the bowl with the stones to Myrad. "Since the dream came first to you, it seems fitting that you cast the stones for each of us." Next, he removed the sash of his tunic and tied it around his eyes, blinding himself with the cloth.

Myrad looked down at the bowl in his hands. "How do I do this?"

"Gather the stones and let them fall into the bowl," Yehudah said. "I will then choose one."

The stones clattered in the stillness, and Myrad held the bowl in front of Yehudah. He bumped it, searching, before he reached in to pluck a stone from the small pile.

Stripping off the blindfold, he held it up for everyone to see. "Aleph." He smiled as if he'd been given the fondest wish of his heart instead of a possible death sentence. He dropped the stone back into the bowl and handed his sash to Dov, who stood on his left.

After eight draws, three of the magi had been chosen to take the journey west to Israel: Yehudah, Hakam, and Dov.

With a smile, Yehudah took the bowl from him and gestured to Harel, who handed Myrad the sash.

He gaped at them. "You're asking me to draw? But the dream came first to me."

Dov reached to squeeze his shoulder. "If the Most High wants you to journey to Judea, then nothing can keep you from drawing the aleph stone."

That they would give him one chance in eight of following the dream he shared with Gershom galled him. "I will draw, but regardless of the outcome, I will go to Judea."

"Will you be like Jonah?" Yehudah asked, his eyes smiling.

Hakam set his jaw. "This is why we shouldn't bring foreigners into our midst."

Stung, Myrad tied the sash around his eyes. The stones were dropped into the bowl, rattling against each other. Despite his vow, if he could not journey to Israel in the company of these magi, how would he get there? He didn't have the money or resources to make the trek on his own. Swathed in darkness, he plunged his hand inside the bowl, the stones shifting and sliding against his fingers. When they settled, he pulled one out.

Hiding it in his fist so he would be the first to see it, he ripped the sash from his eyes and opened his hand. There, black against his skin was the aleph stone.

"Greetings, Yehudah."

The magi started, and Myrad spun around at the familiar voice. When he saw the speaker, spots discolored his vision and he clutched for his knife.

But Yehudah only blinked once, slowly. "Masista."

The man who'd left him to die stepped into the room and paused to give Myrad a slight bow. "It pleases me to find you alive. I hoped you would make it out of the desert."

His rage deepened, casting the room in shades of crimson. "If you wanted me to live, you wouldn't have taken my horse." He clenched his fists at his sides. "The horse was mine, purchased with my father's money. You're not a magus, you're a thief!"

His insult affected Masista as much as if he'd remarked on the weather. "Your anger is understandable but misplaced. A single horse can carry enough weight in silver to purchase a hundred soldiers for a time. You said you wanted revenge. I merely worked to see you get it. Don't blame me for not using methods of your choosing. However, if it helps salve your pride, I did come to regret leaving you behind." He shrugged. "At the time, I didn't think your extra weight was worth the sacrifice of a horse. I see now I was wrong."

"How did you find us?" Hakam asked.

Masista smiled as he dipped his head in Myrad's direction. "Gershom left more than one letter of transfer with his son, but at Nisa I discovered the letter for that mint was gone. Thinking it lost in the desert with this apprentice, I went on about my business in the east. But lo! When I visited the gold merchant here in Margiana to exchange my silver for gold, I was told I would have to go to another banker. Mysteriously, she was unable to fulfill my request." He laughed. "You've left a trail anyone could follow, Yehudah. Tell me, are you still waiting for your Messiah?"

"Are you still conniving for power?"

Masista grinned. "What else is there?"

"I'm afraid you wouldn't understand the answer to that," Yehudah said. "Now, what is it you want?"

Masista held out his hands, palms up, as if the answer were obvious. "I want to force Phraates and Musa from the throne. The Romans have their empire. Let them be satisfied with it. The western satrapies have fallen too far under their influence. It's time to restore the line of Orodes. He's here in Margiana, for a time."

The magi around the table stiffened, but Yehudah merely nodded. "I would imagine he would be very grateful to those who helped him secure the empire."

"My point exactly," Masista said. "Every sword I can put at Phraates's throat is a debt the next king will owe me. Surely you don't believe surrendering to the Romans is in your interests? They take pleasure in what they destroy. What have they done to the land of your God? Tell me, Yehudah, how does Judea fare?"

The planes of Yehudah's face hardened to stone. "If you think I'm going to surrender the Messiah's gifts to help you purchase swords, you're mistaken."

"I have enough men to take them from you if needed."

"Perhaps, but not enough to keep them. Margiana is the largest trading center in the empire. It is crawling with soldiers whose job it is to prevent what you wish to do. This is no petty theft. If word gets out a merchant's goods are unsafe, trade here will collapse. Kings need trade, Masista. All kings."

"There's a war coming. Believe me, if Orodes decides he needs your gold for soldiers, he'll have it."

For a long moment, the two men stared at each other, and although the muscles around Yehudah's jaw bunched, he said nothing.

Masista's outburst of laughter broke the tension. "There's no need for such harsh words, old friend. I have no desire to keep you from your quest. In fact, Orodes wishes to send one of the magi loyal to him with you . . . along with cataphracts to help you guard your gifts."

"Your offer is generous, but we have no need at this point for additional magi or soldiers."

Masista stepped over to the table to pour himself a cup of wine. He paused to sniff it before taking a lingering taste. "It wasn't an offer, my friend. Your route will take you back through the heart of the empire where a single whisper in the wrong ear will bring the masters of the treasury crashing down upon you. I'm sure they'd be eager to renew your acquaintance." He set down his cup with a frown. "Pity. It's a bit stale. My men will join you in the morning. If you try to leave without them, I'll send word to the treasury masters in Nisa and Hecatompylos, letting them know where to find you."

Without waiting for a reply, he stalked from the room, his cataphracts trailing behind him.

"They'll kill us as soon as we leave Margiana," Dov said.

"Perhaps not," Hakam said. "A magus is forbidden to lie."

"You believe him?" Myrad was shocked that anyone would trust Masista. "I wanted revenge for my father's murder. He told me he wanted that as much as I did, yet that didn't keep him from leaving me for dead in the desert."

Shimon, the oldest of the magi, held up a forefinger. "That he wants the quest to succeed is not the same as promising your protection."

"We could hire additional guards," Eliar said.

"Orodes's magi could buy their loyalty," Harel said.

"Then we need allies, not guards," Ronen added.

"I might be able to find some." The group of magi shifted as one to look at Myrad. "I think Walagash is here in Margiana."

"How do you know he's headed in the same direction we are?" Yehudah asked.

"Esai promised him a trial run from here to Palmyra." Mikhael sipped his wine. "The idea has merit. The merchant would take strong exception to anyone who put his caravan in danger."

"Too slow," said Yehudah. "The King's star has hung in the sky for weeks now. Do we want to burden ourselves with camels?"

Dov lifted a hand. "Sure is better than fast."

"Walagash isn't using camels anymore," Myrad said. "He sold them all in Hecatompylos to buy horses."

This seemed to finally satisfy Yehudah. Their leader moved toward the door. "Come, Myrad. Let us seek out this merchant." He put his hand on Myrad's chest. "But allow me to negotiate. You have a tendency to be a bit zealous with your honesty."

CHAPTER 16

They exited the inn and circled around to the southern part of the city where the silk merchants made their camps. Big as Margiana was, Myrad again underestimated its size, and by the time they arrived, his aching foot slowed their progress to a crawl, even with the use of his crutch. They passed one tent after another, whose entrances were flanked by guards and torches in equal measure. When Myrad remarked on this, Yehudah nodded as if he expected no less.

"Trade is the lifeblood of the Parthian Empire, and the silk trade is the cornerstone on which it's built," the magus said. "The wealthy of the world hunger for it and are willing to pay handsomely. Silk merchants aren't just people who trade in a certain good, they're the nobility of merchants. Others curry their favor, and the wealth they accumulate gives them great leverage." His arm swept before them. "You may not see any palaces in Margiana, but you're walking among some of the wealthiest people in the world."

Now Myrad understood. When he'd secured Walagash a chance at entering the silk trade, he'd effectively elevated the man to the highest plane a merchant could desire. No wonder he'd offered Myrad a place in his tent. "I was a fool." He didn't realize he'd spoken out loud until Yehudah answered him.

"How so?"

"Walagash offered to bring me into his tent for helping him secure a place in the silk trade. I lost a father and God immediately provided me a friend." He shook his head in disbelief. "And I threw that aside for a chance at vengeance, manipulated by Masista's worthless promises."

They continued on. Most of the tents they passed were quiet, holding about themselves a sense of emptiness. Perhaps the pain of his journey clouded his recollections, but he remembered Walagash's tent having more life.

"Over there," Yehudah said. "I see a tent with red-and-white stripes."

As they came closer, Myrad heard music and laughter coming from within the large tent. When they entered the pool of light cast by torches by its entrance, he saw Aban and Storana standing guard on either side. The couple took turns peering inside, entertained by what they saw there.

Aban was the first to recognize him.

"Myrad!" The soldier smiled. "It is good to see you alive."

Storana turned from the interior to regard him. "The touch of your God must be on you," she said, serious as ever.

"Aban. Storana. It's good to see you again as well." Myrad gestured to the tent. "May we see Walagash?"

Aban's expression became wry, as though he harbored some jest he wished to share. "Abide a moment and let me tell him you are here." He disappeared into the tent.

A moment later, a roar exploded from the interior just before Walagash burst into view. "Myrad!" He lunged forward and pulled him into an embrace, threatening to crack his ribs. "Come. Come. Bring your friend." He laughed. "I can't explain it, but your God has seen fit to bring you to my tent at the perfect time." He held Myrad at arm's length, his gaze settling on his sunburned face. "The mark of the desert is upon you. Come, tonight we celebrate my entry into the silk trade. And more."

They stepped into the warmth and light of a dozen braziers. Rich carpets covered the floor of the entire tent, and wines and cups covered a number of low tables surrounded by deep cushions. Aromatic smoke from water pipes filled the air with earthy scents of clove and cinnamon while musicians played the lyre and tambour. The center of the tent had been cleared, though no one was dancing.

Walagash led Myrad by the arm to a table at the edge of the clearing. A hundred or more stares from men and women in shimmering silks followed them, and conversations stilled. "Here," Walagash said.

Yehudah, obviously more comfortable with their circumstances than he was, dropped to a reclining position on the pillows with the grace of a dancer. But when Myrad moved to follow, Walagash held him upright. "My esteemed colleagues," he said in a voice that filled the ample tent, "this is the man I told you about, the one who traded on my behalf so that I might join your exalted company. This is Myrad ben Gershom."

To one side, a man stood, his hands raised high in a sign of blessing, and Myrad turned to see Esai looking at him, his eyes welling above his smile.

Across the clearing a dark-haired merchant with chiseled features stolen from a sculpture of Apollo pulled a pipe from his mouth and smiled. "From your description, Walagash, I expected him to be a giant."

Walagash's brows rose. "Is he not, honored Dariush? Do not judge by appearances, my brothers." He tapped Myrad's chest. "There is courage enough here for a whole pride of lions."

154

The merchants clapped their approval while Myrad's face flamed to match the braziers. "I need to speak with you, Walagash," he said amid the applause. "About business."

"Tonight, business must wait," Walagash replied. "Thanks to you I have the chance to enter the silk trade. In the morning I will be leaving for Palmyra." He grinned as he squeezed Myrad's shoulder. "I hope you can come with us."

"Walagash!" several of the men in the tent called.

The newest silk merchant of the empire turned to face his guests. "But these are concerns for another day. Please, rest with your friend."

Myrad lowered himself to the cushions, resigned to wait out the celebration.

"Enough," Dariush called. "Where is this desert flower you've promised?"

Walagash laughed, his face beaming. "Honored guests, tonight we celebrate my daughter's naming day."

Myrad started. *Daughter?* He hadn't seen any women in Walagash's tent during their journey together.

Walagash clapped with a sound like thunder, and the musicians on the lyre and the tambour struck a tune with a lilting, rhythmic beat. From the far side of the tent, a young woman appeared, dressed in beautiful silks and veiled so that only her dark brown eyes showed. Thick, black hair ran halfway down her back and matched the texture of her garments. Her feet were bare, but she wore anklets that rang out in time to the music. She gazed over the crowd, her eyes challenging each man there, yet they passed over Yehudah and Myrad without notice.

She bounded into the cleared space at the center as the pace of the music doubled. The shimmering silks flowed through the air like a waterfall as Walagash's daughter spun and leaped in counterpoint to the beat. Myrad was entranced by the sight as the young woman's arms and hands created tales without words. For several moments, all those in the tent reveled in the music and the tinkling of her anklets, watching her dance with rapt attention. Then the music entered its coda and the dance ended with her standing still in the center, her head held high, challenging.

Everyone cheered and raised their cups in salute.

"There, my fellows!" Walagash said. "Is she not a worthy bride?"

Myrad spluttered, spilling his wine. Wiping his face, he saw Walagash escort his daughter to the table where Dariush waited.

"Walagash has given you quite an honor," Yehudah said, then took a sip of wine. "Surrounded by the richest merchants in the empire, he's giving you the chance to bid for his daughter's hand."

Myrad choked again, clumsily setting his cup down. "Did you say *bid*?"

Yehudah nodded and pointed at the other tables at the edge of the clearing. "That's why he offered you a seat here in front, so you could watch his daughter dance." He took in Myrad's confusion with raised brows. "I told you the silk merchants were practically nobles, did I not? They marry among themselves to strengthen their position and to keep from diluting the trade. You didn't know this?"

He shook his head slowly, helpless. "What could I possibly offer Walagash for his daughter?"

Yehudah laughed. "The customs of the Parthians are not those of the Hebrews. Women choose their own husbands. It's not Walagash you're bargaining with, it's her. What does she want?"

Myrad craned his neck, his gaze following her. "I don't even know her—"

At that moment, Walagash's daughter removed her veil to speak with Dariush.

Something must have happened to the air in the tent. Myrad couldn't seem to breathe. "Roshan?" he rasped.

She turned, her hair flowing, then laughed a split second later at the recognition in his eyes.

"So you do know her," Yehudah said.

He didn't remember sitting down, but an instant later he was staring up at Roshan and Dariush across the tent. "I thought she was a boy."

Yehudah smiled at his discomfort. "It's not uncommon for young merchant women to pass themselves off as boys. It avoids certain problems on the road, though it's quite embarrassing if they are found out. The Romans in particular don't afford their women the standing Parthians do."

He watched, dazed, as Roshan made her way around the circle, stopping to speak with each merchant, hearing their offers. Though she smiled and nodded as each man presented his case, her posture remained neutral, noncommittal. Myrad drew a deep breath of scented air, which did nothing to clear his head.

Roshan was not a boy, but a girl. A *woman*.

The same "boy" who'd mocked him, who'd massaged his foot and ankle with camphor oil and given him poppy tea for his pain. A dozen confusing memories from their time together on the road resolved into clarity. His head hurt.

He looked at her, dressed in the silks Walagash had purchased from Esai, her hair framing her face, and he admitted she was more than mildly attractive. He searched the tent for Walagash, his head swiveling, before he spotted him at the entrance. Stumbling with shock, he made his way there.

"Walagash, we need to talk."

Walagash put a hand weighing half a talent on his shoulder. "Later. Do you not wish to bid for Roshan's hand?"

"Even if I wanted to marry, what could I offer her that would compare with the richest men in the empire?"

Walagash smiled. "What did you offer Esai?"

Laughter spilled from him. "I don't have another Torah, and I don't think that is what she'd most desire."

The merchant stroked his chin as if Myrad's helplessness were some deep wisdom. Why did everyone seem to find his ignorance amusing? "True. Do you find the prospect of marriage unpleasant?"

"I've never considered it. Gershom told me he would pick a wife for me when the time was right."

"I invited you into my tent. What did you think I was doing?" Walagash shrugged. "But the decision is hers, and Roshan is a woman of strange inclinations, perhaps because I raised her in the caravan." He nodded toward the center of the tent. "I think she's ready to hear your offer. That is, if you wish to make one."

Myrad turned to see Roshan speaking to the last merchant of the inner circle. The others had resumed their seats with airs of confident or hopeful expectation. His head spinning, Myrad worked his way back to the table he'd shared with Yehudah.

"Are you married?" he asked the magus.

Yehudah nodded. "I was. She died while giving birth. I still miss her."

"You didn't remarry?"

"No." He smiled against the grief in his eyes. "I needed time. I still do. Perhaps someday I will find one who will capture my heart as thoroughly as Hannah did. You know, it's the custom of our people for a man to abide in his tent with his new wife for a year so they can come to know each other." He looked up and around. "This is a very nice tent."

"What could I offer her?" Myrad asked.

Yehudah looked him in the eyes. "The desire of her heart."

The tinkling of bells warned him of Roshan's approach. He rose, turning to see her staring at him, the face the same and yet completely different, framed by long lashes and lustrous hair. Idly, he wondered if she had a knife secreted away in the folds of her silks.

"Do you wish to make an offer for my hand, magus?" Roshan asked. She made a sweeping gesture. "I've been offered jewels, horses, servants, gold, even a palace. And my prospective husbands have promised to lavish me with all the attention I desire. What do you offer?"

"Would you want a man like me for a husband?" He bit his lip, frustrated he'd spoken the thought aloud.

She leaned in closer so that no one else could hear them. "Don't you really mean, would I be willing to marry a cripple, a man with a clubfoot?"

He nodded.

Her shoulders rose and fell, dismissive. "Foolishness. Now, if you didn't know how to ride a horse, that would be another matter." She smiled. "*Can* you give me the desire of my heart, Myrad?"

The way she asked the question told him none of the other men had managed to offer her what she most wanted. He thought back to their time on the road. She'd always seemed content in her father's caravan. With a flash of insight, he remembered the horse trader in Hecatompylos, the woman who'd surpassed her uncle.

He lifted his head to see Roshan waiting, her lips parted, ready to accept or deny him.

"If you marry me," he said, "I will hold you equal to me in everything, and where your wisdom exceeds mine, I will defer to you."

Her eyes widened, and the beginning of a smile curved her lips. "I'm afraid such vague promises won't suffice, honored magus. You will have to be more specific."

"The caravan is yours."

She nodded. "A worthy beginning, but what about you?"

He thought for a moment about what Yehudah had told him. When he spoke he ducked his head, too afraid to meet her gaze. "I'm yours as well, if you'll have one such as me."

"Closer," she said, "but I want you to prove you know my heart and mind."

"This"—his gesture encompassed the tent—"wasn't what you wanted. You said so. Here in this tent you may choose your husband, but it's not really your choice. You have to pick a silk merchant. This is why you wanted your father's linen. I am not a silk merchant. In truth, I'm not a magus either. You would be hard-pressed to find someone poorer than I. Why would you want me?"

Roshan lifted his chin, her hand soft, her eyes kind and luminous. "I saw a depth of courage in you I never expected to see. Day after day you endured torture to keep yourself and the rest of us from being discovered." She moved closer until she filled his vision. "I would be honored to have one such as you."

Myrad glanced around the tent. All eyes were on Roshan, all awaiting her decision. "What do we do now?"

By way of answer, she kissed him.

CHAPTER 17

Myrad stood with Yehudah just outside of Wala-gash's tent before dawn, waiting for the merchant to emerge. Myrad tried to draw a deep breath and winced, gasping when a needle-sharp pain lanced across his middle. "I think Walagash cracked a rib. Maybe two."

Yehudah nodded. "The Parthians are a demonstrative people, and the merchant is big enough to make his enthusiasm danger-ous. Take shallow breaths."

Ignoring the advice, Myrad tried to take another deep breath in an attempt to clear the effect of countless toasts from his head. The hour was either very late, very early, or both.

"Look there," Yehudah said.

Myrad looked to where his friend had pointed. There, two hands over the western horizon, the King's star shone with a pure and steady light.

"It appeared at sunset," Yehudah said, "and the star hasn't moved all night."

Wonder filled Myrad as he gazed at it. "Like the mariner's star."

"Except this one is down near the horizon."

"It frightens me a bit," Myrad admitted.

"Understandable," Yehudah said. "Fear of such a mystery—

such power—should be felt by any man with sense. God has touched His creation with His own hand. Who knows what will happen?"

"Is the calendar wrong?" Myrad asked, but inside, his question went further. Had Gershom given his life to a mistake?

Yehudah took his time before answering. "I don't think so. It's been kept by hundreds, even thousands over the centuries, constantly checked and double-checked to ensure not even one day was lost."

"Then what does the star mean?"

The magus smiled. "If the Most High wills it, we'll find out."

The flap to Walagash's tent fluttered and the merchant emerged, his scowl hinting at the consequences of the previous night's excess. Even by torchlight his eyes looked bloodshot. When he saw the pair of them, he brightened. "Myrad, you and your friend are up early. Come, we will eat and greet the eternal fire of the day together."

"Walagash, please, we need to talk."

The merchant halted his advance, his gaze taking in Yehudah. "This business you spoke of, it involves your friend here?"

"Yes." He stopped. Now that the moment arrived, words failed him. He looked from Yehudah to Walagash, but the two men simply waited. "I'm one of the magi who keep the calendar."

"I know this," Walagash said.

Again, Myrad tried taking a deep breath but to no avail. "I have had a dream, a dream of a light in the heavens, with the voice of God telling me it's the Messiah's star and that I should go and see."

The merchant's expression clouded. "You're not coming with us?"

"I am." Myrad searched for some combination of explanation

and apology to satisfy him, but his thoughts became a jumble. "I also have to go to Judea."

He expected anger. Instead, Walagash grew still. "Your dream is telling you this?"

"Yes. It's the same dream I had the night before Gershom was killed." He gestured toward Yehudah. "The same dream the other magi have had, and it's what made me seek you out here in Margiana . . ." He stopped.

Walagash waved his hand at him. "Go on." His voice sounded neutral, though a storm seemed to be gathering in his expression.

With a nod, Myrad continued. "We're hoping to travel together as far as Palmyra. After that, I will journey to Judea with Yehudah and the rest of the magi."

"What of Roshan?" Walagash asked. "Do you still want her for your wife?"

The thought of her, how she'd fooled him for weeks, made him smile. "Yes. When I've satisfied the command of the Most High, I will return."

Walagash leaned forward, his gaze intent. "And be part of my tent?"

This was no simple question; Walagash sought a commitment. "If the Most High allows it, I will return to marry Roshan and be part of your tent," Myrad promised. "It shouldn't take too long. Jerusalem is but three weeks from Palmyra. I won't be more than two months behind you."

Walagash paused, then nodded his concession. "Who am I to argue with your God? But if you do not return to us within six months from our parting, I will allow Roshan to choose another. Now," he said to Yehudah, "there are those seeking Myrad's life. Do they seek yours as well?"

"The magi with us are no friends to Phraates and Musa, but we do not have their attention as Myrad does. Without our circlets, no one we're likely to encounter will recognize us."

"And what do you offer in exchange for traveling with my caravan?"

The magus bowed. "My cataphracts will travel with me, and they will guard your silks as if they were my own."

Walagash extended his oversized hand. "We have an agreement."

They gathered to leave later that morning. This time there would be no camels. Their cargo, a supply of silks of middling quality, lay strapped to sturdy packhorses bred for the task. If for any reason they needed to travel with speed, they would be able. Yehudah, along with his cataphracts and the other magi, left momentarily to claim their gold from the banker. When they returned, Masista and three additional cataphracts rode with them.

"You're the one going with us?" Myrad said.

The magus smiled. "With the silver from Hecatompylos secure, Orodes is considering other options. He thought it best if I personally oversee the success of your mission."

Roshan reached over to squeeze his hand. Her other hand was on her knife.

Yehudah seemed to take Masista's company in stride. "I'm surprised Orodes would sacrifice the counsel of such an esteemed magus." He shrugged. "Perhaps with the delivery of the mercenaries you supplied, he no longer sees you as indispensable."

Masista's smile never wavered. "Your mission is more valuable to Orodes than you imagine, and at more risk. If you wish to travel through Judea, you will need someone who speaks fluent Latin. The Romans are unforgiving of offense. Who knows? Perhaps, with my help, you will be able to claim a part in the rebirth of the Parthian Empire." He held an arm up in invitation. "Shall we journey forth?"

"Not just yet," Yehudah said. "We'll be traveling with the good merchant Walagash." He eyed Masista's cataphracts. "Under the circumstances, I thought it best to travel in strength."

When Masista pivoted to consider the cohort of guards assembled there, his expression darkened. "We don't have time to plod along with camels."

"Of course." Yehudah gave him a mock bow. "That's why we've secured passage with a silk merchant. He'll travel quickly and provide us with disguises once we reenter Phraates's territory."

Masista's gaze lightened. "Gold and silk? What a prize you've arranged, my friend. Very well, I consent."

"No," Walagash said. "I will not permit it."

"Permit?" Masista scoffed. He turned to Yehudah. "You haven't told him?"

"Told me what?"

Yehudah inclined his head toward Masista. "Orodes has granted this magus authority to travel with us."

Walagash's voice came out in a bark. "What does Orodes have to do with you?"

With a sigh, Yehudah answered, "Apparently, he thinks our mission may serve his ends somehow, though where he got that idea is anyone's guess."

Masista's smile returned. "It is a mystery."

They departed Margiana an hour later. This time, Myrad rode in the center of the caravan alongside the other magi. They and their gifts for the Messiah were on one side of him, Roshan on the other. Walagash and his guards followed just behind, each man with his bow strung and ready. As they crested a hill, he looked back toward Margiana, whose merchants and soldiers grew increasingly restless. What would war look like?

"If Orodes does not strike quickly, war will come and the Khushan will try to take the city," Yehudah said.

"The first strike will belong to us," Masista said. "And every strike thereafter. The Romans fight well in the hills and mountains, but they are incapable of defeating the horsemen of Parthia in the plains and deserts."

"Perhaps," said Walagash. "But Musa has Parthians to fight for her now, does she not? The real question is, will she learn from her countrymen's mistake, or repeat it?"

Walagash's question penetrated the fog in Myrad's thoughts. "What mistake did the Romans make?"

Yehudah pointed to one of his cataphracts. "Tomyris, I could relate the facts but not their import nearly so well as you, I think."

The cataphract took a pull from his waterskin, then trotted his horse over to ride at Myrad's side. "Most people, even military men, will tell you the Romans blundered when they tried to engage cavalry with foot soldiers, but that reveals a lack of understanding. If Crassus had attacked from the mountains the way those cursed Armenians offered, we would have been hard-pressed to defeat him.

"Mounted men will destroy an army on foot in the plains or the desert, but it takes infantry to besiege and hold a city," Tomyris continued. "The Romans' mistake lay in thinking they could overcome the disadvantage of the terrain with sheer numbers. They assumed at some point, Surena, the general in charge of the Parthian cavalry, would have to engage the Romans in order to defeat them."

That made perfect sense to Myrad. "Didn't he?"

Tomyris gave him a grim smile. "Actually, no, though he tried at first. He sent heavy cavalry against the Roman line, hoping to break through and kill Marcus Crassus in a single stroke. But the Romans held. That was a tactic they were familiar with. Surena ordered a retreat, then sent his light cavalry ahead to rake the lines using the bow. What the Romans never counted on was that Surena brought an almost inexhaustible supply of arrows." The cataphract shook his head. "They crouched behind their shields as death rained down on them, thinking we would run out of arrows. But when the arrows showed no sign of stopping, Crassus grew desperate, and desperate men lose."

Myrad almost felt sorry for the Romans, caught in the middle of the desert, frantic to engage an enemy who remained just out of their reach. "Wait. Didn't the Romans have bows as well? Why didn't they fire back?"

A voice came from behind him. "Because they didn't have these."

Myrad swung around to see Storana holding an unstrung bow made of horn and sinew, its tips almost touching to create a heart shape. "Behold, the weapon that will rule the world."

A few hours passed before Myrad, at a signal from Yehudah, let his horse drift back a few dozen paces to where their conversation would not be overheard. Hakam and Dov joined them some moments later.

"Masista presents a problem," Yehudah began. "Despite his words, I don't think his ends and ours align. Orodes seeks the throne. Even with mercenaries and the eastern satrapies, the issue is in doubt. Indeed, I think Phraates's soldiers will still outnumber his. It looks as though Orodes seeks to create a war or the threat of war between the Romans and the Parthian Empire." Yehudah pointed forward, where Masista's cataphracts surrounded the magi. "Orodes isn't sending a peaceful mission into Israel; he's sending a show of force. He wants the Romans to respond."

Hakam pursed his lips. "Not necessarily. It's possible he seeks to align with Israel simply to keep the Romans there, so they can't serve as reinforcements for Phraates and Musa. Our people"— his glance excluded Myrad—"have always been restless beneath their conquerors."

"Perhaps," Yehudah said. "Once we enter Syria, we will be in Roman territory and Masista will bear watching. My Latin is too weak to prevent subterfuge."

So many questions clamored for attention in Myrad's head, he didn't know which to ask. From the time Gershom brought him into his household, he'd bent to the task of learning the languages of the empire: Greek, Aramaic, and Parthi. Gershom had added Hebrew to the list early on, though few magi and even fewer people knew it. Myrad had become just fluent enough in those languages to begin his studies in history when Musa killed the magi. In every conversation since, he felt as though half of it were taking place in yet another tongue. Merchants and magi made references he couldn't grasp, and before he could ask for clarification, the conversations had moved on.

He and Roshan let their horses drift farther back, past the rear of the caravan where in the past they'd ridden with Aban and Storana. His gaze slipped to his betrothed, noting again the delicate features sprinkled with freckles and the sweep of her jawline, and he laughed at himself in disbelief. More than one veil had lifted with their betrothal. How could he ever have thought her to be a boy?

"What troubles you, *joon-am?*"

His speculations dispersed in an instant, forgotten at her greeting. She'd just called him her life. "There's too much I don't know." More than anything he wanted to understand, yet the pace of recent events had left him reeling.

Roshan's eyes danced with her smile. "You need a diversion. Do you dice?" She dug into the pack behind her and brought out a small, flat board with elevated rims around the sides. Then she pulled out a pair of dice, numbered so that two was on the opposite face from one, four on the opposite side from three, and six opposite from five. Gershom used dice to teach him the rudiments of probability. It had been the study he enjoyed most and he'd taken to it immediately. When he'd learned everything Gershom could teach him, his father sent him to an ancient magus named Otanes, a Mede who bragged he could trace his educational lineage to Archimedes.

Otanes claimed every decision a man made could be aided by analyzing the probabilities involved. Myrad bowed his head in grief. The old magus hadn't foreseen the likelihood of Musa's coup.

"I did once," he replied, "but that was to learn calculations. I don't know much about games."

Roshan laughed lightly. "You diced without gaming? That is like owning a horse without riding. Come, let's play."

Aban caught his attention. "Have you ever seen any of us dicing with her?"

Myrad shook his head. "No."

"You might want to ask yourself why that is."

Roshan gaped. "It's not like we *have* to wager."

"And that's how it always begins," Aban said.

Myrad forced a smile. "Perhaps another time." After Roshan put her dice away, he pointed to the bows Aban and Storana carried. "Tell me about your bows."

Aban reached back with one hand to bring the weapon forward. "Why would a magus wish to know about a bow?"

"My father told me that all knowledge is useful." Storana gave him an approving nod. "How do you make the bow?"

Aban held out his bow, offering it. "It took me a year to make and it's as precious to me as you might expect. What do you see?"

Myrad ran his hands over the weapon, noting the three different materials that had been layered together. When he said as much, Aban nodded.

"And there you have the secret to the power of our bow. The wooden center serves as the structure to which deer sinew and horn are bonded."

"Why do it that way?" Myrad asked.

Aban took back the bow, his hand stroking the outer layer. "As the sinew dries, it shrinks. When the bow is drawn, it stretches the sinew. Likewise, the horn on the opposite side resists compression. The draw is difficult, requiring strength, but the release of the arrow is like nothing the Romans ever saw before. Even riding away from the enemy at a full gallop, a Parthian bow can shoot with enough power to penetrate a Roman shield."

"It's said a Parthian is most dangerous in retreat," Storana added, "and it's true."

Myrad nodded. "Is that what happened at Carrhae?"

"Yes," the two answered in unison.

"When the Parthian cavalry retreated," continued Aban, "the

Roman infantry gave chase. It's difficult for a foot soldier to run and keep his shield up at the same time."

A thought occurred to him. "If cavalry is so superior to foot soldiers and the Parthian bow so deadly, why haven't we conquered the Romans?"

"Because," Storana said, "the Parthians spend too much of their time fighting themselves."

Myrad reminded himself that despite the similarity of their looks, Storana was Scythian, not Parthian.

Aban's eyes narrowed. "That's true enough as far as it goes, but the whole answer is more complicated. The Romans vastly outnumber us, and while they cannot best us on the plain or the desert, cavalry is ill-suited to the forests or the mountains." He tucked his bow back behind him. "And our weapons do not abide moisture. In the desert, the bow will last for many years, but not so in the wetter climates. We took Armenia and Israel from them decades ago, but we couldn't keep them."

"So they can't cross the desert and take our territory, and we don't have the men and weapons to take theirs."

Storana nodded. "Conquering is easier than holding. Someday the horse clans will learn how to do both."

Conversation stilled after that. The sun burned off the cloud cover of the morning and beat down on the caravan as it tracked west until Myrad could feel his scalp burning. Roshan reached up to pat the thick turban she always wore, though now the wealth of her hair cascaded down and over one shoulder in a thick braid. The folds of cloth not only protected the top of her head from the sun but also provided her face and ears a measure of protection as well. "It wasn't just to disguise my hair," she told him. Since Margiana, her smile carried warmth and she took his hand in hers often.

He dug into his pack for his spare tunic and wound it around his head.

"You look like an unmade bed," Roshan laughed.

A flap of cloth flopped down over his eyes, and he smiled as he tucked it back into place. "No doubt I do."

The merchant's daughter tilted her head back until she looked down her nose at him. "Don't you care anything for your dignity, magus?"

He turned to face her. To the east, the wind lifted another of the interminable clouds of dust. "Not at the moment, no." His eyes drifted back to the cloud. The wind had pushed most of it to the south, yet the nearest part was still due west. He pointed. "Someone's coming."

Storana twisted on her mount. "A lot of someones," she growled. She stared at the rising cloud of dust, her gaze intent.

"Horses!" Aban shouted to the front of the caravan.

"Could it be just another caravan?" Myrad asked.

Roshan's mouth went tight. "Caravans don't travel at such speed. It burns through camels and horses alike."

With deft motions, Aban and Storana placed their bows between their legs, their arms straining to bend them in opposition to their natural curve. Before Myrad could count to five, each had their bow strung. They peeled away from the caravan toward the dust cloud behind them, one looping to the north, the other to the south. All along the length of the caravan, Walagash's men fanned out and disappeared over the horizons to the north, south, and west. Only Aban and Storana rode toward the cloud.

"Why aren't they all riding toward the threat?" Worry crackled through Myrad's voice.

Roshan shielded her eyes with both hands, peering along the horizon. "It's the trick bandits know best. They show an attack from one quarter while the main part of their force attacks from another." Concern pinched her face. "Let's pray to the everlasting fire that's not the case here."

"Why?"

She pointed at the growing cloud of dust behind them. "If they have that many men to put into a feint, then we're greatly outnumbered."

CHAPTER 18

Roshan turned to him. "Do you have a weapon?"

Myrad fumbled at the belt around his trousers and pulled free his knife. It looked pitifully small in his grip.

"That's not a weapon," Roshan growled. "That's a utensil."

"I didn't know we were going to be attacked."

"You're one of the magi," Roshan shot back. "I thought your whole reason for living was to know." She reached down and drew her sword, then thrust it hilt-first toward Myrad.

"They have bows!" he said. "What good is a sword?"

The thunder of hooves yanked his gaze toward a line of low hills. Seconds later, with a loud cry, Aban and Storana burst into sight and all thoughts of swords and danger fled from him. Their horses descended a low rise, noses forward, manes and tails streaming into the wind. Their hooves struck the earth in rhythm, hardly touching the ground before they were airborne again.

A moment later, the rumble of pursuit swelled and exploded into view. Aban and Storana nocked arrows to their bows. They drew, their motions as fluid as water, bending the ends of their bows, pulling the shafts back toward their ears. Each turned smoothly and released the instant all four hooves of their mounts were off the ground. Their bows snapped back as the arrows leapt toward their pursuers. A puff of dust shot into the air with a man falling to strike the ground. Calling their war cry, Aban and Storana nocked and drew again.

Roshan growled a curse that broke the spell. "There's too many!" She reached for her bow, a delicate-looking weapon compared to Storana's, and wedged it between her legs, stringing it.

"Where are you going?" Myrad asked.

She clutched his hand. "If they come toward you, lead them away. Aban and Storan are without equal. If we can prolong the attack, we may have a chance." She twitched her reins, and her horse jumped into motion, galloping at an angle toward the guards.

Walagash's bellow followed her but then fell to the dust, unheard.

Aban and Storana split, running their horses at angles to avoid the hail of arrows flying their way, laboring to lead the attackers away from the caravan. It almost worked. The pursuers split as well, a pair of riders pursuing each of the guards, but the main group headed toward the caravan.

Aban and Storana continued to turn and fire at their pursuers. Time slowed as one of the bandits shot, the arrow ascending to hang at its apex for a long moment before it descended and struck home. Storana wobbled, an arrow jutting from her back.

A scream of rage cut through the sound of hooves as Roshan brought her horse alongside the wounded guard, reaching out with one hand to keep Storana on her mount. Neither of them tried to fire.

Wind and dust flew past Myrad as he kicked Areion into a gallop. Ahead of him, Storana and Roshan's pursuer nocked and fired. The arrow flew just wide. Roshan slapped her mount on the hindquarters to gain more speed, but Storana continued to weave, slowing them. In seconds their attacker would be too close to miss.

But Areion was fresh and surged forward with every call of his name. The bandit drew, pulling the bowstring to his cheek. He gave no sign of being aware Myrad was mere paces behind him, but he wouldn't miss again. Myrad screamed.

The bandit jerked, his release spoiled, and the arrow flew high. Myrad held the sword forward, striving to close the distance between them. He pulled close enough to see the attacker search him and then smile at seeing him with nothing but a sword.

Impossibly fast, the bandit nocked and twisted, aiming for Myrad. Desperate, he threw Roshan's sword.

Areion's gallop spoiled the throw and the sword went wide. Spots filled his vision, and he wondered how much dying would hurt. Myrad's brain screamed at him to rein in, jump from his horse, anything, but his body wouldn't move. He sat locked into stillness, his eyes fixed on the man about to kill him.

The soldier smiled and released.

Impact spoiled his aim.

Myrad saw the surprised look at the arrow appearing as if by magic in his chest. Still wearing that expression, he toppled from his horse, rolling end over end to lie still on the earth.

Shimmering light passed him, the sun reflecting from the mail of men and horses as Yehudah's cataphracts surged forward, wheeling to pursue the rest of the bandits to the south. Myrad reined to a stop and watched as the cavalry forced the attackers to flee into a hail of arrows. Men and horses fell until the attack withered. Caught between Walagash's horse soldiers and Yehudah's cataphracts, the surviving attackers retreated to the north. Before long, even the dust of their passage faded from sight.

None of the cataphracts or horsemen pursued. Myrad watched, his breath coming in gasps that didn't meet his desperate need for air. He felt a soft touch on his wrist and started. Roshan drew her horse near, her eyes wide. "They're gone."

Panting, he couldn't seem to make his lungs work.

"You can give me back my sword now."

He nodded, but Roshan's voice came to him as nothing more than a buzz against the pounding of his heart. When she squeezed his hand, he understood. He dismounted and retraced his steps until he found her sword lying in the dirt. When he returned, Aban cradled his wife, his hands applying pressure against a wound covering his fingers in crimson.

"Is she . . . ?"

"She'll be fine," Aban said. "The Sarmatians are a sturdy people."

"I was sturdier when I was younger," Storana mumbled. "Back then a little blood loss wouldn't have kept me from killing him."

"Don't be ridiculous," Aban said. "With an arrow in your shoulder, you couldn't have drawn if you wanted to." He handed her a waterskin she worked to empty.

Aban caught Myrad's gaze. "Thank you for going after her."

"That was the most singularly stupid thing I've ever seen," Roshan said. "What were you going to do, cut him down from behind?"

He nodded. "It would have worked except he was too close to miss you and I had to scream to distract him."

Roshan shook her head. "But why did you throw my sword? Did you really think you were going to hit him with it?"

He lifted his hands. "He had no chance of missing me. I figured throwing the sword was better than doing nothing."

Aban nodded his approval. "A little chance is better than

none. Even great battles have turned on the success of unlikely risks."

They rode at a slow walk back to the caravan with Aban and Storana riding double. "That was the most beautiful thing I've ever seen," Myrad said, "the way you rode over the hill, firing backward at the bandits."

Aban smiled. "It feels beautiful as well."

"Could you teach me?"

"What part?" Aban asked.

He shook his head, still caught in the wonder of seeing their horses riding the wind. "All of it."

Aban laughed. "A dozen journeys from Margiana to Judea might be enough time, but not one."

They came to the caravan where Aban surrendered Storana to Walagash. Dov, his face intent, stood at the merchant's elbow. "I've studied the healing arts since I was a boy," he said. "Bring her."

When Myrad moved to follow, Aban caught him by the arm. "I've never met a healer who wanted an audience. If you want to learn the Parthian shot, perhaps we can make a start to your education. Come with me."

"Where are we going?"

"If we're lucky, to get you a bow and some arrows," Aban said.

Myrad looked out across the dusty scrub, his eyes moving from one still form to another. From this distance, most of them looked like nothing more than piles of rags. He wanted to keep it that way. "We're going to scavenge the dead?"

"They won't mind, I promise."

The rest of Walagash's men rode out as well. When they came to the first body, Aban's expression darkened but he said nothing. He pointed to the fallen soldier and gestured for Myrad to check for weapons.

Myrad dismounted near the body, hanging back. What if the man wasn't dead but only pretending? He drew his knife, the blade offering him no more comfort now than earlier. What was he doing? He knew Greek and Aramaic, not fighting. He stopped. The odd angle of the man's neck made his death plain. Most of the soldier's bow lay trapped beneath the body. Grimacing, he clutched the dead man's tunic and rolled him off the weapon, avoiding the lifeless stare. Hope filled him. They'd found a bow on the first try.

Aban dismounted and joined him. Nothing about the dead man's body seemed to bother him. He gave the man's bow one look before tossing it back to Myrad. "The limb tip's broken."

"The what?"

Aban took the bow from him, pointing to the end. "Here, where the string attaches to the notched end of the bow." He flung the useless weapon away and bent over the soldier. "But it's not a total loss." He tugged and twisted the dead man's thumb until something came loose. "Here." He tossed Myrad a thick cylindrical ring made of some type of bone. "That's a draw ring. You wear it on your thumb to protect the skin when you're shooting. Now we just need to find a bow and a few arrows to go with it."

They moved from body to body. At the fourth they found a bow a dying bandit dropped before falling from his horse. Aban inspected it, his lips pursed, before handing it to Myrad with a nod. "It will be a bit heavy on the draw, but that's any bow for a beginner. You'll get used to it after a few months."

Myrad wandered over to the dead man. "This one also used a bone draw ring." When Aban's face darkened, he asked, "What does it mean?"

"These probably weren't bandits; they were professional horsemen. Not cataphracts but still likely bondslaves to someone with power."

"Musa's men?"

Aban shook his head. "There's no way of knowing."

He didn't respond, but inside, a small voice pointed out that none of Masista's cataphracts had helped fight off the attack.

The next few bodies yielded another bow Aban kept and a few arrows still in their quiver. The last two bodies they came to were Walagash's men. They worked together to put each body on the back of a spare horse, then rejoined the caravan. Aban's expression promised retribution, and he'd demonstrated that he could make good on his threats.

It took Dov an hour to tend Storana's wound, but afterward she managed to sit upright on her horse. Dov pressed a full waterskin into her hands. "Drink as much as you can. You lost a lot of blood." A thick bandage covered her right shoulder.

Yehudah looked at Myrad and then at the bow at his side. An obscure shame came over him, as though he'd deserted his father and his beliefs by taking the weapon. Still, Yehudah's expression held no condemnation, and soon the magus shifted his attention to the caravan master.

With gruff commands, Walagash ordered the caravan back into motion. "The desert is unforgiving of mistakes. We'll speak of this once we're safely at the next oasis."

There was nothing for Myrad to do except resume his ride. He let Areion drift back toward the rear once more, but he couldn't seem to find the peace he'd felt before. His neck hurt from trying to see in every direction at once and he couldn't seem to still his hands. He realized he might throw up.

Aban spoke to him, his voice sounding far away. "Do your insides feel like a runaway horse you can't control?"

Even now, his heart thundered hard enough to shake him. He jerked a nod.

"It takes a while to calm down, especially after your first fight," Aban said. "I couldn't seem to wash the fear and dust from my throat no matter how much I drank."

Storana grunted. "My hands shook for the rest of the day after my first battle, and again after my first kill."

"Aren't you afraid the survivors will bring more men and attack again?" Myrad asked.

"We left a warning for them in the desert," Aban said. "The only bodies in the dirt are theirs."

Storana nodded. "Nothing gives a warrior pause like a gathering of vultures. It still turns my heart cold every time I see them."

Myrad tried not to think of the dead guard he'd put on the back of a horse, a quiet man named Delshan. "Even so, we should be watching."

Aban laughed softly. "Your eyes are good, and right now I don't think there's much chance you'll miss anything." He pointed to the bow still clenched in Myrad's fist. "While you're watching, you can familiarize yourself with your bow. Finding one is not as good as making it yourself, but it will have to do. Draw it until you're too tired to pull the string back to your ear." He smiled as though he'd made a joke.

CHAPTER 19

The cursed bow wouldn't move. Sweat beaded across My-rad's forehead, which had nothing to do with the sun. He grasped the bowstring with the draw ring on his thumb, hooking around it as Aban had instructed, and pulled. Spots bloomed in his vision from the effort, but he kept pulling until the caravan in front of him narrowed to a pinpoint in a field of black.

He took a pair of ragged breaths and bent to attempt the bow again.

"Stop," Aban said.

"Why? I haven't drawn it yet."

"And you won't," the guard said. "Not today and not for some time. You're not strong enough."

"All the more reason to keep trying."

"If it hasn't happened by now, it's not going to happen today. Tomorrow, and even more on the next day, you're going to wake so sore you will think you've been beaten in your sleep." Aban pointed to the rise they'd just begun to ascend. "And we'll be stopping soon. Our way station lies just beyond. Give me your bow."

With annoying ease, the guard slid the bow between his legs and slipped the string from the notched ends. The bow curled into its unstrung shape, though now it reminded Myrad less of a heart than it did the curled legs of a dead insect.

"Here." Aban handed bow and string back to him. "Keep them dry. Wet can destroy a year's work in minutes."

Roshan guided her horse close enough to put her hand on Myrad's arm. "It took me weeks to draw mine, and weeks more to do it without shaking. Be patient."

They turned their caravan to the south, where they dismounted and began unloading the horses before leading them to a long water trough. A man stood at the far end, turning a crank that rotated a tube sloping down into one of the many cisterns dotting the oasis. As the tube rotated, water was pushed upward through the spiral attached inside to spill into the trough.

Someone tapped him on his shoulder. Turning, he saw Walagash standing there along with Aban, Storana, and Roshan. Aban held the reins of the horses holding the bodies of Delshan and Jahan. "You're part of my tent," Walagash said. "Come with us."

"Where are we going?"

Aban led them away from the oasis to the desert. "To lay Delshan and Jahan to peace."

Myrad glanced at each man's horse. "You don't have a shovel."

Aban shook his head. "Our brother guards are Parthian. It's not our way to bury our dead. Instead, we will strip them. The scent of death—"

"And blood," Storana added.

"—will draw scavengers. After a few days, nothing will remain but their bones. We'll pay the innkeeper at the oasis to bury those."

The idea of leaving men who'd been living and conversing just hours ago out in the dirt as carrion struck him as indecent. "You're going to let the animals eat them?"

Storana squinted at him. "Above the ground for animals or below the ground for worms, what's the difference? This is our way. At the next city we will visit the temple where the shining fire burns without ceasing and offer prayers for them."

He followed, watching as Aban took the bodies and placed them in the shade of a stunted acacia tree. Roshan's hand crept into his, and when they stripped the bodies bare, she sobbed, adding her breath to the wind.

Memories of rage rushed to Myrad's mind, but Aban and Storana held nothing in common with the beggars who'd taken his father's clothes. Their movements were solemn, dignified, speaking of respect and ancient ritual. Walagash lumbered forward to close the eyes of the dead men and offer his prayers for their families. After they returned, the bottom edge of the sun kissed the horizon.

Walagash stopped Myrad with one hand. "Bring the magi to my tent. I wish to speak with them about this attack."

Myrad moved to comply, but Walagash's grip stopped him. "Bring Masista as well."

He found Yehudah and the other magi at the inn, sipping date wine in silence. "Come. Walagash desires to speak to us."

"What about?"

"About the men who attacked us."

"The bandits?" Dov asked.

"Aban said they weren't bandits." He held out his right hand to show Yehudah the draw ring he still wore. "All of the men who attacked us had one of these."

"Bandits don't have them?"

"Not made out of bone," Myrad said. "Aban said bandits aren't usually so well-equipped."

Yehudah pursed his lips. "That's good to know."

They entered Walagash's tent bathed in the ruddy light of the afternoon sun. Walagash was already there, sprawled on cushions around a low table that held a pitcher of wine and half a dozen goblets. Masista entered a moment later, accompanied by one of his cataphracts. "What do you want, Walagash?"

"Please," the merchant said, "be seated. Have some date wine. I wish to negotiate." His gaze swept over the cataphract.

The magus nodded and lowered himself on the cushions. He reached forward and filled his goblet, gulping it down and refilling it again. "What negotiation?"

Walagash took a sip of wine. "The price for the lives of my guards."

Masista laughed. "I'm sure your guards knew the risks of their profession, merchant. I fail to see how their death is my concern."

Walagash's eyes hardened until they were chips of obsidian. He extended a closed fist over the table. When he opened it, a half-dozen bone draw rings clattered onto it, the noise loud in the absence of voices. "Those men weren't bandits. They were professional soldiers. I don't think they were after my silk, and none of your cataphracts assisted with the defense of the caravan during the attack."

Masista didn't reply. Instead, the two men stared at each other in silence, each waiting for the other to speak first.

"You've yet to ask me a question, merchant," Masista finally said. "The magi say all knowledge is useful, but I believe some is more useful than others. I have no interest in your speculations."

Crimson crept up Walagash's neck. "I've two men dead, and the price to their families must be paid. Do you think I'm a fool? Those men were soldiers, magus, and I think they were yours."

"If you have a question, merchant, ask it," Masista said, his words clipped. "A magus is not permitted to lie."

Walagash's laughter crackled in the air. "But they're allowed to steal a man's horse and leave him for dead in the desert? No. I have no need for greasy answers." Walagash clenched a fist twice the size of a normal man's. "Know this, Masista. I have given orders to my men. If we are attacked by forces we cannot defeat, their first duty is to see you dead."

Masista's eyes widened until the whites showed all around. "You would make me responsible for your safety? The desert is filled with bandits."

Walagash smiled, though it never reached his eyes. "This is so, and now it is in your best interests to ensure your cataphracts help with the defense. Consider it the price you must pay for abandoning Myrad in the desert." He gestured to the tent flap. "You should go now. You have new orders for your men."

Masista rose to depart, forcing a laugh. "You've misinterpreted events, merchant. My cataphracts are present to protect me, not your silks. I kept them with me during the attack for that reason." He turned to Yehudah. "Did I not say you left a trail in Margiana a blind man could follow? If I'd wanted your cargo, I could have taken it from you in Margiana. I had nothing to do with the attack." He swept from the tent.

With a sigh, Walagash took his cup of wine and drained it. "Perhaps," he said to Yehudah, "I should have Masista and his men killed. Despite what he says, I believe he knew about the attack."

Yehudah shook his head. "No. As much as I might agree with your suspicion, we do not know those were his men." He looked at Myrad. "It is not our way to condemn without proof."

Our way, Myrad noted. Did he mean the way of the magi or the way of the Hebrews, and did he mean to include him? He put the question aside. "What makes you think those were his men?" he asked Walagash.

"Bandits are like jackals," Walagash replied. "They attack when their numbers are great enough to ensure victory. There weren't enough men for that." He leaned forward. "But there would have been had you left Margiana on your own. Four cataphracts and six magi would have been no match for the bandits and Masista's guards."

Realization flooded through him. "He was angry when he found out we'd joined with your caravan. He knew we were leaving this morning and had already arranged the attack. There was no way to call it off. He'd ordered the ambush the night before."

"It fits all we know," Yehudah said, "but it's not proof."

Walagash's knuckles cracked as he clenched a fist. "Where the safety of my tent is concerned, I do not require proof."

"Leave him be," Yehudah advised. "If it was his attack, it's over now. While on the road, he has no opportunity to arrange another."

Walagash's disagreement rumbled through the tent. "What do you say?" he asked Myrad.

All eyes regarded him. Those of the magi held a speculative cast as though Walagash's question posed a test. Could they afford Yehudah's offer of mercy? Could he place the blood of five men on his hands?

In the end, he strove to please both Walagash and Yehudah. "For now, keep eyes on Masista and his men," Myrad answered. "Any attempt to arrange another attack will happen at the oases. If he is caught, he is killed."

Walagash took a deep breath, but his head lowered and Myrad couldn't read the expression in his eyes. Yehudah set his wine cup on the table. "All decisions are difficult. The road to Judea is long. Perhaps by the time we arrive, Masista will think differently."

CHAPTER 20

No attack came against the caravan the next day or the day after. Once a week had passed, Myrad felt a weight lift from his shoulders as though some threat had been averted. Masista and his men settled into the rhythm of the caravan, and if they were not friendly, at least they ceased to be combative. Surprisingly, Hakam became Masista's companion of choice, their mutual hatred of all things Roman serving as the glue that bound them together.

The relative calm that descended upon the caravan after the attack would have been even greater except for the reminder hanging in the western sky each night. As soon as the light from the sun fled, the King's star appeared above the horizon where it hung without moving while the rest of the lights of heaven circled around the mariner's star.

"It unsettles me," Dov said one night between Nisa and Heca-tompylos.

"Why?" Myrad asked.

The magus chuckled, his features drawn in flickers by the torchlight within the oasis. "I've forgotten what it is to be young. I think when a man grows old, the routine of unnumbered days has a way of dulling his sense of wonder." He pointed at the star. "Then, when he comes across the opportunity, he fears instead."

"That doesn't answer my question."

Dov laughed again. "Well spoken. Consider, then, the evidence of your eyes each night. What is the center of the sky?"

Myrad pointed to the sky. "The mariner's star."

"And what about the rest of the lights?"

He shrugged, though the gesture held little meaning in the darkness. "They revolve around the mariner's star like bits of clay on a potter's wheel."

Dov's arm came up as he too pointed. "Fixed in the heavens and yet rotating around a central point. Now, consider what must be happening for the King's star to remain fixed at a single point in the sky while all the other lights move along their appointed rounds."

Myrad raised his arms, his hands moving as he tried to visualize Dov's explanation. Then it hit him. "It's moving. All night long it moves against the current of the stars so that it appears to remain fixed in the sky." He took a long, slow breath. "I still don't understand why that would frighten you."

The magus laughed softly in the darkness, yet the sound seemed directed inward. "In the pride of my knowledge I thought I understood the ways of the Most High God, the rhythm and melody of His creation. Now I am reminded the stars are nothing more than grains of sand in His hand. It's unsettling to know everything can be upended in a mere moment."

Myrad thought about that as he gazed at the light in the western sky, fixed yet moving while all of the surrounding lights followed their routes. "What will we find in Judea?"

"The King," Dov said. For a moment, Myrad thought the poet might leave his answer in those simple terms. "But I hope to find some greater truth. Just as the King's star behaves differently from the rest of the stars, I hope that this King will be different as well."

"Different, how?"

"I don't know. It may be the King will frighten me even more than His star." After a last look, he moved off into the darkness, but Myrad stayed, watching.

Roshan joined him a moment later. She wore the fine linen of a noblewoman, appropriate for a daughter of a silk merchant, her hair thick and loose down her back. His fingers twitched at the sight of it. His gaze traced the arch of her neck. The physical traits he'd once taken for boyish immaturity were in fact feminine softness. The star and her acceptance of him both managed to fill him with a sense of wonder.

"You and the rest of the magi come out of your tents every night to look at the sky," she said. "What is it you see?"

He laughed, surprised that she didn't know of the Messiah's star even after their weeks on the road together. He pointed to the beacon hanging low over the horizon with its steady light. "See that star there, the really bright one? Throughout the night it won't move. While all the other lights of heaven spin in a circle around the mariner's star, that one will stay fixed in the west."

She leaned in closer. "Which one?"

"That one," he said, pointing again. "You can't miss it. It's the brightest star in the west."

She shook her head. "They all look the same to me."

"Perhaps your eyes are too weak to see it."

She laughed and gave him an exaggerated blink. "My eyes are fine. I see at least as good as a magus who spends too much time reading."

Frustrated, he straightened his arm and tipped his head to sight along it, moving until it was aimed straight at the star. "Stand behind me and line up with my shoulder and finger. The star is bigger than any other light in the sky except the moon. If you can see the other stars, you can see this one."

Again she shook her head. "I'm telling you, I see nothing there. Have you been drinking poppy tea for your foot again? I think you're seeing things."

A realization dawned on him then, and the flesh on his neck pebbled in the cool of the evening. "You're sincere, you truly can't see it?"

"I truly can't. Is something wrong?"

He stared to the west, afraid the light linking him to Gershom might have winked out as suddenly as it appeared. While the star still burned, he trusted it less now.

"Myrad?" Roshan's voice brought him back to himself.

"I . . . I don't know." He turned and started toward Yehudah's tent. Days on horseback had restored his foot to normalcy, if not health. Even so, his steps back to the tents still carried the tentative cadence of a man who distrusted his own body.

Inside a tent that rivaled Walagash's for its size, he found Yehudah huddled close beside Dov, speaking in low tones, while Tomyris and the rest of his cataphracts relaxed a space apart. The two magi reclined around a low table. Yehudah shifted at his entrance. "Myrad, welcome. What brings you to our tent? I would have thought you would be using nights such as this to court your betrothed." He gave a weak smile. "A wise man courts his wife for the length of his life."

The sadness in his smile reminded Myrad that Yehudah had lost his wife and child. "I was. We were looking at the King's star. I mean, *I* was. She can't see it, yet her eyesight is better than mine."

The magi didn't appear at all surprised. They both looked at him but remained quiet.

"You knew?" Myrad asked.

They nodded in unison. "Since we first came to Margiana," Dov said.

"How?"

The poet shrugged where he reclined by the table. "Every people and nation watch the stars, and every religion has astrologers who map them and search the sky. We inquired of those in Margiana who follow the shining fire, and none of them knew anything of a new star hanging in the west. None. Then we went to the Greek temples, but it was the same response. No one had noticed anything different about the night sky."

Myrad shook his head. "How can they not see it? And if they can't, how can we?"

"Your question can be debated but not answered," Dov said. "Therefore, the subject is of little use to us."

"Of little use? But what if the star isn't real?"

Yehudah and Dov exchanged a look Myrad couldn't decipher. "He's one of us," Yehudah said. "We found him in Nisa and, if you recall, his dream predates ours. Is that not a sign of God's favor?"

Dov, the oldest of the magi with them, sighed. Sprinkles of gray marked his beard, though his gaze was sharp, even fierce. "Am I real?" he asked Myrad.

Myrad laughed his discomfort. "Of course."

"How do you know?"

He pointed at Dov's chest, picking a point where a splash of wine created another stain on his tunic. "I can see you."

"You can see the star as well."

Myrad looked at Yehudah, and although the conversation seemed genuinely earnest, he showed no inclination to contribute. "But I could walk over and touch you as well."

"Not if I ran away," Dov said. "Let's assume for the moment that these ancient legs are swifter than yours. I grant you, the question is in doubt."

At first, Myrad thought the magus had mocked him and his clubfoot, but there was no trace of humor or derision in his expression. He'd merely stated a fact. "You would leave footprints as evidence of your existence."

Dov nodded as if Myrad made his point for him. "And the star has too. You can see it, but it is beyond your reach. You can't touch it, but you see the evidence of its existence in our shared experience."

"But anyone can see you," he protested. "Roshan can't see the star."

Undeterred, Dov went on. "Tell me, can everyone see the sun?"

"Unless they're blind, yes." He saw where Dov wanted to lead him, yet he refused to follow.

The magus's intended explanation failed to satisfy him. "But even a blind man can feel its warmth."

"The warmth he feels could be from the sun or a fire. I . . ." He stopped. There would be no answers.

Dov sighed. "Stop dressing your fear in logic and arguments that don't mean anything. What is it that troubles you so?"

"It frightens me," Myrad confessed, "Roshan not seeing the star. She's my betrothed."

"For some reason, God has seen fit to reveal the King's star to us but not to others. We don't know if the star is *real*. In the end, it doesn't matter. Whether it's a figment God has planted within our minds, or He's blinded everyone else from seeing it, the end result is the same, is it not? He's communicated His message. It may be that *everything* we consider real is nothing but an image in the mind of God anyway."

"That we can see the star is no credit to us," Yehudah added. "And the fact Roshan can't see it doesn't mean there is anything unfit in your betrothed or God has found her lacking." He paused and smiled. "Of course, you could always ask Him for an explanation." Dov nodded his agreement.

"Now you are mocking me," Myrad said.

Yehudah's smile broadened. "Only a little. I still ask God for explanations of what I don't understand. I'll let you know if He ever gives me one."

Myrad spent his days in the company of Aban and Storana, riding close to Roshan, hoping by proximity to subdue his doubts. He occupied himself with the bow. After several weeks and much practice, he could now pull the string all the way to his cheek. The ache in his shoulders and back he thought would be permanent additions to the one in his foot had subsided at last, and Aban set him to drawing with a nocked arrow. But not firing.

"Pull the bowstring back," Aban instructed, "until you can feel the point where the draw comes easier. Then hold the arrow steady on your target for a count of two, then release the tension."

"When do I get to shoot?"

"When your draw becomes as fluid as wine and as quick as a hare."

He sighed and pulled again.

"Patience," Aban said. "You'll shoot when I think you're ready." The natural tilt of his eyes, the telltale sign of his Parthian heritage, gave his gaze a permanent squint. Now it swept across the landscape. "I think this will do. Leave your bow with Storana and come with me."

Encouraged by Aban's strange invitation, he surrendered the weapon and followed the guard out across an empty section of desert. "If you want to master the Parthian shot, you'll first have to learn how to ride."

The image of Aban and Storana flying across the desert on their horses came to his mind, the horses' manes waving in the wind, the pair shooting like earthly embodiments of Artemis and Apollo. "Shouldn't I have my bow with me?"

Aban nodded. "Yes, if you want to fall and break your neck. That would definitely speed up your training. I told you the Parthian shot takes years to master. Nothing's changed."

"What do we do first?" he asked.

Aban gestured to his horse. "Your mount isn't of Nisean stock, but it's a good, serviceable horse. You have to learn how to guide it with just your legs. Now, let go of the reins and close your eyes."

Myrad did so, and Areion continued to walk, guided by the horse walking next to him. "Now," Aban continued, "with your eyes closed, I want you to concentrate on the pressure between the inside of your legs and your horse. Curl your legs so that you have as much contact as possible."

He could feel Areion's steady breathing through the inside of his thighs, a gentle force of the animal's ribs pushing against Myrad's legs with each breath it drew.

Aban's voice mixed with the whispers of the desert. "Feel the rhythm of your horse's stride. When I tell you, turn your shoulders to the left and let your hips follow." Aban waited a moment, perhaps two, while Myrad rocked back and forth with his horse's stride. "Now."

Myrad shifted on his riding blanket and opened his eyes to find himself angling away from the caravan. Aban paralleled him, his reins loose on the back of his mount.

Though it was a small triumph, it still brought a smile to Myrad's face.

Something in Aban's expression warned him. "Now for the rest." And for the next two hours he taught Myrad the techniques for making Areion speed up, slow down, and stop, but Aban always stopped short of letting Myrad push his horse to a gallop. Bringing his mount to a complete stop without using the reins proved the most challenging.

"You'll have to use the reins and the same vocal command along with the pressure from your legs until your mount understands your intention," Aban said. "It will take a while."

"How do I get him to run?" Myrad asked.

The guard shook his head. "You don't want him to run. Not for weeks, maybe months." Aban must have seen the disappointment on his face. "You're training your horse to react to the pressure from your legs. At a full gallop, an unintentional squeeze will send your horse veering into a turn sure to pitch you to the ground. At that speed you could split your head open on a rock or break your neck. You are just now learning your horse in earnest. Be content and continue to draw your bow."

Myrad nodded. "I'll try."

Aban's dark brows came together over his prominent nose. "You're one of the magi, the kingmakers of the empire. Why is this so important to you?"

Myrad hesitated a long moment before he replied. "When I'm up here," he said at last, patting Areion's neck, "I don't have a clubfoot. I'm like any other man."

CHAPTER 21

The rhythm of Myrad's days became defined by his efforts to master the horse and the bow. His progress in both areas pained him, coming as it did in small increments, and not even Roshan's unfailing encouragement cheered him. At the oases, news of war and fighting came to them, and Walagash made it a practice to send guards out to scout the road ahead and behind. The caravan skirted south of Nisa and began the leg back toward Hecatompylos. The magi, even Masista, took to scouring the horizons for the telltale clouds of dust that would preface an attack.

At an oasis eight days east of Hecatompylos, Storana beckoned to him. Aban and Roshan flanked her. "Bring your bow. We're going to teach you how to shoot."

They walked their horses out to the edge of the oasis until they came upon a date tree growing in seclusion, its serrated trunk and fronds solitary against the backdrop of earth and sand. Storana pulled a scrap of red cloth from inside her tunic and wedged it into a crack head-high between the sections of the trunk. Facing away from the tree, she stepped off fifteen paces. Without hesitating, she nocked, drew, and fired. The arrow flew through the air with a hiss and struck the lower right corner of the cloth with an audible *thunk*. The shaft of the arrow vibrated for an instant before it stilled.

Aban smiled at his wife's skill and held an arrow out to Myrad. "Now you."

His hand trembled as he took the arrow. He missed the nock with the bowstring and tried to ignore the way Storana hung her head. On the second try he managed to get it onto the string. Hooking his thumb with the draw ring around the string, he pulled it back almost to his ear just as Aban had shown him. After many weeks of practice, his arms hardly shook. Taking aim, he let the arrow fly.

He watched as the shaft flew wide and high of the cloth, missing the tree entirely. His face heated as the two guards pursed their lips.

"Actually, that wasn't too bad," Roshan said.

"No," Storana added. "Considering he has no idea what he's doing."

Aban sighed. "Storana is the best shot in the caravan. She believes mastery of the bow is the loftiest goal of a man or woman."

"And I'm right," Storana said. She stepped in and took Myrad's bow. "Everything you've seen of archers standing on the ground you have to forget. Those techniques won't work on horseback. From the moment you reach for an arrow to the moment you let it fly, every movement has to take into consideration you're moving on horseback." Her eyes grew wide. "And we haven't even started on the Parthian shot. Keeping your horse running straight while you turn and fire at a target behind you is a skill unto itself."

For the next hour, Storana and Aban took every movement from taking an arrow from the quiver to firing and retaught them to Myrad. Each time he asked why, they gave the same answer: "Because you're going to be on your horse." In that entire time, he failed to hit Aban's red cloth and managed to hit the tree trunk a single time with a glancing blow that sent his arrow careening off to the right.

As they gathered the arrows by the last light of day, Aban queried him again. "Why is this so important to you?"

Myrad glanced back at Roshan, where she scanned the ground a dozen paces away. His shots covered a wide expanse.

The guard smiled, accentuating the tilt to his eyes. "It has something to do with Roshan?"

"And Walagash. When he and Roshan look at me, they see a lie of their own making. Walagash brought me into his tent because I gave him the desire of his heart." He laughed a little at the memory. "He thought I was being generous. I wasn't. Musa's men were hunting me. Without the caravan to conceal myself, I would have been killed within a day. What value does a Torah have to a dead man? Now, whenever he looks at me, he sees the man who gave him the desire of his heart."

Aban nodded. "Walagash is quick to see the best in men, but he's quick to see the worst as well. Either way, he's rarely in error. What about Roshan?"

Myrad sighed. He didn't want to tell the story, but he wanted even less to carry the weight of the secret. "When the caravan was attacked, I stayed at the rear. Then that bandit went for Storana, and Roshan followed. I understood everything that was happening. He was less than ten paces away when I threw Roshan's sword at him. Nobody could have missed that target except for me. The bandit smiled as he drew, and all the time I was screaming inside to turn aside or duck. Instead I just stayed there, not doing anything, too afraid to move."

"Ah," Aban said. "And Roshan thought you were being brave."

Myrad nodded. "Foolish but brave. When she looks at me, I see the man I want to be reflected in her eyes. I'd like to live up to that image . . . someday."

"It may be that Walagash and Roshan know you better than you realize," Aban said. "Come, let us finish gathering the arrows. I'm hungry, and food awaits."

A week later, they reached the last oasis before coming to the summer capital of Hecatompylos. As date palms and acacia trees resolved out of the shimmering heat of day, Myrad saw throngs of merchants and camel trains lining the watering station, the grounds filled with men and animals like so many crawling insects. The men working the water pumps sweated and strained to keep up with the demand. Not a single space stood empty, with merchant masters cursing and barking orders, and guards shouting for more water. Despite the chaos all around him, the impression of something missing nagged at Myrad. He searched for what that could be, but it eluded him.

"Have you ever seen anything like this before?" Myrad asked Roshan.

Her eyes darted over the chaotic scene. "No."

Walagash's bellow came from the middle of the caravan, calling for Roshan, Aban, and Storana. Riding his mount, Myrad followed her.

The merchant surveyed the oasis. "Roshan, go talk to the merchants. Aban and Storana, talk to the guards and soldiers. Find the cause of this." He turned to address the rest of the caravan. "None of those merchants are staying the night, not even the ones with camels, despite that they have no hope of making it to the next oasis before dark."

"How do you know this?" Hakam asked.

"Tents," Walagash said. "The oasis is overflowing, but no one's putting up a tent."

Myrad dug his heels in to bring his horse to a canter, quickly catching up to Roshan.

"What are you doing?" she asked. Her eyes were sharp beneath the turban hiding her hair, and a heavy plain cloak covered her fine linen.

"I'm going with my betrothed."

The answer surprised her enough to make her eyes widen, but whatever she felt after that remained hidden behind their deep brown. "You're out of place. You should stay with the other magi."

He laughed. "My clothes are covered with the dust of the desert, and my bow is strung and ready. The sun has burned me so that my skin is nearly as dark as your eyes. I couldn't look less like a magus if I'd tried."

She gave him a grudging nod. "Stay on your horse so they don't see your foot."

A month or even a few weeks earlier, he would have taken offense at the remark. Now it just seemed like sound advice. This close to Hecatompylos and the king's mint, they couldn't afford to have him recognized.

Roshan led them toward the main watering trough, leading her horse between a pair of camels toward a merchant dressed in purple and black. "What's happened?" she asked him.

The merchant ignored her and pivoted to continue yelling orders without effect. Roshan reached down from her horse to grasp the merchant's arm. Startled, he wheeled, grabbing the hand on his shoulder and clutching his knife with the other. Caught off guard, Roshan pitched from atop her horse and fell against him, knocking her turban to one side.

Her long black hair spilled loose. She reached up, straining to push her hair back under the turban, but the merchant still gripped her arm. "You're a long way from home, girl." Something hot awoke in his eyes.

Weeks of training set Myrad's hands in motion. Between one heartbeat and the next, he sat with an arrow nocked and drawn, its point trained on the merchant's heart. "Let her go."

The merchant's smile became a snarl. "What do you care? Only one type of woman puts her hands on a man."

"She's not that type. You've made the mistake of putting *your* hands on the only daughter of a silk merchant. We want information and that is all. If we can't get it from you, we'll get it from someone else. Someone breathing." He pulled back the bowstring a little farther.

The man threw Roshan to the dirt. Myrad let the tension in his bow go slack but kept the arrow nocked. If the merchant decided to charge, he could shoot him before he took a second step. He gestured to the crowd and chaos with his arrow. "What's happened?"

"Phraates is dead," the merchant said. "Some say from poisoning, others from a dagger stroke, but they all agree on who did it."

"Who?"

"Musa." The merchant leaned to one side and spat. "Phraates was a fool. His death suits him. Still, his passing will be mourned, even if few people celebrated his life."

"Why's that?" Myrad asked.

The merchant scowled. "Are you simple? Musa and her son,

Phraataces, reign in Parthia now. Her soldiers are sweeping the city. All it takes is the wrong word in the right ear and you're taken to the palace courtyard and killed. If you're lucky they put the sword to you. No one can say the Romans lack imagination when it comes to executing their enemies."

"What about the magi?" Myrad asked. As the merchant's brows rose in surprise, he regretted the question. "My father has friends among the king's counselors," he was quick to add.

"I don't know," the merchant replied. "And no one with any sense will say what they know either. They're too busy trying to escape."

Roshan pulled him away, and the merchant went back to tending his horse. But when Myrad looked back, the man was staring at him. "I think I've made a mistake. That merchant suspects I'm a magus."

She nodded. "The merchant has to find someone willing to pay for the information, and they're most likely still in the city. His fear should keep us safe. We need to let my father know there's trouble coming."

They returned to Walagash and the magi. Myrad expected an outburst from the merchant at hearing the news, but instead Walagash stood by his mount calmly, a mountain in repose. "How much daylight remains?" he asked Roshan.

She peered west, extended her arms, and spread her hands. She counted the number of hands up from the horizon until her topmost hand touched the sun. "Three hours."

Aban and Storana approached at a trot, their expressions grim.

"How bad is it?" Walagash asked.

"Bad enough," Aban said. "For now, Phraataces still has the loyalty of his father's clan. Musa is using that to ensure no one from the family of Orodes is left alive to make a bid for the throne. She seems particularly eager to put her hands on the prince of Hyrcania."

"It's not as bad as having Phraates die without an heir," Storana said, "but it doesn't miss it by much. Anyone with a political score to settle is trying to make the most of the opportunity."

Yehudah sighed. "Caesar's plan has been fulfilled at last. A Roman sits upon the throne in Parthia." Dov nodded as Hakam and Masista growled curses.

Myrad couldn't see what difference the death of Phraates could make. If civil war had already come to the Parthian Empire, what further impact could Phraates's death have on it?

"So," Walagash said, "not a safe environment for buying or selling."

Aban shook his head. "When the merchants started to scatter, Musa closed the city and posted guards around the camps to keep any more from leaving." He pointed at the crowds around them. "These are just the ones who escaped before she shut the gates."

"There's more," Storana said.

Walagash sighed. "There almost always is. What?"

"I spoke with a caravan guard who bribed his way out of the city after Musa posted sentries at the gates. She's stripping the caravans of their guards and impressing them into her cavalry. And she seems to think Parthia needs infantry. Able-bodied men who don't know how to ride are being taken as well."

At that, Walagash signaled Aban, Storana, and the rest of his guards to surround them. "Make sure we're not overheard." After they left, he pointed at the cataphracts. "Merchants have guards, not cataphracts. They have to change. We can hide their armor with the silks, but the lances must be left behind. Leave them in the desert where they won't be found." He turned to the magi.

"The rest of you will need more functional clothing and weapons as well. From a distance you should be able to pass as guards."

"Why not ride north around the Hyrcanian Sea and travel down to Israel through Syria?" Hakam asked.

Walagash's laughter came out as a bark. "Two reasons. First, the Hyrcanian Sea is unimaginably vast. Going around it would more than double the time it takes to get from Margiana to Judea. Second, the northern tip of the sea is controlled by Scythian tribesmen. They're aggressive and ruthless toward outsiders."

"And as good with the bow as the Parthians," Aban added.

Storana smiled, her eyes sharp. "Some of them are even better."

"Let's water the horses," Walagash said. "Then we will cut across the desert to the first oasis east of Hecatompylos."

"At night?" Yehudah asked.

"Yes." Walagash looked at Masista.

"It can be done," said Masista, "if you have someone to guide you."

CHAPTER 22

B y the time they'd led the horses to the watering trough,
the sun was a ball of dull orange resting on the horizon.
Aban and Storana scouted the western edge of the oasis to
listen for the latest news from Hecatompylos. When the horses
finished drinking, Myrad took his place at the back of the caravan with Roshan, but before they could leave, Aban and Storana
came galloping back to the caravan.

"The way west is blocked," Aban said after everyone gathered.
"Musa's men have left the city and have covered the caravan
routes from here to Ctesiphon. Any man who can bear arms is
being taken as property of the empire. The other caravan masters
thought as you did, so Musa's men are sweeping the desert."

Walagash bowed his head and muttered a curse. When he
looked up again, he surveyed the men before him. It was Myrad's
face he settled on. "I'm sorry. We're going to have to go back.
Your dream and mine are over." He looked at the train of horses
with their piles of silk and sighed. "So close."

Myrad followed his gaze. "Can you not sell your goods in
the east?"

He nodded, but his expression never changed. "With the
trade routes cut off by the war, Margiana and the cities of the
east will be awash in silk and every other good coming out of

Qian. It would be a miracle if I broke even, and breaking even was not part of my deal with Esai."

"Go back if you must," Yehudah said, "but we will go on. We have to find a way to Judea and the King."

Myrad sat on his horse, his bow in his lap as it always was now, his clothes along with his crown and the rest of his father's money stashed in his pack behind him.

"What path will you follow?" Walagash asked Myrad.

He looked to Roshan, who was on her mount at Walagash's side, her eyes fixed on her father. Yehudah and the rest of the magi watched him, waiting for him to affirm or deny his place among them. There was no choice. He would follow the dream in all its impossibility, no matter the cost.

"No choice needs to be made," Masista said. "At least not yet."

Walagash's eyes narrowed. "Surely, magus, you don't think I'm foolish enough to trust you. Your place in my caravan was nothing more than a temporary necessity."

"There is a way to get your goods and Yehudah's gifts to the west," Masista said, "if you're bold enough to take it."

For the space of a few heartbeats, Walagash appeared to consider Masista's offer. Myrad watched warring expressions chase each other across his face. "No," he said. "I have no reason to trust a man who finds his friends expendable."

Masista bowed as though the merchant had paid him a compliment. "That I am single-minded is why you can trust me, but if you won't trust me, consider whether or not you can trust the prince of Hyrcania and the kings of Armenia."

"Armenia?" Dov said. "They're aligned with Rome. Going there would be like running straight for Musa's embrace."

Masista shook his head. "You're one of the magi. You should know better." He turned to Yehudah. "What do you say?"

Yehudah jerked his head once in assent. "There's merit to what Masista says. The prince of Hyrcania is of the same blood as Orodes. His territory skirts along the southern edge of the sea and would bring us to the border of Armenia. The Armenians"—he sighed—"are unpredictable."

Masista smiled. "I know them. They will bargain. From there we can journey west to Syria and the border of the Roman Empire. Just because the roads in Parthia are closed to merchants doesn't mean the roads in Armenia will be."

"But what of Tigranes and Erato?" Dov asked Yehudah.

The magus shrugged. "That's a cast of the lot. They may be disposed against Rome as Masista says, but political alignments in Armenia are even more ephemeral than Parthia. Their survival is based on their ability to play the two empires against each other."

Masista's gaze sought out each of them. "As I said, there's a plan if you are bold enough to take it. Sell your silks directly to the Romans and your profit is assured."

By way of answer, Walagash checked the position of the sun. "We can't stay on the road and we won't be traveling through the desert. Who will guide us through the forests?"

They polled their men and found no one with knowledge of Hyrcania. Walagash appeared undecided. Then, like a man shouldering a burden he knew to be too heavy, he straightened. "Our first priority is to get off the road and away from the eyes of Musa's men. Put the horses to a steady trot until sunset."

They rode north out of the oasis. Within minutes, the terrain changed from desert to rolling hills covered with scrub and wayfaring trees. At Walagash's command, they rode four across to ward off attacks by leopards. They ascended a wrinkle in the hills, then dropped into a swale between two folds of the land.

When they ascended again, they heard sounds of fighting, the distant clash of swords coming from the oasis behind them.

They paused to look back, but dusk blurred the torches of the oasis into smudges of wavering light. The sounds of war stilled a few moments later until there was nothing but silence. "Musa has taken the oasis," someone said. No one needed confirmation. They turned their horses toward the next hill north. Minutes later, the sky darkened and night sounds filled the air. Soon the guards out front could no longer see the steps their horses took, and they stopped to light torches.

Walagash wheeled his mount to peer back the way they'd come. Myrad followed his gaze. There, in the distance below them, burned the lights of the oasis, the individual torches small like candles and as fragile. The merchant muttered a curse.

"What's wrong?" Myrad asked.

Walagash's arm rose to point. "If we can see their lights, they can see ours. We'll have to make camp in the dark."

"Is that bad?"

Walagash nodded and ordered the torches extinguished. "Leopards can see in the dark. Pray to your god we haven't stopped in their hunting range. Perhaps a cold camp will work in our favor."

They unloaded the horses by the light of a crescent moon and bunched them together instead of placing them in a picket line. Walagash barked orders in the darkness. "Every man stands watch tonight. All night."

Masista's objection came immediately from Myrad's right. "Are you not overestimating our danger, merchant?"

To his credit, Walagash responded to Masista's question instead of his arrogant tone. "Perhaps. I have camped in the hills north of Hecatompylos only once before, when I was new to the road. It wasn't quite the same. We had camels, not horses, and we thought we were safe enough to have a fire at night." His words hinted at a story left unspoken.

"What happened?" Myrad asked.

"Two of our men died by snakebite and one more was dragged away by a leopard. He screamed for a long time." The pitch of Walagash's voice dipped to a murmur. "Keep your sword out and forward."

Myrad stared out over the end of a sword given him by one of Walagash's guards, or imagined he did. He strained to see, but his eyes couldn't penetrate the deepening gloom. Three, perhaps four hours in, long past the point where the pain in his clubfoot had become a stab of fire, he noticed shadows of black within the night, suggestions of rocks or horses depending on where he looked.

Aban's voice came out of the darkness. "We've been seen, Walagash. Men are headed this way from the oasis."

The merchant spun to stare south. Pinpricks of light bobbed in the distance, floating toward them, with more appearing every second that passed.

Walagash spat in the dirt. "Your plan isn't starting off so well, Masista."

"Bold moves require sacrifices," the magus replied.

Quickly lighting a torch, Walagash turned to Aban and Storana. "Get a dozen guards with torches mounted and lead the pursuers away from here. Head north, then east. As soon as the sun comes up, we'll head west."

Aban glanced back at the bobbing lights. "They'll find you."

Walagash shook his head. "It will take them an hour or more to get here. We'll be hiding."

The look on Aban's face spoke as eloquently as words of his thoughts on the plan. He nodded and turned to go.

Walagash ordered the rest of them into a line toward the thickest part of the forest. "Get the rest of the horses as far into the forest as possible."

"What about the gifts?" Hakam asked.

Walagash huffed. "Cargo doesn't make much noise. Take it a short way into the trees. As long as they don't stumble over it, they'll never see it."

Roshan sidled up to her father. "That's a lot to move in not much time, and we're going to have to feel our way in the dark."

Myrad stepped forward over the uneven ground, desperate for some task to distract him. "What do you want me to do?" he asked Walagash, but it was Roshan who answered.

"Find a couple of good horses and follow me."

The lights of Aban and the other torchbearers faded. Before absolute night fell over them again, every man grabbed the reins of as many horses as he could hold. Roshan led Myrad into the forest. Myrad felt his way, praying any snakes would be scared away by the approach of hooves. After fifty paces, Roshan stopped. Her voice came to him a moment later. "Hand me your reins."

Myrad held out his arm toward the sound of her voice until they bumped hands. She tied his horses to a nearby tree.

For the next hour, they crept back and forth with more horses as the lights of the approaching soldiers inched closer. Walagash and the rest of the caravan paralleled them, moving the heavy loads of cargo into the cover of the trees. No matter how many trips they made, it seemed the number of horses to move never changed.

In the distance, he could make out hints of faces and bodies surrounding the torches. He tasted bile at the back of his throat. This was no scouting party. Over a thousand men were

211

heading their way. Steel reflected the light of their torches. In minutes the soldiers would be on top of them. If any horses or cargo were discovered, their ruse would fail. Escape in the dark would be all but impossible, especially for a half-lame magus.

"Faster," Roshan urged.

They led horses by groups now, hurrying across the rocky ground. Twice Myrad stumbled and fell, pitching headlong. The second time he landed on a sharp rock and cut open his arm. Breath hissed from him as he struggled not to scream. By the time he got his feet underneath him again, blood tracked its way to his hand.

He felt along the ground with his feet, working to get the horses deeper into the forest, when a hand to his chest stopped him. "Be still," Roshan whispered into his ear. "They're here."

He looked back the way he'd come and saw men picking their way among the rocks by torchlight. Tracking.

"Where are Walagash and the others?" Myrad whispered.

"Around us. Hiding."

The soldiers approached the place where they'd intended to camp, their horses slowing. By flickers of torchlight Myrad could see them pointing at the ground. It wasn't until his vision narrowed to a pinpoint that he realized he'd been holding his breath.

"There were riders here," one of them said. In the stillness, his voice sounded close enough for Myrad to reach out and touch him.

The scouts for the soldiers—four men holding torches as they studied the ground—split up, searching. Roshan reached out, found Myrad's hand, then pushed the hilt of a dagger into it. One of the men twitched the reins of his horse, moving toward their hiding spot. Any second now he would stumble across them or their cargo and they would be discovered. Then they would die.

"This way," one of the other scouts called, pointing north.

The long column of horses passed by even as the scout nearest them lingered. Myrad stared at him, transfixed by his danger. Roshan's whisper warmed his ear. "Close your eyes. They reflect torchlight, and he can feel you looking at him."

Myrad squeezed his eyes shut, trying to hear, but the thunder of his heartbeat drowned out every other sound. He cracked one eye open, just enough to count the riders passing by their hiding spot. An eternity later, a few men shy of two thousand, Roshan's whisper came to him again. "They're gone."

"What do we do now?"

"We wait for dawn and hope Aban and the rest can lead them away."

He slumped against the tree, his eyes on the night sky.

A nudge in his ribs brought him to wakefulness. A predawn sky lightened to gray showed figures moving through the trees. They brought the horses out of the forest to the trail leading north and headed out before the sun broke the horizon. Myrad and Roshan rode next to Walagash in the center of the caravan. The cataphracts rode in the front while the remainder of Walagash's men covered the rear. "Are we safe now?" Myrad asked.

Walagash cocked his head to one side. "Safety is measured by comparison. We're safer than we were last night, but those men are in the forest with us."

"What do they want?"

"I thought at first they desired nothing more than to force the guards and cataphracts into the service of the queen." He rolled his huge shoulders. "But there are too many. Now I think we have a common destination."

They continued north, riding into a narrow ravine whose sides grew steeper as they proceeded. By midmorning, clouds blotted out the sun, cooling the air. Storana handed Myrad a piece of thick, oiled leather. "Wrap your bow and bowstring in these. Rain will ruin them."

He wrapped the bow and tucked the weapon beneath his riding blanket just before the rain began to fall. A few moments later, it was pelting him and his horse. He peered ahead but couldn't make out the trail anymore. A wall of gray obscured his vision, and a rushing sound filled his ears. Amid the deluge, claps of thunder rolled across the sky from the north.

"Get out of the ravine!" Walagash shouted. He waved his arms, working to be seen.

The torrent of water was so heavy that Myrad could hardly breathe, much less see. A bolt of lightning stabbed through the sky to strike a tree beside him. Blinded, he threw his hands up to cover his ears as Areion reared and bolted. By chance or miracle, he managed to stay mounted. He heard screams to his left but couldn't see anything but afterimages of lightning. Areion ran to higher ground. He and the horse crashed into a copse of trees, shielding them from the worst of the storm.

Myrad wiped the water from his eyes. He was alone.

A brief lull in the storm allowed him to see more clearly. The rest of the caravan paralleled him on the opposite side of the ravine. All of them but Dov. The magus lay in the stream at the bottom of the defile, his horse nowhere in sight.

Myrad kicked his horse into motion as the storm surged again, down the steep slope toward the magus. Before he got halfway there, a roar came from the north and he looked to see a wall of water rushing downhill, churning and carrying broken tree limbs as thick as his waist. The stream at the bottom of the ravine swelled. Roshan and Aban rode toward Dov from the other side of the ravine.

Before any of them could reach him, the wall of water came crashing through, lifting the unconscious magus and carrying him away. Myrad drove Areion toward his friend, but the flood continued to swell and strengthen, swallowing him. His body submerged, bobbed once to the surface, and was gone.

Myrad watched in horror as the storm raged around him. He heard screaming coming from Roshan on the far side of the flood. "Hurry!" She pointed to a sheer wall of rock twenty paces behind him.

Horror struck him. If he couldn't get to the other side, the floodwaters would trap him against the rock wall and sweep him away.

He dug his heels in, desperate to cross the stream. Areion responded as if he understood their danger, his hooves pounding the earth, working to find purchase. Myrad leaned forward and shouted, urging his horse on to greater speed. He looked up to see grief etched on Roshan's face. He was still ten paces away when the flood turned the river into a seething cauldron that filled the bottom of the gorge.

Water lapped at Areion's knees. Myrad jerked the reins and reversed direction, begging his horse for all the speed it could give him. Areion fought for every inch of ground he gained, his hooves slipping against the rain-slicked rocks. Then he stopped, unable to climb any farther.

The water roared through the defile, growing, reaching for them. Myrad dismounted, gripping the reins, struggling to pull Areion higher up the side of the ravine. But each time he planted his right foot, he slipped farther back. His ankle wouldn't bend.

Then the water hit him, knocking him from his feet. He slipped beneath the flood clutching at the reins. The rush of water threw him against a tree and he grasped at the trunk with his free hand, clawing at the rough bark until his head broke the surface. He sucked air into his starving lungs. Areion still stood, but the water continued to rise.

"Hi-ya!" he screamed, but the animal didn't move.

He could either cling to his horse and try to make for higher ground or let the animal loose while he tried to climb the tree. The water surged higher. In moments it would reach Areion's belly, sweeping them both away. He'd begun unwrapping the reins from his hand when his gaze fell on the wrapped bundle of his bow and his pack with his father's calendar in it. The flood would take everything from him.

"No." He raged at the storm. "NO!"

Using his horse as an anchor, he pulled himself hand over hand up the reins until he stood at the horse's head. "HA!" he yelled, pulling the horse forward and upward. Areion scrabbled to find purchase on the rocky ground beneath the water. When the animal stilled, Myrad used the reins to pull himself even, then repeated the process.

They didn't escape the rising waters, but inch by excruciating inch they managed to keep pace with them. Then Areion stopped, lungs heaving, refusing to move any farther. A wall of jagged rock rose above them, blocking their way.

Peering into the downpour, Myrad could see no end to it. It ran as far along the ravine as he could see in either direction, looming twenty feet above him. It might as well have been a hundred.

"Is this how it is?" By way of answer, the water continued to rise. "I should have expected as much." Yet the instinct of survival refused to let him surrender, and he worked to get Areion as close to the rock wall as possible. Pushing and shouting commands, he turned his horse so that it faced the flood, keeping the rushing water from hitting him broadside. He fought his way until he stood in front of his horse and angled his body to direct the force of the water out, away from the wall.

Then he waited, fighting to stand against the water's rise.

CHAPTER 23

He and Areion fought to hold their footing as the water rose higher. Inevitably, his bad foot, stuck on the downslope of the ravine, betrayed him. A branch swept by, clipping his foot. Myrad plunged beneath the water, the reins around his arm going taught. Struggling to find purchase with his feet, he got his head above water again. He saw Areion's forequarters slipping from the wall, dragged away by his weight.

"Hold on!" he cried to the horse. But it was no use, and he let loose of the reins. The water closed around him and swept him downstream. Rocks battered his legs, and tree limbs scratched at his face as the flood pushed him onward.

In the distance he heard a roar like a thousand storms. He spun, struck by a limb, and peered into the gloom. Two hundred paces ahead, the flood disappeared from the horizon, dropping off into nowhere. The flow of the water forced him inexorably toward the roaring sound.

Ahead, a solitary tree, thick and broad-limbed, rose in defiance of the flood. Myrad paddled toward it, striking the water with clumsy strokes. The trunk came at him like a giant fist, but he kept his eyes open even as it hit him.

Struggling to breathe and stay conscious, he wrapped his arms and legs around the rough bark, inching his way around the trunk until the water pinned him in place. Branches and debris struck him in the back, raking at him, but he held on. Pain tore snatches of prayers from his lips. Then something hit him in the head and the world darkened to a pinpoint. He fought to stay conscious, his sight spinning.

After an eternity marked by blows, he slipped down the rough surface of the tree trunk. Then his feet touched the ground. The rain slowed to misting, then stopped. For over an hour he watched the flood recede, leaving behind a mass of branches and weeds at the high watermark. His weight hit the ground, yet his legs refused to bear him. He landed half in, half out of the water. Uncaring, he slept.

He woke to the smell of detritus benath his head. The water at bottom of the gorge muttered now instead of roaring but still held swift runoff. He struggled to his feet and made his way upstream, searching for Areion. He had no idea how far he'd been taken downstream or if his horse had managed to keep from being swept away as well. He scanned the slopes of the ravine. Nothing looked familiar. If he couldn't find his horse, he would have to walk until he came to a village, assuming he could find one or make it that far.

After an hour of searching the ravine, or perhaps a bit more than a mile later, a soft whicker sounded above him. There, a few paces away from the shelf of rock where he'd left him, stood Areion. A sense of loneliness he hadn't known he carried lifted from him, and he stumbled forward with a sob. When he came within reach of his horse, he put his arms around Areion's neck and hugged him tight, muttering words of comfort more for himself than for the horse.

"We're going to get out of here," he said, but before he mounted, he unwrapped the oiled leather from around his bow.

When he opened the folds, he found water had worked its way through, but thankfully only a small amount. He did his best to dry the weapon by wiping it with his hands and shaking it.

Painstakingly, he led Areion down the slope toward the water. It took no more than a glance to confirm he couldn't cross anytime soon. Debris still littered the water, pieces of deadfalls floating along the surface. At least the ground was more level here. He mounted Areion and rode north at a walk.

He hoped to find help before sunset, but the ravine continued to stretch before him with no end in sight. The sun vanished below the crag to his left and plunged him into dusk. Myrad surveyed the woods around him. No sign of the caravan or their pursuers. Except for himself and Areion, the forest lay empty. He dismounted and tied the reins to a tree, then stripped off the riding blanket to drape it over a low branch to dry. Moving to his pack, he opened it to discover the ruins of Gershom's calendar, the parchment and ink destroyed beyond salvage by the rain. Resigned, he pulled out his spare clothes, careful to safeguard the last of his money, and wrung the water from them before hanging them next to the dripping blanket. Next, he removed his wet clothes. Shivering, he twisted as much water from them as he could before putting them back on. The forest would become completely dark soon, so he found a pair of sticks while he could still see, stuck them into the ground, and upended his boots on top of each stick.

Myrad couldn't recall ever feeling this exhausted. Not knowing what else he could do at the moment, he lowered himself to rest on an outcropping of rock next to Areion and waited for sunrise.

By the light of early dawn, he dressed and packed his things and then set out to the north. Gradually, the heat of the day finished drying his clothes. He stopped and changed, using the opportunity to flip the riding blanket. The second time he stopped, he heard the distant sounds of horses on the opposite side of the river. He scrambled into the nearest copse of trees, hiding to avoid being seen. The sounds grew louder. Soon the horses and riders passed him by a few paces, then continued south. He heard voices as well, faintly, yet the ones speaking were too far away to make out what was said. After they faded and rode away, he came out of his hiding place.

Hour after hour, he followed the winding course of the river upstream. That sameness lulled him into a false sense of security and betrayed him. He came to a bend in the river where the ravine narrowed and the trees and brush hid everything beyond, and when he passed through the vegetation, he found himself in a broad valley running east and west. In the far distance, he saw what looked like a road. No merchants traveled on it. Instead, hundreds, perhaps even a thousand soldiers on horseback filled the road, all of them in formation. Every man had his bow strung and ready. Tension radiated from them, their horses shifting nervously.

By the time it occurred to Myrad to retreat to the defile, he'd been spotted and it was too late to run. His heart began to race as five men peeled from the group, galloping toward him. There was nothing for him to do but wait. Areion shied beneath him. He patted the horse on the shoulder to calm him. The men coming for him wore the road-weary look of those who'd been on horseback overlong.

They drew closer, slowing their horses to a trot. One of the riders moved to cut off his escape into the ravine. The man in front made no move to draw his weapons. A glance over his shoulder told Myrad why. The man behind him sat with an arrow nocked to his bow. In an instant he could draw and release at a distance even Myrad couldn't miss.

"What business does a lone soldier have in Hyrcania?" the man asked him.

The creed of the magi that Gershom had instilled in him prevented him from lying, and he could think of no deception that might fool these men in any case. "I was accompanying a caravan. We were headed north, but the storm caught us in the ravine. The flood swept me away from the rest of the caravan. When it subsided, I wandered here."

"You were caught in the flood?"

He nodded, and the man edged his horse closer while Myrad concentrated on keeping his hands still, trying to ignore visions of being stabbed or shot with an arrow. When they were near enough for their knees to touch, the man drew his knife and leaned over until his nose practically touched Myrad's tunic. He sniffed.

"You have the smell of floodwaters on you. You're fortunate to be alive."

The soldiers' neutral expressions indicated they believed him. Still, they made no move to withdraw and let him pass. "My caravan is hours ahead of me by now. I need to catch up to it."

The leader shook his head. "You may be a scout for our enemy. Tell me who you serve, whose bondslave you are."

Myrad held his hands up in surrender. "I'm a free man from the city in the employ of a silk merchant."

The man's brows, dark and heavy, met in disdain. "Do you think I'm a fool? Silk merchants don't wander the ravines of the Elburz Mountains."

"They do if they're being pursued by Musa's men."

The man straightened on his horse, his expression opening in surprise. "Musa? What of Phraates?"

"Phraates is dead. *Musa* and her son rule now," Myrad said. The queen's name fell from his lips like a curse.

Several of the men spat at hearing this news, but the leader's gaze never left Myrad. "What did Phraates and Musa do to earn your hatred?"

"They killed my father for voting against Musa's elevation."

The leader held a hand to his own chest. "I am Nimar. What is your name, traveler?"

He gave his name, confused by the shift in temperament.

"Welcome to our company."

A few of the soldiers nodded their agreement. "I don't understand," Myrad said.

"You will stand with us. A large force of Musa's men is coming this way."

Myrad looked across the valley and compared the number of men before him to the soliders he'd counted the previous night. "You're outnumbered, Nimar. They have nearly two thousand men."

"And that's just this force," Nimar said. "Our scouts tell us another is approaching Hyrcania from the southwest. String your bow and offer your prayers to the god of the shining fire to deliver us from the hands of our enemies."

Myrad shook his head. "Even before the flood, I could barely draw my bow, and water from the storm may have ruined it. Either way, I'm of little use to you. I'm no soldier. I wear these clothes to hide myself from the men who killed my father."

The leader's face darkened as he reached for Myrad's bow. With a quick, fluid motion, he strung the bow and nocked an arrow. He twisted, sighting just over Myrad's left shoulder for an instant before he let fly. The arrow flew so close to his face, Myrad felt the wind of its passing. The arrow struck a tree trunk dead center where it lodged with a low vibrating note. The message was impossible to miss. *Join us or die.*

"Your bow is dry and working," the leader said. "You serve Artabanus, the prince of Hyrcania now."

CHAPTER 24

With no other choice, Myrad rode back with them toward the main party. Water splashed in every direction as they galloped across the wet ground, churning the earth into mud. Once they'd slowed to a trot, he posed a question. "Why are you fighting if you're so outnumbered?"

"Musa hopes to take Artabanus and ransom him against Orodes. We're buying him time to escape east. To a man, we are his bondslaves." Nimar stopped to give him a level stare. "If you try to flee once the battle is under way, I will ride you down and kill you myself."

Myrad swallowed his fear, but the panic he expected failed to materialize. Perhaps encountering more danger after he'd just survived the flood muted its intensity, or possibly he was too tired to care. His body screamed for food and sleep. Whatever the reason, he found himself concentrating more on how he might live than the certainty he would die.

"Do you have any food?" he asked. "I'm hungry."

Nimar offered him bread and water, and Myrad took a mouthful, his thoughts working in time with his jaw muscles. To the west, a pair of riders entered the valley at a gallop. Their horses were of Nisean stock whose coats shone like burnished

225

gold. They flew across the terrain, and even from this distance Myrad could sense their haste. An idea occurred to him, spurred by the memory of a tale Gershom once read to him, a tale of a battle between Greece and Persia. "Have Musa's men seen your forces?" he asked Nimar.

"No," he said, and offered nothing more.

"The walls of the ravine where you found me are steep."

"I have not seen them, traveler, but I will take you at your word. Why tell me this?"

"In Thermopylae, a few hundred men held their ground against thousands. Men hidden on the upper slopes of the defile I rode through would wreak havoc on Musa's forces."

"A Parthian fights from the back of his horse," Nimar said.

"Should a bondslave die for his master?" Myrad asked.

Nimar and the men around him nodded with resolute expressions.

"Or should he make sure his enemy does?" Myrad added.

After a long moment, Nimar spoke to his men. "If the traveler attempts to run, shoot him." He nudged his horse to ride toward the center, where he waited.

After the scouts arrived, Myrad watched as Nimar engaged in an extended conversation accompanied by much pointing. Then he rode back, barking names that pulled men from all across the line to follow him. He returned with over a hundred men.

"It is as you've said. We are outnumbered. Our commander has agreed to your plan." Nimar's face became like flint. "I've been told to kill you if it does not succeed." He turned to issue an order, and his men set out, racing for the narrow canyon. Myrad's horse, spent from its fight against the flood, lagged behind. Nimar stayed by him.

"Why these men?" Myrad asked.

"These are the weakest archers from horseback among us," Nimar answered. "They see this duty as a dishonor, pulled from their horses to fight with their feet on the ground like a Roman." He looked east over his shoulder. "We must hurry."

Their horses pounded through the mud until they entered the ravine. Nimar gave more orders that split the men into two separate groups, and they spent the next few minutes coaxing their horses up the walls of the ravine until they were twenty paces above the bottom. There, they tied their horses to the nearest trees and waited. Myrad dismounted and ran his hands along Areion's forequarters. "I owe you a good brushing and a bucket of fresh oats," he told his horse.

Nimar nodded. "A wise man is kind to his mount."

"He's saved my life at least twice," Myrad said. "Oats and kindness are a small price to pay." He looked back through the mouth of the ravine toward the valley. "How long will we have to wait?"

"That will depend on the strength of the enemy. The greater their number, the more likely they are to believe in our retreat and pursue. This deception must cost us some men, but hopefully fewer than before."

Myrad thought about that for a moment. "But if they flee too soon, won't Musa's men ignore them and continue on toward Artabanus?"

"Yes," Nimar said. "This trap you've suggested must be delicately balanced. We must lose enough men to make retreat convincing and yet retain enough men so the enemy cannot afford to leave us alive behind him."

A half hour later, the sound of muted thunder could be heard. Nimar pulled a deep breath. "They are coming."

Myrad stood on the slope of the ravine with his bad foot

anchored behind a rock, his bow in one hand, an arrow in the other, and his quiver propped against a nearby sapling. Absurdly, he counted his arrows as if knowing the quantity might somehow keep him from being killed. Forty-seven. Part of him wondered if the number held any significance, while another part chided him for becoming distracted. The men around him seemed to have more arrows than he, but he doubted if it would make much difference. His skills with the bow were still limited to shooting in the general direction of his target.

The thunder of hooves grew louder.

"Hold until the enemy is completely within the walls of the ravine!" Nimar called. "Slow shoot."

The soliders around him nocked their arrows. "What does 'slow shoot' mean?" Myrad asked.

Nimar's eyes narrowed. "Perhaps you were telling the truth. In battle, a group of warriors will practice a quick shoot, usually four shots at the enemy, then a retreat. This creates a storm of arrows that cannot be dodged, but it also depletes the supply. We have only what is in our quivers. Slow shoot, then, means to pick a single target and aim well."

Myrad could hear the ululating cries of horsemen. He nocked an arrow and waited. The thunder of hooves came closer, yet from his perch he could see nothing. Panic and realization hit him as one. "How will we know our targets?"

Nimar raised his voice above the clamor and shouts of the approaching horsemen. "Our men wear black on their sleeves."

The soldiers of Artabanus came rushing into view with a hail of arrows chasing after them. Myrad saw a soldier go down, taken by an arrow to the back. He struggled to crawl away, but the horses behind trampled him. A cry filled the air before it was cut off.

Myrad put an arrow to his string and drew. Too soon, those who wore black armbands passed by, less than half the number he'd seen in the valley. And more were falling. "They're being slaughtered."

Nimar's scowl promised retribution. "Survival was never our purpose."

The first rider without black on his arms came into view. Nimar put his hand on Myrad's arm as he prepared to fire. "Patience. Give the trap time to work."

They waited until Musa's last rider entered the ravine and then a hundred men placed on the hillside let fly. The ordered column of horsemen erupted into chaos. Men toppled from their horses before they could bring their bows to bear. Farther up the ravine, those who fled from Musa's men turned, hiding behind whatever cover was available to fire into the front ranks. Withering fire answered them, but they held.

Musa's column of riders collapsed from back to front. A stray arrow flew by Myrad, but only one. His hands found their rhythm—nock, draw, aim, release—as over and over again he fired into the column, sighting along his arrow and aiming slightly to the right as Aban had taught him. He never checked to see if his arrow struck true, an admonishment from Storana. The screams of men and horses filled the canyon, then echoed from the rocks in weak imitation, turning plaintive.

And just as suddenly as the battle had started, it ended. Men descended from the hillside in pairs to dispatch enemies or succor allies. The dead were left lying on the ground for scavengers.

Sweat streamed from Myrad's face into his eyes, and his back ached from drawing the heavy bow. A trickle of sweat worked its way down between his shoulder blades.

"You told the truth," Nimar said.

"I'm bound to," he said without thinking.

"You fought with discipline," Nimar went on as though he hadn't spoken, "but you ride and shoot as one new to the craft."

They followed the surviving men down the hillside, where the others busied themselves looting the dead. Of the one hundred men Nimar placed on the hillside, only two had been lost, one to a stray arrow that took him through the eye and another to one of Musa's men who killed him as he lay injured. Of those men who'd led Musa's soldiers into the trap, only fifty remained.

They rode back into the valley with a long train of riderless horses in tow. Nimar pointed to them. "Your idea was timely. A warrior should have a horse beneath him fast enough to carry him to safety. I offer you the first pick."

Myrad had spent enough time with Aban and Storana to appreciate the honor Nimar bestowed on him. He bowed low enough to touch his forehead to his horse's mane. "Thank you, but any of these fine horses would be wasted on me. It will be years before I master the Parthian shot." He smiled and patted Areion on the neck. "My horse may not be the swiftest, but he has saved my life, and it would be poor thanks for his loyalty to trade him for another. But if you could spare some oats for him, I would be grateful. He's earned that and more." He swept his arm from left to right to indicate the possible directions from the valley. "Where will you go now?"

"To tell Artabanus the way east is open."

"I can't go with you. The caravan I was separated from will be headed west."

Nimar shook his head. "Where you go or do not go will be determined by Artabanus, but I will tell him of your aid." He smiled. "And that neither you nor your horse are suited for battle. Did you watch the flight of your arrows?"

"My teacher told me not to. It would only slow my release."

Nimar chuckled. "That part is true enough. You never struck a man, though twice you came close enough to frighten their horses. Your lack of skill may be what saves you from being pressed into Artabanus's service."

CHAPTER 25

For the next two days they rode northwest at a canter, switching horses to quicken their pace. They traveled ancient roads fallen into disuse as the seat of Parthian power moved west and south from the district of Parthia on the eastern side of the Hyrcanian Sea to the satrapy of Babylon. By the time they arrived at the ruins of Zadracarta, the smell of salt hung heavy in the air.

They emerged at dusk from the forested roads onto a flat shelf of land filled with the gray, broken remains of a city. Guards ghosted into view from behind trees, rocks, and the carcasses of buildings. Whispers of movement behind them brought an itch to Myrad's back, but when Nimar called out a phrase in Parthian Myrad didn't understand, the guards relaxed and a pair of men came out from the shadows of the nearest ruin to meet them. The larger of the two, a man who wore authority as naturally as the thick beard proclaiming his Persian heritage, greeted them warmly.

"Nimar, this is an unlooked-for pleasure. Was Phraates's force smaller than we reckoned?"

"No, Sharif. If anything they brought more men than our scouts reported, but the fates offered us a means toward victory. None of their men survived. The way east is open, for the moment."

Sharif's eyes widened for an instant before he smiled. "Come," he beckoned. "I will let you bring Artabanus this news yourself. He will want to reward you, I think. There is food and water near the center of the city for your men and horses to take their rest."

Nimar pointed to Myrad. "If I may have that man join me, honored Sharif, I believe Artabanus will wish to hear what he has to say."

Sharif eyed Myrad, noting his clothes and appearance the way a merchant might examine an item before purchase, but any conclusions he drew were kept from his expression. "A mystery answered and another posed," Sharif said.

Myrad surrendered his horse to one of the guards, with Nimar stepping in beside him. "Give this horse fresh oats and a good brushing as if he were the finest Nisean mount in the desert," Nimar told the man.

"Thank you," Myrad said.

They caught up to Sharif, who led them deeper into the ruined city. As night fell, they came to a large building without a roof, which had managed to retain all four of its walls. Sharif took them inside to where the prince of the Hyrcanian satrapy held an improvised court. They approached a circle of light. There at the center, a man was seated, impressive in stature, speaking to other men of similar bearing to Sharif, all of them surrounded by guards. Sharif stopped at the outer edge of the light and waited until they were beckoned forward.

Myrad felt a touch on his sleeve. "If you are familiar with the throne room of Phraates," Sharif said, "then you would do well to behave likewise here. The prince of Hyrcania holds similar power, if on a smaller scale."

At last they were called forward. Sharif led them into the lighted circle, and Myrad gaped. Though younger by twenty years or so, the prince of Hyrcania bore a stunning likeness to Phraates, the dead king.

"Greetings, Nimar," the prince said. His gaze, piercing in the subdued light, sifted them with a glance. "Are you here in retreat? Your orders were to hold as long as possible and then lead Musa's men away."

Nimar bowed. Myrad rushed to mimic him, holding his torso parallel to the broken stones of the floor. "Retreat and deception were both unnecessary, my prince. Musa's cohort lies dead in a ravine. Not a man of theirs escaped."

The prince's brows rose. "How was this accomplished?"

Nimar straightened from his bow. Again, Myrad mimicked him. "I was reminded of the power of a deceptive retreat," Nimar said, favoring Myrad with a smile.

"Speak plainly," the prince commanded.

Chastened, Nimar ducked his head toward Myrad. "This is Myrad, my prince. He rode into the valley where we chose to make our stand after being caught in a storm. He suggested using the ravine that was nearly his death to trap our enemy. We engaged as planned in the valley, protecting the road. Then, when the timing was right, we fled into the ravine, making sure we had enough men to remain a threat if we were not pursued. The enemy took the bait. They came after us, pursuing where we had archers waiting on the sides of the canyon. After all of Musa's men entered, we turned and boxed them in. None escaped. The way east is open, at least until word of the defeat reaches Musa or her forces."

The prince stood, musing on this news. Myrad watched with interest. For the second time, Nimar referred to their enemy by

Musa's name, not Phraates's, and again the prince showed no surprise. He knew. Somehow word had already reached him of Phraates's death.

"That is well," the prince said. "Musa's second force is no more than two days south of here. When they arrive, I want to make sure we're not here and they cannot determine which way we've gone. See to it."

Nimar pivoted on one heel and departed, but when Myrad made to go with him, the prince's voice stopped him. "You will remain."

The echo of Nimar's footsteps followed him out of the derelict building while the prince reseated himself on the makeshift pile of stones and allowed himself the leisure to examine Myrad. "Where does a youth come by the knowledge to give instruction to one of my captains?"

Myrad bowed before he spoke, unsure of the correct response. "My father was one of the magi. He taught me as much as I could learn before he was killed at Musa's command. Some of the Greek stories he read to me were about war and how smaller forces defeated larger ones."

The prince registered this in silence before he spoke again. "A caravan stumbled into our perimeter a day and a half ago, trying to reach the coast of the sea and the Hyrcanian road. Several of their number petitioned me for permission to search east and south of here for one of their number who'd been lost."

Myrad's heart leapt within him and he took a step toward the throne before he realized it. Guards in heavy armor on either side stepped forward to block his way. He quickly retreated, bowing his apology. "Roshan? Walagash?"

The prince nodded. "I see you are familiar with them." He turned to one of his guards. "Bring the merchant and the rest."

The man left at a run.

"You should know," the prince continued, "I have commanded the loyalty of the merchant and everyone with him to help break through the forces Musa sent to keep me from gaining the east."

Myrad dipped his head at the expected moment, but his response seemed to irritate the prince.

"You have nothing to say? According to this merchant, you have orchestrated not one but two daring thefts from Musa's treasury, not only providing the eastern satrapies of funds to buy men and weapons but also depriving Musa of the ability to do the same. You look ordinary enough. From the merchant's description I expected something closer to the divine to walk among us." The prince stared at him for a heartbeat before he continued. "Most men would protest they'd already rendered more than enough service. Yet you stand there in silence as if the gods have taken your tongue."

He groped for words. "I . . . I should be dead," he said finally. "Abandoned in the desert, hunted by Phraates, caught in a flood. My prince, I can't tell you why I'm not, although those with me would tell you it's the favor of God." Weak laughter caught him by surprise. "It doesn't feel like favor, my prince."

"And how would a mere apprentice to the magi, and a lame one at that, come by such favor?" the prince asked.

Myrad held his hands out, palms up, the gesture of ignorant surrender he'd seen Gershom use countless times. "I don't know. God gave me a dream of a star and told me to follow it to His King."

"One of your company told me of this dream. This is true?"

Myrad nodded. "The dream is true, my prince, yet I cannot tell you if the interpretation is sure. I'm only an apprentice."

Artabanus took a deep breath to continue, but noise at the entrance to the roofless building stopped him, and movement there set the torches to guttering. "Stand behind me," he ordered. "Stay hidden until I signal you."

Myrad complied, stationing himself next to one of the massive guards whose hands never left his weapons.

Walagash, Hakam, Yehudah, and Masista stepped into the circle of torchlight and bowed to the prince.

"I have considered your request, and I still deny it," the prince said. "I cannot spare any men to search for your friend. The fight against Rome's influence is too important to have them out looking for a single magus."

Hidden in the shadows, Myrad could read the expressions of each man standing before the prince. Walagash seemed utterly stricken, pain wreaking violence on his bluff features. Next to him, Yehudah appeared perplexed, as if the deaths of Dov and Myrad himself served to undermine a fundamental belief. Hakam and Masista wore identical expressions of resignation.

The prince waited, but none of the men before him spoke. The pressure of the silence built until it became an unwelcome guest. Masista took a half step forward. "My prince, please reconsider my request."

The prince cocked his head to one side, the resemblance to Phraates surfacing again. "You wish for me to allow a gift of armed men and gold we cannot help but need to slip through my fingers?"

Masista nodded. "Yes, if these gifts can persuade the Armenians to throw their weight against Rome. A few more men can hardly compare to the advantage gained if Musa is forced to fight a two-front war."

The prince laughed. "You expect the family of Tigranes to

commit to the weaker side? I thought the magi were learned men. The Armenians have ever been allies of circumstance, and circumstances change. I am more interested in this messiah in Judea. The Hebrews are not so numerous, but they have a history of rebellion that could prove useful. Even an unsuccessful uprising would serve to pin Roman forces there instead of bolstering Musa's claim."

"Forgive my surprise, my prince," Yehudah said, "but I don't understand why you would consider an option you previously mocked as a fable contrived to secure our release."

"Your story was impossible to confirm, magus," the prince replied. "Only those in your company, and not all of them, can see this star, and I've heard nothing of any prince in Judea to challenge the might of Herod and Rome." He paused. "Our situation has changed, however. It may be the god of the shining fire or the god of the Hebrews has smiled upon us. My men have utterly defeated Musa's force to the east. I no longer have such pressing need for a single group of caravan guards. Though I think you have little chance of convincing the offspring of Tigranes to aid us, you now have the luxury of making the attempt."

From his vantage point in the shadows, Myrad saw Walagash's eyes go wide. "You said their story was impossible to confirm. How have you verified it, my prince?"

Seated, the prince didn't turn, but his right arm came back to beckon him. Myrad stepped forward into the pool of light.

And he found himself in Walagash's crushing embrace. He fought to pull air into his lungs. "I can't breathe." His voice came out in a whisper.

Smiling, the prince rose. "Take your caravan and those of your tent into Armenia, merchant. I'll give you a warning by way of recompense for the apprentice's aid. Mount your horses and do not let your feet touch the ground until you've left Hyrcania. Musa's larger force is coming from the south." He stepped forward to take Myrad's forearm in his grip. "If you and I survive, your counsel would be welcome in my court."

CHAPTER 26

Myrad stumbled after Walagash and the other magi, buoyed by their joy, but so weary he would have gladly dropped to the dirt and slept for a week. Nimar himself brought Areion to him. True to his word, his chestnut coat gleamed, and bits of oats dropped from his lips as he tossed his head in recognition. Myrad patted him on the neck.

Still, his body cried for sleep, and he wanted nothing more than to collapse in his familiar corner of Walagash's tent. But more than sleep, he needed to see Roshan. When they arrived at the square within the abandoned city where Walagash and his company had been placed, she waited.

There were strangers present, so he didn't call her name. Then, at the sound of their approach, she turned toward him. Her eyes widened, and her expression opened for a fraction of a moment until she recovered herself. She came toward him with the gait of a colt whose desire was to break loose of its halter and run. Her footsteps, the swing of her arms, the way her hands clenched and released all spoke of a need for haste. Regardless, she kept herself to a walk.

When she stood no more than a pace away, she glanced once at his face before her stare took in the mud and stains of battle.

"I prayed to every god who might hear me that you would live." Her voice rasped, and she refused to let her gaze meet his.

Unsure of how to respond, he stood there discomfited beneath the stares of Walagash, the magi, and his betrothed. They seemed to be waiting for him to say something, but no one asked a question and fatigue left him unsteady on his feet and muddled in his thoughts. "I wasn't sure I would, but I had reasons to fight," he said, surprised by how much he meant it.

The magi left, and the tension of the moment passed somewhat. "We will leave as soon as there is light enough to travel by," Walagash said to him. "Roshan, see to your betrothed." He pointed to a building retaining a bit more of its structure than its neighbors.

"Come," she said. "I'm sure your foot pains you. I'll see what can be done."

She led him toward the tent, her hand straying from her side several times to take his, but each time she halted before they touched. They stepped through a doorway, and Roshan retrieved a pair of torches and wedged them into niches in the ruins of a wall that shielded them from the rest of the company. Even so, she checked to make sure no one could see them before she threw her arms around him.

"We looked for you. We didn't abandon you." Her voice caught. "Please don't think we abandoned you."

"I think I may have heard you." He sat on a pallet of blankets, which seemed to have happened without transition. "I hid in the trees, thinking it might have been Musa's men." Every time he blinked, he struggled to open his eyes again. Roshan pulled off his boots, and the smell of liniment wafted through the cool air. "I got . . . caught . . ." Her hands kneaded away the pain in his foot and ankle and carried his consciousness with them.

He found himself on horseback almost before he realized he'd awakened. A hand caught him when he wavered, righting him. He blinked, struggling to wakefulness against his body's need for more rest. They rode with the first hint of sunrise on their left, the smell of the sea growing stronger. His eyes swept across the center of the caravan, where Walagash and the magi rode, and he pulled a breath to ask after Dov before he remembered the small, gentle man had died, swept away by the flood. They set off at a trot, afforded by the extra horses from the defeat of Musa's soldiers. By noon they passed through a strip of thick woods and underbrush and reached the sea road, an ancient track of packed earth and stone that hugged the coast of the Hyrcanian Sea.

Walagash gazed across the expanse of dark blue-green water with the expression of a man tasting gall when he'd expected honey. "I spent years building a reputation as a shrewd trader. Here and there throughout the empire are men who have matched me in a trade, but I've seldom been bested," he said in a soft voice. He shook his head. "Until now. This trip will take twice as long as it should have."

"Don't come," Myrad said. "When I asked for your protection, I never imagined any of this would happen. At worst I thought I would make my way east and spend the rest of my life hiding there." He sighed. "I release you from your vow, Walagash."

If he'd expected gratitude, he was mistaken. Walagash, towering over him on his larger horse, looked affronted, his eyes stern. "There is no other chance for success. I must find a way to sell Esai's goods for a profit or forfeit my place in the silk trade. And I do not grant you the power to release me from my word. I brought you into my tent and gave you my daughter. Where you go, we go. If you turn left or right, we will follow you, and if you have set your face toward Jerusalem, we will go there as well."

The merchant's regard was too much for him. He turned toward the ancient road stretching out ahead of them. "How long will it take to get to Armenia?"

"Weeks, at least a full turn of the moon, perhaps a bit more. Then, if Tigranes grants us passage into the Roman Empire, at least twice that to make it to Jerusalem." At the look of surprise on Myrad's face, he laughed. "I remember a time when I thought the world was a much smaller place. The more I travel, the more I learn it is both larger and smaller than I imagined."

"You said *if*. . ."

Walagash nodded. "The prince of Hyrcania is wise. The kings of Armenia have ever played the Parthians and Romans against each other. They have switched allegiance so many times, the word no longer has any meaning for them. I think they might be insane."

Myrad started to laugh, thinking Walagash joked with him, but the merchant's face might have been cast in iron for all the humor it showed. "Truly?"

He shrugged his massive shoulders. "They've adopted the practice of intermarrying. Tigranes is married to his sister, like his fathers before him. The custom leads to certain mental deformities as well as physical ones."

Myrad kept his head still but worked to flex his right foot. It didn't move, of course. Soon after birth the ligaments locked, freezing his foot into the shape it had been ever since. Was that what happened? Did his mother marry a brother or cousin and give birth to a deformed son?

It took no more than a heartbeat for his speculations to change from considering his physical defect to weighing the possibility of a mental one. Had God really spoken to him or had his mind simply conjured the dream, a product of unfortunate parentage? He pulled his gaze up from his foot to see Walagash staring at him. The merchant clapped him on the shoulder. "It's a custom reserved for royalty. Common-born people have no need to guard their power in such a way."

They set off again with guards scouting before and behind them. Walagash pointed to the strip of forest that bordered the sea, a verdant partition between it and the mountains. "At least we can hide if we encounter soldiers. But if they spot our tracks, we'll be impossible to miss."

Myrad fell back to his accustomed spot at the rear of the caravan, where Roshan took his hand in hers as if she intended to never let go.

Day after day passed as they followed the curves of the sea westward and then north into the satrapy of Media, provisioning the caravan at a handful of villages along the way. While they encountered other caravans, only once did they need to hide from soldiers when the rolling thunder of thousands of horses passed them heading east.

The cohort was so large they had more than enough warning to leave the road and slip into the forest before they arrived. Curious, Myrad dismounted and followed Aban on foot to watch them from the cover of thick scrub. Horse soldiers and cataphracts comprised the army in roughly a five-to-one ratio, and the sheer number of men left Myrad shocked. It made the force they'd defeated in the ravine seem like nothing more than a scouting expedition.

"That's welcome news of a sort," Aban said. "Musa has emptied Media to fight the threat against her in Bactria."

Myrad couldn't take his eyes from the seemingly endless line of horsemen. "If these are just the men from Media, how can Orodes and Artabanus hope to stand?"

"They're not as outnumbered as you might think," Aban said. "And the satrapies to the east have ties in Indus and Khushan." He shook his head. "Yet there's bad news here as well. If Musa has pulled her forces from Media, it means she has no fear of the Armenians attacking in their absence. We'll have to be careful."

They watched until the soldiers' horses finally passed by and the sound of countless hooves faded. Myrad made to rise from his place of concealment when Aban grabbed his arm. "Wait a few moments longer."

They remained flat on their bellies overlooking the road until a trio of riders appeared. "Rear scouts," Aban whispered. "Their commander is a crafty one. There's no force here that can rival his, but he's taking no chances."

Myrad posed a question that had nagged at him for months. "Who are you?"

"What do you mean?" Aban turned to smile at him, the same smile Myrad had seen a thousand times before. But behind Aban's eyes danced uncounted memories and a clarity of thinking Myrad saw only in the most intelligent magi.

"You know more about horses and weapons and strategy than any other man in the caravan, and Walagash listens to you as if your word were law. Not once have I seen him go counter to your advice."

Aban's smile faded, replaced by guarded speculation. "Is there anything else?"

"Yes," Myrad said. "One other thing. Storana. Around everyone else in the caravan, she's casual, practically insolent, but not around you. And it's more than just that she's your wife. Every time she looks at you, it's as if she's saluting."

Aban chuckled. "Gershom chose well when he adopted you." He took a last look at the road, then stood. "We have to go. We have days to Armenia yet and countless days more to Israel."

In the next instant, Myrad was on his feet and working to catch up. "You didn't answer my question."

"Humph. Very well. Here's a lesson any man with enough years could teach you. The merchant? The cataphracts with their armor and lances? The horse soldier with his bows and arrows?" He gave Myrad a direct look. "The apprentice magus with the clubfoot? All of these have a past and a story beyond expectation and imagining."

They strode down the backside of a hill to where the caravan awaited. Aban lapsed into silence and remained there.

Yet Myrad felt emboldened. "You still haven't answered my question, Aban."

Aban sighed. "Your story is compelling for one so young, and every man, woman, and child would sit rapt for the telling. What would happen if your story were to fall upon the wrong ears?"

Myrad slowed. "I understand." A few feet farther on, he settled on a different question. "Will you still train me to shoot and ride?"

The man next to him smiled deeply, and a vast array of lines appeared on his face, each wrinkle hinting at a story. "Of a certainty."

CHAPTER 27

The caravan followed the road along the shore of the Hyrcanian Sea for weeks, a time Myrad filled with riding and archery. Roshan took to riding near him whenever he strayed from the rear of the caravan. She never offered a reason why, but her presence both pleased and discomfited him for reasons so subtle he couldn't put a name to them. When she spoke, it was to instruct him on the details of running a caravan.

"Every man or woman in your caravan, from the lowliest guard to the most exalted guest traveling with you to share your protection, is under your authority."

He nodded, half listening. Walagash had already demonstrated as much. "And?"

She gave an exasperated little sigh and glared at him, an expression mixing fire and intensity. Words spilled from him before he realized he'd spoken aloud. "You're beautiful like that."

Taken off guard, she softened. "Like what?"

"Angry. Intense." He shrugged. "Most of the time you look like anyone else, seeing things you've seen before that hardly hold your interest, but when you get angry, it's as if you're completely present and I see the real you."

Her gaze went flat in a different kind of anger, attractive

but not as pretty as before. "You think I'm beautiful when I'm angry?"

He smirked. "Yes. I think the trick will be to keep enough people around to irritate you so that I don't have to." He let his smile grow. "That's probably not going to be too difficult." He pointed toward the caravan. "Now, you were telling me something I needed to know."

The squint around her eyes went through phases until she settled on a look of vague suspicion. "Those men with you are a danger."

"How so?"

She shook her head, annoyed. "Have they told you what they intend to do once we leave Parthia?"

"Our sole purpose is to follow the star, to look for the King."

Roshan sighed, then looked sideways at Aban. "You tell him. Maybe he will believe you."

Aban's eyes narrowed. "Understand, the magi are kingmakers. They're accustomed to wielding power, and men with power don't care to surrender it. Artabanus had us in the palm of his hand, willing to force us into his army to fight his way through to the east. He wouldn't have surrendered the guards or the magi unless he thought there was power to be gained by doing so. Tigranes will think similarly."

Myrad mulled this over before urging his horse forward to the middle of the caravan. When he pulled alongside Yehudah and Hakam, he found them comparing calendars.

"There's no mistake," Yehudah said. "The King doesn't appear for another thirty years."

Hakam refused the assertion. "There must be. How many times in the history of the magi has the same dream come to so many? Eight, Yehudah. There were at least eight of us who dreamt of the King's star. If there's no mistake in the count, then we must have chosen the wrong starting point. It must have been earlier."

"The prophecy was too specific. It said when the *city* was ordered rebuilt—city, not temple. The count started the day Artaxerxes granted Nehemiah permission to rebuild Jerusalem."

Hakam persisted. "Something's wrong."

Masista, riding behind them with his four cataphracts, laughed at their argument. "In my experience, prophecies are vague, nebulous things."

"Your experience does not include the Most High God," Hakam said.

Hakam's anger only served to deepen Masista's smile. "Perhaps. But imagine how it would be for the Hebrews to spend over four hundred years waiting for their King, only to discover their prophecy was no more substantial than smoke. You would be better served offering your gifts to Tigranes in exchange for an alliance with Artabanus."

Yehudah favored Masista with one slow nod. "So that's what you intend? To betray us to the Armenians?"

Masista's smile slid from his face. "By no means, Hebrew. I gave my word to see you to Judea with your treasure, and I will do so. But I said nothing about not trying to persuade you to a more sensible course of action."

"We will follow the star to its end," Yehudah said. "Then we will see what we should do next."

To Myrad, that last statement held more doubt than he'd heard from Yehudah in their entire time together. He cleared his throat to get Yehudah's attention.

"Yes? What do you wish, Myrad?"

He nodded to the pages of the calendar still in Yehudah's lap.

"I lost Gershom's calendar in the flood. I feel I should rebuild it so I can help keep the count."

Hakam's expression filled with refusal, but Yehudah silenced him with a gesture. "What of your desire to become a horseman like Aban or Storana?"

Myrad glanced at his bow. "I can do both."

"Perhaps," Yehudah said, "but I think, sooner or later, a man must choose his master."

Stung, Myrad lashed out at both men. "I have chosen. At every turn I've followed the dream of the star despite every misfortune." His laughter rasped against his throat. "Look at the two of you, clean and safe, lecturing me from the comfort of your circumstances." He gave them a mocking bow. "With your permission, O exalted magi, I would like to keep the calendar as my father, Gershom, instructed. At least until some other disaster strikes."

Hakam spat and urged his horse ahead.

Yehudah dug into his pack. "Here," he said and handed Myrad several sheets of blank parchment. "When we stop for the night, you can begin. I should not have presumed to judge your intentions."

They debated the routes through Armenia, but in the end, circumstances made the decision for them. At a fold in the hills that looked like any other, they encountered a cohort of soldiers guarding the road. Their captain, an older man with scars on his face and recognition in his gaze, insisted on escorting them to the capital. While he made no threat, the posture of the guards with him couldn't be misinterpreted.

On a clear morning, thirty-four days after they set out from

Hyrcania, they arrived at the court of Tigranes in the Armenian city of Artaxata. They rode through the narrow streets toward the acropolis, walled and set on the highest hill of the city. Houses, shops, and government buildings had been built against the exterior of the wall, following the contours of the land. It took them another half hour to navigate the crowded city and terrain before they came to the arched entrance of the acropolis on the southern side. Passing through, they discovered the city's defenses were comprised of an inner and outer wall. At the second entrance, they encountered soldiers posted at the gate, bearing bows and iron-tipped lances.

Masista dismounted and stepped forward to speak to the captain of the guard. When he returned to the caravan, he wore the look of a man who was pleased with himself but trying not to show it.

"You're playing a dangerous game, magus," Walagash said.

Masista's dark eyes danced. "That's the only kind worth playing, merchant."

Walagash shook his head in disgust, and they settled in to wait for the king's answer.

"What game is Walagash talking about?" Myrad asked Aban.

Aban sighed. "Tigranes and Armenia hold less power than Rome or Parthia. What power they do have stems from uneasy truces between the two. If something should upset that balance, then Armenia will find itself under the heel of one empire or the other. Masista seeks to use this insecurity to wrest aid from the Armenian king." Aban's voice dipped. "But if Tigranes believes he can curry favor with Musa by handing us over to her as a prize, he will do so." He spoke of the king of Armenia in a familiar tone as if he knew him. "He has little choice."

"Can't he see his only hope is Musa's defeat?" Myrad asked. "If the Romans control both empires, Armenia will be crushed."

Aban nodded. "Any sane man would see that in an instant. The only problem is Tigranes may not be sane."

Speaking in Greek, the captain of the guard ordered their company to follow him to the king's palace.

They passed dozens of massive decorative columns until they entered a broad L-shaped building, the court of Tigranes and his sister-queen, Erato. Guards formed up around them with military precision to escort them along the colonnade to a pair of gilded thrones, twins in every respect. At a distance of five or six paces, the king held up one hand, his expression stern and forbidding.

To Myrad, it seemed a poor start.

"What do you want, magus?" the king asked Masista.

Masista smiled and bowed until his hair almost touched the floor. "I merely seek your favor on behalf of our caravan, my king."

"Your king?" Tigranes mocked. "Have you become Armenian then? Changing your allegiance according to your own need?"

Masista bowed deeper still. "I only meant to offer you the respect you deserve."

Tigranes's gaze darted from man to man. "By bringing an army of men into my kingdom?"

Aban, standing next to Myrad, muttered something in Parthian.

"An army?" Myrad whispered.

Aban gave him the briefest of nods. "Do you remember what I said about the kings of Armenia?"

"Is he insane?" Myrad asked, keeping his voice low.

"In this matter, not so much," Aban whispered back. "Kings live under the threat of death every day. Consequently, Tigranes sees threats everywhere. He's probably correct."

Masista gestured to the men arrayed before the king, a small number compared to the guards surrounding them. "Surely Your Majesty cannot mean these caravan guards."

Tigranes thrust his weak chin forward. "I know cataphracts when I see them. You've brought threats into my throne room. You are ever crafty, Masista. My kingdom is caught between the might of Rome and Parthia. You may be here to assassinate me. Why should I trust you?"

Masista bowed once more, then straightened. "The conflict between Rome and Parthia is the very reason we are here, Your Majesty. We seek passage to the Roman Empire." He swept his arm in an arc encompassing Yehudah, Hakam, and Myrad. "These three magi have received a dream from their God of a king arising in Israel."

"You expect me to believe that?"

Queen Erato reached across the narrow space between the two thrones to lay her hand on the arm of her husband. "Hear them, brother. Any offer of aid is welcome."

He jerked his arm away from the sister-queen's touch and glared at her. "Can they offer anyone whose word I can trust?" Before she could answer, the king shook his head. "No. The world is filled with traitors. I know none of these men." His gaze darted around the throne room, fear in his expression, before it came to rest on his lap. The queen called his name softly, but Tigranes appeared incapable of hearing her.

She straightened on her throne and surveyed the men before her. "Speak to me of this king in Israel," she ordered. "I will hear you while the king ponders your case. Leave nothing out."

Yehudah stepped forward and related their tale, taking time to emphasize the slaughter of the magi and Myrad's escape. At the end, Erato nodded, her expression thoughtful. "Is this Myrad among you?"

"He is." Yehudah signaled Myrad forward.

When he moved forward, the queen's eyes slid from his face to focus on his feet. "Why do you walk that way?" she asked.

His face flushed as the entire populace of the throne room followed the queen's gaze. "My right foot is crippled, twisted since birth."

The queen's gaze softened, looking on Myrad with a certain kinship. "Are you of the royal line then?"

Myrad stifled a laugh, not knowing how it might be interpreted. But he couldn't help but smile. "No, my queen. I know only my mother, a poor merchant in Ctesiphon."

Her eyebrows rose. "Why give an honest answer when a lie would have served you better?"

"When my father brought me into the magi, my queen, he stressed the importance of our creed to tell the truth always."

The deep brown of Erato's eyes took on a distant look. "Would that kings and queens had such luxury." She glanced at Tigranes, who still mumbled to himself in his seat, unaware of their conversation. "The king's foot is also deformed, and his mind has aged before its time. His clearest memories are those of years ago."

"Can you grant us passage to the Roman border, Your Majesty?" Yehudah asked. Sensing his interview with the queen to be finished, Myrad stepped back to stand next to Aban.

Erato shook her head. "I will not presume on the king's indisposition."

"Is there any way to gain his confidence?" Masista asked.

"Only if there is one among you he knows from his youth."

On Aban's far side, Storana turned to regard her husband, obviously waiting. After a long moment, he sighed and stepped forward. "May I speak to the king, Your Majesty?"

The queen took in his plain clothing, dusty and worn, at a glance. "The king knows you?"

Aban bowed from the neck. "Perhaps. Our encounter was brief and long ago."

The hint of a smile brightened the queen's eyes. "A mystery then. Remove your weapons and approach."

Aban left his sword and dagger in Storana's hands and ascended the dais, where the king continued to murmur against unseen threats. "Tigranes, it is done."

The king's stream of nonsense syllables stopped, and his eyes flicked back and forth, searching. "Who speaks? What is done?"

Aban cleared his throat. "It is as King Artavasdes and King Phraates agreed. Marcus Antonius's baggage train is destroyed. The Romans will have no choice but to withdraw."

The distraction cleared from the king's demeanor, sharpening into something too close to anger for Myrad's comfort. "Artavasdes will blame me for our retreat," Tigranes said, "though the deception was his idea." His face twisted into a snarl. "And Phraates will crown you with glory for the victory our retreat hands you."

"The Parthians do not crown our heroes as they do in Rome. You remember Surena, do you not?"

The king's expression softened. "Ah. The only thing that threatens a king more than failure is succeeding too well." Tigranes straightened and looked around the throne room as if becoming aware of it for the first time. When his gaze fell on Aban, he squinted, peering at him. He lifted one hand, making gestures in the air as if he were smoothing away the wrinkles on Aban's face. "Bahram?"

"My name is Aban now, Your Majesty, as it has been since Marcus Antonius retreated from our lands."

"You pressed for speed against the Romans," Tigranes said. "Advice Phraates ignored. The only thing worse than disagreeing with the king is being right when you do it." His eyes lowered to take in Aban's clothes. "You became a common horseman."

"It was necessary to blend in with the tribes north of the Hyrcanian Sea." Aban glanced at Storana and flashed her a smile. "I would hesitate to call them common. And you became a king."

"I did," Tigranes said. "What is it you need?"

"Passage through Armenia and into the Roman Empire," Aban said. "Nothing more."

The king waved a hand toward the captain of his guard. "Done. The gods dealt unfairly with you, Bahram. Your destiny should have been a better one."

Aban shrugged. "It's been a good life, Your Majesty. I have many friends, and the worries of armies and empires are no longer my concern."

CHAPTER 28

Myrad stared across the expanse of the Euphrates, remembering a time months ago when he almost boarded a ship to let the river take him far away from Ctesiphon and so escape his past. The idea still held some appeal.

"It's beautiful," Yehudah said. They'd risen together early that morning, Hakam scowling at them both, to pray to the Most High God and to keep the calendar. "To cross the Euphrates is to cross from the east into the west, from the lands of Qian, Khushan, and Parthia into the Roman Empire."

"What is it like?"

Yehudah shook his head. "I don't know that my putting the experience into words will help you."

The magus's answer surprised him. "But most of what we learn is by reading or hearing from others."

With a smile, he said, "Knowing *of* a thing and knowing the thing are very different. Many people know of the Most High God. The Hebrews have been scattered across the world by conquest like the wind sowing drifting seeds of grass. Whatever foreign soil we've fallen upon, there we've taken root, bringing the knowledge of the Most High to those around us. Many know of Him, but few know Him. The two are vastly different."

"Do you know Him?"

Yehudah gave a slight shrug. "As much as I can."

"Is that what this journey is for you?" Myrad asked. "A chance to better know your God?"

"And yours as well."

"I'm Persian, or have you not heard Hakam's reminders?"

"Hakam's lineage is Hebrew, though his birth is Median. He . . . struggles with his identity, and the result is sometimes harsh. I hold a belief some may not agree with," Yehudah said, "that the title Most High means our God is the God of all people, and that we have been conquered over and over again and taken away to Assyria, Babylon, Egypt, Parthia, and Rome to take root and spread the knowledge of Him."

To Myrad, this sounded as if it were a harsh way for God to spread the knowledge of himself. "What do you believe is the Messiah-King's purpose in our journey? Why go to Judea if the Hebrews and their knowledge of the Most High are already there?"

Yehudah seemed not to have heard the question. "Have you ever wondered why we refer to the land of our ancestors by two different names? We call it Judea, as you just now did, and in the next breath refer to the place as Israel? I think, though, there is wisdom in that confusion. Judea is a restless province beneath the heel of the Roman Empire, whereas Israel is the kingdom of the people of God. My hope is that the Messiah-King will restore Israel to its intended destiny, as a light shining to the world to bring all peoples into the knowledge of God." Yehudah shifted from his contemplation of the river to meet Myrad's gaze. "I don't know why we've been told to go. I've never been to the land of my fathers, nor do I have any idea what we will find once there." A rueful smile overtook his features. "I have the feeling that when you ask the question 'Why us?' what you really mean is 'Why me?'"

Myrad nodded.

"I don't know," Yehudah confessed. "I have the same question."

They led their horses forward to board the ferry, a wide raft that would carry them into the lands of the west.

Six weeks later, with their guards and cataphracts dressed in their full panoply, they arrived in Antioch. The city sprawled along the road before them, and Myrad found himself struggling to see everywhere at once. They passed a huge oval construction towering over the road on their way to the western part of the city to sell Walagash's silk. Myrad marveled at its size. "What do they do there?"

"Chariot races," Aban replied. "Only the Circus Maximus in Rome is greater. But the finest horses in the world come from Persia and race here, proving their worth before being taken to Rome. They're a commodity some value even more highly than silk."

They rode across one of the bridges over the Orontes River into the expansive trading grounds, which reminded Myrad of Margiana. Up ahead of them, Myrad could see the tension building in Walagash's posture. "Will he be able to get a good price for his silk?"

Roshan shrugged. "It's impossible to know until we speak with the silk merchants. Supply and demand ebb and flow with circumstances. Father may go completely broke with this venture."

"That doesn't concern you?"

"Not overly much. My father is a shrewd trader, just as he has taught me to be. If we cannot trade in silk, there are plenty of merchants who will allow us to trade in something else." She paused and added, "Perhaps spices. They're almost as profitable as silk and they smell nice."

The caravan stopped, and Walagash came striding back to them, worry etched across his face. "I don't know anyone here," he said to Roshan and Myrad. "Discover what you can of the silk prices in Antioch." When Myrad turned to leave, Walagash caught him by the sleeve, his voice low. "But do so discreetly and without drawing attention."

The two of them ventured farther into the market on foot, Roshan keeping to Myrad's stilted pace. Without delay, she led them to a horse trader on the far side of the market. There were no traders of other goods anywhere close, much less silk. "Why him?"

Roshan smiled. "We're planning a sneak attack of sorts on the silk merchants here. It would be unwise to announce our presence too soon."

"You make it sound like battle," Myrad said.

She gave a little laugh. "Compared to trade, battle is driven by random circumstances despite a captain's intentions to plan for them. This is more a contest or game of strategy, a match of wits where those with the best information and strongest nerves prevail. That is why we're going to an isolated horse merchant first. He's unlikely to communicate our presence to the silk merchants. Even so, we'll take other measures too." She bit her lower lip, and an eagerness came into her stride. With her face glowing in anticipation, she became transformed, beautiful.

"You love to play this game of strategy then," Myrad said.

Roshan nodded. "Trade is everything. There is nothing like it."

Now he understood why she'd chosen him. He'd given her exactly what she most desired and it had been by blindest instinct. "What you most wanted," he said out loud.

She stopped and faced him. "What?"

"It's why the silk trade means so little to you. The game you speak of can be played with anything—silk, spices, even grain. You chose me because I promised you this."

"Yes. Every other man in Margiana wanted to keep me in his tent or house and give me gifts I didn't want. You saw what I desired most, and you were courageous as well."

They came to a tent leaning against the entrance to a broad pen where they waited for the merchant to finish haggling with a Roman soldier over a bay stallion. After a few moments, the soldier left with his purchase.

The trader turned to them, searching their faces and clothing before he gave them a nod. "Welcome to the pens of Licinius," the man said in Greek. "How may I serve you?"

Roshan ducked her head, playing the part of the embarrassed youth. "Your pardon," she answered in the same language. "My master is new to Antioch and unfamiliar with its market. Where would one go to purchase silk?"

Licinius made a vague pointing gesture. "Ordinarily you'd go to the north end of the trading grounds closer to the palace and circus, but I'm afraid your master is in for a bitter disappointment. The only silk left in Antioch is on the backs of those who wear it. Haven't you heard?"

"Heard what?" Myrad asked.

"There's war in Parthia. The caravans haven't made it through in weeks." The merchant frowned. "You didn't know? You have the look of Persians."

"You have a good eye, but we've only just come from Armenia."

Roshan glanced westward. "What about ships? Surely some of them have dared the voyage around Arabia."

Licinius made to turn away. "You won't find any silk for sale here. Storms off the peninsula have delayed everything. Silks and spices from the east are so scarce, they're almost nonexistent."

Roshan tendered her thanks and spun on one heel, her face the picture of restraint, but a tremor worked its way into her voice. "I think Father will be pleased." She reached out with a surprisingly strong grip and pulled Myrad along until he asked her to slow her pace.

Yet when they reached Walagash and shared the news, instead of celebrating, he became still. Roshan stepped closer to him. "What's the matter, Father?"

He scanned the crowd, distracted. "There's danger here."

"In the market we used to say desperate men make for great customers," Myrad said.

"We say the same on the trade routes," Walagash said, "but these men will be more than desperate, and we're foreigners in a Roman city." He looked around again, likely searching for the guards. "We must hurry. If any of the guards or magi have let it slip we're hauling silk, we're in danger."

When neither Myrad nor Roshan stirred, Walagash brought his hands together in a thunderclap. "Move! We have to get the caravan to the silk merchants."

A half hour later, with the guards posted around the caravan as if they were expecting an attack by bandits any moment, they entered the trading ground set aside for the silk merchants. There they waited in silence as Walagash fumed. "Too scarce and too slow," he said. Despite their efforts to be circumspect, word had raced ahead of them of a silk trader's arrival, yet there were no merchants waiting. The prolonged absence of goods from the east had emptied the trading grounds.

"What do we do now?" Roshan asked.

Walagash handed her a purse that clinked with silver coins. "Hire runners to find the silk merchants. Tell them we've arrived and bring them here. Give each messenger a drachma up front, another when the merchant arrives, and two if they're here within the hour."

They stood with the cataphracts and guards posted around the horses and the crowd looking on. "Would they attack the caravan in front of this crowd of people?" Myrad asked.

Walagash barked a humorless laugh. "That was never a danger. My fear is that one of the silk merchants makes a charge against us with the Romans. They might plant some stolen goods in our packs as proof. Then when the centurion places the charge, the merchant relieves us of our cargo."

"They would do such a thing?"

Walagash nodded. "Search the packs. See if anything has been placed within them."

The urgency in the merchant's voice set Myrad's heart to racing, and the looks from the gathering crowd took on a menacing cast. He moved from horse to horse as quickly as his foot allowed, unfolding the heavy oiled cloth that protected the silk and searching for any sign of tampering. When he came to the rear of the caravan, he spotted a corner untucked, fluttering in the wind. Moving his body so as to shield the pack and avoid the eyes of the crowd, he thrust his hand into the piles of silk. There! His fingers brushed something hard. Tugging at it, he pulled a stoppered bottle loose from within the folds of silk.

When he brought it forth, an invisible hand squeezed the air from his lungs and kept him from breathing. A light yellowish-red powder filled the bottle. Standing close to the packhorse, he worked the stopper free. The powder gave off a sweet grassy smell. Using his little finger, he tasted a tiny amount of it. The substance was bitter on his tongue. Saffron. Tucking the bottle into his tunic, he wrapped the oiled cloth over the silk, repacking everything tightly, then hurried back to Walagash. As his eyes darted over the crowds of people, he prayed no one had seen him.

A few moments later, he tapped Walagash on the shoulder and pulled open the right side of his tunic to show him the bottle of saffron.

A low, guttural stream of curses spilled from the merchant. "They'll command a search of the horses. When they don't find this, they'll search the guards. Get that away from here."

"What should I do with it?" Myrad asked.

Walagash snorted. "Dump it, throw it in the river, I don't care, but don't sell it or let anyone see it." A shift in the noise of the crowd around them broke their attention. In the distance, a group of men approached. Walagash put his huge hand on Myrad's shoulder. "Hurry. If they see any member of our caravan leaving, they'll come under suspicion."

Myrad left in the opposite direction, keeping a casual pace, but every stray touch as he moved through the crowd stilled his breathing. He wedged the bottle of saffron between his arm and side. The feel of eyes on him raised the hair on the back of his neck. Thirty paces farther on, he stopped, pretending interest in a display of knives, and searched for anyone following him. Not far away, a thin, dark-haired man with a wispy beard mirrored his movements, pausing to look into a blue-and-black-striped tent.

Myrad stepped through the front entrance of the tent, but as soon as he slipped into the shadows, he rushed out the back entrance. Beyond, he lost himself in the crowd, turning at random. By luck or by fortune, he found himself amid the spice merchants. He slipped into the nearest booth, its shelves nearly empty, and searched the crowd from the shadows.

"How may I assist you, young master?"

Myrad spun around. "I'm looking for a quantity of ground saffron. Would you happen to have any?"

The merchant sighed. "A small amount is all. With the delay of the Parthian caravans, I'm afraid the cost is prohibitive."

Myrad pretended disappointment. "Might I see it anyway? That way I can tell my master's wife I bargained in good faith."

The merchant brought forth a large jar with the expensive powder filling the bottom eighth of it. When he leaned over to smell the contents, he unstopped the bottle under his arm and quickly poured the saffron into it. "Ah," he said. "There's no finer spice on earth." He tucked the empty bottle in his tunic and straightened. "What is your price?"

The merchant quoted an exorbitant amount. "You see?" he said as if to make clear his predicament. "Please offer a prayer for the shipments from the east. Until then, I'm cursed to disappoint my customers and they're cursing me for it."

When the merchant moved to put his precious spice back on the shelf, Myrad slipped away, dropping the empty bottle in the press of the crowd to be trampled underfoot.

He returned to Walagash to find him sitting on a stool, a dozen men arrayed before him. A Roman centurion stood to one side, next to a merchant who sat with one hand pointing in accusation.

CHAPTER 29

The centurion addressed Walagash in Latin first, then switched to Greek when he failed to get a response. "This merchant claims you've stolen from him."

Walagash spread his hands. "We've only just arrived from Parthia." He pointed at the packhorses still carrying their burden of goods. "What need would a silk merchant have to steal anything?"

The centurion's brows rose. "You're carrying silk?"

Walagash gave the same smile to the Roman soldier as he would a potential customer. "Indeed." He motioned to the group of men before him. "We were just about to open negotiations for my goods when you arrived."

The centurion turned to the merchant who had brought the complaint. A nervous tic worked its way across his cheek. "You have proof of this theft?"

The merchant nodded. "Search them. If you find saffron, it's mine."

Walagash scowled. "Expensive, but many merchants carry their own spices to flavor their meals, and the best saffron comes from my country. Who is to say it's not mine?"

The merchant pounced on the question. "The bottles have the brand of my house on them."

The sea of people wavered in Myrad's vision. *Bottles?* He'd found only the one.

The centurion signaled to a pair of soldiers, who began unloading and searching the first horse. Walagash stepped forward so quickly, the centurion's hand flew to his short sword.

Walagash stopped and lifted his hands. "No threat is intended, Centurion, only a request."

"What is it?"

"May I have my own men unload the horses for your inspection?" He gestured at the merchants still seated and waiting. "We were just about to do so, and my cargo is quite valuable, as you can imagine."

Under the watchful stare of the centurion, Walagash ordered Aban and Storana to remove the oiled cloth to reveal bundles of shimmering off-white fabric. Myrad stared at the untold wealth the fabric represented. Then he caught sight of the merchants. Each man leaned forward, his expression hungry.

Even the centurion gaped, and his hand brushed the fabric with a gentle motion. "I can see why the emperor and his favorites clothe themselves in it."

Walagash laughed. "This is nothing, Centurion. When the dyers and weavers of Rome are finished with it, the silk cloth will glimmer and shine like the stars themselves in colors we can scarcely imagine."

One by one, Aban and Storana unloaded the packhorses and unrolled the bolts of fabric for inspection. As they came to the last horse where Myrad had found the bottle of saffron, the merchant accusing Walagash straightened, his sharp features avid.

Myrad licked his lips. He'd found only one bottle, yet was there another hidden deep inside the bundle of silk that he'd missed? He watched his friends carefully unroll the folds of expensive fabric, waiting for a bottle of saffron to tumble loose. But when the silk was completely unrolled, no bottle appeared. Myrad breathed a sigh of relief.

The centurion turned to Walagash. "My apologies, merchant. When there is a theft, it is natural for some men to blame the strangers among us."

Walagash didn't move, though his fists were clenched. "Especially if such a claim might personally enrich oneself."

The centurion left, the accusing merchant trailing after him.

Walagash signaled to the cataphracts around him to post themselves near the merchandise. "Now that the play has reached it conclusion, we can begin. You've seen the silk, and I'm well aware there is a shortage in the market." He paused to look each man in the eye before he went on. "If I deem the bids insufficient, I retain the right of refusal."

While several of the traders groaned, the hunger never left their eyes.

Myrad stepped over to where Aban and Roshan stood, but as he approached them, Roshan turned away and left, darting into the crowd. "I thought there was another bottle in there," he whispered to Aban.

Aban took a deep breath and stretched, appearing bored, but his gaze measured the distance to those around them. "There was."

"What? How did you keep them from finding it?"

"Not me. Storana."

Myrad looked at the Sarmatian, who grinned back.

"My fingers aren't as nimble as they used to be," Storana said, "but almost anyone could have palmed that bottle. Every time we unwrapped a bolt of silk, the crowd could see nothing else."

"Where's the bottle now?" Myrad asked. "If the merchants see it, they'll call the centurion back."

Aban smiled. "Roshan is getting rid of it. The merchant who accused Walagash of stealing is having a very bad day. He's lost his chance at the silk, along with a considerable sum in spices."

The negotiations dragged into the late afternoon. The merchants, each unwilling to let such a prize escape them, began forming cooperative groups to purchase the cargo. Often they spent more time bargaining with each other than with Walagash. Roshan stood next to Myrad, her attention fixed on the negotiations taking place. Every time Myrad's focus drifted elsewhere, she gave him a smack on the hand.

"Watch them," she insisted.

"Why? They've been at this for hours now."

She shook her head at him. "Because you're watching a master at work. If you could hear the best musician in the world play his instrument, would you leave in the middle of the performance?"

Myrad frowned. "But he's hardly doing anything."

"Aren't there silences in a piece of music? Notice, every time the merchants' negotiations with each other threaten to break down, my father says just enough to keep them in cooperation. These men are rivals. Look at the way they sit, leaning away from each other, and their expressions when they speak. Most likely some of them hate each other, yet Father has spent all afternoon building their alliance until they can bid as a single unit."

Myrad observed Walagash as he offered a well-chosen word, a smile, or a frown whenever negotiations appeared to be breaking down. "Amazing," he whispered. "They'll pool their bids to keep from losing out altogether. How much will he get?"

"No one back east, except for Esai, will believe him, but this sale will establish my father in the silk trade for the rest of his life." Roshan smiled, her face flushed with excitement. "And we've been here to see it."

An hour later, ten of the eleven merchants agreed to a price for the lot, with the condition it would be split based on each man's contribution to the purchase. Roshan practically crowed at the price. "Three-eighths of a talent of gold for each talent of silk." She turned to Myrad. "That's as much as the finest grade would bring."

After the crowd dispersed and the transaction was finalized with weights and scales, Walagash sought out Myrad. "A difficult journey but a handsome price."

Myrad nodded. "You were brilliant. I didn't even know what I was seeing until Roshan opened my eyes."

A grin split the huge man's face. "I have learned to take what's been given me and make the best of it." He pointed to his face.

Myrad shook his head. "I don't understand."

Walagash winked at him. "I think you do. I still look like a wrestler, big and brutish. People often assume big men have small minds. They don't stop to think that a man who looks like he can break rocks with his hands might be shrewd as well."

Myrad looked down at his right foot. "What do people think about the lame?"

Walagash's grin faded, but light still danced in his eyes. "You tell me."

"They tell me I'm cursed by my God, shunned for some sin of my parents or my own." His feelings of being blemished and insufficient still lay beneath Gershom's lessons to the contrary. "You're telling me that's not true?"

"I'm telling you exactly that," Walagash said. "You see yourself as a man cursed with a clubfoot and beset by trials at every turn. You've been hunted, hurt, drugged, abandoned, and caught in a war having nothing to do with you." He laughed. This giant in linen robes had the audacity to laugh at Myrad's struggles.

"That is what *you* see," Walagash went on. "But I see a man who has triumphed over every obstacle placed before him. By the god of the shining fire, you should be dead five times over. Yet here you stand, alive, and part of one of the richest caravans in the empire."

"That's your fortune, not mine."

Walagash burst into laughter. "Sometimes I forget that this life is unfamiliar to you, Myrad. Even as a member of my guard, you would be paid handsomely for your part, but you've done much more." He leaned forward and whispered a number that left Myrad's mouth hanging open.

Afer sunset, Myrad went looking for Yehudah. He found the magus with Hakam in the broad courtyard of their inn, staring into the sky. He looked up and saw the King's star blazing as usual just above the horizon, though it no longer shone west of them but instead burned to the south.

"It's beautiful," Yehudah said.

Hakam pointed to the sky. "And right over Jerusalem." He glanced at Myrad, then looked away without saying anything, but his dismissive expression said what his mouth hadn't. Myrad was no Hebrew and could claim no part in the plan of God.

"What will we do?" Myrad asked. Not for the first time, he mourned the loss of Dov. The quiet poet had always accepted him, and the peace he'd carried calmed Myrad's fears even when he offered no answers to his many questions.

Yehudah lifted his gaze to the star once more before he responded. "Follow where the light leads, of course. Once we find the King, we will serve Him."

"How?"

Hakam gave a brief shake of his head as if to say the question wasn't worth answering. "If God can give us a star to guide us to the Messiah, then He can provide a direction for us once we arrive there. Imagine it," he said to Yehudah. "The land of our fathers cleansed of Roman rule once and for all."

Yehudah nodded, but Myrad saw hesitation in the gesture. Hakam departed, leaving Myrad with Yehudah to admire the star that had guided them to this land hundreds of miles away. He stayed just long enough to verify the Messiah's star didn't move while the rest of the lights in the heavens did. Then he returned to the inn.

Myrad heard voices as he mounted the wide stone steps, voices hinting at conflict. They were hardly more than murmurs floating in the darkness. Creeping within the shadow of the eave, he made his way toward the sound.

". . . an end to Roman power as much as you." *Masista.*

"Our goals are not aligned. Despite the adage, a common enemy does not make us friends." *Hakam.*

Masista's voice dropped into a lower range. "I'm not speaking of friendship; I'm merely stating a fact. The Romans are a disease that has conquered every nation and land bordering the Great Sea. Your messiah will need allies."

Hakam snorted. "And you're proposing Parthia as an ally to Judea?"

Myrad could almost see Masista's ingratiating nod. "Consider how a Roman attack on Parthia emanating from Judea would serve us both. Musa would find herself fighting a two-front war, and your messiah would find conquest of Judea far easier with most of the garrisons dispatched to the east."

Myrad listened for Hakam's response, but the silence stretched without interruption. It was Masista who broke it.

"I was one of the emissaries to Armenia and the Roman Empire before Musa elevated herself to the title 'queen of queens.' If you think Parthians and Persians are harsh, shall I tell you what I've seen of Roman cruelty?"

"There's no need," Hakam said. "They occupy my homeland. That is more than enough to earn my hatred."

"A magus should be equipped with knowledge. If one of their prized virgins knows a man, they bury her alive in a wooden box tall enough for her to stand in. Others accused of crimes are sealed in an oxskin with dogs and vipers and thrown into the river to drown."

"Stop," Hakam said, his voice rough.

But Masista persisted. "Their favorite form of execution is strangulation, but this doesn't tell the whole story. The Romans are creative. If a people dare to assert their right to be free, people like the Hebrews, the Romans will crucify them. But the guards aren't allowed to leave the condemned while they live, so they take an iron club and—"

"Stop!" Hakam's voice cracked like a whip.

Myrad waited, tense, but neither of the magi made to leave. After a moment, he left them to their mutual hatred and withdrew, seeking his bed.

Sleep and the dream came to him almost without transition. The star burned above the western horizon as before, its corona flaring in the night now as though urging him haste. There on the sands of the desert, Yehudah and Hakam flanked him on either side, staring. "Behold," the voice said, "the promised one has been born."

CHAPTER 30

After Jesus was born in Bethlehem in Judea, during the time of King Herod, Magi from the east came to Jerusalem. . . .

Matthew 2:1

Myrad rolled from his blankets as soon as wan sunlight brought him to wakefulness. Without pausing to put on his sandals, he padded the narrow hallways in search of Yehudah. He found the magus at the front of the inn, speaking with Hakam. "I understand," Myrad said as he came to the edge of their table.

Yehudah nodded and even Hakam jerked his head in agreement. "The star was to announce his birth. Hakam and I had the same dream."

"So the calendar is correct after all," Myrad said. "We're on our way to see a child." Disappointment warred with relief. Gershom had been right all along.

"The messiah has been born," Yehudah said, "but it will be decades yet before he is revealed."

The muscles along Hakam's jawline bunched. "It will take

years for the rightful king of Israel to throw off the yoke of Rome."

"We've come thousands of miles over the course of months to see a child," Myrad said. "Why?"

Yehudah shrugged. "Doubtless, the Most High God has a reason for bringing us here. Perhaps, in time, we will even know what it is."

The caravan departed the next morning with half their horse train bearing riders, goods, or gold. With Walagash's business completed, the magi rode toward the front just behind Yehudah's cataphracts, whose armor and plate mail gleamed in the sun with a thousand flashes of light. Masista's soldiers, similarly arrayed, brought up the rear just behind the packhorses. After them came Aban and Storana, who took turns scouting, though there seemed to be little need. Roman cavalry patrolled every mile of the Via Maris, the road along the sea that the Romans called the Mare Nostrum.

At intervals, a plumed officer would ride by, leading a group of thirty or so mounted men. Each time, the officer and his men would slow their pace to eye the cataphracts and their horses the way dogs eyed wolves. Yehudah's men merely stared back, expressionless, until the Romans moved on. But the threat of confrontation wore on them all, and when they stopped at the end of each day, Myrad was exhausted.

They continued south with the Great Sea on their right for nearly two weeks, following the Via Maris while the star shifted from directly in front of them to shine on their left. The night they came to Jaffa, the star burned a pair of hands above the horizon directly to the east.

"Jerusalem," Yehudah said.

"Where else would the Messiah-King be?" Hakam asked.

Masista had taken to joining them each morning and evening as they marked the position of the star, and the man's frustration at his inability to see it became palpable.

"Herod is there," Masista said. "Perhaps he will be the one to throw off the Roman yoke."

Hakam turned on him, his face twisted in disgust. "Herod is no Hebrew! He's a mongrel, a dog from Edom."

"Pardon my mistake." Masista bowed. "Perhaps I was unaware of his origins." He turned and left while Hakam went back to his contemplation of the star.

Myrad considered the two men before him. Yehudah seemed as placid as ever, but Hakam's anger troubled him. Masista's litany of Roman atrocities had stoked the magus's fury until it burned in the depths of his eyes. Even Yehudah's disagreement earned Hakam's scorn now.

"What of the calendar?" Myrad asked. "Why did God bring us here early?"

Yehudah continued gazing at the star. "The acts of God are difficult to understand before they occur, clouded as they are by our preconceived notions. Yet after they have happened, they seem obvious." He rolled his shoulders as he shifted his weight. "The prophecy says the *coming* of the Messiah-King, and within those words are any number of interpretations."

"Any Hebrew king will have to cleanse the land," Hakam said. "The Roman Empire is vast. Conquering them could take thirty years."

The pronouncement could have come from Masista. "You believe the Messiah-King will defeat the Roman Empire?" Myrad asked. He would have laughed, except Hakam was in earnest.

"Israel is a small strip of desert and little else. It took us months to get here but less than two weeks to cover half the kingdom. How can they fight the Romans?"

Hakam's eyes traveled to Myrad's clubfoot and back up to his face. "You know nothing of Israel. Nothing! Egypt was once an empire much like the Romans, yet they couldn't keep their slaves from escaping to freedom. Because the Most High God was on their side."

With an effort, Myrad kept his voice even. "I know more of Israel than you suppose. Even before Gershom taught me the language, he told me the stories. How many times did the kings of Israel and Judah presume God's favor only to be defeated in battle?"

"You think to lecture me?" Hakam spat. "You're a Persian, born in the gutter, and blemished. You're not alive because of God's favor. You're alive because He won't accept the sacrifice of a cripple."

Myrad took a deep breath to ward off the truth and hurt of Hakam's words. "And yet the dream came to me, a Persian boy from the street, long before it came to you, O exalted magus." He didn't wait for a response. Instead, he strode away.

When he entered Walagash's tent, Roshan came to him, her eyes searching. Then, without speaking, she reached up to caress his face, her hands moving to erase his scowl. "What happened?"

In halting language, he told her of the exchange with Hakam.

"Hakam's hatred of the Romans is poisoning his heart," she said. "What would Gershom tell you?"

"To honor God and not worry about what others say."

"Wise advice." Her brow furrowed. "Remember, I chose you rather than the richest merchants in the empire, and God chose you as well."

Later, when he lay in his bed, sleep took him despite the anger that still made his heart pound. Without transition, he found himself standing on a hill beside a circular palace overlooking a strange city. Yehudah and Hakam stood next to him. Before he could speak, the King's star appeared in the heavens. They watched as the star left its place where it had hovered over Jerusalem and moved south. A voice encompassed the heavens, which Myrad felt as much as heard: "Find the child who has been born king of Israel."

Myrad awoke the next morning to find the room he shared with Aban and Storana empty. The guards were gone, perhaps to check their mounts before departing. He dressed and went in search of Yehudah. In two days' time they would be at the end of their quest, once they found the Messiah-King in Jerusalem, but they were headed straight into the seat of Roman power. Myrad swallowed past a knot in his throat.

He descended the stairs into the stable yard of the inn and stopped. Walagash, the magi, and all the guards were there. Surrounded by Roman soldiers.

Myrad started to count but stopped when he saw a man with a red horsehair crest atop his helmet, running from ear to ear. A centurion. Here in the heart of Israel, they were hopelessly outnumbered.

Masista and Hakam sat on their horses with disdain, their backs straight. Walagash and Yehudah wore looks of calm concern. The cataphracts and guards were still armed. Myrad moved off the porch, his footsteps tentative. A Roman soldier brought him his horse.

"Ah," the centurion said upon seeing him. "A welcome morning to you." He spoke in flawless Greek. "King Herod sends his greetings and his escort to our guests from Parthia. He requests the favor of your presence, that he might hear the news of your homeland."

Behind the cordial centurion, dozens of Roman cavalry sat on their mounts, their faces like iron. Roshan sidled up to him. "Get on your horse, Myrad," she murmured. "The invitation isn't optional."

Myrad mounted up, and the Roman cavalry led them out of the yard with a third of their force up front and two-thirds at the rear. They set a steady trot that would have them in Jerusalem by nightfall. Myrad waited until the streets of Jaffa were behind them before he spoke to Roshan. "What happened?" he asked in Persian.

"They were in the courtyard when I woke," she answered in the same language.

"They came two hours before dawn," Aban added.

Roshan's hand took his for a moment. "They didn't wake anyone or threaten the guards keeping watch over the horses. They just waited until everyone woke. Then they extended King Herod's invitation, along with his welcome to emissaries from a sister kingdom."

"Sister kingdom?"

Aban yawned and stretched, looking at the rolling hills around them and the mountains to the east, before he said in a subdued voice, "There's no way of knowing. It may just be Roman flowery, or it might mean he believes Musa has control of Parthia and we're her loyal subjects."

Myrad glanced toward the front where the magi rode next to Walagash. When his gaze fell across Hakam, his heart stumbled in its rhythm. "I have to speak to Yehudah."

Aban leaned across his horse to put a hand on Myrad's arm. He nodded toward their escort. "Be careful. These men are soldiers, and we've been their sworn enemy for hundreds of years. In close quarters, those short swords of theirs are deadly."

"And watch your words," Roshan whispered. "I think I saw more than one look of recognition when we switched to Persian."

Calmly, Myrad urged Areion forward until Walagash and the magi took note. The merchant and Yehudah parted enough to allow his horse between theirs. Masista rode just ahead. At a nod from Yehudah, the cataphracts surrounding them let their mounts drift ever so slightly. The result was a space in which they might be able to speak without being overheard.

"What are we going to do?" Myrad asked.

Yehudah's brows lifted. "Go with our escort and meet King Herod. What else can we do?"

"But what are we going to say once there?"

Masista turned on his horse to meet Myrad's gaze. It flicked briefly to Hakam before returning. "The truth," he said in a normal voice loud enough to be overheard. "Magi can do no less. We're here so that you three may visit the land of your fathers. By happy circumstance, your betrothed's father is a silk merchant."

Walagash's cheeks bunched with a too-big smile. "A very happy circumstance. Trade here on the outskirts of the Roman Empire has proved lucrative. Well spoken, magus."

The shift in Walagash's demeanor toward Masista caught Myrad by surprise, but the company of Romans offered no opportunity to pursue it. He leaned forward to press the question, but Masista cut him off. "I understand the prospect of speaking to the king makes you nervous. Would you like for me to speak on your behalf?" He leaned back toward Myrad and added in a low mutter, "Herod is sick, close to dying, and he's not going quietly. A wrong word could kill us all."

So many undercurrents to the conversation confused Myrad, yet only a fool could miss the suppressed rage in Hakam's posture. Yehudah caught his eye and gave a slight nod. For some reason, everyone present save Hakam had conceded to let Masista speak on their behalf. Even Walagash.

"Thank you," Myrad said. Gratitude tasted like gall on his tongue, but the prospect of being held prisoner or killed at Herod's command settled the issue. "You may understand why royalty makes me nervous."

They all smiled, except for Hakam.

The caravan kept up its steady trot forward. They stopped once to water and change horses at a small village, Emmaus. Afterward they continued on toward Jerusalem, climbing from the basin bordering the sea into the hills of Judea. They came to the city just before sunset while they could still see flat-topped buildings nestled among the hills and winding roads that ran between them like water. Somewhere in the distance, someone blew a horn. Next to him, Yehudah murmured a phrase in Hebrew as a tear tracked through the dust on his face.

"What is that?" Myrad asked him.

"The call to prayer."

They ascended a steep hill toward a massive retaining wall that defined the border of the city. They followed their Roman escort around to the northwest corner, where three towers built with enormous, fitted stones loomed over them like a threat. The last rays of the day faded as they came to an entrance on their right and were led inside the walls of Jerusalem.

"The Old City," Yehudah said.

"The City of David," Hakam corrected. "And it will be his

descendants' city." He drew breath to continue, but sharp looks from Yehudah and Masista reduced him to glowering silence.

They entered through the gate and doubled back toward the wall until the three towers cast them in shadow. Climbing a steep road, they came to a broad archway lit by giant braziers tended by Romans in glittering armor.

Their commander spoke to them in a language Myrad supposed to be Latin, but he didn't need Masista's translation to understand the dark looks the sentries shot toward the cataphracts and caravan guards. The composite bows in particular held the Romans' attention.

"Veterans," Yehudah said.

Masista nodded. "They know who we are. Keep your hands in sight and don't make any move they might perceive as a threat." His face stretched as he donned his customary smile, only here it looked forced. "King Herod has favored us with this invitation. Let us behave as honored guests."

Hakam jerked at the use of the word *king* and mouthed curses. They waited as the sky darkened, their horses stirring beneath them, restless. Masista, his smile wilted at the edges, addressed the head of their guard, speaking in Greek, "Is there a problem, Centurion?"

The man's scarlet crest waved in time to his denial as he spoke in the same language. "King Herod is a busy man. Though your arrival is expected, there are doubtless other details of governance requiring his attention."

"Your Greek is more fluid than my Latin." Masista bowed. "My compliments."

The centurion nodded but otherwise ignored the flattery. "I was born in Athens. It should be."

At last, a soldier appeared at the entrance and waved them

in. They dismounted to pass through the walled entrance and long colonnade into a paved courtyard between two multistory buildings. Fountains burbled, and the scent of unfamiliar plants perfumed the air. Braziers burned brightly every few feet, banishing the darkness. People filled the space, some reclining as they ate from delicate bowls, others moving about and conversing with one another. To their left sat Herod on his throne, situated at the top of the first set of stairs leading up to one of the buildings. A century of soldiers were arrayed before him, each holding a bow.

"Come, my guests," Herod called, waving them forward. A smile etched with pain stretched his face into a parody, and one hand darted to his lap, scratching at some affliction.

They edged forward with Walagash and the magi in the front row, flanked by Yehudah's cataphracts on the right and Masista's on the left. Behind them, the caravan guards formed up in a box.

Sweat poured from Herod's brow, down the pasty contours of his cheeks and onto his robe. Silk, Myrad noticed. "Your presence in Judea is an unexpected pleasure." He smacked his lips. "A delicacy. I have hungered for news from the east, and the gods have delivered it to me." His dark eyes glittered with the reflected light of the braziers. "Tell me everything."

CHAPTER 31

Then Herod called the Magi secretly and found out from them the exact time the star had appeared.

Matthew 2:7

Masista bowed, imbuing the gesture with servitude. "How shall I begin, Your Majesty? Events in Parthia are as vast and complex as its borders."

Herod smiled like a man taking up an expected and hoped-for challenge. "Rumors have reached my ears that our country-woman, Musa, has been named queen. Tell me, how does she fare?"

Masista nodded. "More than queen, Your Majesty. With the death of Phraates, Empress Musa, queen of queens, rules the Parthian Empire jointly with her son, Phraataces."

Herod leaned forward, his enthusiasm battling obvious discomfort. "Does it not trouble you, magus, to see your country fall to the rule of a child of Rome?"

Masista waved away the king's question. "Magi have never been overly concerned with the origins of our rulers, Your Majesty. Phraataces is half Roman and half Parthian. His parentage on his father's side is more than enough to secure the loyalty of the Parthian clans. Most of them anyway."

"Most?" Herod asked.

Masista gave a small shrug. "There are some clans in the far east, near Bactria, that have yet to accept Musa's rule. A temporary circumstance, nothing more."

Disappointment wreathed Herod's expression. As if the deprivation of a contest of wills reminded him of his affliction, a spasm of pain made him wince. "You," he said to Walagash. "I have heard of your exploits in Antioch. What favor did you earn from the queen that allowed you, among all the silk merchants, access to our markets?"

Before Walagash could respond, Masista sidestepped, interposing himself between the merchant and the king. "Pardon, Your Majesty, but our merchant is most comfortable speaking Parthian, the language of his birth."

Herod's eyes narrowed. "No matter, magus," he said in perfect Greek. "Any merchant will speak enough Greek to suffice, and a man with a limited vocabulary is often more . . . forthright." His smile conveyed his sense of victory. He repeated his question in simpler phrases as Masista stepped back to his place.

Myrad glanced around the courtyard. The soldiers stood at attention, their hands on their weapons. He and the rest of the caravan had been escorted into a trap, built upon Herod's suspicions.

Walagash bowed. "In truth, Your Majesty, I did not gain the queen's attention so much as I avoided it. The war with the clans of the east necessitated Musa's acquisition of additional horses and men from the caravans as soldiers. I elected to go through Armenia."

Herod's smile returned. "Interesting. With one breath you tell me Musa is hardly opposed and in another you confirm to me her opposition is strong enough to warrant impressment." He shifted his attention to Yehudah. "Why are you here, magus? You are from Parthia, but your face hints at Hebrew ancestry."

Yehudah bowed. "Your Majesty is perceptive. My ancestors are from Judea as well as Parthia." He inclined his head toward Walagash. "I by chance came to meet the merchant here, and when I discovered his intended destination, I persuaded him to let me travel with him so that I might see the land of my fathers."

Herod's smile twisted until it became predatory. "I know something of your customs. It's said a magus is forbidden to lie. Is this true?" At Yehudah's nod, he continued, "But a man could refrain from telling the *whole* truth. I find it hard to believe a wish to see the land of your fathers is sufficient to bring you all the way to Judea, especially in the midst of war. Does your queen not require the counsel of her wise men?"

"Of a certainty, Your Majesty, she does. And she has it. The queen may believe a great many things about the countries around her, but wisdom would dictate sending out merchants or magi to see them firsthand and report back."

Disappointment flashed in Herod's eyes as he turned to Hakam. "You, magus, have a look on your face I have seen everywhere in the streets of Jerusalem, the look of a man whose food is bitter. It seems most Hebrews have no love for Rome."

Hakam stood before the king and nodded.

"Can you not speak?" Herod asked.

"Assuredly," Hakam said, his voice rough. "To any question the king poses, I will answer."

Myrad winced at the acid tone.

"Any question," the king purred. "Then tell me, why are you here?"

"It is as the magus Yehudah said. We wish to visit the land of our fathers."

Myrad felt panic shooting through his chest. The king had found the weakest link among them, and he leaned forward wearing a victor's smile.

"I have a report from the Roman centurion who searched your caravan in Antioch," the king went on. "Among the silk you carried, he also found a large quantity of gold and spices, strange gifts for a simple visit to the land of your fathers."

Hakam didn't reply, but his face reddened, and beneath the onslaught of Herod's gaze he began to tremble.

"What brought you to Judea, magus?" Herod pressed.

Hakam's head came up, losing its deferential cast, until he stared at the king eye to eye. "We received a dream from the Most High God."

Herod leaned forward, all signs of pain from his affliction absent. "What was this dream that brought magi all the way to Judea with such extravagant gifts?"

The courtyard stilled until nothing but the soft crackle of the burning braziers could be heard. Myrad closed his eyes and prayed Hakam would find some answer that would satisfy the king and let them live. The tone of his first words dashed his hopes.

"A dream of the voice of God." Hakam paused, but the lot was cast. There was no way to keep Herod from the whole truth now. Hakam's voice sharpened until it cut the air like a Roman gladius. "We have come searching for the one who has been *born* king of the Hebrews. We have seen His star in the east and have followed it here that we may worship Him."

Myrad couldn't breathe, and sudden spots swam in his vision. The fool had just sentenced them all to death.

Herod's laughter, caustic and tinged with physical distress, filled the courtyard. "And *this* is the truth you thought to keep from me? By the time the child is grown, I will be dead." His laughter scaled upward until it echoed among the buildings. "I wish your god luck in finding one who can wrest Judea from the grip of Rome." Then his mirth softened and he became dismissive, waving away the magi and Walagash's company. "Come, my guests, let us eat and celebrate the peace, however temporary, between our kingdoms."

Myrad and the others were escorted to an area to one side, where servants brought them dishes of food and wineskins. After a few moments, the tension in Herod's courtyard eased and Myrad was able to breathe freely again. The meal stretched for hours into the evening, the Romans showing no signs of retiring.

At one point during the meal, Myrad glanced toward the dais only to find it empty. "He's gone," he said to Masista.

The magus nodded. "The king left an hour ago."

Despite his dislike of the man, Myrad found himself seeking Masista's reassurance. "Are we in danger?"

The magus's smile held none of its usual superiority. "We were always in danger, but your friend Hakam has made sure that Herod sees us as an enemy."

At the mention of Herod's name, a centurion emerged from the crowd to address them at their table in Latin. The only word Myrad understood was *Herod*.

Masista stood, signaling Yehudah, Hakam, and Myrad to follow him. "King Herod desires to speak with us privately." When Walagash and the guards moved to rise, he held out a hand. "He bids the rest of you to finish enjoying your meal. He requires only the magi."

"My own astronomers have said nothing to me of this star," Herod began. He was perched on a thickly padded throne, his body slanted forward. Braziers heated the room to a stifling degree. Already Myrad could feel the sweat rolling down his neck and into his tunic.

"Only certain magi can see it," Hakam said.

"Ah. Of course," Herod mocked. "Tell me, how long ago did you first receive this so-called vision?"

Now, after the damage was done, Hakam demurred from answering. He turned to look at Myrad. Everyone else in the room did the same.

"A bit over a year ago, Your Majesty," Myrad said.

"And do you know where the child is?"

Myrad shook his head. "Not yet, Your Majesty. The star keeps moving."

"How inconvenient." Herod held Myrad's gaze for a long moment, taking his measure, then leaned back finally. "Take your report back to Queen Musa. Her goodwill is important to the Roman Empire. As for your child and his star, you may find that when you're as close to riding with Charon as I am, your priorities change. I've taken steps to craft a certain reputation, but now I find myself with a different perspective." He took a shuddering breath as another spasm of pain contorted his face. "When you have found the child, bring your report back to me so that I may worship him as well."

Even Hakam had sense enough to bow. With a clap of the king's hands, their escort formed up around them and escorted them back to the courtyard where they were reunited with their party. They retraced their steps to mount their horses, and the Romans led them back outside the walls of the City of David. They headed west, descending toward the floor of the valley until they came to a fork in the road. There, the centurion issued orders to his men to disassemble. With a nod to the magi, he prepared to depart.

"Centurion," Masista called after him. When the Roman turned, Masista pointed toward the city. "Where might we find an inn to accommodate us?"

"There's an inn along the road to Lydda, at the northwest end of the valley."

"Will they have room for all of us?"

The centurion nodded. "It's large enough to hold you, and we're in between holy days. There should be room enough for your party."

The soldiers and the centurion melted away into the darkness, taking the west fork of the road.

"What do we do now?" Myrad asked Yehudah.

Masista spoke first. "Exactly what the centurion said."

Hakam drew breath to object, but Masista interrupted, cutting the air with one hand. He lowered his voice and echoed, "*Exactly* what the centurion said."

When Walagash and Yehudah added their support to Masista, Hakam held back his objection.

They rode until they found the inn, large as promised, and negotiated rooms for the night. The horses were unloaded, the gifts carried inside to rooms guarded collectively by the cataphracts. The magi, along with Walagash and Roshan, met in a room, with Aban and Storana posted outside the door to keep anyone from listening.

Masista raged at Hakam as soon as the door closed behind them. "You fool! What insanity possessed you to cast your defiance into the king's teeth?"

Hakam refused to be cowed. "We have no need to answer to an Edomite. Herod's a pig."

"You think everyone who's not Hebrew is a pig," Masista shot back. "He's *king*."

"No," Hakam said, "he's a usurper. The true King has just been born."

"Your true king is but a babe, a child who doesn't command a single soldier," Masista said. "You've put the edge of the sword against our necks. Herod has no interest in worshiping your messiah. He's going to follow our every move until he can find the child and kill him."

"If you were concerned about being watched, why did you bring us to the inn the centurion suggested?"

Masista shook his head in disgust. "How simple are you? If we hadn't taken the centurion's suggestion, they would have doubled whatever watch they assigned to us."

"A word, if you please," Walagash said. Neither Hakam nor Masista appeared ready to relinquish their argument, yet they paused long enough for the merchant to continue.

"We need to know for certain if we're being watched." When everyone else in the room assented, he turned to Roshan. "Go. Take Aban and Storana with you."

Roshan slipped out of the room.

Walagash sat and stared at Hakam. "When did Masista convince you to defy Herod?"

Hakam bristled. "I don't need Masista's counsel. Herod sits on the throne that rightfully belongs to the descendant of David."

Myrad stepped forward from the edge of the room. "You took advantage of his hatred," he said to Masista. "You stoked it with tales of Roman brutality until it was impossible for him to hold his tongue."

After a moment, Masista laughed, his anger gone. "Of course I did," he said. "I'm trying to save Parthia, along with Judea, from the Romans. With the combined might of their legions and the cavalry of Parthia, they'd sweep across the world like a plague."

"All empires are an abomination," Yehudah said.

Masista laughed. "Strange words for a man who's come to worship a king, but some empires are worse than others. What the Parthians and the Persians conquered, they left in peace, allowing people to worship their own gods and even serve their own kings. The Romans, on the other hand, take pride in what they can destroy."

"You're playing with our lives, magus." Yehudah's hand tapped the hilt of his knife. "Herod could have just as easily killed us."

"A risk that had to be taken," Masista said. "With any luck, Herod may decide to attack the western edge of Parthia, but at the very least he will keep his garrisons here in Jerusalem. Doubt about Musa's intentions will eat at him as surely as his disease."

Yehudah's voice hardened. "You've placed the Messiah in danger."

"Herod is insane. Don't you see? From the moment we were taken, your messiah was threatened. Herod would have ferreted out the truth eventually. As it is, he saw exactly what he expected to see from a Hebrew magus—a frothing zealot who can't hold his tongue."

Hakam spewed Hebrew curses at Masista until the air dripped with vitriol.

Masista dipped his head as if to acknowledge a compliment. "We need to slip away from whoever is watching us. Your messiah's family must be warned. Herod will be looking for the child."

Myrad blinked, confused. "Why do you care what happens to the Messiah?"

"If Herod finds and kills your messiah, the threat to his sovereignty has been eliminated," Masista said. "He will be less likely to march on Parthia." He glanced toward the door. "We must get away from the soldiers they've posted to watch this inn."

A light knock at the door prefaced Roshan's entrance. "We have a pair of guards watching the inn," she said. "If we're going to leave, we'll need a distraction."

"Can they be drugged?" Walagash asked.

Masista shook his head. "They're Romans. They won't accept food or drink from a stranger while they're on guard duty."

Roshan pointed back the way she'd come. "When I passed through the inn's kitchen, I saw the innkeeper's servant preparing food and drink to take outside. When I asked him about it, he said it was for the Romans keeping watch."

"It seems your God is with us," Masista said. "We have lax guards standing watch."

"How long before they bring them the food and drink?" Yehudah asked.

Roshan shrugged. "An hour perhaps."

"Do what you need to do," Yehudah said, rising to his feet. "I'll rejoin you as quickly as I can."

"Where are you going?" Masista demanded.

"We need information of a different type, and we're not going to get it from Herod or his Romans." He looked at Roshan and Storana. "How long will the guards sleep?"

"As long as we wish."

"Two hours then," Yehudah said.

"Shouldn't someone go with you, magus?" Walagash asked.

Yehudah shook his head. "The guards won't follow one man, but they might split up to follow two." He slipped out of the inn.

Roshan and Storana left the room too but headed for the kitchen, leaving the rest of them to wait. An hour later, they returned. "It's done," Roshan said.

Before long, Yehudah returned as well. Nothing in his expression provided a clue as to where he'd been or what, if anything, he accomplished there. Moving as quickly as the demand for silence permitted, they left the inn. To Myrad, the clatter of hooves as they rode away screamed for attention, but there remained enough traffic on the streets of Jerusalem to cover their noisy departure. After a brief conversation with Yehudah, Walagash ordered the caravan to go back the way they'd come, taking the road to Emmaus.

"If we are seen or someone remembers our passing," Yehudah said, "we don't want to give Herod any idea which way we've gone."

Once outside the city, they stopped to muffle their horses' hooves with strips of cloth. Twice after they departed from Jerusalem, they left the road in secret and hid, waiting for signs of being followed. None came.

Next to Myrad, Roshan breathed a sigh that carried regret.

"What's wrong?" he asked her.

"The men assigned to watch us will be put to death."

Hakam twisted to look at them, his mouth twisting. "They're Romans."

Storana's eyes narrowed to mere slits. "They were men doing their job—"

"Look," Yehudah interrupted. By the light of a gibbous moon, Myrad saw him pointing back toward Jerusalem.

Hanging in the sky above Herod's palace shone the King's star. It bobbed once, moved southward, then stopped. The star stayed there in its new position as if waiting for them.

"What do you see?" Roshan asked.

Myrad pointed. "The star's moved."

"What does it mean?" Walagash asked.

"It means the Messiah's not in Jerusalem," Yehudah said.

Hakam's voice carried a note of justification. "And Herod's place has been given to another."

The caravan took the southern road, with Aban and Storana riding ahead and behind to give them warning of approaching riders. They skirted the western edge of the Hinnom Valley.

Myrad strained to hear the approach of soldiers, hardly daring to breathe. "Herod must know we've slipped away by now," he whispered to Roshan.

She shook her head. "It depends on how long our guards were supposed to keep watch and if they were discovered sleeping. If they wake on their own, they may hesitate to make a report, wanting to avoid Herod's wrath."

That sounded to Myrad like wishful thinking, but he latched on to the idea nonetheless. Two hours before dawn, the star moved again, this time from in front of them to the east.

Yehudah tugged at the merchant's tunic. "That way."

"Ride forward and bring back Aban," Walagash said to Roshan.

She'd just pulled her horse out of the caravan's formation when Walagash spoke again. "Wait. There's no need."

Within seconds, Aban came riding back to them, manifesting himself in the spare moonlight. "The road forks, and I spotted lights to the east. I think there's a village in that direction."

CHAPTER 32

After they had heard the king, they went on their way, and the star they had seen when it rose went ahead of them until it stopped over the place where the child was. . . . And having been warned in a dream not to go back to Herod, they returned to their country by another route.

Matthew 2:9–12

With his eyes fixed on the star moving ahead of them, Myrad urged his horse forward until he rode shoulder to shoulder with Yehudah and Hakam.

Yehudah smiled, basking in the radiance of the light only the three of them could see. "That shouldn't be possible."

"What?" Myrad asked.

"The way the light moves. It shines like any other star, and yet the heavens are unimaginably distant." He pointed at the King's star. "Yet while this one appears the same as its kindred, it guides us as intimately as one of Walagash's guards."

Myrad looked again and saw it was true. While they had been speaking, the light had settled in the sky directly over the town. As they trotted together toward the village, Myrad watched in amazement as the star moved in ever finer increments in response until it shone over a single house.

"Walagash, Masista, I think we're here," Yehudah said. "Wait a moment while Myrad and Hakam accompany me." He smiled as he twitched the reins and moved off to the left. Myrad followed, curious as to where the magus might be leading them, but Yehudah corrected him in the midst of his joy. "Not me. Keep your eyes on the star."

Nodding, Myrad saw it hovering over the same house. They turned right at each street they came to until they arrived back at the caravan. At every turn, the star appeared both impossibly far away even as it seemed to remain right over the top of the house.

"This is the house of the Messiah," Yehudah said as they rejoined the party.

Masista grimaced as he regarded the simple dwelling. "*That* is the birthplace of a king?"

"Our God is not your God," Hakam said, though his expression mirrored Masista's from only a moment before.

Yehudah dismounted and strode back to the packhorses. With the help of his cataphracts, he began unloading a portion of the gifts they'd brought.

Holding the reins of his horse, Hakam moved to Yehudah's side. "How should it be done?"

"The gifts?" Yehudah asked.

Hakam nodded.

For the first time, a bit of the joy faded from Yehudah's countenance. "With the loss of Dov, we are three. Let each of us offer a gift to the Messiah-King. My men can carry them."

Myrad expected Hakam to argue, but instead he stepped over to the horses laden with gold. "I will offer gold for our King, our deliverer from the Romans."

Yehudah's expression said he expected no less. "I will bring the incense for our Priest, our intercessor with the Most High." Even in the sparse light of the village and the moon overhead, Myrad thought he caught a hint of shadow falling across Yehudah's eyes.

Myrad recalled then the seller's reaction on the day they'd purchased the myrrh. "Will it seem strange," he asked, "that I'm offering a child embalming spices?"

"Perhaps," Yehudah said, "it's meaning will become clear in time." He looked as though he might say something else, but with a small shake of his head, he dismissed whatever it was.

"Myrrh is the gift for a prophet," Hakam said.

"I would say it's an interesting coincidence that your name has the same root," Yehudah had said, "except I don't believe in coincidence."

Gershom had told a younger Myrad of the prophets of Israel and Judah, the true prophets. "They kill them, don't they?" he'd asked his father. "The prophets?"

Gershom had sighed. "Many, yes, but not all. Truth has never been popular or well received."

Now the three magi approached the heavy wooden door of the house, the cataphracts just behind them, bearing the gifts. Yehudah knocked on the door. Below the door, light flared and guttered before it steadied. Then a man, perhaps in his thirties, appeared in the doorway. He had the hands of a laborer, his dark eyes showing concern as he beheld the number of men with weapons before him. A woman stood and came to his side, hardly more than a girl, of an age with Roshan, holding a child of a year, possibly a little more. The woman looked at each of them in turn, her expression grave.

"May the favor of the Most High God rest on you and your

house." Yehudah bowed low to the ground. "Is there anyone else here?"

The man's eyes narrowed at the question before he shook his head. "No."

The star above the house flared, casting light even a full moon could not have matched, overwhelming their torches and casting shadows of them all on the rough stones of the street. Myrad trembled beneath the overpowering sensation of being in the presence of something or someone holy.

As one, the company fell to their knees, overshadowed by the light of the star bathing the child in radiance. Prayers spilled from Myrad and all around him. He heard those of the caravan giving glory to God with songs and praise in Parthian, Persian, Greek, and Aramaic. Time ceased to have any meaning. One moment the light of the star filled him, and in the next he stood, waiting, as the man's gaze took in their clothes and armor, so different from that of the Romans.

"I suppose you've come a very long way," the man said.

Walagash's laughter rumbled in the still air. "The tale of our journey is too long for what remains of the night."

"Come in. I'm Joseph." He nodded toward the young woman at his side. "And this is my wife, Mary."

"The child," Yehudah said before they rose to their feet, "what is his name?"

"Jesus," Joseph replied.

"The language of Israel is known to most of us," Hakam said. "What's the child's name in Hebrew?"

"Yeshua," Joseph answered.

They entered, as many of them as could fit, and spread throughout the room until there hardly remained any place to stand.

Yehudah smiled. "Please, tell us of the child's birth."

"I can only tell you of my part and what the angel of God chose to tell me," Joseph said. "Mary will tell you what the angel Gabriel said to her."

Myrad stood listening with rapt attention, unconscious of any discomfort in his ankle as the two shared their story of shame and triumph and travel to Bethlehem leading up to the child's birth. When they finished, he was filled with utter amazement, the vision of the tale coming to life in his imagination.

"Tell me of yourselves," Joseph said, "and how God brought you to us."

In brief, halting sentences, Yehudah related their own tale, yet his face showed traces of concern. "Herod knows of our intention. He may be searching for us even now." He moved to one side, signaling the cataphract behind him forward with a portion of the gold they'd brought with them. Hakam and Myrad mimicked him. Joseph and Mary watched as the soldiers offered their gifts. Their eyes grew big when the soldiers made repeated trips to the packhorses.

"Why?" Joseph asked, but it was Mary who answered.

"Because He is the Messiah. *Immanuel.*"

Myrad studied the child's face, searching for some mark of the destiny that lay upon Him. Surely some hint of the child's future would reveal itself in His visage. How could it not? The Most High God had moved events on earth and in heaven for this child. Yet other than the wide-eyed gaze that took in everything around Him, the child appeared no different from any other. Myrad struggled to reconcile the flesh-and-blood babe before him with the witness and behavior of the King's star that had guided them for months.

Late into the evening, they listened once more to the extraordinary tale of the child's birth. Afterward they bedded down on the floor and slept for the remainder of the night. Slumber washed over Myrad like a wave, and he floated unaware of kings or plots. Standing in the desert again, he blinked, unsure if he was dreaming or if he'd stumbled to this place in a waking daze. He searched the sky for the King's star, but the pinpoints of light he saw were all unremarkable and familiar. The star had vanished.

Then he remembered. They'd found Him. Mary had told them how she'd been forced to give birth in a stable, as if the child were nothing more than one of the animals. Hakam appeared angry while Masista seemed amused, but Yehudah only nodded, understanding. Something had spoken to him.

Myrad stood beneath the sky, waiting for the voice and wondering. What could God possibly have left to say? Without transition, the rest of the magi stood with him along with their guards, staring into the sky, waiting. A hand, small but strong, crept into his. Roshan stood next to him, her hair loose, her face turned upward.

"Do not return to Herod," the voice commanded, and Myrad's entire body resonated with the words spoken. "He will seek to kill the child."

He waited, listening, but nothing more was said.

Myrad awoke to a sky lightening to gray and the stirring of their company.

"You must safeguard the child," Yehudah was saying to Joseph. "The Most High God has told us that Herod means to kill Him. Even faced with the certainty of death, the king will tolerate no rival."

Concern etched lines into Joseph's face. "God's hand is on the child. The angel of the Lord spoke to me. We will flee to—"

"Don't tell us," Yehudah said. "If we are taken, we cannot reveal what we don't know." For a moment, he looked as if he wanted to say more, but then he suddenly turned to leave. "Tell no one we were here, not until it is safe."

They left the house at dawn beneath a slate-gray sky. Each of them, even Masista, glanced back at the house numerous times, their gazes filled with awe. Myrad couldn't seem to order his thoughts. The star he'd beheld in his vision had descended on the child. How did one simply resume his life after coming into the presence of the divine?

"There's a storm coming," Walagash said with a look to the sky. "That will help us." They mounted their horses and left the village of Bethlehem. Soon they were back at the fork in the road.

"The choice before us seems clear," Yehudah said. "Either we follow the road apart from Jerusalem or we continue on to Egypt and take to the sea. What is your advice, merchant?"

Walagash nodded. "The road would have us back in Parthia sooner, but I think you should take the sea. Our return to the empire is sure to attract notice. It would be foolhardy to escape Herod by the intercession of God only to put yourself in Musa's hands."

"Well-reasoned. But right now I want to make sure that if we're found, it's not anywhere near here."

Walagash reached into his pack and pulled out a map, unfolding it. "Hebron lies less than half a day's ride from here. From there we can ride west to the sea road, which will take us to Gaza and beyond Herod's reach."

It took them ten days to make the journey from Bethlehem to the port of Aelana on the Red Sea, during which they spent every moment watching for signs of pursuit. When they reached the port serving as a major trading post for the sea routes from Arabia, Walagash approached Myrad, his expression clouded.

"We must sell the horses," Walagash said, looking stricken by shame. "No sea captain would be willing to take them for a reasonable price."

Myrad put his hand to Areion's neck. "Then I will pay an unreasonable one. I won't surrender my friend here without a fight."

Walagash's face softened. "Speak to our captain. Your share of the profits is substantial. Perhaps the right amount will persuade him."

They walked the length of the pier, commenting on the tapered lines of the ship at both the bow and the stern. Walagash smiled and nodded, but Myrad knew too little of ships to understand what exactly the merchant was noticing. Gershom and the rest of the magi expressed little interest in the sea or ships.

"What do you see that has you nodding your approval?" Myrad asked.

Walagash grunted. "A ship to a captain is like a horse to a warrior. Both show lines and temperaments. I know little enough of the sea, yet it's plain to see excellent breeding in either case."

A man standing nearby, dark-skinned with glossy black hair, overheard the comment and approached them. "You have a good eye for a land merchant. I'm Sareshta. Are you looking for passage?" A blood-red stone shone in his right earlobe.

"Perhaps," Walagash said. "If our destinations align. Where are you going?"

Sareshta waved a hand at the expanse of water stretching south and west away from them. "Wherever the wind is willing to take us."

"I was hoping for something more definite," Walagash said.

The captain laughed. "Pardon my poetic turn. We're currently empty. The *Star* will be running before the breath of the gods to Egypt, where we'll pick up grain and then sail around Arabia to my homeland of Indus."

"Do you have room for passengers?"

When he nodded, Myrad stepped forward. "And one horse as well?"

"I've boarded horses before," the captain replied, "the finest Nisean mounts in the world. The Romans pay well for them; they race the horses in the great circus. I thought to make a handsome profit of it, but I found it's much cheaper to transport them overland. That way, they can graze most of the journey and move around freely."

"How much?" Myrad asked.

Sareshta glanced at Walagash. "He's a bit quick to the negotiation. Haven't you taught him one should sneak up on that conversation?"

Walagash smiled. "There's been little time for that. This is my daughter's betrothed, Myrad. He has a unique gift for negotiation I've found most useful."

Sareshta's eyes flashed to Myrad and back again. "I'm intrigued. What would this gift be?"

"He has a way of finding a man's greatest desire and fulfilling it."

"He sounds more like a *djinn* than a man. Still, the price for bringing his horse will be commensurate with the accommodations we'll have to make. We'll need to wall off a portion of the hold so the horse is kept away from the grain."

"Make it so that I can bring him up on deck in calm weather," Myrad said. "Areion needs sunlight."

"This horse is a close friend?"

"You're willing then?" Myrad asked.

"For a price," Sareshta agreed.

Myrad reached into his tunic to retrieve the purse holding the last of his father's inheritance. It was painfully depleted.

Sareshta pursed his lips. "I doubt there's enough coin in there to make it worth my while."

Myrad opened the drawstring and peeked inside. Only the two stones remained. He took the lesser of the two, a ruby whose hue matched the one in Sareshta's ear, and brought it forth.

"For a friend," Myrad said, "who's saved my life at the risk of his own."

"Done," Sareshta said with a smile for Walagash. "And your future son-in-law has nearly granted my wish, as you said."

"How so?"

"The jewel in my ear represents my rank. I captain one of the finest ships sailing the coasts of Indus, Arabia, and Egypt. To wear the second jewel, I would have to own another. It took me my entire life to build up to this, but I would need to haul something more profitable than grain to earn the second."

Myrad caught Walagash's eye. "The civil war in Parthia could come to an end at any moment . . . or the fighting could go on for a while yet."

Walagash's eyes danced above his smile. He put a hand on Sareshta's shoulder. "Tell me, Captain, how quickly can you make the run from Indus to Egypt?"

"If the winds are favorable, the voyage can be made in six weeks."

Walagash's grin widened as he walked with Sareshta toward his ship. "Captain, allow me to propose a negotiation. You may find yourself with that second jewel sooner than you expect."

CHAPTER 33

Walagash and the captain emerged hours later, wearing smiles of smug satisfaction.

"What did you agree to, Father?" Roshan asked.

"Carrying weight back to Indus," he said.

Myrad shook his head. "What does that mean?"

"The captain carries grain from Egypt to Indus, which explains the size of his ship. To be profitable, he must carry a lot of grain. Based on future considerations, the captain agreed to let us travel back with him for carrying weight plus water and meals."

Myrad understood the explanation no better the second time around, but Roshan's eyes widened in surprise. "He's charging us based on how much we're costing him based on our weight in grain?"

When Walagash confirmed this, she scoffed. "That's hardly worth the time he spent negotiating."

Walagash held up a forefinger. "And also future consideration."

Suspicion narrowed her gaze. "What consideration?"

"A chance to carry silks from Indus to Alexandria." He rubbed his hands together with a rasping sound. "With the profit from this trip, I'll be able to procure a tenth of the stock in Margiana.

If Musa is still impressing the caravans into her army, they'll practically force their silk upon me."

Roshan scuffed the deck of the ship with one foot. "Only the most desperate silk merchants use ships, Father. One shipwreck and you're ruined."

He nodded. "Which is why we should employ Captain Sareshta. This is one of the largest ships plying the coastline. In the twenty years Sareshta has been sailing this route, he's never lost a cargo."

After Walagash left, Myrad took Roshan's hand, marveling at the feel of it in his own. "What is it that concerns you?"

She gestured at the ship without meeting his gaze. "I love the trade routes and the caravan, and I've heard too many tales of the sea to be comfortable with it." She turned to face the sea, shaking her head.

They boarded the ship early the next morning. Myrad settled Areion in his spot in the hold, which Sareshta's men had fashioned into a kind of stable, complete with oats and extra water. Myrad brushed Areion's coat until it gleamed while the horse nuzzled and pushed at him with his nose.

When they cast off, Myrad could hardly tell they were moving. He ascended to the deck to behold Aelana diminishing into the distance behind them. A soft breeze filled the triangular sail, sending the ship southwest toward the middle of the Red Sea.

They stopped after two days in Egypt, where Sareshta filled his hold with grain from the Nile Valley. Myrad watched in wonder as the ship settled lower in the water by minute increments. Once they pulled away from the dock twelve hours later, the ship's movements could only be described as ponderous.

Roshan took to dicing with anyone foolish enough to play the game. This was most everyone, owing to the encroaching boredom while at sea. Myrad found Yehudah by the helmsman's hut in the bow, peering out across the water.

"What do we do now?" he asked the magus.

Yehudah turned and made a wry face. "There's only a 'we' if that is what you want. As for me, I will return to my lands in the eastern satrapy of Bactria and continue to keep the calendar."

Masista's words haunted him. "How will he ever be able to throw off the yoke of Rome?"

Yehudah shrugged. "Alexander managed to conquer the entire known world in the blink of an eye. That's a task for God's anointed. Our job is to count the days."

Yehudah's calm assertion brought Myrad back to the essential question, which had been bothering him for a long time now. "Why does the Most High need us to keep the calendar? They have the prophecies in Israel. What do they need us for?"

"Because they don't understand," Yehudah said. "After we left Herod's palace, I went to the synagogue and spoke with the scribes and Pharisees." He shook his head slowly. "They hope for the Messiah to come . . . and yet they're not expecting Him to."

Myrad shuddered. It was as if the words were an axe blow to the roots of his belief. Gershom had been so sure. "How can they not understand? They have the same prophecies you do. Did you show them the calendar?"

Yehudah flinched like he'd been slapped. "No! And I did everything in my power to keep them from coming to the conclusion there might be one. And I said nothing of our dream."

"Surely they'll hear something of it from Herod," Myrad said.

Yehudah conceded the point. "Rumors of us will undoubtedly reach the ears of the Sanhedrin. Even so, nothing will come of it."

"How can you be certain?"

The magus took a deep breath and blew it out. "How can I explain? Have you ever spoken to a blind man?"

"Before Gershom adopted me, my mother and I worked the market near a man named Shahram." He smiled at the memory. "He could identify his regular customers by the sound of their footsteps."

"Exactly," Yehudah said. "Yet despite his skill, he couldn't see, and no amount of explanation could make him see."

They departed Egypt, running crossways at the shallows to reach the deep channel running through the center of the Red Sea. The coast of Arabia crept along their port side. Walagash gazed out over the rail, smiling, almost trembling with excitement. True to his word, Sareshta's ship glided along through the waters of the coastline before the wind.

"Will we always go so slowly?" Myrad asked.

Walagash turned on him, his eyes wide. "Don't you have any idea how fast we're going?"

"About as fast as a horse can walk." He waved at the shoreline passing by. "*Any* horse."

The merchant laughed. "Ships don't stop at night, or ever. We won't stop until we reach Barbaricon at the mouth of the Indus River."

Myrad looked up at the bellied sail with newfound respect. "How far is that from here?"

Walagash grinned. "About three thousand miles."

The math was so simple, most anyone could have done it.

"Fifty days? We're going to cover three thousand miles in fifty days?"

"Plus or minus a week, yes. And Sareshta assures me the journey can be made this quickly all year round. It's a thousand miles from Barbaricon to Margiana, which will take another sixty days, but we can put goods at Margiana into Roman hands in the Egyptian city of Myos Hormos in less than three months."

"I don't understand the advantage over using camels to take your silks to Palmyra."

Walagash leaned forward, his eyes alight. "The farther we penetrate into the Roman Empire, the greater our gain. Our goods exchange hands any number of times. Every set of hands we eliminate increases our profit. In a few years I may be able to buy out Esai's portion of the trade."

Myrad woke each morning to a changing landscape. He spent his days in Roshan's company, learning the trade of a merchant. But more important, he was becoming acquainted with the young woman who would one day be his wife.

"How long will we be betrothed?" he asked.

Roshan blinked at him in surprise. "You mean you don't know?"

When he shook his head, she huffed. "That is just like Father, to assume you know as much as he does. Of course you don't know. How could you? You're Persian, not Parthian." She shifted from her vantage point at the rail to face him head-on, her deep brown eyes luminous in the sun. He felt a sudden urge to remove her head covering and let the wealth of her thick, dark hair come tumbling loose.

"Once the details of the betrothal have been completed, the groom decides the date of the wedding," she explained.

"You speak of our betrothal the same way you describe a negotiation."

She looked at him as if this should have been the most obvious thing in the world. "It is."

"Didn't we already negotiate when I competed for your hand in Margiana?"

She smiled. "That simply means I chose you from among the others. Now we must negotiate the terms of our marriage."

He fought a sinking feeling, like a man stepping unexpectedly from the shallows into deeper waters. "What do you want?"

She laughed a sound that should have been too rich and deep for her diminutive stature. "You've already given me most of what I want, Myrad."

"Running the caravan?" he asked.

She nodded.

"What else do you want?"

She made a vague pointing gesture to the north. He wasn't sure if she meant Parthia or Rome or Judea. In another day, they would round the hook of Arabia and begin their journey northward.

"I didn't know until I saw Mary holding the child . . . the Messiah."

Myrad's heart shifted in tempo, trying to find its rhythm. "You want a child?"

Her face flushed, adding crimson to the tan of her skin. "No. I mean, I do want children, someday. But not yet." She sighed. "The caravan is no place to raise a child." Then her chin lowered and she looked away. "You would be within your rights to break our betrothal without loss, for having a wife who refused to bear you children right away."

"What do you mean?"

"You would retain your rights to the silk trade as if you were my father's son." She swallowed, her eyes still fastened to the decking of the ship. "Father would side with you in this."

He reached into his purse and pulled out the single remaining stone, the last of his inheritance from Gershom. He pressed it in Roshan's hand and then gently lifted her chin until she looked him in the eyes. "Everything I have is yours. I don't want anyone else. It will take me years to learn how to be a merchant, even with your lessons." He smiled. "I'll make sure of it. Once I've learned the trade, there will be children."

Her eyes narrowed in disbelief. "Every man wants a son."

Myrad could have laughed. For the rest of his life, the memory of her entering the tent in Margiana would be at the forefront of his thoughts. "You are worth more to me, Roshan, than many sons."

She took his face in her hands and kissed him. "This may be what I love most about you," she said. "Nobody surprises me. No one but you."

They made port in Barbaricon forty-three days after they had set out, beating Sareshta's estimate by a full week. With the aid of oars, their ship glided up alongside one of the huge stone quays that lined the harbor, and they tied off. Built into the rock of the pier were long, sloping ramps that permitted ships to load and unload with ease whether at high or low tide. At the stern, a set of steps had been carved into the rock to serve a similar purpose for passengers.

Myrad led Areion off the ship. The horse tossed his head and nickered like a colt, butting his nose into Myrad's chest whenever he ventured too close. "I know," Myrad said to his friend. "It's good to be back on solid ground again." Even as he said it, his legs wobbled, working to adjust to a surface that didn't pitch or roll.

Masista rushed past him, making his way toward the city without a backward glance. Yehudah came up beside Myrad, his hand stroking Areion's long neck. Myrad pointed at the retreating figure.

"Masista is aching to know what's happening in Parthia," Yehudah explained. "Any news he learns will be weeks old but still more recent than anything we know." He placed a hand on Myrad's arm. "What will you do now?"

"I will continue with Walagash and take Roshan to be my wife."

Yehudah glanced in their direction. "God spoke to you. You have no wish to serve Him as one of the magi?"

"To what end?" Myrad asked. "Phraates and Musa killed my father. I'm not like you or Hakam. I have no wish to influence the course of empires. Can a man not serve God as a merchant?"

"What about the dreams?" Yehudah asked. "They've marked you as a true magus, a spiritual descendant of the prophet Daniel."

Myrad thought back on his journey to Judea and shook his head. It all seemed so unreal to him now. "The ways of the Most High God are more than a little strange to me. He saved me from the desert, the floodwaters, even the rulers of empires. But why? I'm just a clubfooted Persian boy whom Gershom pitied. It's almost as if God takes delight in accomplishing His ends in the most unlikely way possible." A thought struck him then, and he made a gesture toward the western horizon. "The Messiah, the child who is to deliver Israel from the Romans, was born in a stable."

Yehudah listened intently like a man preparing to argue before a judge. Then all expression fled from his face and shutters fell across his eyes, hiding his thoughts. "Will you continue to keep the calendar?"

He couldn't stop the helpless laugh that prefaced his answer. "I will do my best. In the year since Gershom died, circumstances made it impossible."

Yehudah nodded. "God understands, even if Hakam doesn't. I will send messengers to you, so you can keep the count calibrated. Where should I send them?"

Myrad thought for a moment. "Have them seek me in Margiana. If I'm not there, they can leave word." He then returned the question to Yehudah. "What will you and the rest of the magi who did not support Musa do now?"

"We will stay in the east for now. If the day comes that Musa and her son are overthrown, we'll return to the seat of power and ensure Daniel's prophecy is safeguarded."

"Are you sure there's still a prophecy?" Myrad asked. "Could the Messiah's birth have fulfilled it?"

"No," he said, his voice soft but resolute. "Did that look like the coming of a king to you? The prophecy is intact. If the Most High is willing, we will live to see its fulfillment."

CHAPTER 34

Myrad waited for the moment all four of Areion's hooves left the ground, a fraction of a second defined by hurtling free fall, and fired. His arrow leapt from the bow to streak across the intervening space toward the target, but like its kindred, the arrow flew wide. Myrad slowed his horse to a walk, both of them covered in sweat, and went to collect his arrows.

"You missed," his son, Aban, said. "I've never seen you miss so often."

They began the trek back to the earthworks of Margiana. Myrad's gaze drifted over his son's body, clean-limbed and perfect since the day he'd been born over twenty years ago. Together, father and son rode at a trot toward the house Myrad shared with Roshan and the rest of their children.

Utab, the youngest son of Myrad's factor, rushed forward to take his horse. "Thank you, Utab," Myrad said. The boy of nine or ten smiled and bobbed his head, his eyes never leaving the ground.

"You're allowed to look at me, Utab."

The boy ducked his head and almost fled with Areion in tow.

"I don't understand," he said after the boy's retreating figure.

315

"Father, you're the richest merchant in Margiana," Aban said. "And he's just a boy. It's natural for people to be a bit intimidated in your presence."

Myrad sighed. "I just wish it didn't take so long for them to speak."

Stepping into the tiled entryway of the house, he moved onto a thick carpet in the hall with relief. His foot bothered him more with age, though that didn't explain his performance today. He should have expected it. They found Roshan busy reading the latest reports from their factors in Antioch and Palmyra.

"There you are, my two favorite men in the world." She rose and went to embrace both of them. "How was your shooting?"

Aban opened his mouth with a sidelong look at his father before smiling. "I'll let Father tell you. I need to check the shipments to Barbaricon."

Myrad watched him go. How could a doubt-riddled man like himself have raised such a confident son? "I missed," he said, "almost every time." There was no point in offering an explanation; she would know already. He pointed to the reports. "Is there any news of the Messiah?"

Roshan put a hand to his cheek. "It's impossible to say. Our partners in Palmyra and Antioch paint the same picture: Judea is a cauldron about to boil over, and the Romans are clamping down to keep it in check. The news coming out of Jerusalem changes by the day."

He chewed his lip. Less than a year remained on the calendar. Even after thirty years, he could see Gershom in his mind, marking the passage of each day one patient stroke at a time. Had he been wrong? Had all the magi been wrong?

"Father's going with us."

He sighed. "It would take death itself to keep me from making the trip. This is the culmination of Gershom's work and our dream, but you and Walagash don't have to go."

She smiled. "Walagash and I have worshiped the Most High since that night in Bethlehem. Who wouldn't want to witness the culmination of a prophecy?"

Her words carved an unexpected hole in his chest. "I haven't had a true dream since then," he said softly. "It's been thirty years. Sometimes I can scarcely believe it all happened."

She pulled him into another embrace and rested her head against his chest. "If your God hasn't spoken to you since, perhaps it is because He doesn't need to."

They found Walagash in a courtyard near the gates of the city, talking with the other merchant leaders. He broke off in the middle of a conversation about the trade routes through Bactria, his gaze steady beneath hair gone gray to look to Myrad. "It's time?"

"If we're to meet up with Yehudah, we have to leave now."

Walagash rose ponderously from his seat. "I have everything ready." He patted his belly. "Including a pair of strong horses for me."

"Who will oversee the caravans?"

Walagash shrugged his massive shoulders. "Aban."

"Isn't he a little young for such a task?"

Roshan and Walagash both laughed. "He's older than you were when I brought you into my tent," Walagash pointed out. "The caravans for the next year are all arranged. Any mistakes made will be small ones."

They met up with Yehudah two days outside of Margiana on a morning that promised fair traveling weather. As before, he was flanked by four cataphracts, and with the exception of Tomyris, these men were young.

It would take them nearly four months to travel to Jerusalem, but this time there were no goods or silks to guard, only themselves. And Myrad counted himself nearly as skilled with the bow as their guards or the cataphracts Yehudah brought with him.

"What do you think we will find?" he asked the magus.

Yehudah shrugged, but in the depths of his eyes, Myrad saw a sudden discomfort. "Something unexpected."

The silence after his response grew, and Yehudah seemed in no hurry to fill it. "I remember Dov saying the same thing," Myrad said at last. "Artabanus is old, as is Tiberius in Rome. Will God's Messiah rule the world? Will the Romans accept a Hebrew king?"

Yehudah's discomfort seemed to double, his hand fluttering as he tried to wave the question away. "Who can say?"

When he said no more, Myrad let his horse drift back to ride at Roshan's side. After nearly thirty years of marriage, coming into her presence no longer sent his heart racing but instead calmed him, bringing with it a sense of peace. They dropped back out of earshot of the rest of the caravan.

"Something troubles you," Roshan said. "You've got that tightness around your eyes as though you are striving to see something in the distance."

Ordinarily, he would have laughed at her teasing. "It's Yehudah. There's something about the appearance of the Messiah-King he's afraid of, but he won't say what it is. He won't even admit his concern. You would think that the fulfillment of a prophecy over six hundred years old would fill him with joy, and yet it doesn't."

"What *does* the prophecy say?"

She'd watched him keep his calendar for decades and knew the prophecy as well as he did. "Gershom told me only the one. I have no idea what else the Hebrews know."

"Then it does no good to worry about it," Roshan said with a shrug.

"I'll try not to," he replied.

When they reached Hecatompylos, two men joined them, hailing Yehudah from the entrance of the inn where they'd chosen to spend the night. Their faces tugged at Myrad's memory, like seeing his own writing in a letter that had become unfamiliar due to the passage of time. Then their names clicked into place from some obscure corner in his mind. "Eliar. Mikhael."

They turned to him, and Myrad waited to see if they recognized him. Instead, they responded without hesitation.

"Myrad," they said in unison.

He ran his hand along his jaw. "Have I changed?"

They both laughed. "You're nearly fifty years old," Eliar said. "Of course you've changed, but Yehudah sends us letters."

He glanced at Yehudah on his right. "Letters?"

Eliar nodded. "The magi continue to keep their count. Our group will grow somewhat as we travel west. The Messiah is coming! Every magus who's kept count is making the journey."

"Have any of you had a dream about the Messiah since then?" Myrad asked. As they shook their heads, he felt both relief and disappointment. Had God forgotten about them?

Before they departed the next morning, Hakam, his face serious with expectation, and two younger men joined them. He took one hard look at the group in which Myrad rode with Roshan and Walagash and led his horse to the opposite side of their caravan next to Mikhael.

"I remember that one," Walagash said, "and how he always looked at you with an expression of soured milk."

"Much changes," Yehudah said with a nod, "and much does not."

They traveled west without incident, though Eliar, carrying more years than any of them, tired quickly each day until he required help to mount and dismount his horse. They slowed their pace from a trot to a walk, but by the time they reached Rhagae days later, even with the slower pace, the skin on Eliar's face had become gray and slack, hanging from his bones like wet cloth. When they gathered the next morning in front of the inn, Eliar wasn't among them.

After an hour, he came out of the inn with his arm draped across Yehudah's shoulders. His gaze flickered from his horse to the ones waiting without appearing to see anything. Yehudah bore most of his companion's weight, and the two men carried the burden of a running argument between them.

"You have to rest," Yehudah insisted.

Eliar's voice wheezed with the effort of speaking. "And will the Messiah wait for me to get better before He appears? I think not."

Yehudah shook his head. "I can hear your breath whistling in your lungs. If you don't stay here and rest, you'll die."

"And if I do rest, I won't die? Everyone dies. No. I will make it to Jerusalem."

The argument continued until they arrived at Eliar's horse. One of Yehudah's cataphracts scooped Eliar up in a single, fluid motion and set him on the animal. The rest of their party stood by their horses, waiting for some signal no one seemed prepared to give.

"Are you waiting for me?" Eliar snapped. "The Messiah is coming, and we are wasting precious time."

Yehudah sighed and grabbed a handful of his horse's mane as he jumped and swung his leg over. Myrad, settled on Areion, leaned across to Roshan. "Do you remember how you helped me when we first met?"

Her brows dipped in mock anger. "Do you think I could forget? Father couldn't have devised a better plan to make me fall in love with you if he'd tried."

"Do you have anything that might help Eliar?"

"I can try, but he's old, Myrad. No medicine in the world can cure that."

They approached Yehudah with the suggestion, and the magus only confirmed Roshan's suspicions. "Our bodies wear out. To tell you the truth, I don't know Eliar's age. But he seemed old to me when I met him over thirty years ago. There's nothing wrong with him that I know of, yet he barely sleeps."

Roshan pursed her lips, then nodded. "I will seek him out when we stop for the night. I have herbs that will help him rest peacefully."

By the time they reached Ecbatana ten days later, Eliar appeared to have recovered some measure of strength. He sat on his horse like a shriveled lump of incarnate will and even managed to engage in their speculations.

"You're wasting your time," he grumbled after Hakam once again predicted the expulsion of the Romans. "We have no idea what He will be, nor what He will do."

Hakam bristled. "You've spent too much time among foreigners."

"Ha!" Eliar barked as if Hakam made his point for him. "I've spent *all* my time among them, as have you. The Most High God does not move in ways we expect. When you are old like me, you will learn the futility of your opinions."

Most of the magi laughed, and even Hakam mustered a small smile. Yet a shadow passed across Yehudah's expression.

They continued west for another ten days until they reached Ctesiphon. During their journey, winter lost most of its grip, and Emperor Artabanus no longer held court there. Still, Myrad eyed the city with suspicion. In thirty years of travel, he always bypassed this city. This was the first time he'd returned since Gershom's death and his desperate flight.

Arriving at their inn, one of the few that could house their growing company, they were soon joined by Harel and Ronen. Still in the service of the empire as administrators, the two magi took their places among them.

"Where is Shimon?" Yehudah asked. "He said he would meet us here in Ctesiphon."

The two men bowed their heads as one. "Shimon has passed," Harel said.

"He won't be seeing the Messiah," Ronen added.

"You think not?" Eliar said. "If that is true, then our belief in the resurrection stands refuted."

Awkward silence filled the room, broken by the sounds of the servants who brought them food and drink where they reclined next to low tables. "Such a gathering has not been seen in thirty years," a voice said from the entrance.

Before he turned, Myrad knew whom he would see.

Masista stood limned in the doorway with a pair of cataphracts, his fists on his hips, surveying the assembled magi and former magi as though he'd called them there for his pleasure, but when his roving gaze fell on Myrad where he reclined with Walagash and Roshan, Masista bowed, and there was nothing of condescension or mockery in the gesture.

Myrad stifled a decades-old distrust of the magus.

CHAPTER 35

Masista laughed. His beard, once as black as a starless night, now held streaks of gray. But he still had the poise and bearing of an athlete, all coiled muscle. "Pardon the intrusion. I merely wish to convey my respects to old friends and bid them a fair journey to the land of their fathers." He paused to take in the room, but his movements carried too much artifice, as though they'd been rehearsed. "I would also speak to a few of you in private."

"That's likely not good," Roshan said beside him.

Myrad sighed. "Is there anything we can do to avoid it?"

Walagash shook his head. "Probably not. Masista has done well for himself. He's the king's chief advisor."

Yehudah, Myrad, Roshan, and Walagash followed Masista and his guards to a private room of the inn, where the king's chief advisor dropped all pretense. "Artabanus is old."

"It happens to us all," Yehudah said. "Even you bear the mark of the years you carry."

Masista nodded. "He is a different sort of man than we've had as king for a long time. He thinks."

Yehudah cocked his head to one side. "And what thought of his has sent you to us?"

"That Tiberius in Rome is also old. Artabanus is a student of history. Empires grow, stagnate, and then fall. He sees within the Parthian and Roman Empires the signs of decay, which will lead to their destruction."

"What does this have to do with us?" Yehudah asked.

Masista's smile showed too many teeth. "You were more subtle once. Surely you surmised I've told Artabanus of your trip to Judea. While not convinced, he is . . . curious to see if your messiah could be a man to unite the empires and stave off their decline."

Myrad tried to reconcile Masista's proposal with the memory of a simple man and his young wife holding a wide-eyed baby. That anyone would propose the idea shocked him. That it would come from Masista shocked him ten times over.

Yehudah's eyes narrowed. "What do you wish for us to do?"

Masista held his palms up. "Nothing more than you would have done already. Watch and see if your messiah appears. If he can take control of Judea while the Romans occupy the land, then he demonstrates a power to be reckoned with."

"And will Artabanus and Tiberius consent to throw the kingdoms of the world at the Messiah's feet?"

Masista surprised them all when he agreed. "I can't speak for Tiberius, but Artabanus was always a different kind of man."

Myrad's surprise increased when Yehudah agreed as well. "We will watch, and if the opportunity warrants, we will speak to the Messiah on behalf of the king."

"I can ask no more." With a smile and a parting bow, Masista left.

Watching him leave, Yehudah turned to Myrad, Roshan, and Walagash. "Speak of this to no one, especially not Hakam."

⤜⋙⋘⤛

They left Ctesiphon the next morning, thirty current and former magi, along with a dozen cataphracts. Twenty days later, they came to the bank of the Euphrates, where they looked across the mighty river toward the fortified walls of Dura Europos, the city defining the military boundary of the Parthian Empire. The mercantile edge of the kingdom lay somewhat farther west at Palmyra, where Parthian caravans surrendered their goods to Roman merchants who then transported them around the Great Sea. They dismounted near the gate on the west wall of the city, Yehudah helping Eliar down from his horse. The ancient magus looked like a man so used up, recovery was impossible. Yehudah didn't so much help him into the inn as carry him, and grief etched itself across his face as though he anticipated mourning the loss of his friend.

Myrad pulled his attention from watching Yehudah to Roshan at his side. "Would you be willing to accompany me on an errand?"

"Of course," she said, but her brows came together. "We have nothing to sell here, and there's not much to buy."

"True, and I would rather do this in Palmyra, but I may not get the chance."

After Yehudah and Eliar disappeared into the inn, he gestured toward the heart of the city. "I made a mistake thirty years ago I need to correct. I'm hoping to find some information."

"What are you after?" Roshan asked.

"The prophecy of Daniel." His stomach twisted at the thought. "Gershom used to read it to me because my Hebrew was too weak. Have you noticed how a shadow passes over Yehudah's expression every time we speak of the Messiah? And when Masista told us Artabanus would consider handing the kingdom to Him, Yehudah advised us to keep quiet about it." Myrad shook his head. Too many questions needed answers. "It's taken me thirty years to understand the hints Yehudah has dropped along the way. I suspect I've never heard the entire prophecy."

Roshan fell in step beside him. "What makes you think you'll find it here?"

"I may not, but the closer we come to Judea, the greater the concentration of Hebrews in each city." They came to an intersection of streets where he turned a slow circle without finding his intended direction. "If their synagogue is large enough, they may have an entire Tanakh and not just a Torah."

They made their way to the market, a much smaller affair than Margiana, where they found a trader in jewels who gave them directions to the synagogue. The designers of Dura Europos had long ago laid out the city with military precision. Only a couple of streets farther on, Myrad and Roshan stood at the back of a stone rectangular building with a flat-topped roof. They made their way around to the entrance that faced southwest toward Jerusalem. It was the fourth day of the week and no one stood guard, but the open door revealed light within.

They passed by a pool Myrad imagined immersing himself in and came to a second entrance that revealed columns with ascending rows of stone benches around a central court with a stone dais. A feeling of emptiness bordering on desertion pervaded the synagogue, but when they went forward to stand among the columns, a voice called out to them.

"There's no one here, of course."

Standing by a closet, a short man bent from age stared at him, his head continuously nodding assent to some unheard question. He fussed with a door that wouldn't stay shut. When he opened it to examine the jamb, Myrad glimpsed a pair of heavy wooden dowels holding weathered scrolls.

"If you're looking to hear the teaching, you'll have to wait until they come back," the man said, then struck the stubborn door with the side of his fist.

"I'm looking for Daniel, the prophet," Myrad said.

The old man stopped and turned to face them, his lips quivering. "You're in the wrong place. He's with God." He wheezed with laughter at his own joke.

Myrad smiled. "I apologize. I meant the prophecies of Daniel. Do you have them?"

The old man pointed to the scrolls standing upright on their dowels. "We have the Torah and the Haftarah, but our Haftarah is the writings of Isaiah only." He shrugged. "Our synagogue is rather small."

Disappointment settled over Myrad. "Do you know the prophecies of Daniel?"

The man's unending nod grew in strength before he managed to interrupt it. "Once. My memory isn't what it was. My daughter tells me I talk to people who aren't there." He laughed. "For all I know you might be one of them."

"Is there anyone here who knows the prophet Daniel?"

"No. They've left for Jerusalem, for Passover. More than usual this year."

"Thank you," Myrad said.

They retraced their steps past the pool of cleansing and back out into the streets. "We were so close."

Roshan squeezed his arm. "Be patient, Myrad. You can try again when we reach Palmyra."

He nodded. The city of Palmyra boasted a population nearly as large as Antioch, composed of a huge merchant class and all the people it took to support it. The synagogue there would likely be several times larger than this one, with a more complete set of Hebrew scrolls. Still, his chances at gaining access to them or to someone who would read the words to him weren't good.

They would make Palmyra in seven or eight days, and Jerusalem three weeks after that. This would give them two weeks to spare once in the Holy City before the appearance of the Messiah. Myrad tried to comfort himself with the knowledge that if he didn't find success in Palmyra, he would seek the answers to his questions among the people of Jerusalem.

Eight days passed, and Myrad stopped at the end of the Syrian Desert to gaze at the sprawling city of Palmyra, shrouded in palms and tucked between sand to the southeast and mountains to the north and southwest. He'd visited the city on numerous occasions over the past thirty years. A massive colonnade ran the length of the main road running east to west, and temples to Bel and a host of other gods vied with each other for size. Palmyra never failed to impress. Yet for all of its mercantile might, it made him homesick for the less polished environs of Margiana and its wild, unpredictable surroundings.

They found a suitable inn at the edge of the city closest to the gate of their intended departure and stopped for the day. Myrad glanced at the half disk of a crimson sun vanishing into the horizon and sighed. There would be no answers until they arrived in Jerusalem.

They entered the inn, Yehudah half carrying Eliar, who protested he didn't need help even as his legs failed him. Myrad took his dinner with Roshan and retired to bed with his questions and disappointment. The air in the inn felt heavy, as if it couldn't contain the expectations of the people assembled within it. He stared at a ceiling he couldn't see. Whose expectations would be met? Hakam's? Would the Messiah appear and amass an army to drive the Romans from Judea? Would He be a poet like Dov?

What did Myrad expect? He almost laughed at himself. What could a man expect from two ordinary-looking people like Joseph and Mary? It occurred to him then that one's expectations and hopes depended on what was wanted. What did he want?

Myrad shook his head in the dark. He wasn't sure.

Eliar died in the night.

Yehudah found him on the floor the next morning where he'd crawled from his bed as his heart gave out, his face toward Jerusalem. Without discussion or a vote, the magi elected to stay in Palmyra an extra day to prepare his body for burial.

"We will need oil and spices to prepare him," Yehudah said.

"We?" Hakam asked. "But we'll be unclean for a week."

Yehudah's expression became flint. "We have two weeks or more to Jerusalem. Eliar was one of us who saw the dream of the Messiah's star long ago."

Roshan interposed herself between the two men. "The markets of Palmyra are known to Myrad and me. Tell us what you need to prepare your friend and we will get it for you."

Yehudah smiled his thanks, and moments later Myrad rode next to his wife toward the market to purchase oil and myrrh. "Why would the Messiah need myrrh?" He wasn't even sure he'd spoken until Roshan answered him.

"It has other, less well-known uses, and now is your chance to find out." She reached out to take his hand in hers. "As familiar as the markets are to me, it will take some time to gather the oil and spices we need."

She almost made him smile through his grief. "Is it any wonder I prize you above all others?"

"You say that all the time."

"Is it not true?"

She gave a small laugh. "It is. Go find your answers."

He left her at the next major intersection, where a vendor of cured meats gave him directions to the synagogue that lay deeper in the city.

The layout of the building echoed that of the synagogue in Europos Dura, except that it was bigger. The benches where the people sat to hear the readings of the Torah and Haftarah stretched nearly twice as long to accommodate the Hebrews of Palmyra. Even so, the echoing of footsteps against the stone floor spoke of emptiness. Thinking his errand wasted, he turned to leave when a man emerged from the shadows near where Myrad stood by the synagogue's entrance. After a brief silence during which he noted the man's sleeveless vest, Myrad bowed. "Peace to you, Teacher."

The man dipped his head in greeting. "You know the correct form of address despite your having the appearance of a Persian. What brings you here?"

"I have a question that my father, Gershom, left me . . . before he died. It concerns the Haftarah."

The teacher's brows rose. "Your father was a Hebrew?"

"Yes. Tell me, do you have a complete Haftarah?"

"We do, but like most synagogues outside of Judea, we have only the one in Greek. If you desire the words in Hebrew, you will have to travel farther west."

"Is there much difference?" Myrad asked.

"Sometimes. Concepts are like water, a certain volume but susceptible to influence by the language they are expressed in, the way a container molds the shape of the water."

Myrad thought about that. He'd heard men in the market switch from Greek to Parthian, noting subtle changes in their personality as they did so, assuming it was the merchants who influenced the language. Perhaps it also worked the other way around. "I think I understand. Do you have the writings of the prophet Daniel?"

"In Greek, as I said. Follow me."

He led Myrad to the back of the synagogue where he took a key from within his vestment and unlocked a door to reveal myriad wooden dowels with scrolls on them of varying diameter, all arranged vertically. He lifted one and untied its ribbon holding in place a protective cloth, moving closer to the light cast by several tall candles. "It's not very long," the teacher said, "but if you want me to read the entire scroll, we'll be here for some time."

"No," Myrad said. "Can you read the portion that speaks of the sixty-nine weeks?"

"Ah," the teacher said. "I know the reference. You mean the seventy."

Myrad covered his surprise with a nod. "Yes." *Seventy?*

The teacher began reading aloud, and while Myrad was still more comfortable in Persian, many years of negotiating had sharpened his skill with the language to easy familiarity.

"Seventy weeks are decreed . . ."

Myrad listened, the words lulling him until the teacher read a phrase that never passed Gershom's lips in his presence. "Stop!" At the look on the teacher's face, he lowered his voice. "Please. I'm not sure what that word means."

"Which word?"

"*Kopto.*"

The teacher nodded. "It is nearly as fluid in Greek as it is in Hebrew. It means *cut off.*"

Myrad's vision swam, and he gripped the edge of the table holding the scroll to steady himself. "What did you say?"

"In this context it usually implies exile or execution." The teacher's voice never changed. It barely wavered from the cadence he used when reading from the scroll.

"It says the Messiah will be exiled or killed?" Myrad asked. "How could that happen?"

The teacher smiled. "The prophecies of God can be difficult to interpret, and Daniel has troubled more than one of us. When the Messiah comes, He will explain the books of God. He will interpret the words, the letters, and even the spaces between the letters. Until then—" he stopped and shrugged—"it's no use trying to guess exactly what will happen. Now, do you want me to continue?" He lifted the scroll a fraction.

Myrad nodded, but as the teacher read on, nothing else in the words of the long-dead prophet struck him.

He stumbled out of the synagogue into too-bright sunlight and found his way back to the market where Roshan waited, her arms filled with the oils and spices for Eliar's burial.

"Did you find your answer, Myrad?" she asked.

"Yes, I believe so."

CHAPTER 36

A very large crowd spread their cloaks on the road, while others cut branches from the trees and spread them on the road. . . . When Jesus entered Jerusalem, the whole city was stirred and asked, "Who is this?" The crowds answered, "This is Jesus, the prophet from Nazareth in Galilee."

Matthew 21:8–11

They left Palmyra by the southwest gate and journeyed eight days to Damascus, passing between a short range of mountains on their right and lower hills on their left bordering the desert. Then, still east of the Jordan River, they journeyed south for seven days along the King's Highway until they were due east of Jerusalem. The closer they got, the more crowded the roads became. Myrad avoided Yehudah and discussions of the Messiah, instead searching the faces of the rest of their party for some hint of what was to come. For thirty years he'd honed his ability to read the expressions and mannerisms of others, training himself to interpret why someone might look away, scratch the neck, fold the arms, or make a hundred or more similar gestures.

Yet for all his experience and intuition, Myrad could read nothing more of his companions' expressions than wasn't readily apparent. Most of the magi wore the same expression as Mikhael, who'd set his sights on Jerusalem like a man returning home from a long journey, one that had taken him far away for too long. Hakam's countenance was more avid, his eyes burning with thoughts of retribution toward the Romans.

Even Walagash's guards seemed eager for the culmination of their journey. Except for Yehudah. Pressed for the reason behind his silence, he claimed grief at Eliar's death, taken from their company at the doorstep of the journey's conclusion. But Yehudah had shown this same demeanor the entire time of their travels. The closer to Jerusalem they came, the more shadows gathered behind the clear brown of his gaze.

They crossed the Jordan River just north of the Dead Sea close to sunset. Three miles later they came to Jericho, a city full of tales that were centuries old. Beggars lined the streets, filling the spaces between uncounted palm trees from the city gates to the threshold of Herod's winter palace. Conversation between the magi stopped, drowned out by the cries of the blind, lame, and ill for mercy and money.

The crowds of pilgrims heading toward Jerusalem forced them to divide and stay in different inns. After a moment of hesitation, Myrad and Roshan changed groups so they could stay with Yehudah. As he came alongside, the magus's gaze cut to him and he slowed. The others pulled ahead. "Tomorrow we'll be in Jerusalem," he said after a moment.

The two of them walked side by side with their heads toward the ground. "Certainly an easier trip this time," Myrad said.

"Is it?" Yehudah asked. "I suppose that depends on what we find."

"What *will* we find?"

"The Holy One of God," Yehudah said, "if our count is correct."

Myrad almost laughed. "You mean after all this time, even after finding the Messiah beneath the star, you're still not sure?"

"Doubt, even doubt in the face of overwhelming evidence, is the human condition," Yehudah answered.

Myrad forced the question past the knot in his throat. "Will . . . the Messiah be exiled or executed?"

Yehudah stumbled, the toe of his sandal catching in the dirt. "None of the magi have said anything about such an event." Even as he offered his denial, he curled his shoulders like a man expecting blows.

"And that," Myrad said, "is the crux of *my* doubt. Why? Because I found Daniel's prophecy in Palmyra. It's not hidden; it's right there for everyone to see. Unless the wording in Hebrew is somehow different than it is in Greek."

Yehudah sighed. "No. If anything, the words are more emphatic in Hebrew. I've been hoping, praying, that my fears are misplaced as simply the dread of an old man who fears too easily."

"How can you hope that?" Myrad asked. "It's written right there with the rest of the prophecy."

Yehudah sighed. "I'll try to explain. You found the prophecy in Palmyra. Did you read it yourself, or did one of the teachers there read it to you?"

"One of the teachers."

The magus nodded. "Did it trouble him?"

"Not at all," Myrad said, his voice rising. "And I don't understand why it didn't."

"You have the advantage of limited information."

Myrad could do nothing with this except shake his head and wait.

"Do you think Daniel is the only prophet to speak of the Messiah? The scrolls are filled with the signs of His coming. The prophets tell us He's to be born in Bethlehem and yet He comes from Egypt, and He will be called a Nazarene. They trumpet the fact He will be King forever, but He will also be exiled or executed. One says He will judge the nations from Jerusalem, while another says we will be healed through the beating He takes." Yehudah's words spilled from him in a torrent. "Are you beginning to understand?"

"No," Myrad said.

Yehudah nodded. "That's the point. Neither do we. Our God has given us so many seemingly contradictory prophecies, we have no idea how they can all be fulfilled. Most men are like Hakam, who read the prophecies of triumph and place their hopes on a conquering Messiah."

"But not you," Myrad said. "Why?"

"Because that is the world's measure of a man."

"Dov," Myrad said simply.

"Yes." Yehudah sighed. "I still miss him. He and I were of a mind in numerous ways, but he saw more deeply than I, past the despair of the prophecies to hope."

"Why didn't you tell me? We rode together for weeks. You knew what Gershom kept from me, knew of my ignorance for decades but never said a word."

They approached the steps of the inn, where servants came to take their horses. "I was afraid."

"Of what?"

"At first, of undermining Gershom's intent. I intended to tell you more at some point, but the time came and passed, probably somewhere on the road to the Messiah's birthplace. By then my reticence had taken root and I was unwilling to share my fears. If it is any consolation, I haven't shared them with the other magi either."

"Eloquent," Myrad said, "but not good enough. You say it's possible, even likely, you might be wrong, yet your eyes fill with grief as if the Messiah's death were already written in history. Why?"

"Daniel," Yehudah replied. "It always comes back to Daniel."

He paused again, and Myrad clenched his fists, wanting to scream his frustration. "Stop making me drag this out of you. Speak plainly."

"There's not much left to tell. In his writings, Daniel referred to earlier prophecies. He actually received one in the midst of praying for the fulfillment of another given nearly seventy years prior." Up to this point, Yehudah had answered Myrad's questions while staring straight ahead. Now he turned to face Myrad like a man accepting the burden of his beliefs. "Every time we read of a prophet interpreting prophecy, the words are read literally with events taking place exactly as it was spoken."

"You mean they're all true?"

Yehudah lifted his hands, palms up. "I can come to no other conclusion."

"How can that be?"

"I don't know."

It was during the evening meal, among the muttered echoes of the other guests' conversations within the inn's walls, that they heard the first mention of Mary's son.

"Will he be there, do you think?" a woman asked.

The man next to her lifted his hands. "The Pharisees speak against him. He should stay away."

Another man, younger, with a beard as wild as the expression in his eyes, leaned forward. "Yeshua has the people on his side. The Pharisees would not dare harm him."

An older woman seated close by shook her head at him. She might have been his mother. "The people are but sheep."

The young man bristled. "Watch. Someday the people will take up arms and throw the yokes of the Romans and the Pharisees from our necks."

Across the room, Myrad overheard another conversation. A man with a thick bandage around his eyes, his hands fumbling to eat the food in front of him, spoke to the woman on his left. "Can he heal me?"

She patted his hand. "They say the carpenter's son has healed the blind and the lame. Even raised the dead." While her words flowed with the practiced ease of a Greek actor, doubt filled her eyes.

Myrad tried to close his ears to the hopes and animosities of the people around him. It all weighed too heavily upon him.

They approached Jerusalem from the east, circling the Mount of Olives where tents dotted the hillside, and riding across the Kidron Valley to enter the city through the Water Gate. The streets teemed with Roman soldiers, who marched in a straight line through the crowds of people, all of them parting for the soldiers like water flowing around boulders. Yet the soldiers, beneath their looks of stoic disdain, seemed uneasy.

Next to Myrad, Walagash said, "When I was young, before I became a merchant, I earned my living as a wrestler. We would work the crowd, stoking them so the wagers would be larger. A few times they would riot when the match didn't go the way they wanted. No one was safe."

His father-in-law's observation required no explanation. Myrad spotted a slim opening and urged his horse through it until he came to Yehudah's side. "The city is filled to bursting," he shouted above the din. "Where will we stay?"

"I've made the trip since the Messiah's birth," Yehudah said. "Several times. I sent letters ahead to make arrangements with a friend. He has a small inn. Space will be tight, but we won't have to camp on the hills outside the city."

They came to a low building with a flat roof owned by a man named Silas and his wife, Rachel. The innkeepers greeted them with smiles, explained by the amount of silver Yehudah gave him as they entered. "Yehudah, it is good to see you. Another week and I would have given your place to another."

"As agreed. The city is overflowing already."

Silas scoffed, even as his smile grew. "This? This is nothing. We're still nearly two weeks from Passover. Wait a few days. Jerusalem will be five or six times its usual amount of people, but there's much more tension this year. The zealots are more active than usual, and the Romans are crucifying so many criminals that the carpenters can hardly keep up."

Yehudah kept his expression neutral. "We heard talk in Jericho of a man, Yeshua."

Silas's eyes widened. "Ah. That one. Even some of the Pharisees speak of him as if he's a prophet. But he doesn't speak like any prophet I've heard. I don't know what to make of him and I don't think anyone else does either. They say he works miracles. Some of the zealots want him to rescue us from the Romans, while the Pharisees accuse him of being in league with Satan."

"What do you say?" Myrad asked.

Silas shrugged. "Who am I?"

"Is he in the city?" Yehudah pressed.

"No, not that I've heard." Silas pointed to a hallway. "Your rooms are there."

After thanking the hosts, their party moved to get settled when Yehudah called for everyone to linger a moment longer. "I would like to compare calendars once more. And make a plan."

"To what purpose?" Hakam asked. "We know who the Messiah is. We have only to wait for Him."

"But what will He do?" Yehudah asked. "The city is so crowded, we might miss Him."

"No," said Mikhael. "If He is the true Messiah, we will not miss Him. God will not allow it." His expression softened. "Still, it won't hurt to compare the calendars again."

Each of them retrieved parchments with columns of numbers and tick marks. Myrad, his parchment newer and showing fewer marks than the other magi present, counted the days remaining.

"Seven," each of them said. Myrad counted and added his voice to theirs, his heart confused, beating in anticipation one moment and stilled in the next with fear.

"Just as we planned," Hakam said. "At least a week to spare until Daniel's vision is revealed."

They spent the next seven days in the inn, venturing out in groups of two or three to buy food and listen for news. Day by day, tension in the inn tightened like a rope under too much load until tempers frayed. Then, when it seemed they would descend into fights of their own to mirror those in the city, the sun broke the horizon on the day of Daniel's fulfillment. Enduring the night without sleep, Myrad rose from his bed, put on his boots, and shuffled quietly from the room. He found Yehudah and Mikhael at one of the low tables, their heads close together over their parchments.

"Today," Mikhael said. "The Messiah will reveal himself today."

Yehudah nodded. "The count is complete. Sixty-nine sevens of years have passed."

"What do the prophecies say will happen next?" Myrad asked.

Though the question was aimed at Yehudah, it was Mikhael who spoke. "So much it's impossible to guess."

"What do we do?"

Yehudah smiled. "I've sent my men to each quarter of the city. Until one of them returns to us with his report, we wait."

An hour later, Yehudah and Mikhael still sat, unconcerned, wrapped in a silence that drove Myrad to his feet to pace the room despite the ache in his foot. Outside, a pair of women, their voices carrying the excitement of the day, rushed down the slope of the street to the Water Gate. The women were soon followed by a quartet of men. Then the trickle became a flood, as if the city were trying to empty itself in a rush of bodies.

Tomyris filled the doorway, his bulk blocking the morning light as his hands gripped the lintel. "He's coming!"

CHAPTER 37

Now there were some Greeks among those who went up to
worship at the festival. They came to Philip . . . "Sir," they
said, "we would like to see Jesus." Philip went to tell Andrew;
Andrew and Philip in turn told Jesus.

John 12:20–22

They rushed the street. Magi with their guards and families exited the inn only to be engulfed in the crowd sweeping toward the gate. Myrad gripped Roshan's hand as eddies and accidents in the press of people worked to pull them apart. Outside the Old City, they pushed north along the Kidron, paralleling the walls until they came to Gethsemane. There, with the throngs pouring in from the Tekoa Gate farther south, they merged with crowds still coming from the Golden Gate . . . and then stopped. Men and women yelled over the din as they shoved one another, trying to gain a better view.

Ahead, from the road circling around the Mount of Olives, came singing. Near him, a woman, her gray hair framing her lined face, cried out in a voice like a child's. "There he is!"

Myrad strained to see while all around him men and women jumped and stretched as the singers drew closer.

Roshan, diminutive by any standard, pulled him up the slope toward the Golden Gate, farther away from the road. With each step, people flowed around them, filling the space they vacated. Before long, they found themselves just outside the gate, perched above most of the clamor. But he still couldn't make out the center or cause of the commotion.

A few seconds later, the crowd shifted, revealing a man riding a donkey, surrounded by others who looked around in fear. Before them, the road filled with palm fronds and colorful clothes as thousands of different voices sang and coalesced into a single unified voice until the hills echoed the refrain.

"Hosanna! Blessed is he who comes in the name of the Lord. The king of Israel."

The celebration grew until it became a living thing, feeding on the rejoicing of the people. "Look!" Roshan shouted in his ear. He turned to see her pointing at the Golden Gate, where men in dark robes stood in a knot of silence, glaring at the crowd.

When Yeshua came near, they screamed, their necks corded with the effort to be heard above the noise. "Rabbi! Rebuke your followers!"

Silence fell across the multitude closest to him, though in the distance singing still echoed across the valley. Myrad held his breath, standing among a crowd of people waiting to see if the man before them would take up the title they'd sung.

"I tell you the truth," Yeshua said in a voice that carried despite the clamor, "if they were to keep silent, even the stones would cry out."

The people erupted all over again, and Myrad covered his ears as cry after cry went up to announce the King and Messiah.

He glimpsed Hakam, trailing after the men surrounding Yeshua, his expression brimming over with triumph and retribution. The procession swept past the Pharisees and through the Golden Gate.

"He's going to the Temple," voices cried through the singing.

Myrad moved to follow, but too many people were squeezing into too small of an area. Each time they tried to step forward, they were swiftly pushed back. He became aware of a persistent tug on his sleeve and a voice calling his name. Roshan pointed back behind them to where a man with a red plume on his helmet watched the crowd, his features menacing. All around him, Roman soldiers stood ready and watchful against attack, their short swords drawn.

"We have to leave!" she yelled. "One rock or dagger will turn the streets into a killing ground."

They retraced their way to the Water Gate, moving into the shadow of the tower that protected it and back into the lower city. Myrad's throat hurt, though he couldn't remember at what point he'd added his voice to the thousands around him. When they arrived at the inn, no one was there, not even Silas or Rachel.

"Lie down," Roshan told him. "You've walked too far on uneven ground. I can see pain written in your eyes." She took two pillows and stacked them beneath his right foot, then disappeared into the kitchen to return with a full wineskin and two cups. The deep red liquid burned his throat, but he finished the cup and asked for more. He drank in silence while she took oil and massaged the pain in his clubfoot away.

"What did you see?" Roshan asked him after a long while.

He lifted his cup to his lips, stalling, overwhelmed. "A king," he finally said. "Did you see them? Calling the man's name,

'Yeshua!' and throwing their garments on the ground before him for a donkey to trample on? If he hadn't complied, they would have ignored him and made this man their king regardless."

"What . . . happens now?" Roshan hesitated to ask.

Myrad couldn't seem to bring order to his thoughts. Then it struck him to the core, the truth, and he believed. "It *happened*. On the very day Daniel predicted, He appeared."

"That surprises you?" Roshan asked. "You kept the calendar faithfully, along with the rest of the magi."

A helpless laugh he couldn't contain burst from him. "Of course it surprises me! It should surprise anyone."

"Perhaps this Yeshua knew about the calendar."

"That thought did occur to me, but how do you account for the crowds? They didn't just proclaim Him, Roshan, they were *worshiping* Him. I didn't think there could be a power strong enough to cast the Romans from Judea. Now . . . I'm not so sure."

The light streaming in from outside dimmed as a figure filled the doorway and Yehudah entered, his eyes filled with too many thoughts and emotions for Myrad to count. His guards and Mikhael came after, along with several others, but not Hakam.

"Did you see him?" Mikhael asked.

"Yes, but we couldn't follow through the Golden Gate for the crowds. What happened? Did He go to Herod?"

Mikhael gaped as though he could scarcely credit his own memory. "No. He went to the Temple and drove out the money-lenders."

Yehudah's head dipped. "Zeal for my father's house will consume me," he said. The magus sounded as if he were quoting someone else.

Myrad's attention kept slipping to the street outside the inn, where people passed singly or in pairs with their heads close together, their lips relating wonders. "Where are the others?"

"When the Messiah left the city, they followed Him," Yehudah replied.

Mikhael's mouth pinched in disapproval. "You should have stopped them. It is not their place to tell the Messiah His role."

"I have no power to stop them."

"What are they going to do?" Myrad asked.

Mikhael's frown deepened. "They wish to make the Messiah a prince of Parthia, so that when Artabanus dies, He will contend for the throne."

"What? None of the families would have Him."

Surprisingly, it was Yehudah who disagreed. "They would. Many of the families remember the civil wars after Musa killed Phraates. They're tired, Myrad. They want peace. Many of them would support a man who can inspire whole populations the way Yeshua did today."

"Will He accept?"

"We have only to wait and see."

It was well past dark when the rest of the magi came back to the inn, led by Harel and Ronen, disappointment engraved on their faces. Hakam wasn't with them. They took their places around the table and asked that food and wine be served them. Myrad waited for their tale, impatient to hear more of the man who could command such adoration from an entire city.

"He refused," Harel said. "The Messiah—"

Ronen held up his hand. "They deserve the entire tale."

Unshed tears pooled in Harel's eyes. "Will any amount of context make it bearable?"

"Still," Ronen said.

"Then you tell it. I have no heart for it."

"We followed the Messiah from the Temple back to Bethany," Ronen began. "The crowd thinned as we left the city when it became apparent He wouldn't challenge Herod today. When He passed through the village of Bethphage and it became obvious He meant to continue, most of those remaining turned back to Jerusalem. We continued to follow Him, hoping to approach Him quietly. He stopped in Bethany, at the house of friends."

"*The* friend," Harel corrected. "Tell them."

Ronen took a half step forward. "We spoke with those close to Him: Mary, Martha, and Lazarus." He shook his head. "How can I say it? Lazarus died."

Yehudah leaned forward. "While you were there? What did the Messiah do?"

"No," Ronen said. "He *died*. This Lazarus fell ill while Yeshua was away. They buried him. The Messiah raised him from the dead, days after Lazarus had been placed in the tomb."

"There were witnesses?" Yehudah asked. When the magi nodded, Myrad saw unfamiliar hope flare in his eyes. "What happened next?"

"We found a man, Philip, who knew His disciples, and we asked to see the Messiah."

"And he denied you?" Yehudah asked.

"No," Harel answered. "He saw us. He *knew* us. How could He not? Even His friends proclaimed us magi by our dress and speech. We went before Him, dropped to our knees, and asked Him to be a prince of Parthia, that He might take the throne and rule its kingdoms . . ."

When he stopped, Yehudah's hand made tiny circles in the air. "And?"

Hints of anger or defiance came into Harel's expression. "He declined. He said He'd already been offered that and more. Then He spoke of death. His death."

Ronen nodded. "We heard Him, then heard thunder from a clear sky. We were fools. If He can raise a man from the dead, what need has He of Parthia?"

Harel rounded on him, and the tension bubbling between the two men boiled over. "If he's the Messiah, he's King! He's supposed to rule!"

"If?" Ronen shouted back. "Are we not here on the appointed day? Did we not draw lots and send magi here thirty years ago? Is this not the selfsame man they saw as a babe?"

Harel growled his disbelief. "I wasn't there. I didn't see it."

Shouting filled the inn then as those present weighed in on one side of the argument or the other. Out of the corner of his eye, Myrad saw Yehudah slip away. The argument pummeled him with blows, driving him from the room to the comparative silence of the street. He followed Yehudah and found him a few paces away, speaking to Walagash. They spoke in quiet tones, made all the more remarkable for the noise he'd just left.

"The mood in the city is turning ugly," Walagash said as Myrad stepped within the circle of their conversation. "He didn't do what they expected."

"Or us, it seems," Yehudah said.

"I've traveled enough to see what happens to a city with too many angry people in it, and this one is filled to bursting with them," Walagash said. "We should leave."

Myrad was tempted to add his voice to Walagash's, but then a feeling of incompleteness filled him and prevented him from speaking.

Yehudah shook his head. "We will wait for a resolution," the magus said. "Yeshua has declined to take up the mantle of

Parthia, and His ire seems to be directed more at the Pharisees than Rome."

"This city is tinder, and your messiah is the match." Walagash turned to Myrad. "What do you say?"

Myrad tried to put words to the sense of deficiency he felt. He'd seen a star descend and alight on the child. What would the man do? He groped for words, but no answer came.

After a moment, Walagash sighed. "Very well. If you stay, I stay." He strode up the hill toward the inn's entrance with his head down, his effort apparent.

"How much of what's happening is in the prophecies, the ones outside of Daniel?" Myrad asked.

Yehudah's head swept back and forth. "Probably all of it."

That shook him. "You don't know?"

The magus pulled a breath that seemed to last forever. "The demarcation between the prophetic books and the rest is blurry, difficult to define. Even the songs of King David may be prophetic."

The city of Jerusalem, still swarming with people, stepped back from the precipice of riot. But the mood remained hot, a cauldron over a low flame ready to boil over again at any moment. They spent most of the next two days at the inn, with occasional forays into the city to check the mood while preparations were being made for Passover. Myrad, his mind and nerves frayed, distracted himself with the ceremonial search for leaven in the inn. Roshan helped him as he lowered himself to look under cabinets and beds in rooms nowhere near the kitchen, yet questions swam behind her eyes like fish darting in the shallows. Myrad found himself staring at odd moments, remembering Dov and the diminutive poet's hope for a king.

"You're gone again," Roshan said.

He ducked his head, acknowledgment and apology together. "I know. I keep thinking of Dov."

She put a hand to his chest. "There are souls you meet who are too sweet for this world. If they're older, it makes you wonder how they lasted so long."

"I don't think Dov wanted an emperor such as Rome has, or even a king of kings like the Parthians," Myrad said. "He wanted something else. I wonder if Yeshua would have been for him that something else."

Passover came, and they washed their hands and feet, then settled in the eating room. All of them listened as Silas the innkeeper led them through the ceremony, beginning with the curse on leaven. Even the guards listened, who knew little of the Hebrews or anything outside of their own customs and the god of the shining fire. Silas related the tale of the Hebrews' time in Egypt, and Myrad found himself slipping into the rhythm of a ceremony he'd practiced ever since coming into Gershom's house. Yet here it meant more. Jerusalem was the promised city, after all, the reward for four hundred years of exile.

Roman soldiers passed by on the street outside, the clanking of their armor and weapons harsh even through the closed shutters. For an instant, Myrad understood Hakam, even agreed with him in some measure.

After the rituals, the meal, and the dipping of the bread, their host raised his arms high. "'Then I will take you as my people, and I will be your God; and you shall know that I am the Lord your God, who brought you out from under the burdens of the Egyptians,'" he quoted.

Myrad shook his head, the motion exaggerated by weariness and wine. How did the Messiah-King fit into such a promise? Where was its fulfillment? Exhausted, he rose from his spot, took Roshan by the hand, and retreated from the weight of ceremony to the room they shared. There, he collapsed on the bed, letting the food and wine carry him into a slumber.

CHAPTER 38

"Why? What crime has he committed?" asked Pilate. But they shouted all the louder, "Crucify him!"

Matthew 27:23

Rough hands woke Myrad the next morning, shaking him so that his head jerked from óne side to the other. A voice mingled with his dream of a Passover, which repeated itself without end, before his eyes opened and he glimpsed sunlight through the cracks of his shuttered window.

Yehudah was shouting at him.

"Get up! They've taken the Messiah!"

He snapped awake. Roshan was already up and dressed, the alarm in Yehudah's voice enough for her to check the dagger she carried. Myrad swung his feet from the bed and hurried to pull on his boots. The aftereffects of wine muddled his thoughts, yet the magus's words compelled Myrad to ask, "*Who* took the Messiah?"

"The Pharisees," Yehudah replied. "Come. We must get to Herod's palace at once."

He hurried after Yehudah and the others of their party who streamed out of their inn northward from the lower city toward

Herod's palace. Pinpricks of pain shot through his foot at the quick pace. They followed the twists and turns of the streets heading upward, a crowd gathering and joining with them along the way, drawn by the news, while others streamed in the opposite direction where the sounds of doors being shut and barred could be heard.

Walagash kept pace despite his bulk and years, pointing at the closed-up houses along the street. "We should be doing the same, Myrad. The tinder is lit, and the city will burn."

He couldn't deny the prudence of Walagash's warning. Yet he'd passed the point where he could simply turn aside or steal away. Daniel's prophecy—the whole prophecy—had taken root within him in counterpoint to a long-ago dream of a star.

The crowd thickened as they came to the court of Herod's palace, where men and women, their faces so suffused with anger they all looked alike, stood screaming at the man on the balcony before them. He pointed to a figure on his left.

Yeshua.

"I have examined him, and I find no fault in this man," the man declared. Those around Myrad called him Pilate, the Roman addressing them from the balcony.

Myrad watched the crowd in both wonder and horror. Where were the people who had proclaimed Yeshua as king? Were *any* of them here?

"NO!" Several people scattered among them screamed back at the Roman. They shouted the word repeatedly, until soon the entire crowd took up the chant. "No! No! No!"

Someone grasping Myrad's arm drew his attention. Walagash leaned in to speak to him. "Your messiah is in more trouble than he knows," the merchant said. "There are plants all throughout this crowd."

"How do you know?"

"Because they've been placed evenly throughout the court-yard, and they shout in unison."

"But the Roman said he is innocent."

"The Romans are no different from the Parthians, Armenians, or anyone else who holds power. They don't care about innocence so much as they do *order*. If your messiah has to die to keep this city under control, then he's going to die."

Chants and waving arms pulled Myrad's attention back to the throng. The cacophony took bare seconds to resolve into a brutal rhythm. "Crucify him! Crucify him!"

He swallowed, starting to back away as if the crowd might see his distress and attack him for it. Again, Pilate sought to appease the unruly crowd, his expression marked now by concession, surrender. A woman dressed in silk came running forward to whisper in his ear, and a few moments passed before he turned back to the enraged crowd.

"I have found no guilt in this man—" Pilate repeated.

The people erupted, hissing and hurling threats toward the balcony.

"But so that you may be satisfied," Pilate continued, "and because he is of Galilee, I have resolved to send him before the Tetrarch, Herod Antipas. He will determine this man's guilt."

A full score of soldiers rushed forward from the shadows behind Pilate to seize Yeshua, forming up around him with shields and weapons ready. They disappeared back into the palace while the crowd surged east to follow the soldiers with Yeshua in their custody, people from all stations with their ordinary clothes mixed with men in robes and tassels and still others wearing garments nearly as fine as Pilate's. Not all of them wore expressions of scorn, but those whose faces were grief-stricken were few. Here and there, Myrad recognized some of the ones who'd celebrated and hailed Yeshua as the Messiah mere days ago, the day he entered Jerusalem atop a donkey.

The soldiers ascended the street along the city wall toward the Temple, striding with the determination of men under siege, until they came to the palace of the man Pilate called Herod the Tetrarch. The crowd streamed after them, filling the colonnaded courtyard.

A chill spread through Myrad at the sight of Yeshua standing before a man whose dark coloring emphasized a diminutive chin and a mouth that was hardly more than a slash in the face, giving him an appearance of cunning rather than strength. Yet for all of this, he appeared excited, even eager to see the man standing before him. The centurion of the guard stepped forward to give his report, and Herod Antipas nodded, his attention focused on Yeshua and the crowd. When the soldier finished, younger men among the Pharisees shouted accusations against Yeshua, their voices building.

Instead of commanding silence, Herod grinned. "Do you hear the charges these men are making against you?" he asked. Only when he spoke did the men grow quiet, listening.

When Yeshua refused to answer, Herod assailed Him with more questions. "Are you stirring up the people? Have you told the citizens of Judea not to pay their taxes?" Herod paused while muttering swept across the frustrated crowd. "Tell me, are you the king of the Hebrews?"

Still no reply from Yeshua. Herod's lighthearted demeanor never changed, giving the impression his questions meant as little to him as they did to the man standing silently before him. Then his posture tensed, and his head came forward. The crowd quieted again. "If you perform some miracle for me, I will make sure you live."

Hundreds held their breath, but Yeshua, unmoving, said nothing.

The Hebrews dressed in finery yelled, "Fraud! Trickster!"

Herod's mouth compressed until it all but disappeared. He spoke to the soldier at his side, who vanished into the palace only to return a moment later with a robe of purple silk.

As they placed the robe across Yeshua's shoulders, Herod stood and gave Him a mocking little bow. "There. Do I not rightfully dress you as a king? You escaped my father's wrath, and I bestow upon you the honor of your people." He gestured to the crowd with their venomous stares. "Is there no sign you wish to give me to save you from their love and adoration?"

When no acknowledgment came, Herod flung out his hand dismissively. "Take him back to Pilate."

Back down the hill they went, the crowd following the soldiers. The magi clustered around Yehudah, some with unshed tears, some with anger, but most lost in their shock, staring through their surroundings. Within minutes, they gathered again before Pilate's balcony.

Pilate took in the crowd once more, his face twisted in defeat. "I have already told you, I find no guilt in this man." His neck corded with the effort of being heard above the shouts. "Shall I not release him to you in accordance with your Passover?"

"Passover has finished," a number of them said. "Crucify him!"

Pilate's face reddened. "I have no cause! Passover custom allows me to release a prisoner. Would you rather have Barabbas?"

"Barabbas!" they screamed. "Give us Barabbas!"

"You would rather have a murderer of your own people?" Pilate shouted back, incredulous. "I still have no cause."

The people roiled, and fights broke out. Soldiers waded into the melee, dispensing blows. Voices screamed in pain and anger, but a few latched on to Pilate's last statement. "He claimed to be king of the Hebrews. We have no king but Caesar. If you free him, you are no friend to the emperor."

Pilate reeled back as though he'd been struck. Slicing the air with one hand, he silenced the crowd. With a curt order, his centurion disappeared into the palace with the group of soldiers who'd taken charge of Yeshua. Long moments passed until a servant with a linen towel draped over one arm brought a bowl of water and presented it to Pilate, who rinsed and dried his hands. "I am innocent of this man's blood," he announced to the crowd. "See to him yourselves."

The people screamed their approval while the soldiers escorted Yeshua into their midst.

Myrad followed, his mind numb, incapable of reconciling the vision of Yeshua on the donkey and the man being dragged away. The crowd followed as the soldiers took Him into the center of the Praetorium, the stronghold of Rome's might in Judea, where they stripped Him of His clothing, bound Him to a post, and ripped out His beard. One of the soldiers took up a whip of nine strands tied with bits of bone at the ends.

Roshan gripped his hand, pulling him away. Walagash was gone, though Myrad hadn't seen him leave. "Come away, Myrad. Come away."

Some part of his mind acknowledged her even as he gaped, uncomprehending as the crowd cheered while the soldier tested the swing of his whip. For a moment, he dared to hope it was just a dream, that such insanity couldn't happen, but the first strike dispelled his foolish notions of justice or mercy. Blood erupted from the stripes appearing on Yeshua's back while the crowd cheered His agony.

Myrad couldn't seem to make his lungs work. Spots swam in his vision like a mockery of Yeshua's drops of blood. With the next strike, a strip of flesh tore away from the muscle beneath. He couldn't look away. Hands grabbed his face, turning it against the locked muscles of his neck. He found himself gazing into his wife's eyes.

"*Come away*," she repeated more forcefully.

Myrad finally nodded. He and Roshan turned and left the Praetorium to the cries of cheers and of agony.

He didn't start weeping until they were back at the inn, in their room, the door closed. Memories of Gershom, of death he hadn't let himself remember for decades, rushed at him from some hidden recess of his mind and mixed with visions of Yeshua with His face bleeding, the whip descending for another blow. Roshan held him, but his grief wouldn't run its course, refused to be washed away because there simply weren't enough tears. Long after his eyes dried, he lay in her arms, dry sobs wracking his body.

It was still light when Yehudah returned to the inn, his gaze haunted. The magi assembled in the main room, food sitting before them untouched, though some drank liberally from wineskins, not in sips but in desperate gulps.

"It's finished," Yehudah said. Oddly, his voice once again held the inflection of a man quoting another man. "The Messiah-King is dead."

"What happened?" someone asked.

They sat in shocked silence as Yehudah, his voice hollow and small, recounted the moments leading inexorably to Yeshua's death.

Harel, his eyes red from grief, looked around the room at men who couldn't seem to pull their gazes from the floor. "As

Daniel spoke, so it's done. The Messiah-King has been cut off, executed by these barbarians with their swords and spears, the ones wearing the plumes or tassels." He went to take a drink, but his cup was empty. He slammed the cup to the table. "This land is cursed, has cursed itself by killing its Messiah and King. We should leave in the morning. To remain here will only lead to more death."

No one answered.

"A few days?" Ronen whispered. "That's all? Did Daniel know God's Messiah would be with us for such a short time?"

But Ronen's question could no more move the magi to speak than Harel's demand. Yet it stirred something within Myrad and brought forth questions from out of his ignorance. He craved answers that were denied him from his first conversations with Gershom over thirty years ago.

"How much?" he asked, his voice croaking in protest. He took a drink of wine as heads turned toward him without understanding. He tried again. "How much of what happened today was written in the prophecies of the Haftarah?"

"Much," Yehudah said at last. "Especially from the prophet Isaiah." Without meeting Myrad's gaze, he began to quote, "'He had no form or majesty that we should look at him, no beauty that we should desire him. . . .'"

Myrad listened to the recitation. At first, he marked the point in his mind where it followed the events of the day, but after the first couple of minutes, he stopped, the exercise pointless. The account matched exactly, an account written hundreds of years before its occurrence. How?

By the time Yehudah stopped, a fire burned in Myrad's chest, small but growing.

"Not just the Haftarah, but the psalms of David as well,"

Ronen said. "'My God, my God, why have you forsaken me?'" he began, though at first Myrad didn't realize he was quoting.

They continued late into the evening, each of them sharing some passage or snippet from memory while the fire in Myrad's chest grew. When at last their recollections faded, he stood. "You could have told me," he accused his fellow magi. "You *should* have. What kind of God kills His own Messiah?"

Myrad left the room then, carrying with him a grief he could neither shed nor understand.

CHAPTER 39

"Take a guard," Pilate answered. "Go, make the tomb as secure as you know how."

Matthew 27:65

M yrad awoke the next morning to a city as dead as the Messiah they'd crucified. No men called to one another as they passed in the streets, and no women exchanged greetings as they opened shutters to let in the light. Even the sun appeared wan and exhausted, with the demarcation between light and shadow indistinct. Myrad moved through the inn, his steps wandering without a destination.

He came to the stable where he saw Harel with two of the newer magi whose names slipped from him. They were bridling horses. Their movements were quick, nervous. Harel glanced up, saw him over the back of his horse, and looked away without acknowledgment.

Oddly, the need to speak, to put words to the moment overwhelmed Myrad and he limped his way to them. "Is Ronen going with you?" The two men, despite their disagreements, had been practically inseparable during the journey to Jerusalem.

Harel shook his head but didn't speak.

"Why not?"

The magus glared at him. "He's waiting for a sign." His hands stopped, and a bit of his defiance leeched from him, his shoulders dropping. "I cannot bear any more. Do you understand?"

But Myrad's attention was still fixed on Harel's previous statement. "What sign?"

Harel ran his hands down the forelegs of his horse and checked its hooves. "Yeshua predicted His resurrection and His judgment." He sighed. "I cannot take any more."

Myrad understood. Harel wanted nothing more than to leave Judea. He'd had enough of prophecies and Rome and people screaming for death. He looked up to see Ronen standing near the back of the inn. The two men couldn't have missed seeing each other, but nothing passed between them—no waves, no farewells, and no attempts at persuasion either way. Harel and the two magi with him rode away.

"Yehudah has been to the upper city," Ronen said to Myrad on his way back to the inn. When Myrad paused, he went on. "Pilate ordered a guard placed at the tomb. Sixteen men, all Romans."

"Why is that important?"

"They think the Messiah's disciples will try to steal the body to make it look like He's come back from the dead."

Impossible hope flared in his chest and he groaned, envying Harel the courage of his departure. "Do the prophets speak of His resurrection?"

"Perhaps," Ronen said. "Harel and I could not agree. Come, you should see the tomb. It's not a long walk from here."

Myrad pointed to his foot. "I would accompany you, but any walk is long for me."

"We'll take the horses then. It's just outside the Damascus Gate."

Trapped by his own protest, he followed Ronen to the stable where they blanketed and bridled their horses. A measure of unexpected peace stole over him as they rode, and he leaned forward to give Areion a pat on the shoulder. The horse nickered and tossed his head. "I know," Myrad said. "I promise we'll have plenty of time to run once we leave for Parthia."

The route they took through the city too closely followed the path Yeshua took to His crucifixion. Passing through the gate, they came to the side of a hill of solid rock, where almost a score of Roman soldiers stood post. Each man guarded a patch of earth hardly bigger than a single pace wide on each side. "They don't do anything by half measures, these Romans," Myrad commented.

"No," Ronen said. When Myrad moved to dismount to get a closer look, the magus stopped him. "Don't. If you step too close, a firm warning is the least you might expect." He reined his horse to the right, and Myrad followed, and they observed the tomb from a more oblique view. From here, he could see the thickness of the stone covering the mouth of the tomb. It had been rolled down a channel until it stopped at a short abutment, completely covering the opening.

"The tomb's not his," Ronen said. "It belonged to one of the Sanhedrin, those who so skillfully plotted Yeshua's death."

The stone blocking the tomb captured Myrad's attention. He gestured to it and asked, "How much does that thing weigh?"

"As much as ten men, perhaps twenty," Ronen said.

One of the soldiers, dissatisfied with the length of their inspection, waved them away. They reined their horses and retraced their steps to the inn. Myrad spent a few moments with Areion, brushing his coat to keep his hands busy while his mind raced. "Why show me the tomb?"

"Because you were thinking of leaving."

"Why would you care?" Dismissal laced his question. He kept his back turned. "You, Yehudah, and the rest kept me in ignorance, told me nothing about all of this. Hakam I can understand. He can barely stand to be in the same room with me. The only way he'd dislike me more is if I were Roman."

"Hakam is dead," Ronen said.

He lifted his gaze to Ronen's face, but there was no jesting there, just the same hollowed-out expression they'd all worn since yesterday. "How?"

"Something broke in him after Yeshua cleared the Temple of the moneylenders but did nothing about the Romans. He took a sword and attacked a full squad." Ronen shook his head. "He couldn't reconcile the reality with his vision."

"I wish Dov and Eliar were here," Myrad said softly. He missed the two old men, different as they were. Each, in his own way, had known nothing of subterfuge.

He left Ronen to return to the inn where he and the remaining magi nursed their hopes like a man guarding the first spark of a fire. He couldn't say for certain why he stayed. Perhaps it was because the others did, or possibly it was because Gershom still held his heart and loyalty. Or it might have been because the days of Daniel's calendar were complete, and he didn't know what to do next.

The news spread through the Old City faster than fire through brush. *The tomb is empty!* When it reached the inn, the magi assembled to pray and talk, and it was one of Yehuda's cataphracts who argued most fervently. Myrad could hardly conceal his surprise. Yehudah's soldiers guarded their words with as much diligence as merchants did their gold.

"It's true." The assertion from Dariush, his voice resonant, drew every eye to where he stood at the back of the room. "I spoke to a few of the soldiers."

Yehudah's eyes grew wide. "You spoke to Roman soldiers?"

Dariush's nod was shared by the other cataphracts. "Away from the battlefield, soldiers share a common viewpoint that binds us together, even though we might find ourselves fighting each other tomorrow. I asked one of them about the guard at the Hebrew's tomb. He scoffed at the idea the watch fell asleep, ridiculed it as nonsense. Of course, his honesty might have had something to do with the wine I bought him."

"Why is it nonsense?" one of the magi asked.

"Sixteen men watched over the tomb," Dariush said. "By the order of Pilate himself. Do you know what happens to a guard who falls asleep on duty?" He paused before continuing. "Death, along with the rest of the guard who allowed him to fall asleep. That's why they won't eat or drink during their watch. Yet all of the guards posted at the tomb live, separated and assigned to other duties."

The minuscule spark of hope Myrad had guarded for three days suddenly came to life. Dariush's simple denunciation of the rumor Yeshua's disciples had taken His body were axe blows to the root of his doubts.

"What is to be done?" Yehudah asked.

"That's the right question, but the wrong audience," Ronen said. "We should find these disciples of Yeshua and ask them."

One of the magi from Ctesiphon wrinkled his nose. "The fishermen? What could they tell us? They abandoned Him."

"Is there an alternative?" Ronen asked. "If Yeshua has indeed risen, would He go to Pilate? Or Herod?"

"His mother, Mary," Myrad said. "She and the other women stayed with Him until the very end."

The magi nodded.

It took a while for them to find Mary, though in the end they found her and the eleven disciples as well. They were huddled together on the upper floor of a small house at the edge of the city.

When they knocked on the door, it was one of the eleven who opened it. Seeing Yehudah with his guards, the man panicked and moved to shut the door again when a woman standing to the side placed a hand on his arm, halting him. She stepped into the circle of torchlight. Despite the passage of thirty years, Myrad instantly recognized her. Grief and joy had become so alloyed within the lines of Mary's face that they could no longer be distinguished, yet her eyes shone as if lit from within. "It's all right, Simon. They're old friends."

The man called Simon nodded and swung the door wide, allowing them into the crowded room.

Mary turned and addressed the disciples in the room, and the joy emanating from their faces was incomprehensible to Myrad. "I've told you of the men who traveled to Bethlehem from the east after Yeshua's birth and of the gifts they brought, which allowed Joseph and me to escape into Egypt. These are those men."

Looking unkempt in their homespun attire, the men made no reply, but backed up to make room for their guests. A few of them looked on with wary eyes.

Yehudah stepped forward. "We heard that the tomb is empty, and by the testimony of one of our own, we became convinced the Romans—"

One of the disciples, younger than the rest with short, curly hair, held up a hand to stop him. "Your Greek surpasses ours. Do you speak Aramaic?"

Yehudah nodded and switched languages with the ease of a man who'd spoken both for decades. "Is the tomb indeed empty?"

The men looked at Simon, the one who'd answered the door. "Yes. Three of us saw our Lord just after He arose." He gestured to a small group of women there with them. "If you had been here an hour ago, you would have seen Him yourselves. He appeared to us in this very room, though the door was barred and the windows shuttered."

"What did He tell you?" Yehudah asked.

"To wait here in Jerusalem until we were given power from on high."

They spent hours in the upper room, listening to the disciples closest to Yeshua tell of His life, what He'd taught them, whom He'd healed, speaking Aramaic in simple phrases any of them could follow. Matthew, once a tax collector, shared more of the account while speaking in Greek.

At one point, Roshan went to Mary's side and the two women embraced. They spoke together in whispered tones for an hour or so, and then Roshan returned to Myrad's side, her hand slipping into his. Once the disciples finished their chronology of Yeshua's time with them, they asked the magi for the tale of His birth and for passages from the prophets, nodding whenever the meaning became apparent.

Red and orange streaked the sky to the east when the magi

departed the upper room to head back to their inn. Myrad fell into bed next to Roshan, his head heavy with stories and the need for sleep. The shutter over the narrow window allowed scarcely any light into the room as he closed his eyes to rest, but not before he noticed much of the burden of his grief had lifted.

Later, when he rose and left the room in search of food, the sun was past its zenith and shadows in the street were growing in length. Most of the magi reclined by the low tables, eating and drinking, their movements slow and deliberate as if mirroring their thoughts.

Yehudah and Ronen spoke quietly, but their conversation carried a tone of disagreement. When they saw Myrad, they waved him over.

"Help me persuade Ronen to remain," Yehudah said. "He believes our work here is done."

"Isn't it?" Myrad asked. "Daniel's prophecy is fulfilled, and from what I understand, so is Isaiah's. What more is there for the magi to do?"

"My point exactly," Ronen said.

"And mine," Yehudah added.

Myrad shook his head. "You can't both have the same point."

The two men looked at each other, then back at him. "Why not?" they said in unison.

He held out his hands. "Because you disagree."

"We differ in the interpretation, not the point," Yehudah said. "Ronen believes there is nothing more for us to do. This is the end of the magi. Our task was accomplished the day Yeshua rode into Jerusalem." Ronen nodded at this. "While I believe this may be the end of the magi, I think there's still some task yet remaining."

"What task is that?" Myrad asked.

But when Yehudah spoke, he offered no assurance of his position, but struggled to answer, the creases in his forehead deepening. "Because an action should have consequences, and I can't see how having us present for His entry accomplishes anything. We kept the calendar for centuries, and on the day the Messiah was to appear, He appeared. So?"

Ronen lifted his hands, his face the picture of exasperation. "So? That's the point. God's promises are sure, whether they come sooner or later. It's not for us to provide the meaning and interpretation of God's plan. That's for God to do."

Yehudah sighed. "I can only say that something in my heart tells me to stay. To wait and see what happens."

"And how long will you wait?" Ronen asked. "A week? A year? Perhaps you will find yourself here, old and infirm, waiting for events that may take another five hundred years to occur."

"I don't know," Yehudah said. "But there is nothing for me to go back to except lands and cattle and trade. Those things seem unimportant now."

Ronen drew a long, slow breath. "Then I will wait with you, my friend. For a time."

Myrad took a few moments to eat and then rose in search of his wife and father-in-law, to tell them they would be remaining in Jerusalem for a while yet.

CHAPTER 40

*"Aren't all these who are speaking Galileans? Then how is it
that each of us hears them in our native language? Parthians,
Medes and Elamites . . . we hear them declaring the wonders
of God in our own tongues!"*

Acts 2:7–11

Myrad bided his time in Jerusalem along with the
rest of the magi, all of whom seemed content to
wait until Yeshua's promise of power came to pass.
Roshan shared in that contentment, though Myrad caught her in
unguarded moments staring toward the eastern horizon. Walagash, however, came directly to the point.

"We can't stay here much longer," he said. Age deepened his
voice to a low rumble.

In truth, Myrad's feet had started to itch. Or more accurately,
he missed the feel and freedom of being on horseback. "Why
not?"

"Because Aban cannot handle the business all by himself in-
definitely. Sooner or later, he's going to encounter a very great
opportunity or a very great risk, and he's going to have to make

a real decision, not just act as caretaker." Walagash took Myrad's silence for argument. "Why are we staying here?"

When he looked up from his cup of wine, he found Roshan staring at him in a way that told him she shared the question. He set his cup down and voiced his doubts out loud for the first time. "Because I'm hoping that, thirty years after Gershom's death, Yeshua will give purpose to Gershom and all the rest of us who kept the calendar."

Walagash gripped him by the shoulder. "What more purpose do you need? God gave you the dream of His star. You kept the calendar faithfully. You've spoken to those who have seen Yeshua alive again."

Myrad ducked his head, hesitant to put his need into words. "I want something for myself. I want a new task to give meaning to the one before."

He expected Walagash to argue with him. Instead, the old merchant surprised him. "I understand, Myrad. You hope that God will allow you to serve Him."

A hole opened deep in his spirit, a desperate longing. "Gershom adopted me into *his* task. He had the same dream as I. If there had been no threat from Musa, would God have given me the dream as well? I want to know that God can use a man like me."

"We'll stay," Roshan said. The look in her eyes told Myrad she understood the anguish that went with his doubt. He reached out and took her hand in his, still overcome after so many years that she chose him to be her husband. What had he ever done to deserve such wealth?

A few days later, word came to them that the disciples who'd been closest to Yeshua had left the city. The rest of the magi—all of those who still held positions within the Parthian Empire—departed from Jerusalem to make their way back. Only Ronen and Yehudah remained to hold vigil with Myrad, who rose each morning with the same question in his heart. *What am I waiting for?*

Weeks passed with no word of the disciples, the days growing steadily longer and warmer as Judea embraced summer. Then at the end of the Hebrew month of Iyyar, word finally reached them that the eleven were just outside the city.

"Has it happened already?" Ronen asked. "Have they received this power Yeshua spoke of?"

They scoured the city, following rumors like dogs on the scent, until they found them at the Mount of Olives just outside Jerusalem. The disciples waved to them in greeting as they approached, picking their way across the rocky slope. Myrad tried to keep up, but the rocks confounded his gait and slowed his steps. By the time he arrived, Yehudah stood before Simon. Something had happened to the disciples during their time away from the city, but it left the deepest traces on Simon's face. Myrad had never seen peace and grief combined in such strength in his entire life, especially in the expression of one so young.

"We saw him again," Simon said. "Yeshua."

"You had a dream or a vision?" Yehudah asked.

"No. Yeshua is risen! There is no need for dreams or visions. I saw Him as I am seeing you." He reached out to grab Yehudah's shoulder. "I touched Him as I am touching you. He spoke to us as a man speaks. He ate with us." Simon nodded toward the city. "He told us to return to Jerusalem and wait for ten days."

The years of keeping the calendar had ingrained in Myrad a sense of time he would carry with him the rest of his life. In ten days, the city of Jerusalem would celebrate the Feast of Weeks in the Hebrew calendar, seven weeks after Passover.

If waiting was difficult before, now it became a torture unto itself.

Myrad found himself pacing the inn, the streets, and the path to an empty tomb that no longer required mourners to weep over it or soldiers to safeguard it. His right foot ached, and he found rest impossible. The city of Jerusalem filled with those from the surrounding area to celebrate the feast, and he couldn't help but search their faces in an attempt to recognize any from Yeshua's trial and crucifixion, wondering what part they'd played. Finally, mercifully, the day of Pentecost arrived. Myrad woke at first light, though waking would be a charitable description. He rolled from his bed to dress.

"Come, Roshan." He shook his wife's shoulder. "Today is the day."

She stirred, rising. "I remember when you were always last out of bed. It doesn't seem so long ago." She yawned. "That's right, it wasn't."

"Come," he said again, his heart beating against his rib cage. "You can joke later. We have to get to their house."

She rose, still yawning, dressed in her best linen, and ran a brush through the wealth of black hair that still begged for his touch. "Why is this so important to you, to see this coming of power?"

The question brought a stop to Myrad's pacing, providing a means to halt the ceaseless fidgeting that had marked the last ten days. "I've been surrounded by miracles for weeks now. We arrived to see Yeshua, but I never saw Him heal the lame or the lepers. I didn't get to see Him bring Lazarus back from the dead, and in all the times He's appeared to others since His resurrection, I've not been there. I'm always too late, too slow, or in the wrong place."

She shook her head, but her eyes reflected kindness. "But you've had your miracles, Myrad. God kept you alive time after time. In the desert. When pursued by Musa. In the storm and flood. He gave you and the other magi the miracle of the star. I was there."

"That was a long time ago."

She spread her arms. "Has He gone anywhere? He has other people to see to, people who need *their* miracle. Would you have God perform for you the rest of your days just so you can believe? That's not belief; it's the opposite."

"How did I manage to marry a woman so wise?"

She took three steps until she stood close enough to bring him into the circle of her arms. "You gave me the desire of my heart when no one else could. There are two types of wisdom, one of the heart and one of the mind. You've always had the first and most important of them, but now you need the second. See your life for the miracle it is. You've been highly favored by God. Accept it."

He nodded, but inside he still ached for purpose, for some task to replace the one he'd inherited from Gershom.

Walagash joined them at breakfast, and afterward they left the inn, each of them carrying two loaves of bread to make the customary offering at the Temple. They walked the streets with Yehudah and Ronen, none of them speaking. After leaving the Temple, Myrad gave Yehudah and Ronen his answer to Roshan's question. "I'm going home tomorrow."

The magi turned, their eyes full of questions.

"Whatever happens today is enough for me."

The two men nodded, yet it was the feel of Roshan's hand in his that brought the comfort he needed. Her warmth and approval filled him with peace.

An hour passed while others from the city, drawn by instinct or rumor, joined them until soon a thousand or more people surrounded the house. Perhaps it was Myrad checking the position of the sun that allowed him to hear it first: a low rushing sound coming from the clear sky. Soon the sound grew louder until it became a burst of wind through the streets, tugging at his ears with the suggestion of voices.

The crowd swelled as people ran out of shops and homes. Searching for the source, they found themselves drawn to the house where the disciples of the dead prophet were gathered. The wind and the sound continued to grow, and fear replaced curiosity as the onlookers added their cries to the noise.

Then the door opened, and the disciples emerged from the house, each of them wearing a flame of fire above his head. Myrad blinked and the flames were gone. Had he only imagined them? The sound of the rushing wind died then, and the quiet that followed was absolute.

The disciple Simon stepped forward. "People of Jerusalem," he called, "hear me. The word of Yeshua has been fulfilled this day in your presence." Myrad leaned forward with the rest of the crowd to listen to Simon, but he couldn't think clearly. Some inflection in Simon's voice caught his attention, filling him with wonder as if he were a boy in the market once more and Gershom were speaking to him all over again.

Persian. Simon was speaking Persian. Myrad blinked again, this time struggling to reconcile an eloquence that surpassed his own and Gershom's with his memory of the disciples.

The rest of the eleven came to stand beside Simon and added their voices to his. Their words filled the air like a chorus from the streets of every city in the world.

"This Yeshua whom you slew . . ." Simon continued, and the

cadence of his voice shifted. Beside him, Yehudah, Roshan, and Walagash jerked as if they'd been struck. Roshan's eyes grew wide, and her lips parted in shock. "They're speaking Parthi. That's impossible."

On it went for hours, the disciples proclaiming the death and resurrection of their Master in multiple languages, eloquently, leaving every foreigner in the street befuddled. When they switched to Greek, Myrad shook his head, unable to conceal his wonder. This was no pittance of the language a merchant might use to barter with another. Rather, these were the spoken words of men steeped in Greek since birth, educated in it, not the words of fishermen in rough linen. With every shift in language, the men and women around Myrad cried out in wonder and shed tears. As the disciples switched to languages unfamiliar to him, strangers in the crowd wept openly in amazement just as he had.

Finally, the burden became too great and someone called out, "We are undone! What are we to do?"

Myrad heard Roshan and all those around them echo the words. Tears streamed down his face as he added his voice to theirs, and their pleas grew until it echoed in the streets.

"Repent," Simon told them, "and be baptized in the name of Yeshua, and you will receive the gift of the Holy Spirit." He scanned the crowd before him. "The promise is for you and your children and for all who are far off."

Hours later, at nightfall, they met at the inn, each of them speaking of what they had seen, their voices flowing and cascading over one another, mixing and parting like floodwaters. Laughter and tears filled their conversation late into the night until, at last, their excitement ran its course and they quieted in contemplation of the miracle they'd witnessed. Myrad passed a wineskin and loaf of bread to Yehudah and Walagash, who sat beside him. He smiled to himself, looking at the bread, the wine, and everyone in amazement. Would anything be ordinary again?

"What will you do now?" Yehudah asked him.

"Do? What does anyone do with this?" Even as the words left Myrad's lips, the answer came to him. He smiled at Walagash. "Do you remember when we first met and you traded with Esai?"

Walagash nodded. "I bartered your Torah for the chance to trade in silk. I think you did more trading than I that day."

Myrad laughed. It seemed everything brought him joy now. "I'm going to take a lesson from Esai and purchase a Torah, and a complete Tanakh as well. I saw the Messiah the prophets have spoken of for hundreds of years. I want to know everything."

Yehudah smiled. "And what will you do with all your knowledge?"

"Gershom told me that knowledge is only useful if it's shared." He reached out to take Roshan's hand. "A merchant goes everywhere. What I have seen and witnessed will go with me. What about you, magus?"

Yehudah and Ronen exchanged glances, and Myrad got the impression the two had already discussed the matter. "No longer," Yehudah said. "I used to pride myself on that title, on being one of the magi. Call me *disciple* now."

Acknowledgments

With every book I become more aware of how integral to the writing process my wife, Mary, has become. She listens to ideas, encourages me, and helps me proof the manuscript. Thanks also need to go to my agent, Steve Laube, for sharing his wisdom yet still listening to a relatively wet-behind-the-ears writer like me. At Bethany House, I would like to thank acquisitions editor Dave Long, who showed a surprising willingness to listen to my pitch and an openness to a quick deadline. As well, thanks go to Luke Hinrichs, my new editor who pushed me to write the best story I could. New friends are always a joy.

Patrick W. Carr was born on an Air Force base in West Germany at the height of Cold War tensions. As an Air Force brat, he experienced a change in locale every three years until his father retired to Tennessee. After high school, Patrick saw more of the world on his own through a varied and somewhat eclectic education and work history. He graduated from Georgia Tech in 1984 and has worked as a draftsman at a nuclear plant, did design work for the Air Force, worked for a printing company, and consulted as an engineer. Patrick's day gig for the last thirteen years has been teaching high school math in Tennessee. He has a wife and four amazing sons, all of whom are far more riches than he deserves.

Sign Up for Patrick's Newsletter!

Keep up to date with Patrick's news on book releases, signings, and other events by signing up for his email list at patrickwcarr.com.

More from Patrick W. Carr

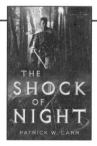

Reeve Willet Dura is called to investigate when a brutal attack leaves one man dead and a priest mortally wounded. As he begins questioning the priest, the man pulls him close, cries out in a foreign tongue—and dies. This strange encounter sets off a series of events that pull Willet into an epic conflict that threatens his entire world.

THE DARKWATER SAGA: *The Shock of Night, The Shattered Vigil, The Wounded Shadow*

You May Also Like . . .

Two women occupy a place in Herod's court: the king's only sister, Salome, a resentful woman who has been told she is from an inferior race, and her lowly handmaid, Zara, who sees the hurt in those around her. Both women struggle to reach their goals and survive in Herod the Great's tumultuous court, where no one is trustworthy and no one is safe.

King's Shadow by Angela Hunt
THE SILENT YEARS
angelahuntbooks.com

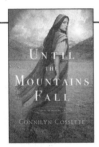

Recently widowed, Rivkah flees Kedesh, refusing to submit to Torah law and marry her husband's brother. Malakhi has secretly loved Rivkah for years, but after her disappearance, he throws himself into the war against the Canaanites and is forced to confront not only his wounds, but also hers—including the shocking truth that has kept her from returning.

Until the Mountains Fall by Connilyn Cossette
CITIES OF REFUGE #3
connilyncossette.com

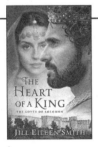

King Solomon could—and did—have anything he wanted, including many women from many lands. But for all of his wealth and wisdom, did he or the women he loved ever find what they were searching for?

The Heart of a King by Jill Eileen Smith
jilleileensmith.com

◊ BETHANY HOUSE